PanEuro

Borrowed Airspace

Thomas Brant

CHAPTER 1 – Ready To Go
Saturday 5th July 2025

"And we're live in 5," Captain James Hart heard from the NBC crew as he stood on the ramp at Las Vegas McCarran, squinting against the rising desert sun. A slick of sweat had already formed beneath his crisp Sprinter US shirt collar, despite the hour; July in Nevada was not for the faint-hearted. He straightened his tie—red, with subtle navy stripes, the one his daughter claimed made him look "very airline-y"—and glanced past the camera operator to where the inaugural flight, Americano 4644, to John F Kennedy, New York, gleamed in the unforgiving light.

The A321neo's fuselage shimmered, the Sprint logo and navy blue livery, with a small "AmericanoAir" badge freshly painted near the front doors, standing out sharp and almost comically clean. Behind the aircraft, a gathering of dignitaries, aviation vloggers, and a scattering of bemused local officials milled in clusters of branded deckchairs and banners, sweating into their plastic cups of weak coffee. It was an event that felt both momentous and absurd—America in the age of TikTok and low-cost air travel, performed for cameras but rooted in a strange, persistent optimism.

Officially, AmericanoAir was a franchise of Sprint Air, the restless Anglo-Lithuanian upstart that had made a name for itself shuttling Britons and Poles across post-Brexit Europe in battered Airbuses. But this was different: AmericanoAir was their attempt to storm the US market, to dress up Sprint's madcap operational genius in the hopeful gloss of American exceptionalism. It was the sort of pivot that would have sounded like satire in 2019—a British-registered, Vilnius-based operator launching a Nevada-headquartered "all-American" airline, staffed by a melange of British, American, Lithuanian, and Brazilian crews. Yet here they were, on a sticky Saturday morning in Las Vegas, being ushered about by an NBC producer and a sharply suited PR consultant whose accent wobbled between Manhattan and Mayfair, depending on who she was speaking to.

Officially his flight was the maiden flight, even though, opposite him, in the sea of Delta, United, American Airlines, Southwest, and even the yellow of Spirit, the American ULCC that everyone hated but still booked, was another Sprint A321neo, which he knew was being Captained by a Nevada former Delta Captain and his First Officer, Theodore Sullivan, a Brit, who, unlike the Texan, had come from some posh airline that was a Pan Am legacy in all but name.

But it was Captain James Hart that the NBC crew wanted, the "face" of the launch: an Iraq veteran who had been USAF, then Frontier, then now a figurehead for this audacious Anglo-American venture. He was well-spoken, square-jawed, unflappably polite—the kind of airline Captain that marketing teams dream of, with enough medals in a drawer back home to pass muster in any crew room bar. James was aware of the theatre, and played his part with understated grace.

The one thing that confused James was why him, why not the Brit with the Birmingham, England, not Alabama, James had to remind himself, accent. Why not the Captain from Chicago, or the Brazilian with the Instagram following? But perhaps that was the point. He was, in some transatlantic way, both ordinary and emblematic: an American with just enough "international" edge, military but not macho, new enough to be unburdened by legacy, old enough to seem reliable. He was the sort of Captain who could, as his daughter once joked, "make a diversion to North Dakota sound reassuring."

The PR woman gave him a nervous thumbs-up from behind the camera, mouthing smile, and he did, as the red tally light blinked on.

"And we're live from Las Vegas McCarran International, for the first ever Sprint—" The correspondent's voice bounced with forced cheer, the words echoing off the tarmac. James hated that name, Sprint. It sounded as if they were trying to pass themselves off as Spirit, the other airline nobody quite admitted flying, unless cornered by their own Amex statement. Still, "AmericanoAir" was little better—a branding brainstorm that, James suspected, had begun as a joke and stuck out of sheer inertia. But none of that mattered now; the red light was on, the world—at least, the sliver of it that watched early-morning cable—was watching.

"And with us, Captain James Hart, the man in command of Flight 4644 to John F Kennedy in New York, set to make aviation history today," the reporter intoned, handing him the microphone.

James mustered a measured smile, eyes flicking to the camera, then back to the crowd. "Morning," he said. "It's a privilege to be here—on behalf of everyone at AmericanoAir, and Sprint, we're proud to bring something new to the skies. We look forward to connecting people, places, and opportunities—"

His prepared words, memorised on the drive from Summerlin, faded into the background hum of cameras, PR flunkies, and the brittle promise of a new airline launch. He shook hands, posed for photos with a mascot in a foam aeroplane suit, and endured the strangest moment of his morning: a selfie with a YouTuber wearing a retro Pan Am jacket and an "*I* ❤ *JFK*" baseball cap.

Out on the apron, the heat radiated off the concrete. The A321neo looked every inch the flagbearer of a transatlantic gamble—clean lines, enormous engines, the navy blue Sprint tail now daubed with a white star. He could see Theo Sullivan, the English FO on the other jet, leaning against the airstairs with a mug of what was probably PG Tips, smirking at the performance.

Theo confused James, not because he was formerly of PanEuro, or that, according to the rumours, he had dated a British easyJet First Officer back in 2022 and, in a heated argument in Athens, finished with her. No. It was that, apparently, he had then started dating a LAPD Metro officer—something that sounded to James like the set-up for a bad sitcom or a very niche daytime drama—and married her to get a Green Card.

The irony that, back in October, Donald J Trump had been elected to return to the White House, and AmericanoAir's "British-branded, Cayman-owned, Delaware-based" status was already the subject of memes and Fox News diatribes, was not lost on James. But when it came to Theo, who, like James, was based at Los Angeles, but would commute to their shared Vegas layovers with the grim efficiency of a man whose entire adult life had been measured in duty hours and reserve callouts, the contradictions didn't matter.

Unlike the European ULCC market, where AmericanoAir's leadership had once been able to hide its chaos in a fog of legal opacity and "let's-just-get-the-plane-back-on-the-line" improvisation, here in the US, the FAA didn't do improvisation. It did checklists, callouts, mandatory union meetings, and a regulatory culture that might have let Boeing sign off on a few too many Maxes but would, nevertheless, rip your AOC out from under you if you didn't file your paperwork correctly. That tension, James knew, ran through every briefing, every morning like this: the performance of American optimism, the operational reality of a business model that ran on the ragged edge of what was legal, let alone sustainable.

The PR teams loved to talk about "democratising the skies," about "legacy disruption" and "pan-Atlantic connections for a new generation." What they didn't love—what none of the marketing gloss could hide—was the creeping sense, shared by every seasoned crew member from JFK to LAX, that this was all a little bit mad. Not that anyone would say so, not while the cameras were on, not with so much of their careers now bound up in the success of this roll of the dice.

James shook the last of the hands, nodded at the mayor of Henderson (who looked as if she'd rather be anywhere else), and took a grateful gulp from the chilled water bottle handed to him by the station manager, an ex-

Southwest dispatcher with the bone-deep calm of someone who'd seen much stranger launches. He checked his watch: 06:42 on the West Coast, which meant that on the East Coast, his flight would be splashed across the breakfast news, perhaps even trending, for a handful of minutes, among the thousands of stories that flashed across America's collective consciousness before vanishing into the digital ether. The PR teams would be pleased. But James was a pilot first, and in his bones, the only thing that mattered was getting the aircraft airborne, on time, and in one piece.

"And now we have the CEO of Sprint Group, Jeff Young, the British entrepreneur behind this entire operation, joining us, along with AmericanoAir CEO Randolph Monroe, firstly, Randolph, what made you partner with the Sprint Group for this historic launch?" The NBC reporter was on autopilot now, voice arch and warm for the broadcast, but James could see her eyes flit, scanning the crowd, the aircraft, always on alert for a PR misstep or a soundbite that could be replayed on Twitter by noon.

Randolph Monroe, a balding man with a tan that belonged on the golf course, grinned for the cameras. "We saw in Sprint a hunger, a nimbleness that the industry needs. We're not legacy, and we're not trying to be. AmericanoAir is about a new kind of connection: American values, global reach. That's why we're standing here today. We're also proud to have Captain Hart flying our inaugural flight, as he is a former US Air Force Major, an American Hero and a Purple Heart recipient, and he symbolises the blend of courage, reliability, and progressiveness that we want to offer our passengers." Monroe's words washed over James with the familiar sheen of American corporate patriotism, calculated to land well on both cable news and the Instagram feeds of newly minted aviation geeks.

"Also, we're glad to partner with Sprint, as their leadership is experienced in bringing British, European and Middle Eastern travellers together. Jeff here cut his teeth at easyJet, a British startup that is now Europe's third largest airline, and their team has a proven track record of doing more with less. Fernando Costas, the Sprint Group Head of Legal, is formerly of Ireland's biggest ultra low-cost carrier, Ryanair, and is, frankly, the most creative lawyer I've ever met. We like that. It keeps us sharp. And today, with AmericanoAir, we're bringing that spirit to the States, with a little more polish and a lot more… American hustle."

"Fernando, you're currently involved in a massive legal expansion effort—one that's generated plenty of column inches on both sides of the Atlantic," the reporter said, turning to where Fernando Costas stood, immaculate in an open-necked shirt, sunglasses perched on a legal pad thick with post-it notes. "What's your vision for AmericanoAir in the US, and what do you say to those who claim this is just regulatory arbitrage?"

Fernando, ever the operator, smiled with the weary charm of a man who had long ago made peace with his reputation. "Well, I'd say the only thing more American than disruption is reinvention," he began, his accent a hybrid of Dublin, Madrid and Heathrow, "and we believe in doing things by the book—just a slightly bigger, more complicated book. The US has always been a market of opportunity, but also a place where you have to be very,

very sharp on compliance. We're here because we're prepared to do both. And if someone wants to call it arbitrage, well, they can call it whatever they want—so long as we're flying people safely, on time, and giving them the kind of fares they'll talk about at every family barbecue, I'm happy. After all, if Trump can get back into the White House and cause chaos, riots in LA and send ICE to arrest innocent British tourists by mistake in Miami, I'd say we're all living in an era of creative interpretation," Fernando finished, a gleam in his eye, the punchline just ambiguous enough to allow for plausible deniability. The camera operator grinned. Randolph Monroe nodded approvingly.

James half-listened, adjusting his tie once more, glancing back at the aircraft as the airport PA sputtered out another Delta boarding call. The performance, he realised, was as much for the staff as it was for the viewers: a ritual of optimism, repeated at every new base, every rebranded jet, every attempt to make chaos look like choreography.

He let the words wash over him, tuning back in only when Jeff Young, Sprint's CEO, took the mic with the calm assurance of a man who'd weathered more bankruptcies and EASA audits than most people had hot dinners. "AmericanoAir isn't just a new logo or a new livery," Jeff said. "It's a statement—about what aviation can be when we refuse to do things the way they've always been done. James here, and all our crew, represent the best of the new transatlantic partnership. We're not just flying from Las Vegas to New York. We're building something that stretches from Birmingham to Boston, from Krakow to Kansas City, from Vilnius to Vegas. After all, what airline apart from Sprint get you from LAX to Almaty for less than $300... subject to optional seating preferences, checked luggage, airport convenience fees, and a surcharge if your name starts with a vowel," he added with just enough levity to generate a smattering of chuckles from the assembled crowd. Even Randolph cracked a grin.

The speech ended with polite applause. Another round of handshakes. Another series of smiling poses for cameras wielded by media interns and travel bloggers. The rising heat shimmered visibly now on the apron, and James could feel sweat beginning to pool in his lower back. There was a line somewhere between inspirational and performative, and this event had tiptoed over it three hashtags ago. He glanced over at his watch again: 06:53.

Time to prep.

He made his way to the base of the airstairs, glancing up at the glinting aluminium skin of the aircraft, a brand new Airbus A321neo, one that had, three weeks ago, been in Toulouse, having been intended for Chinese Nepal Airways, who had decided, mid build, to opt for the A321XLR instead, an extended range variant. It was rumoured that Sprint in the UK and Europe had form for purchasing 'whitetails', aircraft that had been cancelled by original buyers and thus available for a knockdown price, provided one was prepared to take the risk on fit, finish and a paperwork trail that often meandered across three continents.

James climbed the steps, offering a brief nod to the ground handler posted at the top, whose neon vest still read "Sprint" in small lettering over an AmericanoAir sticker, barely concealing its European roots. It was a symbol of everything about this venture: audacious, opportunistic, and perpetually one step from exposure.

Inside the jet, the air was blissfully cool. The interior had the air of being hastily installed—rows of blue and white leather seats, slightly mismatched lighting panels, and the new AmericanoAir logo on the headrest covers, some slightly askew. The galley still smelled of new plastic and packing tape. James set his bag in the flight deck and took a long, slow breath. Here, at last, the performative chaos of the ramp faded, replaced by the familiar order of checklists, flows, and systems. He let his hands move through their rituals: logbook, flight plan printout, radios on, fuel confirmed—each tick on the list settling his nerves.

His First Officer, Sarah Rojas, arrived with her usual cheerful energy, hair neatly pulled back and her accent revealing years split between Miami and Bogotá. She had joined AmericanoAir after five years with Avianca, lured by the promise of a US base and higher pay—though, as she often joked, it was "gringo pay in theory, chaos in practice."

"Morning, Cap," she greeted, dropping into the right seat, already thumbing through her iPad for the day's NOTAMs.

"Morning, Sarah. Ready to make history?" James tried for levity, but it came out sounding a little more tired than intended.

Sarah just grinned. "If by history, you mean doing the world's fastest turn at JFK, followed by the world's slowest taxi in New York traffic—then sí, Cap. I'm ready."

They ran through their pre-flight flows with a practiced economy, trading checklists and paperwork while the purser—an ebullient New Yorker named Letitia who'd previously wrangled crews at JetBlue and could spot a difficult passenger at fifty paces—popped her head in.

"We've got a camera crew doing a little piece on boarding, Cap. PR says it's mandatory. They promised not to film the cockpit, just some 'friendly faces' in the cabin. And we have three vloggers, two 'TikTokers'—one who claims to have twenty million followers and asked if he can do a 'safety dance'—and someone from Aviation Week who wants to see our SOPs."

James blinked. "Just keep the TikTokers away from the overwing exits, Letitia. Last thing we need is a mid-Atlantic dance-off."

Letitia cackled. "Wouldn't be the strangest thing I've seen. Anyway, boarding starts in ten. Manifest shows a full press pack, the Chief of the LVPD, the Mayors of both Vegas and New York, Jeff, Randolph, Fernando, and a Mr Josh Cahill."

James offered Letitia a weary, appreciative smile, watching her retreat into the corridor of the forward galley, her radio already chirping as she relayed instructions to the ground staff in that precise, world-weary manner unique to senior cabin crew everywhere.

The cockpit, temporarily, was silent but for the soft whir of the avionics fans and the distant echo of ramp activity. James could hear, faintly, the PA of a Southwest 737 barking out group numbers, and further away, the first note of "Viva Las Vegas" drifting from a portable speaker somewhere amongst the media scrum.

Sarah was methodical, efficient, and—for all her easy charm—immune to distraction. She scrolled through the ACARS printout, annotated the weather page, and ran a hand along the side panel as if checking it for structural reassurance. James let his gaze linger on the familiar curve of the A321's flight deck, taking comfort in the subtle differences between this airframe and the last: the new electronic displays, the unscuffed centre pedestal, even the faint aroma of adhesives and new leather in the jump seat.

He cleared his throat, willing his mind into the narrow focus that decades of flying had drilled into him. "Let's have the full briefing, Sarah. Standard departure, ATC have us runway 26 Right, Las Vegas Two departure, climbing to seven thousand, initial squawk four-seven-zero-one. Alternate is Phoenix. Fuel's bang on the plan, plus a splash more for taxi. Weather at JFK's showing VMC, but they're talking about possible thunderstorms late afternoon."

Sarah nodded, a small crease of focus appearing on her brow. "And the NOTAM about the JFK T8 taxiway? They've closed Bravo between Yankee and Sierra after some muppet in a Global Express took out a sign last night. Looks like we're routing round via Zulu, so could be a long taxi."

James allowed himself a soft chuckle. "Nothing says New York like arriving late and blaming it on the infrastructure. We're booked a remote stand, and then a short hop in rev service to EWR for a trip to Dulles this evening."

"Great, I love it when the plan involves JFK, EWR, and IAD on the same pairing," Sarah replied with a dryness James immediately appreciated. "You know, just to really make us feel we're earning our money. Why on earth do we have a JFK to Newark passenger flight in the first place?"

"Think that's bad? I've got a Hobby to DWH on Tuesday evening," James said, sighing. "Something about cheap fuel and slot hoarding—Sprint's real masterplan. Nothing says 'disruptor' like running flights nobody needs, but the FAA loves an operator that makes the slots look busy. We're living the dream, Sarah."

Sarah grinned, ticking boxes on her digital checklist. "As long as the dream comes with good coffee and nobody live-streaming their emotional support lizard, I'll take it. Did you hear about that one Brit Sprint employee who had to deal with an emotional support snake at Luton? I saw it on TikTok. Poor supervisor looked like she was ready to strangle the passenger with her own lanyard."

James snorted, shaking his head. "I did hear about that, actually. Something about a woman with a Tupperware box full of snake, demanding to see the captain. Makes me grateful for the TSA, for once. At least they draw the line somewhere—usually."

Sarah laughed, the sound bouncing off the cockpit bulkhead and out into the stifling quiet. Outside, boarding had started. Through the open cockpit door, the hum of voices—American, British, Spanish, and a smattering of what sounded like Polish and Lithuanian—rose and fell, punctuated by the call of "Welcome aboard AmericanoAir!" in varying accents. James watched the stream of passengers filtering in: a blur of caps, pressed shirts, gym shorts, sunglasses, and that tell-tale modern aviation mix of excitement and weariness. Somewhere in the background, a child wailed; someone's suitcase caught on the aisle armrest; a media intern directed a camera crew in a low, frantic whisper. The airline's future, James thought, would live and die on days like this: not just the big, glossy launches, but the ability to get a full plane boarded, seated, and airborne on time.

A PA announcement from Letitia, all Brooklyn vowels and well-practised cheer, welcomed passengers and began the safety script. "We know you have a choice when you fly, and we're grateful you picked the only airline whose founders once bought an Airbus on eBay…"

Sarah, peering down the manifest, grinned again. "Full load today—business types up front, vloggers mid-cabin, everyone else in the back. Do you want to bet how many are just here for the points?"

"None," James replied, smiling faintly. "Because we don't do loyalty schemes like Spirit or Frontier, and the tech stack is based on the Euro Sprint website, so the best they'll get is an email with half the diacritics missing and a voucher for three pounds off a duty-free scratchcard.

And you know what? As passengers are trained by Spirit
to take it like a man, they'll accept it."

****

CHAPTER 2 – Day Two: Tarmac Tantrums and Take-offs

Sunday 6th July 2025

Stepping on board an Airbus A319neo at Denver, Colorado, for the second day of his AmericanoAir pairing, Captain James Hart was reminded how every aircraft type carried a personality of its own, and the A319's was, without question, a touch apologetic. He had flown bigger and smaller, newer and older, but never one quite so short on both stature and pretence: a stubby-fuselaged Airbus, all earnest effort and very little glamour. It had a humble honesty about it. If the A321neo was the flashy MBA cousin—glossy, ambitious, the one you put on the front of a company prospectus—then the A319 was the middle manager, dependable but doomed to be overlooked, always a rung below the glory.

The cabin smelled faintly of reheated coffee and industrial disinfectant — not the sharp new-plastic tang of Toulouse delivery, but the lived-in aroma of an aircraft already doing too many sectors for its age and utilisation profile. This one, James knew from the tech log, had been on the line in Europe less than three weeks earlier, operating point-to-point flights between Baltic cities whose names most Americans couldn't pronounce and didn't care to try. Now it wore AmericanoAir titles stuck over ghost outlines of Sprint's European branding, the vinyl already lifting at the corners like an afterthought.

"Morning, Captain."

The greeting came from a man in his late forties, standing by the forward galley with a tablet tucked under one arm and a coffee in the other. Stocky, balding, with the kind of face that suggested decades of weather exposure and disappointment rather than stress. He wore the AmericanoAir uniform correctly but without enthusiasm, shirt sleeves rolled up just past regulation, epaulettes slightly skewed.

"Morning," James replied, pausing. "You must be—"

"Mike. Mike Hanlon. Cabin Manager today." He extended a hand. "Welcome aboard, sir."

The handshake was firm, neither forced nor limp, just the matter-of-fact pressure of two men who had both been up since before four and had stopped pretending otherwise. Mike Hanlon wore the slightly crumpled look of a career crew manager in his late forties, salt-and-pepper stubble shadowing his jaw, a lived-in uniform with creases in all the right places. James found himself instinctively liking him.

"Thanks, Mike," James replied, swinging his overnight bag just clear of a cart full of bottled water. "All calm so far?"

"Only if you're measuring against yesterday," Mike said, with a half-smile that was equal parts resignation and gallows humour. "Manifest says we're full, but I've only counted about eighty-five souls checked in. Still waiting on a family of seven with a stroller the size of Nebraska. You know, I did a seat count of the number of seats on this flying bus. 156 seats, all 28" pitch, all midget sized Recaros."

James laughed, shaking his head. "You know, the last time I flew a 319... well, I haven't, as I was separated from the USAF when Frontier was pulling their 319s. You know we're in their turf right now," he said, pointing out through the window the line of Frontier A320s and A321s that was on the tarmac like a flock of migratory birds, tails emblazoned with cartoon foxes, bears, and, in one memorable case, what looked like a confused raccoon.

"Yeah, and every single one of them's delayed. That's progress for you," Mike replied. "But don't let that worry you, Cap. At AmericanoAir, we're always on time — as long as you redefine time as 'eventually'."

James grinned. "That's the spirit." He then sighed. "So, what's your hours on type like?"

Mike looked skyward for a moment, as if consulting the gods of scheduling. "More than I care to remember, sir. I'm ex Spirit, made redundant when they went into Chapter 11 last year, went back to a regional for a bit, then joined Sprint as they were poaching any regional, Spirit and Frontier folk who could find Denver with an iPad and show up for recurrent training with a smile. Y'know, I can't believe its Day 2 of actual passenger operation and not just us shadow running putting planes in places ready for service this past week."

James chuckled at that, as he remembered the past three weeks of moving planes around the US to create the illusion of a network: night sectors with no passengers, repositioning flights flown on minimum fuel and maximum optimism, crews shuttled between bases that existed more on PowerPoint slides than in any physical sense. Aircraft had appeared at gates like stage props wheeled into place just before curtain up. AmericanoAir had not so much launched as materialised.

The flight deck of the A319neo at Denver International felt at once familiar and alien. James had never quite understood how a cockpit, designed to be identical across so many variants, could develop its own idiosyncrasies—leftover coffee stains, the click of a slightly sticky rotary knob, the faint impression of a prior captain's cologne, all part of the inheritance passed along with the airframe. He settled into the left seat, dropping his flight bag to the floor with a practised thud, then running a palm over the smooth, if slightly worn, armrest.

The sky was flawless: Colorado blue, the kind pilots compared to the fake backdrop in flight sims, so vivid it bordered on the absurd. Out on the ramp, a convoy of luggage carts scurried past, chased by an airport maintenance truck whose hazard lights blinked in nervous apology. Through the side window, James could see the endless sweep of the Rockies, their snow-streaked shoulders only just visible above the summer haze. This, he thought, was the promise of flying in America: impossible scale, infinite horizon, and always the vague, nagging sense that everything—crew schedules, airline fortunes, personal histories—could change overnight.

He powered up the displays, watching as the familiar Airbus boot sequence blinked to life. The screens, he noted, were not original. The right-hand display bore a sticker—SPRINT EU PROPERTY—partially removed, the edges gummy with residue. He reached over and flicked it off with a fingernail, dropping the scrap into his flight bag. Little things, he thought. Always the little things.

A minute later, his First Officer arrived—a woman in her early thirties with cropped black hair, dark brown eyes, and the brisk, slightly wary energy of someone new to both the airline and the country. She wore the AmericanoAir uniform with that same blend of pride and disbelief James remembered from his own early days at Frontier: the excitement of a new badge, the private fear that it might not last.

"Good morning, Captain. I'm Zahra Mirza. FO today."

"Zahra—welcome. You flown much on the 319 yet?"

"Plenty on the 320, a few jump seat rides on the 321. This one—" She patted the sidewall of the cockpit. "—I think she's got a bit of a sense of humour. Controls feel lighter than the 320, but the pitch trim wheel's got a bite. I had her yesterday on a Boston run, so she's already had her proper American welcome—late push, short turn, three lav maintenance stickers, and the catering loaded for the wrong sector. She flies all right. If you're gentle."

James smiled, appreciating the candour. "Gentle, then. I think I can manage that. Glad you're here, Zahra."

She took her seat, began her flows with efficient muscle memory. There was an ease to her presence, and James recognised in it something both familiar and foreign—the quick-study confidence of an FO determined not to look out of place, not here, not today. He glanced at her ID clipped to the yoke, a new badge, the AmericanoAir globe logo sharp and barely scuffed. The lanyard was still Sprint-issue, as it had the Sprint S logo on it.

"Where were you before?" James asked, as Zahra keyed in her login to the FMS.

"Riyadh. Saudia for a couple of years, then some ACMI work for Sprint. Been bouncing around Europe, Middle East… now, finally, the States. It's a long story."

"All the best ones are," James replied. "You based here?"

"Boston. I'm part of nearly 3000 crew based there."

"Boston, eh?" James grinned, slotting his sunglasses onto the brow of his head. "Proper city, if you like your weather as unstable as your roster. I was based at Vegas, back in my Frontier days."

The hum of the Denver ramp rose as the sun crept higher over the Rockies. In the cockpit of AmericanoAir 1218, James and Zahra settle into the gentle ballet of pre-flight checks, their movements a kind of quiet resistance against the chaos outside. The airport was alive with the clatter of baggage carts and the distant wail of ground service vehicles, the faint rumble of a departing Dreamliner shaking the glass of the jet bridge. James let the routine settle over him, grounding himself in checklists and flows, muscle memory kicking in after so many years, so many flights.

"Hydraulics… green," Zahra said, ticking boxes on her iPad. "Check fuel and trim."

James glanced over. "Fuel's up, trim's set. We're good for power-on. You're flying, I'll monitor."

The A319neo's flight deck had the peculiar atmosphere of a rented flat: functionally familiar but never quite home. James leaned into the left seat, adjusting his headset, a battered David Clark that had seen more oceanic crossings than most of the airline's executives. Next to him, Zahra scrolled through her tablet, ticking off her flows with that mixture of wariness and determination that James recognised from every new recruit thrust into the deep end of a startup airline.

The cabin manager, Mike Hanlon, ducked his head into the cockpit. "Ops says they want push in twenty. Still holding for two bags and the world's slowest stroller."

James nodded. "Let 'em know we'll need a minute. No point getting out there just to burn APU time."

Mike's lips twitched into a smile. "I'll tell 'em. By the way, catering loaded one too few water bottles for the jump seat crew. If anyone's dying of thirst, blame the union, not the company."

Zahra chuckled. "Union? Bah, Sprint have already broke BALPA by refusing to recognise it properly. They're running this whole show on Omani trade union loopholes and a prayer."

James raised an eyebrow, amused by Zahra's bluntness. "You've done your homework on Sprint's corporate gymnastics, then?"

"Had to," Zahra replied, not looking up from her tablet. "When you've worked ACMI contracts across three continents, you learn to read the fine print. Sprint's not the worst I've seen, but they're not exactly Virgin Atlantic either. Half the crew in Boston are still trying to figure out if their payslips are in dollars, pounds, or Lithuanian litas."

Mike snorted from the doorway. "Litas? Mate, you're lucky if it's not crypto. Last month, I got a payslip with a QR code for 'crew appreciation tokens.' Thought it was a scam till HR swore it was real." He shook his head, retreating to the galley with the air of a man who'd seen too many payroll experiments.

James leaned back, letting the cockpit's hum fill the silence. The A319neo was alive now, systems purring as the avionics fans spun up. Outside, the Denver morning was heating up, the ramp shimmering under the relentless Colorado sun. A Frontier A320 taxied past, its tail sporting a grinning wolf that seemed to mock the patchwork ambition of AmericanoAir's operation. James couldn't help but feel a pang of nostalgia for his Frontier days—simpler, in a way, despite the grind. At least back then, the airline's chaos was confined to domestic routes and didn't involve transatlantic dreams or corporate sleight-of-hand across three jurisdictions.

"Alright," he said, snapping back to the present. "Let's run the briefing. Denver to Boston, flight 1218, A319neo, full load, 156 passengers, weather's clear at both ends but with a chance of convective activity over the Great Lakes. Departure runway 35 Left, initial climb to 9,000 feet, squawk 4723. Alternate is Cleveland, fuel's on plan with a bit extra for holding if those storms kick up. Any NOTAMs we need to watch?"

Zahra nodded, her fingers dancing across the iPad as she pulled up the latest updates. "Nothing critical. Denver's got some taxiway work on Echo, so we're routing via Foxtrot to the runway. Boston's reporting a bird strike issue near Logan's approach path—mostly gulls, so keep an eye on the engines during descent. Oh, and the usual: don't expect ground control to sound happy about anything."

James chuckled. "When do they ever? Alright, you've got the leg. I'll handle the radios and keep the vloggers from storming the cockpit."

The cockpit settled into a rhythm, the pre-flight checklist a kind of liturgy that James had always found grounding. It was the one constant across airlines, continents, and decades: switches flicked, numbers cross-checked, systems humming to life. The A319neo, for all its middle-manager humility, was a reliable beast, its CFM LEAP engines spooling up with a reassuring whine.

"Right, we've got 15 minutes until pushback, so let's make sure we're buttoned up," James said, his voice steady but carrying the weight of a captain who knew the next few hours would test both crew and aircraft.

The A319neo's cockpit was a cocoon of controlled chaos, a microcosm where the absurdity of Sprint's transatlantic gamble felt distant, manageable, even if only for the duration of a flight.

Zahra nodded, her focus unbroken as she cross-checked the flight management system. "FMS is loaded, Denver to Boston, direct route via SID to STAR. Fuel's confirmed at 12,500 pounds, plus 2,000 for contingency. Trim's set for take-off, and I've got the performance data for runway 35 Left—V1 at 142 knots, VR at 145, V2 at 152. We're good for a standard departure unless ATC throws us a curveball."

James gave an approving nod. "Sounds solid. Let's keep an eye on that convective activity over Lake Michigan. If it starts building, we'll need to coordinate a deviation early. Boston's got enough going on without us dodging thunderstorms on final."

The cockpit door swung open again, and Mike Hanlon reappeared, this time with a clipboard and a look of mild exasperation. "Right, Cap, we're fully boarded. Family with the stroller finally showed up, but they're kicking off because their pram won't fit in the overheads. I've got-"

"FUCKING GET OUT OF MY WAY!" The shout, sharp and unmistakably American, sliced through the hum of the cabin, audible even in the cockpit. James and Zahra exchanged a glance; the kind pilots share when they know something's about to escalate. Mike Hanlon froze mid-sentence, his clipboard dangling, and leaned out the cockpit door to peer down the aisle.

"Bloody hell," Mike muttered, his voice low but carrying the weary tone of someone who'd seen this movie before. "Sounds like we've got a live one already."

James unbuckled his harness, standing to get a better view through the open door. Down the length of the A319's narrow cabin, a man in a red polo shirt—mid-forties, sunburned, with the build of someone who'd once played high school football but hadn't seen a gym in a decade—was jabbing a finger at a young cabin crew member. The crew member, a woman with a tight ponytail and a name tag reading "Clara," stood her ground, her posture calm but her eyes betraying a flicker of tension. Behind the man, the family with the oversized stroller hovered awkwardly, their kids staring wide-eyed at the unfolding drama.

"Problem?" James asked, his voice steady but loud enough to carry authority without stepping into the fray just yet.

Mike turned back, shaking his head. "Same old, Cap. Guy's pissed because he wants an exit row seat, but he didn't pay for it, and now he's claiming Clara's 'disrespecting' him. Reckon he's one of those 'I know my rights' types. Clara's handling it, but he's loud enough to wake half of Colorado."

Zahra snorted softly, still focused on her checklist but clearly listening. "Bet you ten bucks he's got a TikTok account with three followers and a bio that says 'patriot.'"

James allowed himself a faint smile, but his attention stayed on the cabin. He trusted his crew to manage passenger disputes—Mike and Clara had the experience to de-escalate without making it a spectacle—but the last thing AmericanoAir needed on day two of operations was a viral video of a meltdown at Denver International. The airline's launch was already a tightrope walk; one misstep, and the vloggers and aviation geeks circling like hawks would have a field day.

"Mike, keep an eye on it," James said, settling back into his seat. "If it escalates, let me know. I'll do the captain's walk of shame if I have to."

"Roger that," Mike replied, already halfway out the door. "Clara's got it under control, but I'll hover in case he decides to storm the galley for 'justice.'"

The cockpit door clicked shut, muffling the cabin noise but not entirely silencing the low hum of passenger chatter and the occasional clatter of overhead bins. James adjusted his headset, glancing at Zahra. "You ever miss the days when the biggest problem was a late catering truck?"

Zahra laughed, her fingers pausing over the FMS. "Miss it? Cap, I never had those days. My first gig was flying Hajj charters out of Jeddah. You think this guy's loud? Try 300 pilgrims arguing over who gets the window seat to Mecca. This—" She gestured vaguely toward the cabin. "—this is just Sunday morning."

James chuckled, the tension in his shoulders easing slightly. Zahra's bluntness was a tonic, a reminder that aviation, for all its chaos, was a shared language. He turned his attention back to the flight deck, running his eyes over the displays. The A319neo's systems were green, the fuel load confirmed, the weather reports stable for now. Outside, the Denver ramp was a hive of activity: ground handlers in neon vests darted between baggage carts, a fuel truck disconnected with a hiss, and a pushback tug rolled into position, its driver giving a lazy wave to someone out of sight.

"Let's finish the brief," James said, his tone shifting back to business. "We've got a full load, 156 souls, including a couple of unaccompanied minors in 12A and B. Cabin crew's got them sorted. Departure's on 35 Left, as you said, but let's double-check the performance data. Denver's hot today—92 Fahrenheit and climbing—so we'll need every knot of thrust."

Zahra nodded, pulling up the take-off performance calculations on her iPad. "Already factored in the temperature and elevation. We're at 5,430 feet here, so runway 35 Left gives us 12,000 feet to play with. TOGA thrust, flaps 2, V1 at 142, VR at 145, V2 at 152, like I said. We're well within limits, even with the full load and the extra fuel."

"Good," James said, scanning the numbers himself. Denver's high altitude and summer heat were a notorious combination, but the A319neo's LEAP engines were more than capable, provided everything went to plan. And that, he knew, was the catch. At AmericanoAir, "to plan" was a phrase that carried the weight of a bad joke.

The cockpit door opened again, and Mike reappeared. "Cap, this idiot is refusing to sit down unless he gets an exit row seat. Clara's explained it's pre-booked and he didn't pay, but he's now demanding to speak to the captain. Says he's got 'rights as a paying customer.' I can keep him contained, but it's getting loud, and we've got a gate agent hovering who looks like she's about to call security."

James sighed, unbuckling his harness again. "Alright, Mike. I'll handle it. Zahra, finish the setup and keep an eye on the clock. We're not missing our slot because of this guy."

Zahra nodded, her focus unbroken. "Got it, Cap. I'll have everything ready. Go play diplomat."

James stepped out of the cockpit, adjusting his cap and smoothing his jacket. The cabin was a sea of faces—some curious, some bored, a few already filming with their phones. The man in the red polo shirt stood in the aisle near row 15, arms crossed, his voice carrying over the hum of the air conditioning. Clara, the young cabin crew member, stood calmly in front of him, her hands clasped, her expression a masterclass in professional restraint.

"Sir, as I've explained, the exit row seats are reserved for passengers who've paid the fee or been assigned by our system," Clara was saying, her voice steady but firm. "You've been assigned 26F, so you need to take your seat so we can prepare for departure."

The man, whose sunburned face was now a shade closer to his polo shirt, leaned forward, his voice dripping with indignation. "I paid for this flight, sweetheart, and I'm not sitting in some cattle-class middle seat just because your system screwed me over. I want to speak to the captain. Now."

James cleared his throat, stepping into the aisle with the measured calm of a man who'd defused more than his share of inflight tantrums. "I'm Captain Hart, sir. What's the issue?"

The man spun to face him, momentarily thrown by James's presence—six feet of pressed uniform, silvered temples, and the quiet authority of a pilot who'd flown through worse storms than this. "The issue, Captain, is your crew's trying to rip me off. I paid good money for this flight, and I'm not sitting in a seat that's basically in the toilet. I want an exit row, and I want it now."

James nodded, his expression neutral but his eyes scanning the man's body language—tense shoulders, clenched fists, the kind of bravado that could tip into a scene if not handled carefully. "I understand you're frustrated, sir. Let's sort this out. Can I have your name?"

"Gary. Gary Whitaker." He jabbed a thumb at his chest, as if the name carried weight.

"Alright, Gary," James said, keeping his tone even. "Here's the situation. Exit row seats come with extra responsibility—assisting in an emergency, which requires specific briefing. They're also premium seats, pre-booked by other passengers or assigned based on our system. Your ticket shows you're in 26F, which is a window seat, correct?"

Gary's eyes narrowed. "Window next to the damn lavatory at the very back. I'm not an idiot, Captain. I know how this works—you're just trying to upsell me. If you don't upgrade me, I'm going to Corporate."

James had to chuckle to himself, as AmericanoAir, or Sprint US, was using the Sprint Europe model, which itself was the Ryanair model of ultra-low cost aviation, where "Corporate" was less a department and more a WhatsApp group staffed by overworked interns in Vilnius. Still, he kept his face composed, the faintest trace of a smile softening the edges of his authority. "I hear you, Gary. Nobody's trying to upsell you. The exit rows are fully booked today, and moving passengers around at this stage risks delaying the flight for everyone. I'm sure you don't want that, and neither do we. Let's get you settled in 26F, or we'll have to call security and have you arrested for non-compliance."

James's voice carried the calm finality of a man who'd learned long ago that authority in aviation wasn't about volume—it was about certainty. Whitaker's face twitched, his bravado faltering under the weight of James's steady gaze and the subtle threat of security. The cabin, momentarily hushed by the confrontation, seemed to exhale as passengers turned back to their phones, their books, or the view of Denver's shimmering tarmac outside. Clara, still standing nearby, gave James a barely perceptible nod of gratitude, her professionalism unshaken despite the verbal barrage she'd endured.

Gary muttered something under his breath—half curse, half surrender—and shuffled toward the rear of the A319, his carry-on bag banging against the armrests as he went. The family with the oversized stroller, who'd been hovering awkwardly during the exchange, seized the moment to scurry to their seats, the mother mouthing a quiet "thank you" to Clara as she passed. Mike Hanlon, clipboard still in hand, leaned against the galley counter, his expression a mix of amusement and exhaustion.

"Well played, Cap," Mike said, keeping his voice low as James turned back toward the cockpit. "You've got the magic touch. That one was about ten seconds from turning into a YouTube special."

James shook his head, a wry smile tugging at his lips. "Just another day in paradise, Mike. Let's get this bird moving before he decides to stage a sit-in at the lav."

Mike chuckled, giving a mock salute before turning to coordinate with Clara and the rest of the cabin crew. James stepped back into the cockpit, the door clicking shut behind him, muffling the cabin's hum. Zahra looked up from her tablet, her dark eyes glinting with mischief.

"Nice one, Cap," she said, her tone teasing but approving. "You didn't even have to pull out the 'federal regulations' card. I'm impressed."

James settled into his seat, adjusting his headset. "Years of practice, Zahra. You'll get there. Just wait till you're defusing a row over an emotional support hamster at 35,000 feet."

Zahra laughed, the sound bright against the steady hum of the avionics. "Hamster? I'd take that over the snake story from Luton. Did you see the TikTok? Poor woman looked like she was ready to quit and join a convent."

James snorted, his fingers moving through the final pre-flight checks with practiced ease. "Yeah, I saw it. Makes me glad we've got the TSA to filter out the Tupperware menagerie. Alright, let's finish up. We're cutting it close for push."

The cockpit settled back into its rhythm, the brief drama in the cabin fading into the background as James and Zahra focused on the task at hand. The A319neo's systems were green, the flight management system loaded with the Denver-to-Boston route, and the ground crew's chatter crackled through the headset, confirming the pushback tug was in position. Outside, the Denver sun beat down on the ramp, the heat haze distorting the outlines of the Frontier jets parked nearby. The raccoon-tailed A321 seemed to stare back at James, a silent reminder of the cutthroat competition AmericanoAir was stepping into.

"Ground, Americano 1218, ready for push," James said into the mic, his voice steady and professional.

"Americano 1218, Ground, push approved, tail south, call when ready for taxi," came the reply, the controller's voice clipped but clear, with the faint edge of someone juggling too many aircraft at once.

Zahra reached for the pushback controls, her movements precise. "Brakes released, steering pin confirmed out. Ready for push."

The A319neo lurched gently as the tug began its work, easing the aircraft away from the gate with the slow, deliberate grace of a beast being coaxed from its stall. James kept his eyes on the displays, cross-checking the systems as the jet rolled backward, the Rockies sliding out of view through the side window. The ground crew's hand signals were crisp, their neon vests glowing in the morning light. For a moment, the chaos of AmericanoAir's launch—the PR circus, the regulatory tightrope, the passenger meltdowns—faded into the background, replaced by the simple, mechanical certainty of getting an aircraft airborne.

"Push complete, brakes set," Zahra announced, her voice calm but alert. "Steering pin's in, tug's disconnected."

James nodded. "Ground, Americano 1218, push complete, ready for taxi."

"Americano 1218, taxi to runway 35 Left via Foxtrot, hold short of Echo, expect departure in five," the controller replied, the words rattling off with the efficiency of someone who'd said them a thousand times that morning.

Zahra taxied the A319 with smooth confidence, the aircraft responding eagerly to her inputs. The taxiway stretched out ahead, flanked by the endless sprawl of Denver International's ramps and terminals, a concrete labyrinth that felt both familiar and faintly hostile. James kept his eyes on the instruments, his hands resting lightly on the yoke, ready to take over if needed but content to let Zahra handle the groundwork.

"Nice touch," he said, glancing at her. "You've got a feel for this one already."

Zahra smirked; her eyes fixed on the taxiway. "She's a good girl, Cap. Just needs a bit of love. Unlike some of the 320s I've flown—those ones fight you every inch."

James chuckled, the cockpit's tension easing as the A319 rolled toward the runway. The radio crackled with a steady stream of clearances and instructions, the voices of other pilots and controllers weaving a tapestry of controlled chaos. A United 737 rumbled past on a parallel taxiway, its livery gleaming in the sunlight, while a Southwest jet spooled up for take-off, its engines roaring with the kind of power that made the A319 feel like a scrappy underdog.

"Americano 1218, line up and wait, runway 35 Left," the tower called, snapping James's attention back to the task.

"Line up and wait, 35 Left, Americano 1218," Zahra replied, her voice crisp as she eased the aircraft onto the runway threshold. The A319's nose aligned with the centreline, the runway stretching out like a promise— 12,000 feet of concrete, more than enough for a hot-and-high departure, provided the numbers held.

James scanned the displays one last time, his eyes flicking over the engine parameters, the flight controls, the weather radar. Everything was in order, the A319neo humming with quiet confidence. "Take-off checklist," he said, his tone shifting to the formal cadence of the cockpit.

Zahra ran through the checklist with practiced efficiency, her voice steady as she confirmed each item. "Flaps 2, check. TOGA thrust, set. Brakes, released. V-speeds, confirmed. Ready for take-off."

"Americano 1218, cleared for take-off, runway 35 Left, fly runway heading, climb to 9,000," the tower called, the controller's voice cutting through the static.

"Cleared for take-off, 35 Left, Americano 1218," James replied, giving Zahra a nod. "Your aircraft."

Zahra advanced the throttles, the CFM LEAP engines spooling up with a deep, resonant growl. The A319 surged forward, the acceleration pressing James into his seat as the runway markers blurred past. "V1," Zahra called, her voice steady. "Rotate."

She eased back on the sidestick, and the A319's nose lifted, the aircraft breaking free from the runway with the smooth, almost effortless grace of a machine doing what it was built for. The Rockies fell away below, their jagged peaks softening into the haze as the jet climbed into the Colorado sky.

"Positive rate, gear up," Zahra said, her hands moving with precision as she retracted the landing gear. The thump of the gear locking into place echoed through the airframe, a satisfying punctuation to the departure.

"Gear up, confirmed," James replied, his eyes scanning the displays. "Climb thrust, set. Heading 350, climbing to 9,000."

The A319neo settled into its climb, the engines humming as the aircraft carved a path through the clear morning air. Denver's sprawl gave way to the endless plains of the Midwest, the landscape flattening into a patchwork of fields and highways. James felt the familiar rush of a clean departure, the moment when the chaos of the ground gave way to the ordered simplicity of flight. For now, at least, the A319 was theirs, and the sky was forgiving.

"Nice work," he said, glancing at Zahra. "Clean take-off. Let's get her levelled off and see what Boston's got in store for us."

Zahra grinned, her focus unbroken as she adjusted the autopilot. "Thanks, Cap. Let's hope Boston's in a better mood than Gary back there."

The cockpit settled into a comfortable silence, the hum of the engines and the occasional crackle of the radio the only sounds. James leaned back, letting his eyes drift to the horizon. The A319neo was a humble workhorse, but it was theirs, and for the next few hours, it would carry them across the country, a tiny speck of ambition in a sky full of dreams and deadlines.

****

CHAPTER 3 – The Atlantic Is a Puddle Now

Monday 7th July 2025

"Newark Tower, this is AmericanoAir Three Four One Two on final approach, confirm runway?" James asked, thumb resting lightly on the transmit switch, voice level, professional, betraying none of the mild irritation humming beneath the surface.

Beside him in the right-hand seat sat his First Officer for the sector, an Alaskan named Evan McCall, early forties, former bush pilot, former Horizon Air, briefly Delta Connection, and now—by a combination of timing, optimism, and AmericanoAir's aggressive hiring net— long-haul narrowbody FO on a transcontinental sector that technically shouldn't have existed yet.

Evan had the weathered look of someone who'd spent half his adult life in cockpits without jet bridges: windburned skin, crow's feet earned honestly, a beard permanently hovering between "approved" and "HR meeting." He wore the AmericanoAir uniform with the faint air of a man still deciding whether to commit emotionally. His accent was Anchorage-flat, vowels stretched thin by years of radio discipline and snow glare.

"AmericanoAir Three Four One Two, Newark Tower, runway Two Two Left, winds two one zero at one five, gusting two two, continue."

James acknowledged, adjusted their track fractionally, and glanced out through the windscreen. Newark lay beneath them in a hazy, shimmering sprawl of concrete, terminals, freight ramps, rail lines and port infrastructure, all softened by summer heat and the late-afternoon Atlantic humidity. Beyond the runways, the Manhattan skyline rose faintly to the northeast, the towers distant and almost unreal, as though painted onto the horizon by a bored stagehand.

"Two Two Left," James said aloud, more for ritual than necessity. "Bit lively down there."

Evan nodded, fingers resting loosely on the sidestick. "Newark likes to remind you it's still got opinions."

The aircraft—an A321LR in AmericanoAir colours that were still faintly too glossy, too new—rode the air with a patient steadiness. She was heavy but obedient, the extra fuel tanks useful for the San Francisco to Newark run.

The approach checklist was complete, the aircraft trimmed and descending cleanly through six thousand feet. The air outside had taken on that particular murk that signalled a New York summer: not so much weather as a simmering atmospheric grudge. Newark's runways shimmered like mirages, painted lines bending in the heat haze.

"Cabin's secure, Captain." Mike Hanlon, today's cabin manager, leaned into the cockpit, his voice pitched low but unhurried. He looked the same as ever: sleeves rolled, tie askew, the picture of seasoned competence in a world full of amateur drama.

"Thanks, Mike. Tell them it'll be a lively roll-out," James replied, scanning the arrival chart again, hand steady on the sidestick. "Not quite Kennedy crosswinds, but enough to keep us honest."

Evan grinned, eyes crinkling behind his glasses. "You ever land here in a nor'easter?"

"Worse. Once did it with one reverser inop and a cockpit full of lawyers from corporate." James allowed himself a thin smile. "Frankly, I'd rather take my chances with the wind."

Below, the patchwork of Port Newark's container yards and chemical tanks slid by in slow procession, the city's faded glamour giving way to hard-edged industry. To the north, a queue of aircraft waited in line for Runway 22L, tails twitching in the heat: United, FedEx, a single Delta 757 edged out of place like a recalcitrant sheep in a flock.

James keyed the PA, dropping his voice a shade, instinctively British in tone despite the AmericanoAir logos everywhere.

"Cabin crew, thirty seconds to landing. Passengers, please ensure seatbelts are securely fastened. We'll be on the ground at Newark shortly."

He flicked off the mic. "Moment of truth, Evan."

The final approach was a negotiation with the wind, a matter of coaxing rather than commanding. The A321LR's wings flexed, spoilers twitching with each subtle gust. At five hundred feet, Newark's runway finally declared itself—a battered grey ribbon, rubber streaks piled upon rubber streaks, a history of arrivals both smooth and otherwise.

"Two hundred… one hundred… fifty, forty, thirty, twenty…"

James brought the nose up a fraction, crabbing into the crosswind, then straightening at the last moment. The aircraft responded dutifully, main gear kissing the asphalt with a solid, unapologetic thump. Spoilers deployed, engines roared into reverse, and a cloud of dust billowed along the runway edge.

Evan called out the speeds: "Seventy knots… sixty… fifty. We're good."

James eased the brakes, guiding the aircraft onto the high-speed exit. The world beyond the glass transformed instantly—no longer sky and runway, but now the world of taxiways, apron buses, marshals in faded orange, and the distant hum of a city that never, ever seemed to sleep.

"Nice work, Captain," Evan said, his admiration understated.

"I'll take that," James replied, pulling off his sunglasses, running a hand across his brow. Sweat and jetlag felt interchangeable now—a product of time zones, humidity, and the relentless American summer.

James released the tiller, letting the A321LR amble through the heat shimmer of Newark's taxiways. To the left, a pair of United 777s loitered at their gates, engines ticking down, while a ground crew in overalls daubed with "AeroFleet" leaned against a loader and scrolled their phones. The radio burbled with clipped American voices: clearance, ramp, push, slot delays, a medley of acronyms. Somewhere behind, an Air India Dreamliner whined and hissed, its nose canted up, its fuselage glinting with thousands of reflective dots—a detail James found curiously soothing, like watching sunlight on water.

Looking round, James noticed 4 of the European Sprint fleet parked on various remote stands, their tails not in the Stars and Stripe but navy blue, like the fuselage, a giant S in a stylised format, on there, a mix of British G and Lithuanian LY tail numbers.

"Look, it's the Sprint invasion," Evan said, nodding towards the remote stands. "I can't tell if that's reassuring or just a reminder that the Atlantic's a puddle now."

James followed his gaze. Four aircraft, all A320 family, none older than a decade but bearing the faded marks of harder lives: the navy blue tails and stylised 'S', two with British registrations, two Lithuanian. A reminder, if he needed it, that for all the rhetoric of 'AmericanoAir', this operation was built on borrowed airframes and stretched paper trails. The transition was not yet complete; even the paintwork had the uncertain sheen of a startup. He wondered if anyone at Newark's ramp noticed, or if all narrowbodies just blurred into the same logistical headache by mid-afternoon.

They taxied behind a Swiss 777, waiting as a ground marshal waggled his fluorescent batons in a kind of exhausted semaphore. As the aircraft idled, the cockpit filled with radio chatter: ramp control demanding a tighter hold-short, dispatch asking for an updated block time, and a stray fragment from Maintenance—something about a misdirected catering cart now lost somewhere on the port perimeter.

"You know, it's funny that our Euro cousins have been going for 3 years, yet we're only on Day 3 of own American saga," James said, half-smiling at the window, watching the Sprint tails shimmer in the afternoon haze. "Suppose that's progress. Or at least, a warning."

Evan grunted in agreement. "At least in Alaska, you knew what'd go wrong. Here, I'm not sure if it's the paperwork or the humidity that'll kill us first."

They followed the Swiss 777 as it lumbered toward the terminal, the taxiway ahead flickering in the heat. The A321LR's nosewheel thumped over the painted lines, and James felt the peculiar shift that came with leaving the world of airborne possibility and re-entering the realm of ground-bound logistics—a world that never seemed to run to plan, even in the best-run operations.

AmericanoAir's gate allocation was at the end of Terminal B: new, efficient, oddly sterile, with a view across to the United fortress gates and a faint chemical tang from the recently installed carpets. As they reached stand, the ground crew materialised in an efficient ballet of neon vests and tired expressions, guiding the aircraft in with measured signals.

"Park brake set. Engines one and two off. Your aircraft, Evan," James said, voice edged with the satisfaction of a landing safely executed.

"My aircraft," Evan replied, running through the shutdown checks, his hands moving with the ease of a man who'd learned to trust muscle memory more than policy manuals.

The cockpit fell into a brief, companionable silence as the A321LR's systems wound down, the hum of the avionics fading into the background clatter of Newark's ramp. James leaned back in his seat, loosening his tie a fraction, the weight of the transcontinental sector settling into his shoulders. The view outside was pure Newark: a sprawl of tarmac, baggage carts darting like ants, and the distant rumble of a departing 737 slicing through the haze. The Sprint aircraft on the remote stands caught his eye again— those navy-blue tails, a quiet reminder of the airline's sprawling, chaotic roots. Three years of European hustle, now grafted onto this fledgling American experiment. Day three, he thought. Feels more like day three hundred.

Evan, still ticking through the post-flight checklist on his iPad, glanced over. "You reckon those Sprint jets are here to help us or just to remind us of who's really running the show?"

James chuckled, the sound low and dry. "Bit of both, I'd wager. Sprint's not exactly known for letting go of the reins. Probably shipped them over to make sure we don't cock up their brand before it's properly Americanised."

Evan snorted, powering down the last of the displays. "Brand? Mate, the brand's a logo slapped on with duct tape and a prayer. Half the passengers think we're a budget Spirit knockoff, and the other half are just happy the fare was under a hundred bucks."

James didn't disagree. AmericanoAir's launch had been a masterclass in ambition over preparation—press conferences with more polish than the aircraft, promises of a "new American dream" that felt like they'd been scribbled on a napkin in a Vilnius boardroom. The A321LR they'd just parked was a case in point: a capable machine, no question, but its glossy livery couldn't hide the fact it had been flying Sprint's European network six months ago, shuttling bleary-eyed tourists between Krakow and Luton. The cabin still had a faint whiff of Baltic catering—pickled herring, maybe, or just the ghost of a thousand budget sandwiches.

"Captain, ground's ready for the passenger count," Mike's voice crackled through the intercom, pulling James back to the present.

"Thanks, Mike. Let's get the numbers sorted," James replied, flicking the intercom switch and glancing at Evan. "Time to face the music."

Evan gave a mock salute, unbuckling his harness. "After you, Cap. I'll handle the paperwork if you deal with whatever's waiting for us out there."

James stood, stretching his back with a faint grimace. The cockpit, for all its ergonomic design, wasn't built for six-hour sectors followed by Newark's bureaucratic gauntlet. He adjusted his cap, smoothed his jacket, and stepped through the cockpit door into the galley, where Mike Hanlon was already coordinating with the gate agent via a crackling handheld radio.

"Manifest says 189 souls, Mike," James said, leaning against the galley counter. "Any surprises?"

Mike snorted, scribbling on a clipboard. "Only if you count the guy in 22C who tried to smuggle a foot-long sub onboard. Thought he could hide it in his backpack.

Smelled like a deli exploded mid-flight. Clara's still fuming."

James allowed himself a grin. "Better than the snake story from Luton."

"Don't jinx us, Cap," Mike said, shaking his head. "I've seen the TikToks. Last thing we need is someone trying to board with a bloody python."

The cabin was emptying slowly, passengers shuffling toward the jet bridge with the dazed, slightly resentful air of people who'd just endured a low-cost transcontinental flight. The A321LR's interior was a study in budget ambition: seats in a tight 3-3 configuration, upholstery in grey and blue, the typical Sprint configuration, and overhead bins that creaked with the weight of overstuffed carry-ons. The air was thick with the mingled scents of recycled cabin air, coffee dregs, and the faint tang of someone's vape that had definitely not been used in the lavatory. James scanned the rows as he moved toward the forward door, noting the usual detritus of a full flight: crumpled napkins, half-empty water bottles, a single sock inexplicably wedged under a seat.

"Captain Hart," came a voice from the jet bridge, clipped and official. A woman in her late thirties, dressed in the sharp navy blazer of AmericanoAir's ground operations team, stood waiting with a tablet in hand. Her name tag read "Vanessa Torres, Station Manager." Her expression was one James recognised instantly: professional calm masking the kind of fatigue that only came from wrangling low-cost airline chaos.

"Vanessa," James said, offering a nod. "Good to see you. How's Newark treating us today?"

She gave a tight smile, the kind that said she'd already put out three fires before lunch. "Oh, you know, the usual. Ramp's a mess, catering's late, and we've got a Sprint crew from the European side kicking off about hotel assignments. Welcome to day three."

James chuckled, stepping aside to let Evan and Mike join them on the jet bridge. "Sounds about right. Anything we need to know before we debrief?"

"Not really. You've got 43 minutes until your next departure, and that's over at Terminal C," Vanessa continued, her voice dropping half a tone as though she were delivering bad news at a funeral. "Gate C-87. They've moved it twice already. United's hogging half of B tonight, so we've been shunted across like the poor relation at Christmas."

James exhaled slowly through his nose. Forty-three minutes to cross Newark Liberty International Airport from the far end of Terminal B to the depths of Terminal C, with a full crew change, a captain's handover, and whatever fresh chaos Ops had queued up. In a sane airline, that would be tight but doable. In AmericanoAir, on day three of revenue operations, it felt like a deliberate test of endurance.

"Brilliant," he muttered, then caught himself and switched back to the measured tone he used in front of ground staff. "Thanks, Vanessa. We'll make it work."

Vanessa gave him the weary half-smile of someone who had heard that phrase far too often. "Oh, and you've got a different A321 for that, it's a Guadalajara run, so you've got the full brief on the Guadalajara customs setup. It's their first rotation for us, so expect some teething issues with the manifest uploads—Mexican side's still using that ancient system that hates our DCS. And, oh joy, the catering's coming from a new vendor down there, so if the sandwiches taste like regret, don't blame me."

James nodded, absorbing the litany with the resigned poise of a man who'd long since stopped expecting smooth operations. Guadalajara—Jalisco's bustling hub, a gateway to tequila country and, apparently, one of Sprint's routes. It seemed, from the route map, that Sprint was trying to compete against the operations of Frontier and Volaris, the two American operating airlines backed by Indigo Partners, the Arizona based low-cost giant that had its fingers in more aviation pies than seemed possible.

James had skimmed the route announcement during his pre-flight brief: AmericanoAir pushing into Mexico with the kind of aggressive pricing that made investors salivate and competitors snarl. Fares starting at $29 one-way from Newark to Guadalajara, baggage fees not included, naturally. It was classic Sprint playbook—flood the market, undercut everyone, and let the ground staff sort out the inevitable mess.

"Guadalajara, eh?" Evan said, falling into step beside James as they descended the jet bridge, the air conditioning blasting a welcome chill after the cockpit's stuffy confines. "Never been. Heard the tequila's decent, though. Have you been?"

"No. Even though Frontier and Volaris are siblings through Indigo, the AOCs and Unions wouldn't allow such easy cross-pollination. Separate AOCs mean separate worlds—crews, maintenance, the lot. You'd think being under the same Indigo Partners umbrella would smooth things over, but no, it's all firewalls and red tape. Volaris runs Mexico like a fiefdom, Frontier sticks to its US backyard with a bit of spillover. We're the interlopers here, barging in with Sprint's playbook."

Evan nodded, his boots scuffing the worn linoleum of the jet bridge as they descended into the terminal proper. "Makes sense. Last thing the unions want is some British-Lithuanian hybrid poaching their slots. Still, $29 fares to Guadalajara? That's got to sting for them. Passengers win, I guess, until the first delay turns into a riot."

James hummed in agreement, his mind already shifting gears to the logistics ahead. Terminal B was a hive of mid-afternoon activity: passengers milling about with the dazed expressions of those who'd just survived security, gate agents barking into handhelds, and the omnipresent scent of overpriced coffee mingling with jet fuel exhaust wafting in from the ramps. The terminal's architecture was a mishmash of 1970s brutalism and half-hearted modern updates—glass partitions here, LED screens there, all under a ceiling that seemed perpetually in need of a fresh coat of paint. Overhead signs directed flows to gates 40 through 68, with clusters of weary travellers huddled around charging stations, their devices plugged in like lifelines.

"Ladies and Gentlemen, Sprinter flight MGT 8903 to Shannon is ready for boarding at gate B-52. That's flight

S0 8903 to Shannon from gate B-52. All paid for priority boarding will commence in approximately ten minutes. Passengers are advised to have their boarding passes and identification ready. Thank you for flying Sprint Air."

The announcement echoed through the terminal, tinny and slightly distorted, as though the speaker had given up halfway through the sentence. James paused, half-turning towards the sound. There, beyond a cluster of United gates, a familiar navy-blue tail loomed against the glass: one of the Sprint A320s he'd spotted from the air.

Evan raised an eyebrow. "Shannon. That's one of their transatlantic feeders, isn't it? The ones they're using to pretend they've got a proper network."

"Yeah, they were, over winter, doing a Keflavík to Newark run, but that's now a direct Shannon to Newark with the A321LRs," James said, completing the thought Evan had started earlier. "They've been using those to feed passengers onto our domestic legs. The whole thing's a patchwork quilt—European crews on the transatlantic legs, American crews on the domestic, and God knows who on the Mexico runs. It's like they're trying to outdo Frontier and Volaris at their own game, but without the benefit of being part of Indigo Partners."

Evan raised an eyebrow. "You think they're worried? Frontier and Volaris have been codesharing for years now—codeshares that actually work. Volaris flies out of Guadalajara like it owns the place, and Frontier's got the US network to feed it. We're the new kid crashing the party with $29 fares and a DCS that probably still thinks it's in Vilnius."

James shrugged as they pushed through the crowds, dodging a family with a double stroller and a suitcase the size of a small car. "Worried? Probably not yet. But if we keep undercutting them on price and the passengers keep coming, they'll notice. Volaris has been the king of US-Mexico routes for years—cheap, reliable, and they know the customs dance inside out. We're going to have to learn fast."

They reached the AirTrain platform, a sleek monorail that snaked between terminals like a silver vein. The platform was packed: pilots in various uniforms, cabin crew dragging rollaboards, passengers with the glazed look of those who'd been awake since dawn. James and Evan squeezed onto the next train, the doors hissing shut behind them. The AirTrain glided smoothly, offering a brief view of the airport's sprawl—runways stretching into the distance, aircraft taxiing like oversized insects, the Manhattan skyline a hazy promise to the east.

"Forty-three minutes," Evan muttered, checking his watch. "We've got to do a crew change, handover, and get to C-87. That's cutting it fine."

"Newark's designed for this," James said, though he didn't sound convinced. "AirTrain every few minutes, and the walk from C station to gate 87 is another ten minutes if we hustle."

The train jolted slightly as it pulled into Terminal C station. They stepped off, the air cooler here, more corporate—United's colours dominated the walls, blue and white, with the occasional United Polaris lounge sign promising luxury that AmericanoAir passengers could only dream of. The terminal was busier than B: business travellers in suits, families with screaming toddlers, and a group of college kids in matching hoodies heading for a spring break flight.

They walked briskly, rollaboards clattering behind them. James's phone buzzed—a message from Ops via Microsoft Teams.

East Coast Ops: *Aircraft swap confirmed. N748SP at C-87. Crew briefing in progress. Fuel uplift delayed due to ramp congestion. ETA 10 mins late already.*

"Great," James said aloud. "We're already behind before we've started."

Evan glanced at the message over his shoulder. "At least it's not a tech delay. We can work with late fuel."

They arrived at gate C-87 with fifteen minutes to spare. The gate area was a scene of controlled chaos: passengers lined up for priority boarding, gate agents arguing with a man who insisted his carry-on was under 10kg despite it clearly bulging like a rugby ball, and a small cluster of AmericanoAir crew waiting for the handover.

Gate C-87 was already a microcosm of the world Sprint had made for itself: two Americans at the front, voices pitched for dominance, a Lithuanian gate agent tapping a battered iPad with all the patience of a man chiselling runes, and a huddle of uniformed Sprint crew—navy-blue suits, gold-trimmed stripes, and the sort of jetlag that never quite wore off, only receded between sectors.

James scanned the gate area, his eyes settling on the cluster of Sprint crew members standing near the podium. They were a mix of familiar and unfamiliar faces, their uniforms a shade darker than AmericanoAir's but unmistakably cut from the same corporate cloth. The navy-blue blazers bore the stylised 'S' logo, and their expressions carried the universal fatigue of low-cost aviation—resigned but ready, like soldiers in a war they didn't start. One of them, a woman in her early thirties with a sharp bob and a clipboard tucked under her arm, caught James's eye and gave a nod. Her name tag read "Lina Kazlauskaitė, Cabin Manager."

"Captain Hart?" she called, her accent lightly Baltic, the vowels clipped but warm. "You're on the Guadalajara leg?"

"That's me," James replied, closing the distance with Evan at his side. "Lina, is it? Good to meet you. This your crew?"

Lina nodded, gesturing to the group behind her. "Most of them. We're short one cabin crew—she's stuck in a security queue back at B. Newark's having one of those days. You've flown with Sprint before?"

"Not exactly," James said, offering a wry smile. "AmericanoAir's my home now, but I've been on the wrong end of Sprint's scheduling a few times in Europe. You're the transatlantic cousins, right?"

Lina's lips twitched, a flicker of amusement breaking through her professional veneer. "Cousins, maybe. More like the ones who show up uninvited with a dodgy bottle of wine and expect a seat at the table. We've been running Shannon to Newark for three years now. This Mexico thing, though…" She trailed off, her eyes flicking to the gate agent wrestling with the oversized carry-on. "Let's just say it's ambitious."

Evan chuckled, setting his rollaboard down. "Ambitious is one word for it. I'm Evan McCall, FO. What's the mood like on your side? Ready to take on Volaris and Frontier?"

Lina shrugged, her clipboard shifting slightly. "Mood's the same as always—survive the shift, don't lose the paperwork, and pray the DCS doesn't crash mid-boarding. Volaris and Frontier? They've got the home advantage, but Sprint's got the fares. $29 to Guadalajara's got people booking faster than we can process them. Problem is that the systems aren't keeping up. You'll see when we board."

James nodded, his mind already ticking through the implications. Sprint's ultra-low-cost model was built on razor-thin margins, which meant every delay, every glitch, every passenger tantrum was a direct hit to the bottom line. The Guadalajara route was a bold move, but boldness without infrastructure was a recipe for chaos. He'd seen it before—airlines stretching themselves thin, betting on volume to outweigh the inevitable breakdowns. Sprint, with its British-Lithuanian roots and now this American offshoot, seemed determined to test that theory to its limits.

"Right," James said, glancing at his watch. "We've got about ten minutes before we need to be on the aircraft.

Vanessa mentioned a fuel delay and some customs quirks with Guadalajara. You got anything on that?"

Lina's expression tightened, just enough to signal she'd been expecting the question. "Fuel's the least of it. The A321 at C-87—N748SP—came in from Boston an hour ago. It's got a minor write-up for a sticky tray table in row 18, but maintenance says it's cosmetic, not a deferral. The real headache's the customs setup. Guadalajara's system is… let's call it vintage. Their DCS talks to ours about as well as a drunk uncle at a wedding. And the catering?" She rolled her eyes. "New vendor, first day. If the chicken wraps taste like cardboard, don't say I didn't warn you."

Evan snorted, adjusting his cap. "Cardboard's an upgrade from what we had on the San Francisco leg. At least it's edible."

James allowed himself a brief grin, but his focus was already shifting to the aircraft. N748SP, an A321neo, was one of AmericanoAir's newer additions, but "new" in this context was relative. Like the A321LR they'd just flown in, it had likely spent its early years in Sprint's European network, shuttling passengers between secondary airports with names like "Berlin Rechlin" or "Liverpool Chester." The thought brought a flicker of amusement—Sprint's knack for branding obscure airfields as major cities was legendary, and now they were bringing that same audacity to the Americas.

"Let's get to the aircraft," James said, nodding to Lina. "Evan, grab the pre-flight brief from Ops. I'll do the walkaround and meet you in the cockpit."

"Roger that," Evan replied, hefting his rollaboard and heading toward the gate podium, where the Lithuanian agent was now explaining to the oversized-carry-on man that no, his bag couldn't be gate-checked for free.

James turned toward the jet bridge, Lina falling into step beside him. The bridge was a tunnel of fluorescent light and recycled air, the kind of liminal space that felt like it belonged to no country, no time zone. The faint hum of the A321's APU greeted them as they approached the aircraft door, a reassuring sound despite the chaos waiting inside.

****

CHAPTER 4 – The Art of Air Marshal Cock Ups
Friday 11th July 2025

Of all the things James could find while in the forward lavatory of his Airbus A321LR, near to the end of a Los Angeles to Washington Dulles flight, as he had needed to go to the toilet, a Federal Air Marshal shield and gun, left in the sink, was not exactly of an outcome he'd have expected. He stared at the silver badge glinting under the lavatory's dull overhead light, nestled awkwardly in the sink basin like a discarded piece of costume jewellery. Beneath it lay the holstered pistol—compact, jet-black, standard-issue Glock. It hadn't been left carelessly on the counter. No, it had been dumped. And whoever had done so hadn't flushed, hadn't wiped the sink, hadn't even shut the lav lid properly. The whole forward lavatory was a portrait of lazy panic.

James didn't move for a few seconds. His first instinct wasn't fear, oddly—it was dismay. The same tired, tight-lipped dismay he reserved for bad rostering, late paperwork, or passive-aggressive emails from Ops. His bladder complained sharply, so he took a hasty step back out of the lav and locked the flight deck door behind him.

He re-entered the cockpit, where the first officer, a 63 year old Detroit native named Carl Jefferson, glanced up from the flight management system, brows already knitting at the sight of James's unsettled face. The autopilot thrummed quietly. Out beyond the windscreen, high summer sun was already burning the last pink off the stratosphere, horizon glowing somewhere over Colorado.

James shut the door softly, lowered his voice and muttered, "Carl, we've got an urgent problem. I've just found an Air Marshal's badge and firearm in the forward lav. Just sitting in the sink."

Carl's weathered features barely changed; only a deep exhale gave him away. "Christ," he said, almost conversational. "Left his shooter in the bog?"

"Worse than that. Looks like he panicked. There's… a mess."

They locked eyes a moment, old and young, both trained to expect every kind of airborne absurdity but still floored by new varieties. James ran through a mental checklist: It was strictly against company policy, let alone FAA regulation, to touch a weapon or federal credentials—doubly so if you weren't the one authorised to carry them. But neither could he leave a loaded firearm unattended in the lav. Even a quick call to the purser would open a nest of procedural hornets. He felt his pulse tick up: this wasn't the sort of decision that made it into the training manual.

"Who's the Marshal on the manifest?" James asked, voice low.

Carl tapped the EFB, squinting at the encrypted section under 'Gov Security Personnel'. "One on board. Name of Harris. Sat row 10C. Quiet chap. Chatted with the FA in the forward galley before we left LA, that's all I know. You know we're nearly at IAD, right. I'm going to raise it with ATC, so they're ready on the ground, but not in the clear," Carl said, his voice taut with the slow patience of a man who'd done this for decades and seen bureaucracy flex its many-tentacled reach. "You want to grab the purser? I'll keep an eye on the cockpit and make sure we don't startle anyone."

James nodded, hand resting on the latch, already building his mental script for the least catastrophic way to break this news. Before he opened the door, he forced himself to breathe slowly, squaring his shoulders to assume the role expected of a captain, not merely a man caught up in someone else's panic.

He stepped into the forward galley, catching the Purser, a young Floridian named Kevin Reid, mid-way through assembling the service trolley for the pre-arrival Buy-on-Board run. Kevin's usual easy grin faltered at the sight of James's expression, replaced by a warier professionalism. The galley thrummed with the vibrations of the big Leap engines in cruise; somewhere back in the darkened cabin, a child cried out, a bell dinged, and a passenger pressed the call button.

"Captain? Something up?" Kevin asked, lowering the can of Diet Coke he'd been ferrying from the trolley to the worktop.

James gestured with a subtle tilt of his head, glancing at the lavatory door. He pitched his voice just above the hum of systems and whispered, "I need you to listen carefully, Kev. I'm closing the forward lav until we land, and enforcing the seat belts. Seems our idiot FAMS officer has left his piece and badge there."

Kevin's face stilled, the gravity settling over him. He glanced involuntarily at the lavatory door, then back at

James, his posture straightening with the kind of self-conscious authority that came with suddenly realising he'd have to act like the sensible adult. "No shit," Kevin whispered, his accent sharpening into something more brittle.

James nodded, his voice a measured hush. "I wish I were joking. Lock it off, and I'll Pan Pan Dulles Approach, have Local and Federal LEO meet us. It'll be a remote stand—don't let anyone near that lav until we're on blocks. If anyone asks, say there's a plumbing issue, leave it at that."

Kevin's eyes darted over James's face, searching for any sign that this was some elaborate wind-up, but found none. He inhaled, then set his jaw, squaring his shoulders with a kind of resigned steadiness you only saw in crew who'd worked through the pandemic. "Alright, Captain. I'll keep the area clear. If the marshal himself tries to get clever, what's your call?"

James considered. "If he approaches, keep it calm, but don't let him in. Tell him Ops wants a word on the ground. I don't care whether he flashes his ID or badge, you don't open that door. He can wait until the authorities are present. This is federal territory now."

Kevin nodded. "I'll get Kayla to mid-cabin, loop Amelia onto the PA for a galley loop. Nobody goes past 1L unless it's crew or med emergency. And Kev? Keep eyes on 10C," James added, dropping his voice as a couple of passengers stirred from slumber nearby. "Don't make it obvious, but if Harris so much as twitches wrong, I want to know."

Kevin gave a brisk, silent nod—gone was the pretence of casual service. He pivoted, lips tightening as he assumed the brisk but undramatic gait of a seasoned purser in the midst of low-grade crisis. The trolley was locked, stowed beside the bulkhead, and within a moment Kevin had quietly briefed the nearest crew member with a murmured "Plumbing fault, don't let anyone up," and an unspoken glance of urgency.

James watched as the cabin theatre adjusted almost seamlessly. If there was one thing he admired about his crew, it was their ability to dance along the knife-edge between routine and chaos, hiding any hint of abnormality from a hundred sets of passenger eyes. No sudden movements, no exaggerated whispers—just a slight shift in the choreography, subtle as a minor turbulence deviation.

He stepped back into the cockpit, clicking the door shut behind him, heart still prickling. Carl's eyes met his with a steady calm. "Sorted?"

"As much as it can be," James said, dropping back into his seat and donning his headset. "Kevin's locked down the forward galley. Nobody in or out. I'll call Dulles on the secondary and let them know we're coming in with a sensitive, ah, security irregularity. I won't use the marshal's name or mention the firearm—just a request for federal LEO to meet at the aircraft and secure the forward lav."

Carl nodded, fingers flicking methodically over the approach brief. "Better they hear it from us than from some Twitter idiot. You want me to pull the cabin video for the last twenty minutes, just in case?"

"Good idea," James replied, already rehearsing the script in his head.

He toggled the radio, switching to Dulles Approach on the backup. Voice carefully neutral, he keyed into his radio mic button.

"Dulles Approach, Americano 723, with a Pan Pan. We've got a situation involving government security personnel—requesting remote stand and law enforcement to meet us on arrival. No immediate threat to aircraft or passengers. Please confirm."

There was a brief pause, the kind James knew meant a controller was pulling a supervisor closer to the screen. The reply, when it came, was clipped, professional, and calm—exactly the way he wanted it:

"Americano 723, copy Pan Pan. Remote stand will be arranged. Law enforcement notified. Advise if further assistance required."

James exhaled, letting the tension settle on his shoulders for a moment. He shot Carl a look of grim appreciation.

"Right. Now we see if our friend in 10C makes a move."

Carl gave a faint, humourless smile. "If he's smart, he'll sit tight and let the system do its thing. If he's not…"

James didn't answer. They both knew how federal ego, fear, or plain old embarrassment could spin a situation out of control. He scanned the cabin camera views—10C was visible in the corner of the forward camera, Harris's posture rigid, head bowed over a battered paperback. If he felt the eyes on him, he gave no sign.

"To be fair, with Trump sacking half the Federal protective service budget last quarter, I'm surprised there's any Marshals left to cock it up," Carl murmured, dry as Nevada gravel. "You know he's sacking the National Park lot soon and going after "To be fair, with Trump sacking half the Federal protective service budget last quarter, I'm surprised there's any Marshals left to cock it up," Carl murmured, dry as Nevada gravel. "You know he's sacking the National Park lot soon and going after the Amtrak police too? Maybe after this they'll come for the stewards on the City of New Orleans."

James managed a bleak smile, the edges of it worn thin. "Suppose next week it'll be us, armed with a bottle of Evian and a sharpened Biscoff."

"Spirit of 2025," Carl deadpanned.

James turned his focus to the pre-arrival checks, ticking through flows by rote, mind still snagging on the pistol in the lavatory, the badge, the mess—what had happened in that cubicle that made a trained federal agent abandon his sidearm like a nervous rookie? The possibilities circled grimly. Panic attack? Illness? Sudden crisis of confidence?

Or worse—what if it wasn't Harris who left it? The thought gnawed, cold and silent. He willed himself not to spiral: chain of custody, that was all that mattered for now.

Protect the scene, keep passengers safe, let the feds unpick the rest.

He thumbed the cabin camera again. Harris hadn't moved, not even a furtive glance toward the galley. Kevin was at the bulkhead; arms folded in the practiced stance of a purser with zero time for chancers.

"Americano 723, you are number one on the approach, expect runway one right, wind zero-niner-zero at six, cleared ILS," the controller's voice crackled in his headset, every word steady with the impersonal assurance of someone who handled emergencies for a living.

James acknowledged with a calm, "Cleared ILS, one right, Americano 723." His voice was neutral but clipped, signalling to the controller that the situation, while unusual, was under control—for now.

He muted the intercom, turning back to Carl, who was already programming the approach into the FMS. James's mind raced ahead through the descent: the checklists, the briefing, the precise wording of his post-landing announcement. He tried to will himself into the safety of routine, focusing on the sequence of procedures that would get the aircraft, its crew, and its passengers to the ground and into the hands of authorities with as little drama as possible.

The next ten minutes passed with a kind of brittle, contained tension. Kevin moved with clockwork precision, his cabin crew deploying the seatbelt sign early under the pretext of a minor turbulence warning. Passengers murmured but complied, and Harris remained unmoved in 10C—if anything, his stillness was now unsettling, his book propped open but unread.

Through the forward camera, James watched as a young mother argued gently with her toddler, who wanted to use the loo. Kevin intervened, offering a quietly firm apology about the "plumbing" issue. The mother grumbled, but returned to her seat, shooting Kevin a tired, suspicious look. In that moment, James felt a pang of sympathy for his crew, forced to police a situation none of them had created, spinning calm out of uncertainty like magicians with battered hats.

The approach into Washington Dulles was smooth, the air eerily calm as the plane broke through the lower cloud deck and the lights of the city came into view. Carl handled the radios with his usual unruffled confidence. James ran the before-landing checklist with the fluidity of a thousand flights, each step a touchstone against the rising thrum of adrenaline.

As they intercepted the localiser, Carl's voice was low but steady. "You want me to call the tower direct? Make sure the law's waiting at the stand?"

James nodded. "Let's make sure they don't get clever. If there's a delay on the ground, it's on the feds, not us."

Carl made the call, keeping the details vague: "Dulles Tower, Americano 723, confirming law enforcement requested on arrival, security issue isolated to forward lav. Crew request no approach to aircraft until LEO is in position."

"Americano 723, roger, security will be in place. Taxi as directed."

The descent played out in efficient silence. Flaps set, gear down, landing checklist complete. James stole one more glance at Harris on the cabin monitor—still statue-like, knuckles white on his paperback. The landing itself was textbook, the main gear kissing the tarmac with only a faint thump, reversers spooling up as the A321 decelerated towards a remote stand lit by the fierce glare of ground floodlights.

As they rolled clear of the active, a string of marked SUVs and one unmarked black sedan became visible on the ramp, blue strobes reflecting on the wet apron. James felt the muscles in his jaw tighten; whatever came next was out of his hands, but he would see it through on his terms.

He taxied to the stop point as directed, set the brakes, and announced to the cabin, "Ladies and gentlemen, welcome to Washington Dulles. For operational reasons, please remain seated with your seatbelts fastened until the seatbelt sign is switched off. Thank you for your cooperation."

Carl ran the shutdown flows while James keyed the interphone. "Kev, stand by. Feds are outside. Nobody off, nobody in the forward. You alright?"

Kevin's reply came, clipped but steady: "All good, Captain. 10C hasn't budged. I've got Amelia posted at 1L, and Kayla's locked down the mid-galley."

Outside, the floodlights intensified as ground agents motioned to the jet bridge crew to hold back, keeping the stand clear for the swarm of uniforms now massing just beyond the nose of the aircraft. Through the window, James could see an ATF officer in a black windbreaker, a pair of US Secret Service agents and someone in an FBI trench coat, huddled around a radio. Not the sort of reception that boded well for a routine handover. A police dog sat beside the SUV, nose lifted, bored and expectant.

James ran through a last checklist in his head: cockpit locked, CVR marked, incident time logged, chain of custody for the lavatory scene unbroken since his initial discovery. He caught Carl's eye, reading the same exhausted resolution in the old FO's face. They'd both flown into their share of storms, literal and metaphorical; this one, at least, was nearly down to its last act.

A sharp knock sounded at the forward left door—two beats, then three, the sequence agreed for law enforcement presence. Amelia, standing poised by 1L, glanced to Kevin, who had assumed the role of doorman and bouncer both. James pressed the interphone, voice level but insistent.

"Cabin secure. Who's on the other side?"

A clipped reply filtered through the reinforced door, relayed by the agent holding up his credentials to the fisheye peephole: "Special Agent DeSantis, ATF. We have the manifest and are here for the security irregularity in the forward lavatory, Major Hart."

James did a double take, as it was rare for someone to address him by his Air Force rank on a civil flight deck, but DeSantis looked the sort to have done his homework, or at least to have trawled the TSA's security profile list before boarding an aircraft surrounded by this much muscle. James exchanged a glance with Carl, who gave the faintest, slowest of shrugs—let the federales play their game.

He keyed the interphone: "I'll open the cockpit. Cabin door remains locked until I say so."

James stood, tugged his uniform jacket straighter, and exited the cockpit into the forward galley. He met Kevin's eye, steady as granite, and signalled to Amelia with a tilt of his head. "You'll open on my word. Only for the ATF."

A tense, mechanical hush fell as the door slid back with a double thunk. The corridor beyond seemed flooded with authority. Special Agent DeSantis, trim and balding, stepped through flanked by a larger man in an FBI windbreaker and a short, severe woman with USSS credentials and her partner, a youngish USSS agent whose expression betrayed the double fatigue of a long shift and the premonition of paperwork yet to come. They moved with that precise, slightly over-practiced choreography of federal law enforcement: aware of their own spectacle, careful not to spook the civilians in the rows beyond.

James kept his voice low and courteous, the accent crisp, a little tired but unflinching. "You're here for the security item?"

DeSantis nodded, producing a small evidence bag with one gloved hand, the other holding a digital notepad. "Major Hart, appreciate your cooperation. You have not touched the item since first discovery?"

"Correct," James said, gesturing to the lav door. "I entered, saw the weapon and badge, left immediately. Nobody else inside since. I locked the door and briefed my purser—he's kept the area clear."

The woman from the Secret Service took a small step forward, her presence exuding the quiet confidence of someone long-accustomed to being the only adult in a room full of adrenaline. "Can we get visual confirmation before we break the seal? For our chain."

James produced the cockpit iPad, calling up the internal video, and handed it over. The agents watched in silence for a moment: the timestamp, the way James had discovered the lavatory, the subsequent securing. The FBI man grunted, scribbling on a legal pad.

"Alright, we'll open up now," DeSantis said quietly. "Captain—stay close, but out of the line of sight. Purser, you as well. Nobody else up here."

He nodded at the DHS agent, who reached up, broke the lavatory seal, and swung the door open with a crisp, deliberate motion. The interior was just as James had left it: the badge still glinting, the holstered Glock positioned awkwardly atop a balled paper towel, the air tinged with the scent of stale soap and panic sweat.

For a moment, all four agents simply stood there, weighing the scene. Then the FBI man murmured, "Photograph first," and they snapped a sequence of forensic images before the ATF agent reached in, gingerly plucking the badge and firearm into separate evidence bags. The whole sequence took less than two minutes, but James knew it would be replayed in reports for weeks.

DeSantis turned to James. "Captain, thank you. We'll need statements from yourself, your purser, and your flight crew. Your first officer as well. We'd prefer to do them on the stand, if you don't mind, while memories are fresh."

James nodded, masking his irritation—every minute this dragged, the more questions would circulate among passengers, and the less he could control the narrative. "I'll need to brief my FO and the crew, but we'll comply."

The Secret Service agent stepped closer, voice pitched low. "And the Marshal? He's onboard, yes?"

James met her gaze squarely. "Row 10C, name of Harris. He hasn't left his seat since the incident. We've kept it that way, at my direction."

A brief silence passed, weighty with unspoken protocols. The FBI agent gave a terse nod, flipping his badge open with an audible snap. "We'll speak to him now. Please keep your crew and passengers seated until we advise otherwise."

James watched as the agents filed down the aisle, an unmistakable ripple of tension trailing behind them. Kevin hovered at his side, posture braced. "You think he's going to make a scene?"

"Doubt it," James replied, sotto voce. "But he'll know his career's hanging by a thread."

The walk down the aisle had the strange, slow-motion quality of all true moments of crisis: James watched as the federal trio passed, their presence drawing wary eyes from those passengers close enough to spot the lanyards, sidearms, and crisp windbreakers. To most, it would register only as the usual dance of authority in transit—lost property, medical issue, a celebrity needing privacy. But those who did clock the serious faces and the unyielding posture would know something was very, very wrong.

James stayed at the forward bulkhead with Kevin, hands folded over his tie to stop them trembling. He could feel his heart kicking at his ribs, his mind split between the relief of passing the problem to those paid for it, and the dread of what might still go wrong. He could see, two-thirds down, the shape of Harris—stocky, close-cropped, somewhere between ex-military and failed gym enthusiast—glancing up as the lead agent stopped at his row.

The agents spoke quietly, but there was an unmistakable change in the atmosphere. People craned in their seats, subtle as ever. Harris's face moved through a series of emotions: confusion, dawning panic, and finally a sort of hollow resignation. He did not stand up, did not argue. He nodded, lips pressed tight, and submitted to the requests for ID and credentials with hands that shook just enough to betray him.

The FBI agent produced a set of cuffs—a quick, discreet flick—and Harris was quietly asked to stand. His head hung low as he was ushered forward, murmurs rising and falling as the trio blocked him from view. There was a brief, half-hearted protest—"I need to speak to my supervisor"—but it died almost instantly, as if Harris himself already knew there was no story he could tell that would let him out of this with dignity or job intact.

James felt a sudden, jarring sympathy for the man. However badly Harris had screwed up, nobody put themselves through FAMS training to end like this: handcuffed in a public aisle, reputation shot to hell, weapon bagged up by strangers. Kevin seemed to sense it, too, glancing sidelong at James with a look that blended compassion and weary disgust.

"Seen a lot, but never this," Kevin muttered, his voice pitched for James's ears only.

"Nor me," James replied. "But let's keep our bit clean. I'll deal with the paperwork; you watch the cabin."

The agents led Harris forward, carefully shielding him from passenger view with their own bodies. The Secret Service woman signalled to Amelia to crack open 1L just enough for them to slip through. The second they vanished, the hum of speculation started: the low rumble of cabin chatter, the beginnings of TikTok videos no doubt already being drafted in heads across row after row.

James slipped back into the cockpit, glancing at Carl, who was quietly collecting his headset and stowing paperwork. The first officer's voice was gentle, almost too neutral. "Harris?"

"In custody. Calm enough. No drama. They'll want us out for statements."

Carl grunted, the sound halfway between relief and annoyance. "You think this'll make the news?"

"Give it fifteen minutes. Depends on if anyone films the next bit," James replied, mouth twisting. "You alright to come out, or want me to go first?"

Carl shook his head, gathering his jacket. "We'll do it together. Not our circus, not our monkeys, but they'll try and say it is if we're not careful."

James allowed himself a thin smile. "Let's be careful, then."

He keyed the PA; voice modulated for calm. "Ladies and gentlemen, apologies for the brief delay. We have a minor security issue being handled by authorities. Please remain seated until instructed by crew. Thank you for your cooperation."

He let the mic drop, heart drumming, and stepped into the forward galley with Carl at his side. Kevin had already mustered the rest of the crew near the L1 door, all postures radiating a cool professionalism.

"Statements?" Kevin asked, already resigned.

James nodded. "They'll want your version, Carl's, mine, and anyone who touched the front galley. You, Amelia, Kayla, possibly whoever walked past the lav last. I'll make sure they keep it to just the facts. Nobody speculates. If they ask, just stick to what you saw or did."

Kevin nodded, eyes scanning the gathering outside the aircraft. "Want me to brief the rest?"

"If you would. No heroics, no filling in the gaps. Just facts."

Carl reached across and squeezed James's shoulder—a small gesture, but a steadying one. "You did it by the book. Don't let them say otherwise."

James managed a grateful nod. "Let's get it over with."

****

CHAPTER 5 – The Day Things Changed
Saturday 12th July 2025

"These losers in the cartels are going to see my big, beautiful US Air Force, and the servicemen who risk their lives, take the action to the border and beyond," the voice of President Donald J Trump on the television of the crew room at Fort Lauderdale International Airport. "and we're not going to apologise for defending America. You've seen the numbers, the planes, the jobs. Everyone's talking about it. Except the fake news, who are very bad people. But we're going to do it anyway. Thank you, God bless you, and God bless the United States of America."

A half-hearted applause filtered out from the TV's tinny speakers, mingling with the buzz of the flickering overhead lights. The CNN chyron, all-caps and hysterical, crawled past

TRUMP ORDERS FULL ENGAGEMENT AGAINST MEXICAN CARTELS - MILITARY DEPLOYMENT TO SOUTHERN BORDER.

No one in the Fort Lauderdale AmericanoAir crew room seemed to pay the broadcast much attention. They'd seen this all before: Presidents making threats, cable news in meltdown, the airline bracing for "operational impacts." Outside, subtropical rain lashed the apron in thick, metallic sheets, and on the windowless wall, a roster screen blinked yellow and red with delays. Across the city, even the iguanas had gone into hiding.

James slumped deeper into the sagging brown sofa, idly rotating his airline badge on its lanyard, boots on the edge of a battered coffee table. Today he was on milk runs, doing Fort Lauderdale to Miami to Havana to Miami to Governor's Harbour to Miami to Kingston back to Fort Lauderdale, the sort of schedule only an airline that was determined, in its first week of operations for a European ULCC brand that wanted to kill Spirit, who had back in February, came out of Chapter 11 Bankruptcy, and absorb the yellow fleet, could inflict upon its crews. The irony, James knew, that the two low cost carriers, Sprint and Spirit, sounded almost alike, and therefore almost certainly confused the public, had long since stopped being funny. Passengers booked Sprint thinking they were on Spirit, or vice versa, and AmericanoAir, as the operator of the Sprint branded services, had borne the brunt of it, even though they had signed the franchise agreement, with operations starting less than a week earlier.

That meant that there were Spirit, Sprint, Frontier and Breeze Airways all competing for the Summer traffic in the US, with Sprint the only one, via AmericanoAir, to serve Cuba and the Bahamas, unlike Spirit or Frontier, who had terminated their services to both certain "unprofitable" Caribbean points after the latest round of regulatory chess. AmericanoAir's version of Sprint was, technically, the first European airline in decades to operate scheduled flights from the US to Cuba, albeit via a brand nobody on the island had heard of, and with an aircraft that was navy blue.

"What a dickhead," James's First Officer, a Jamaican born pilot named Kofi looked up from his phone, snorting as the President's voice faded into a cacophony of punditry.

Kofi was thirty-five, as easy-going as he was precise, with an accent that seemed to modulate effortlessly between Montego Bay and Miami, depending on whether he was talking to a passenger, a dispatcher, or, as now, just venting to James.

James grinned, but said nothing. The airline world, as always, kept spinning regardless of presidents or policy or TV drama. What mattered was weather, rosters, delays, paperwork—those things you could actually touch.

Kofi stretched, long legs uncoiling from beneath the battered crew room table. "You know, man, I came all the way up here from Kingston for this job. Thought it'd be all sunshine and smooth flying, get a break from the politics back home." He thumbed his badge. "Turns out, it's just politics in a different accent."

"Welcome to Florida," James replied, with the faintest attempt at a smile.

Rain hammered the tin roof overhead, as if to punctuate their collective misery. Out on the ramp, a navy blue A319neo shimmered in the Floridian sunshine, its navy blue fuselage with stars and stripes tail glinting in brief bursts between the rain. The Sprint logo, in yellow, was prominent as usual while there was a small AmericanoAir logo on the forward passenger door, so subtle most passengers never noticed it until they were posting complaints online. Next to it, another Sprint Airbus A319neo, James knew, was slated to do runs to Grand Turk, San Juan, Sint Maarten, St. Croix, Key West, Naples and West Palm Beach International for its final for its final round of island hopping before being sent north to Boston, the next city in Sprint's American experiment. The Sprint tailfins looked out of place amid the tail parade of Spirit yellow, Frontier raccoons, and the more conservative white of Delta and American. To the untrained eye, it was chaos. To James, it was just another Saturday.

The crew room filled with the scent of burned coffee and stale cookies, the remains of a pilot's breakfast that no one ever actually enjoyed but always nibbled at, out of habit more than hunger.

Kofi glanced up at the screen, then back at James. "You reckon the bosses know the difference between a hurricane and a presidential order?"

James snorted. "They'll blame the weather, same as always. Cheaper than paying delay comp." He checked his watch, then the group chat on his phone, where the WhatsApp crew group was a scroll of memes, passive-aggressive "operational reminders" from management, and the usual dark banter about FTL limits and the latest rumour from Miami ATC.

The purser for today's flight, Marisol, breezed into the room with a clipboard and a look that managed to be both cheerful and exasperated. "Alright, gentlemen, the bus is here in five. We've got N742SP to start—she's on Gate F7, catering's late, the Havana paperwork's wrong, and Ops say the Miami slot is, quote, 'flexible'. In other words, chaos as usual." Marisol's dark hair was still damp from the rain outside, her uniform blazer hung over one arm, revealing a faded sprint-logo polo beneath.

James sat up a little straighter as Marisol rattled off the morning's complications. He offered her a weary smile—the sort you gave to people you'd see again in some other crew room, in some other city, with the same broken coffee machine and the same sense of impending disaster.

"Flexible slot means 'don't leave the gate until we beg,' right?" Kofi asked, already tucking his iPad into his flight bag.

"Flexible slot means Operations forgot to file for one," Marisol replied, dropping her bag at the table's edge. "Miami's gridlocked, ATC are playing musical chairs, and AmericanoAir Ops South has said that we're still running to Mexico UFN."

James let out a quiet groan. "How many times have we told them—'UFN' is not a plan, it's just a way of saying 'we'll tell you when we know ourselves.'"

Marisol's laugh was quick, bright but edged. "You want a plan, go work for Delta. Here we do improv, every day."

Kofi zipped his flight bag with a theatrical flourish. "Improvisation, man. That's how you know it's authentic."

As the crew filed out into the humid corridor, the conversation faded to a rhythm of routine: bag, badge, pass, scan. Security in South Florida had become a theatre of the absurd since the new border orders. TSA officers checked crew IDs with a nervous gravity, their eyes flickering to the TV screens behind them, as if expecting a presidential address to suddenly rewrite aviation law mid-shift.

James felt the gentle weight of fatigue settle on his shoulders. He had never felt this kind of tension before— not during the pandemic, not even after 9/11. This was different. The news wasn't something distant and abstract; it felt like a curtain about to fall, a before and after. But for now, all that mattered was the next leg. The flight deck, at least, was a world he understood.

Outside, the ramp crew battled wind and rain, darting between puddles, yellow vests glowing in the murk. Their aircraft, N742SP, was already being refuelled, a catering truck hissing as its hydraulic lift juddered upwards. Two airport police officers watched from the shelter of a golf cart, one eye on the crew and the other on the lightning tracker.

James caught Kofi's eye as they trudged up the airbridge. "You ever wonder if it was all easier in the old days? Before, you know… all this."

Kofi shrugged. "I wasn't alive in the old days. But I heard they didn't have WhatsApp groups. Maybe that was the real golden age."

The cockpit was cool and dry. Familiar. James slipped into the left seat, stretching his arms overhead as he surveyed the panels. The Airbus A319neo still had that faint 'new aircraft' smell, tinged with cleaning chemicals and something uniquely synthetic. He began the flows, fingers flicking over switches, as Kofi loaded the EFB and checked the weather radar.

Marisol poked her head into the cockpit, her tone suddenly serious. "We've got three deadheading Sprint

Europe crew, as they're doing a MIA-Shannon-BHX run and Sprint Ops Dublin booked their hotel here in Fort Lauderdale by mistake—again. They're in 14A, B, and C. One of them, Captain, is wearing, and you'll love this, a RAF roundel pin badge."

"What's the names?" James asked, looking at her manifest, more from habit than curiosity. International dead headers always brought an element of unpredictability to an otherwise formulaic day.

Marisol squinted at the list, her voice dry. "Let's see—one 'S Marsh', who's a FO, a 'H Whiteman', who's a Captain, and a 'P Ryan', who's a lead FA. Marsh is the one with the roundel, apparently ex-RAF, and she's got a carry-on bag with a Sprint Europe sticker that's seen better days."

James gave a soft chuckle at that, turning in his seat to glance at Marisol. "Well, at least if the apocalypse kicks off mid-Atlantic, we'll have a backup pilot with proper war stories."

Kofi's fingers were already dancing over the MCDU, checking the new batch of NOTAMs. The US border states were a glowing mess of red triangles, half warning about temporary military zones, the other half showing "presidential activity" in airspace close to the border. The cockpit windows shuddered under another blast of rain.

"I'll try and find them in the terminal before we go. They're sitting in the galley with the cabin crew, talking about tea and actual biscuits, so don't be surprised if you hear about scones or 'the proper way to fly an approach into Birmingham'," Marisol quipped, before heading aft.

James's gaze lingered on the ramp a moment longer, watching a National Guardsman direct a convoy of Humvees around the cargo perimeter. Another sign of the times: soldiers everywhere, half of them so young they looked like they'd got lost on the way to prom.

Kofi craned his neck, lowering his voice. "You think we'll get caught up in it? All this Trump stuff, the border, the war talk?"

James didn't answer straight away. He was studying the weather radar, but the truth was he'd already asked himself the same question a dozen times. He'd flown in more places than he could name—seen airports shut down for hurricanes, watched politicians make empty promises on TV—but this felt different. Something was shifting.

"We'll keep our heads down, do our jobs," he said finally, more for himself than Kofi. "That's what we always do."

Kofi grunted, unconvinced, but let it drop.

* _ * _ * _ *

The pushback was delayed, of course—fuel paperwork didn't match the upload, catering had delivered extra Halal trays instead of the kosher ones for the Miami-Havana sector, and the 'flexible slot' at Miami became a full ground stop just as they finished the walk-around. Out the window, James watched lightning fork between clouds beyond the airport perimeter, feeling the static prickle across the skin of his hands.

The PA crackled to life. Marisol's voice was the model of calm: "Ladies and gentlemen, welcome aboard this

AmericanoAir Sprint service to Miami. As you may be aware, weather and air traffic conditions in South Florida are causing delays today. We appreciate your patience and will update you as soon as we have more information."

The usual ripple of sighs, murmurs, and WhatsApp messages followed from the cabin. James imagined the three deadheading Brits, enduring it all with that particular brand of irony he'd seen from European crews before. He found it oddly reassuring.

He glanced at the flight plan—still the same: Miami, Havana, Miami, Governor's Harbour, Miami, Kingston, back and then a deadhead on a late Sprint service to DC to pick up tomorrows set of crews. Six sectors, three countries, four sets of ground handlers who never quite got the memo that Sprint wasn't Spirit, and not a single leg where he expected anything to run on time. In other words: a normal Saturday in AmericanoAir's brave new world.

He scrolled through the dispatch remarks again, half-hoping for something actionable, half-hoping for a new excuse to scrub the whole day. Instead, he found the usual nonsense: "Ops monitoring situation. Maintain flexibility. Expect increased ramp checks at MIA and HAV. Overflight permits confirmed. Do not discuss military activity with passengers. Crew—refer to manual section 12.3 for media protocol." As if a laminated section in a battered blue manual would cover the day when the world started coming apart.

There was a tap on the door. Marisol leaned in, her expression somewhere between weary and apologetic.

"Captain, catering says it'll be another ten. Miami ATC just put a freeze on all inbounds—some story about a Cessna busting airspace, but everyone's saying it's Secret Service rerouting the President's convoy. Weather's going nowhere. Shall I do a pre-board walk or…?"

"Let's wait. If we start, we'll just have them all stuck on here. Tell the gate we'll do final paperwork and call them in ten."

She nodded, closed the door behind her. Silence again. Outside, a ground crewman in soaked hi-vis overalls gave James a thumbs-up through the rain-streaked glass, his breath fogging the window. James saluted back, for no reason except habit, and watched the young man hustle back to shelter.

Kofi sighed. "Back home, man, they'd call this a blessing. Delay means time for another coffee. But here? Delay just means someone in Ops is going to be texting us every five minutes."

James grinned. "Yeah, and none of them actually here in the rain." He peered at the flickering EFB screen. "Got your jump seat briefing ready for the dead headers?"

"Reckon I'll just tell them not to touch anything, and if they want tea they can have what passes for it in the galley. You ever had those British crew try to fly the sim? They can't help themselves—always think they know better."

James snorted. "I flew with a bloke out of Stansted once— spent forty minutes arguing about the best way to intercept the localiser at Malaga. In the end I just turned the autopilot off and let him sweat."

Kofi laughed, his accent veering towards London for a heartbeat. "Proper education, that is."

"You know, I'd have been getting ready to deploy against the cartels, had I still been in the USAF," James said after a few minutes of silence. "I don't think I'd be able to do it now, though. I remember when I was back in Syria and Iraq, how the briefings always started with something about 'surgical strikes' and 'precision targets'—as if that made the mess any less bloody once the wheels left the tarmac. At least here, all you can kill is time and maybe your sense of optimism."

Kofi's eyes flicked up, both sympathetic and shrewd. "You think any of those pilots out west actually want to be flying over Mexico? Dropping JDAMs on cartel convoys, then home in time for the evening news?"

James shrugged. "I doubt they get much choice. Most of 'em just want to keep their heads down till it all blows over, like the rest of us. Orders are orders, until you find out they've changed and no one told you."

The cockpit settled into its ritual hush—James flicking between checklists, Kofi prodding the weather radar for optimism where none existed. In the galley, muffled voices—Marisol greeting the deadheading crew, someone making jokes about Brexit and hurricane protocols. The aircraft had that liminal, in-between feeling of every delay: ready to move, but held tight by invisible threads.

By the time catering arrived—trays clattering, tempers frayed, one container slightly steaming from a short-circuiting oven—the rain had slackened to a mere drizzle. Rampers in waterlogged boots gave up all pretence of running and slogged through puddles, ground handlers barked at each other in the particular Florida-Cuban-English that passed for ramp protocol, and the hum of the APU became the day's only constant.

James flicked his phone off airplane mode for a moment and glanced at the crew chat, already fifty unread messages deep with speculation.

Kofi was scrolling through TikTok—aviation memes, mostly, a wry smile playing at the edge of his lips. "You see the one about the pilot who tried to cross into Mexico on a JetBlue pass and got detained?" he asked, showing James a pixelated video of a man in a captain's hat arguing in Spanish with a confused border guard.

James only shook his head, the gallows humour too familiar to sting. "Wait till we get rerouted and end up in Nassau. Then we'll see who's got jokes."

Marisol returned, ushering the cabin crew with brisk efficiency. "Boarding in ten. Miami want us to taxi but not depart—so, scenic views of the ramp for everyone, free of charge."

A new face, one of the deadheading European crew, lingered near the cockpit, peering in with a slightly dazed, curious look—pale, short hair, a bright roundel on her lanyard.

"Sarah Marsh," she introduced herself, the vowels clipped and brisk, "Sprint UK, Manston base. They told us Miami, but nobody said anything about thunderstorms or Fox News on every telly."

James noticed the way she stood, and clicked from her posture and "attention" stance that she was former military, not just in the badge. He extended a hand, half rising. "James Hart. AmericanoAir. Welcome to Florida, where the only thing we control is the humidity."

Sarah shook it firmly, eyeing the cockpit with a quick, tactical scan. "Heard you've got border delays, presidential flyovers, and a catering mutiny—all before noon?"

Kofi grinned, already liking her. "You forgot the flight plan bingo. Place your bets—Cuba, Nassau, or two laps of Miami holding?"

She gave a dry smile. "As long as we don't end up in Santiago de Compostela, I'll count it as a win."

James gestured to the observer's seat. "You're welcome up front any time. We've got coffee that tastes like jet fuel, and the entertainment is just watching Ops try to spell 'Havana'. You on the Shannon from Miami, right?"

Sarah nodded, dropping her battered Sprint Europe-issue overnight bag at the cockpit bulkhead. "Aye. Miami–Shannon, then on to Birmingham. If Ops don't change it again." There was a flicker of something in her voice— weariness, but underneath it, a streak of amusement that James recognised from every career crew: the deep-rooted knowledge that the universe was in on the joke, and the only way through was to play along.

"We'll make sure to send you off with a full complement of complaints about the coffee," Kofi said, already warming to her.

Sarah flashed a grin. "We're used to it. Last week, our galley oven started a fire in row 32 and the only thing that burned was the gluten-free scones. Crew ate the rest."

"Forgive me for asking, but did you serve?" James asked, curious if his "Forgive me for asking, but did you serve?" James asked, curious if his instinct was right. He watched Sarah's face carefully—a flicker of surprise, then a half-nod that was all admission.

"RAF. Typhoons mostly. Few years. Washed up in the world of LCCs when I realised that I preferred four hours to Palma over four months in Oman. That and Covid cuts because Boris spaffed the money on parties. Never thought I'd miss the sand, but here we are."

James grinned, suddenly feeling less isolated by his own past. "USAF here, 77th Fighter Squadron, Shaw AFB. Tapped out at Major."

"Ah, I finished as a Flight Lieutenant. 5 years in Typhoons on QRA and 5 in Tornados, including Syria. I can't believe Trump has decided the cartels in Mexico are fair game, especially as a couple of weeks ago he'd had the Spirits bomb the Iranians nuclear sites and nobody in Ops even knew which airspace was going to be closed next," Sarah replied, her tone halfway between sardonic and deadly serious. "I was on a Muscat to Skardu when the Iranians fired at Al Udeid Air Base."

"Skardu? Where the hell is that?" Kofi interrupted, eyebrows raised.

"North Pakistan," Sarah replied, matter-of-fact. "Sprint do a once weekly to Islamabad from Muscat and a once weekly to Skardu, as the Omanis were keen to impress the Pakistanis. Came in to Skardu just as Iran fired at Al Udeid and the airspace between Bandar Abbas and Muscat was closed with five minutes' notice. had to divert to Karachi and wait for Oman to reopen the corridor. It's amazing how fast airspace can go from open to closed just because some old men in government decide to start a proxy war. And here we are, thinking Miami thunderstorms are a big deal."

James let out a low, commiserating whistle. He saw the same glint in her eye that he recognised in so many ex-military pilots—never quite at ease, always holding back a few stories, always able to find the bleakly comic side of international chaos. Sarah Marsh fit right in. He gestured again to the jump seat.

"You ever want a change from British rain, you could always try Floridian rain. I swear it's wetter," he said, with a thin smile.

"Just wish it washed the politics away as easily as it soaks your socks," Sarah replied.

Kofi watched their exchange with open curiosity, then glanced down at his EFB as the boarding chime rang. Outside, the rain was easing, and the light took on that distinctive Florida post-storm hue: everything sparkling and momentarily clean, the world scrubbed but never really changed.

"Boarding commencing," Marisol's voice echoed from the interphone, and soon, the familiar parade began: harried families with massive strollers, businessmen pretending not to sweat through their shirts, elderly couples clutching Miami Dolphins cushions, and a handful of confused tourists who seemed to think Havana would be just like Key West. A pair of TSA officers hovered at the jet bridge, eyeing everyone with the pained look of people who long ago lost the will to intervene.

The deadheading Sprint Europe crew filtered into the back rows, swapping banter with Marisol and the local FAs, instantly at home in the strange in-between world of airline crewmembers everywhere. Sarah lingered in the forward galley, sipping a scorched coffee and watching the controlled chaos unfold.

By the time James had finished the last of his pre-flight checks and Kofi had fended off three separate calls from Miami Operations ("Just checking if you're still here?" "Yes, still here." "Okay, great, keep us posted..."), the jetway was retracting. The purser, Marisol, stopped by the cockpit for a final nod.

"Full house," she said, ticking something on her tablet. "Thirty-eight through connections for Cuba, twelve going just to Miami for onward Spirit flights, and the rest all local. We've got a pair of non-revs from headquarters, too—something about 'observing the operation'. Not our problem. You want a run at the PA?"

James winced, but nodded. "Might as well let them know what they're in for."

He lifted the handset, pitched his voice to that calm, dry register only true airline pilots could ever quite manage. "Ladies and gentlemen, from the flight deck, this is your captain speaking. We're just about ready to push back here in Fort Lauderdale, but due to weather and ongoing air traffic delays, we'll be holding for a short while longer. We appreciate your patience. Our route today will take us south and west toward Miami International, where we expect further holding due to presidential flight restrictions and a number of, ah, operational impacts. We'll keep you updated as things develop. In the meantime, sit back, relax, and enjoy the sound of Florida rain on the fuselage."

He clicked off, and could almost hear the collective sigh from the cabin. Passengers these days didn't expect good news, only that they'd eventually be told something.

The engine start sequence began, predictably, with another delay: Miami ATC called up, apologetic, reporting that the presidential convoy was rolling down the Dolphin Expressway with the full array of FHP outriders, causing Miami's entire arrival corridor to freeze. The ground controller's voice, a mix of Cuban drawl and weary amusement, barely rose above the background static.

"Americano Seven-Four-Two Sierra Papa, expect pushback in approximately twenty. You are number four in sequence for release to the ramp. Advise if you need anything. Sorry about this—El Presidente, you know how it is."

James simply acknowledged, routine professional patience masking the steady thrum of irritation. He cut the intercom and glanced sidelong at Kofi. "Bet you a Cuban sandwich that by the time we get to Miami, they'll be sending all traffic to Opa-locka just to keep the optics clean."

Kofi rolled his eyes. "If we get sent to Opa-locka, I'm putting in for double pay and a week on a beach. But sure, you're on."

Sarah, now settled with a takeout coffee and one leg crossed over the other in the jump seat, smiled faintly at the exchange, her gaze flicking between the MCP and the APU page on the overhead.

"Is it always like this?" she asked, dryly. "Back in Europe we just blame the French ATC and call it a day."

James grinned. "Here, it's always the weather, the politicians, or—if all else fails—the catering. At least the French have the decency to tell you they're on strike. Here, you only find out when you're on short final and the tower tells you they're closed for a 'VIP movement'."

The cabin was a gentle buzz behind the locked cockpit door: the shuffle and click of seat belts, the distinct rustle of service carts, the murmur of low conversation from a galley where Marisol and the Sprint Europe crew were already swapping union stories and finding out what—if anything—could pass for proper tea on an AmericanoAir aircraft. It was, in its own odd way, soothing. As long as the cabin sounded like this, nothing truly catastrophic was happening outside.

****

CHAPTER 6 – The Cockpit Incident
Sunday 13th July 2025

"Newark Tower, this is Americano 5231, approaching via Juniper, established on the ILS two-two, requesting permission to permission to continue approach," James Hart spoke with the crisp clarity honed by two decades in the left seat.

The flight, AmericanoAir 5231, was already 4 hours late because, in the infinite wisdom of Washington Dulles, and a Royal Jordanian 787 causing a nuisance of itself on the taxiway at Dulles, causing everything from their flight to half of British Airways, United and even Lufthansa's Atlantic operation to grind to a halt. It had taken two ground tugs and a maintenance crew with more optimism than mechanical insight to tow it clear of the active runway, and by then Americano 5231 had missed its original slot by a smooth three hours and forty-five minutes.

As James turned onto final for Runway 22 at Newark Liberty International, he shook off the exhaustion of the day behind him. He was paired with a decent First Officer today—Andreas Carlsen, a quietly competent Scandinavian with a love for weather charts and a tendency to mutter METARs to himself during descent. Their interaction had been professional, almost boring in its routine. After the last few weeks, boring was a blessing.

"Flaps full, gear down, landing checklist complete," Andreas called out calmly.

James acknowledged it with a nod, hands light on the side stick. The aircraft, a brand new Airbus A321LR, fresh from the Airbus factory in Mobile, Alabama, responded like a dream to every nudge and correction. After the run of rickety, inconsistent airframes they'd been flying through late June, it felt like steering a thought made metal.

"Americano 5231, continue approach, winds two-one-zero at five, cleared to land runway two-two," came the reply from Newark Tower.

"Cleared to land two-two, Americano 5231," James replied. Then, to Andreas: "I have control."

James cradled the side stick as they dropped down the glideslope, feeling the latent tension of a day spent waiting and shuttling through operational hell. He let his gaze sweep across the clean horizon of the Newark basin: the toy skyline of Manhattan shivering in humidity, the chemical blue of the Passaic River to their left, and the haze-smudged outline of Liberty State Park. Below them, the tarmac and taxiways writhed with a ballet of delayed jets and irate ground controllers, all of them prisoners to a day that had gone awry from the start.

"Speed's good, localiser captured," Andreas intoned, glancing between the flight director and the instrument panel, confirming what James already knew. The Scandinavian was solid, a steady pair of hands and temperament, and a reassuring presence amid AmericanoAir's recent revolving door of pilots.

James reflected for a moment on the churn that now defined their daily life: faces cycled out from one rotation to another, CVs with histories as patched as the airline's business plan, a who's-who of ex-regional and furloughed pilots all trying to make the best of Americano's ambitious chaos. Andreas, at least, came from the old school—ex-SAS, then Air Sweden until their abrupt collapse, before being poached by Sprint Group for the US launch. Professional, unreadable, and exactly as Scandinavian as the name promised.

James let his feet rest lightly on the pedals, coaxing the nose through the last mile as the radio altimeter ticked down, numbers falling away with a lulling certainty. There was comfort in the ritual: the hum of the engine, the checks flowing like a litany, the knowledge that for these last few minutes, nothing existed but the approach, the aircraft, and the unspoken trust between pilots.

"Two hundred," Andreas called, tone unchanged.

James glanced over at the FO's hands, curled in his lap. No nerves, no tension. He smiled to himself, the first real one he'd managed all day.

"Approaching minimums. Runway in sight."

"Landing," James confirmed, and brought the throttles back, guiding the A321LR through a final, gentle flare. The mains met tarmac with a muted bark, reversers opening with a whine. They rolled out smooth, spoilers biting the thick New Jersey air, tyres hissing over the seams in the concrete.

"Sixty knots," Andreas said, hands still on his knees. "Manual braking. Vacate left?"

"Vacate left," James echoed, guiding them off the active. He toggled the radio. "Americano 5231, clear of two-two at Juliet."

"Americano 5231, taxi via Juliet, hold short Alpha. Contact ground on one-two-one point eight."

"Juliet, short of Alpha. Ground on one-two-one point eight, Americano 5231." James set the frequency, released a soft sigh, and finally let the muscle ache in his right calf register. He shot Andreas a grateful look.

"Nice flying," Andreas murmured, in the noncommittal way of a man who had seen too many good landings to care for unnecessary praise.

James grinned, unclipping his harness. "You kept me honest. Sorry about the delays—none of it's on you."

The FO gave the faintest shrug. "If you fly in America, you must become one with the delay."

James chuckled, tension ebbing now that the hard part was done. They ran through the after-landing checklist in crisp monotone, the unspoken code of old pros. Lights, flaps, spoilers. APU on, transponder to standby, radios handed back to company. Ground control, when he finally got through, was as brusque and overworked as ever, chivvying them into a hold near the midfield cargo ramp, then directing them to Gate 74 at a stately crawl behind two JetBlue Embraers and a rogue Southwest 737.

From the left window, James watched the ragged parade of airline logos and delayed flights—United, Air India, British Airways, the ever-present whiff of jet-A and the sense of enforced waiting that defined American summer travel. Crew buses trundled past, ground staff in reflective vests standing with arms folded and faces blank, every one of them dreaming of clocking off.

Once they finally parked, chocks in, the ground crew opened the forward door, and the weary dance began. Andreas handled the shutdown, while James busied himself with paperwork and the last bits of communication with Ops, fielding a barrage of company messages on his tablet. Most were redundant—apologies, rescheduled block times, and an endless stream of queries about catering, missing bins, and why the hell the RJ 787 had been allowed to block a taxiway for four hours.

Passengers deplaned in various shades of muted resignation. Most offered the blank-eyed nods of the internationally delayed, but a few managed a quick "thank you" or even a weak joke as they trudged past. The purser, Natalie Tremblay, lingered a moment in the doorway, her French-Canadian accent softened by fatigue.

"James, you have another sector today?" she asked, brow creased with the unvoiced question of whether he could talk her out of being rostered to Miami.

He shook his head with a half-smile. "Ops have me swapping aircraft and picking up the late Miami. New FO. You, by some stroke of mercy, are done for the day."

She grinned. "Tell them I said 'merci beaucoup'."

He offered a salute. "I'll trade you Miami for a New York hotel."

She laughed, rolling her eyes, then disappeared into the boarding bridge, shepherding her crew.

James stayed in the cockpit until the last passenger had gone, double-checking the cabin with Natalie, then collecting his flight bag and heading into the terminal with Andreas. At Crew Ops, he signed the usual forms, swapped a few pleasantries with the overnight dispatcher, and checked his phone for new messages—only to find the Miami sector had shifted gates again, and he'd be flying with a new First Officer: Bryce Keegan.

He groaned, quietly. He'd flown with Keegan only once before—a brash, restless thirty-something who had recently made the leap from a regional jet operator in the Midwest, and whose reputation for high spirits and lax professionalism preceded him. In a different era, Bryce might have been "one of the lads" at PanEuro or Sprint, but AmericanoAir was not short of chaos, and James had little appetite for games.

Still, he squared his shoulders, mustering professionalism as he made his way to Gate 88, where a fresh, factory-clean A321neo awaited them for the sector south to Miami. Another four hours, another hundred and eighty souls, another iteration of the great AmericanoAir experiment.

The late afternoon heat pressed against the jet bridge as James strode down, flight bag over his shoulder, tie slightly askew from the humidity. He checked his watch—boarding wasn't due to start for another thirty minutes, but he'd long ago learned the value of being early. It gave him time to settle, to check the tech log, and, most importantly, to meet his new FO on his own terms.

The A321neo was pristine—newer even than the LR they'd just brought in. It still smelled faintly of synthetic leather and glue, the aroma of Airbus branding and a hasty American retrofit. He nodded to the ground staff, offered a quick hello to the cleaning crew bustling in and out, then strode up the air stairs and through the forward door.

The cockpit, however, had the sounds of heavy breathing, squealing and "harder, harder," coming from it. James knew that this was a breach of FAA regulations, especially as the 'sterile cockpit', a protected environment required from pushback to 10,000 feet and below again on descent, was sacred in both law and culture. He paused just inside the threshold, the snap of the door's handle loud in the silence between the moans. The voices—one male, one female—were unmistakable, their urgency all the more jarring for being so brazen, and so close to the start of another rotation. The compartment air, thick with sweat and the synthetic tang of new Airbus plastics, seemed to freeze around him.

James took two deliberate steps forward, past the forward galley jump seat, his hand tightening on the grip of his flight bag. Every second made the scene more surreal. He was a veteran of every flavour of cockpit farce—lecherous captains, inebriated first officers, even the occasional impromptu therapy session with a sobbing cabin crew member—but never, in all his years, had he actually encountered this: a full-on, in-progress tryst, just minutes before boarding, and in full violation of every regulation he'd ever held dear.

He rapped the side of the open cockpit door, not gentle. "Excuse me?"

The movement within stopped at once, a gasp followed by a muted curse. There was a scrabble, the thump of a knee or elbow against a side panel, and a frantic shuffling of uniforms. The male voice, its Midwestern drawl barely suppressed, hissed a whisper that was supposed to sound authoritative but came out sheepish: "Hold on—just—one second, Captain—"

James could feel the prickling heat of a nascent migraine bloom behind his right eye. He fought the urge to bark. "You have exactly one second, Mr Keegan. Make yourselves presentable."

He stood square in the doorway, arms folded, waiting. The woman—junior cabin crew, James guessed from the shape of her uniform tunic—emerged first, her face with cum all over it, her shirt, as, unlike other airlines, Sprint's uniform that it forced AmericanoAir to use was unisex, was only half buttoned, and showing a thin lace bra, one which, as a married man, James hardly wanted to see, and certainly not in the sanctity of his own cockpit. He forced his eyes to a neutral point, scanning the overhead panel instead, as the junior flight attendant—he recalled her name from the crew manifest, *Lena*, barely twenty-three and new to both aviation and, apparently, discretion— hurried past him. She mumbled a mortified "Sorry, Captain," eyes fixed firmly on the floor, hastily dragging a makeup wipe across her face and struggling with the buttons on her tunic as she squeezed through the narrow gap between the galley and the flight deck door.

Keegan followed a beat later, still tucking in his shirt, his tie nowhere to be seen, cheeks florid with the telltale mix of exertion and embarrassment. He moved with the casual arrogance of the young and the heedless, offering James a sheepish half-smile that did nothing to improve the situation.

"Sorry, Cap," he tried, voice too loud, too jovial for the gravity of what had just happened. "Didn't realise you'd be on so early. Just, uh, running through some—"

James silenced him with a look that had cut short many a career misstep. "You'll want to shut the cockpit door, Mr Keegan, and take a seat. Now."

He waited until both had vanished—Lena all but fleeing for the aft galley, Keegan slumping into the right-hand seat—before stepping inside himself, closing the door with a deliberate click. The silence that fell in the cockpit was brittle, edged with the static charge of a storm barely avoided. James dropped his flight bag with a controlled thud, settled into the left seat, and took a long breath, willing his pulse to steady.

He began his flows—oxygen, circuit breakers, battery master, IRUs—moving with a mechanical precision that let his mind race in parallel. What he wanted to do was rage, to let loose on Keegan with every iota of old-school, PanEuro-bred invective he could summon. What he *had* to do, for the sake of the operation and the airline's already precarious standing, was maintain control.

Keegan, to his minor credit, at least had the decency to look chastened. He busied himself with the OFP and tech log, not meeting James's eye.

It was James who broke the silence, voice low but hard as iron filings. "Mr Keegan, you and I are going to have a very direct conversation before boarding starts. You are aware, I assume, of AmericanoAir's policies regarding crew conduct, cockpit discipline, and the sterile environment rule?"

Keegan squirmed, eyes fixed on the FMS. "Yes, Captain. Just—got carried away, I guess."

"Carried away," James repeated, tone flat. "On an aircraft about to be loaded with passengers. In violation of every federal regulation on the books. Not to mention the professional standards you are paid to uphold."

A flush crept up Keegan's neck. "I get it. It won't happen again."

James leaned forward, voice softening only slightly. "You're new here, so let's be clear. What you just did could end your career. FAA, EASA, the company—they do not look kindly on what they would call 'lewd and disorderly conduct' on a revenue flight. If you or Miss Reznikova—" (he checked the crew list again for Lena's surname) "—want to carry on like twelfth graders, do it on your own time. Never again in my cockpit. Am I understood?"

Keegan nodded, eyes finally meeting James's, and for a second, a flicker of actual contrition showed. "Yes, Captain. I'm sorry. Properly."

James held his gaze, making sure the message landed. "Good. Because if there's a next time, I won't be having this conversation in private."

He let the silence settle, then turned back to his pre-flight checks, logging into the company EFB and flicking through the telexes and MELs for the Miami sector. The professional rhythm reasserted itself: fuel checks, weather at MIA, alternate planning (Fort Lauderdale, Key West, Tampa), route amendments. All the while, Keegan worked in stony silence, the easy bravado of five minutes ago wholly evaporated.

As the routines of preflight filled the air, the adrenaline drained and left in its place a leaden, professional quiet. James relished the habit and ritual of checklist discipline, letting the recitations of procedure bleach the memory of what he'd walked into. He reviewed the log, checked the fuel slips, double-checked the last company message from Ops ("Expect more weather on descent into Miami—plan for holding, possible ground stops due TSRA"). There was always weather, always chaos, always another variable.

After a minute or two, the cockpit's hush was broken by the tap of Lena's knuckles at the door—an uncertain, "Captain?" that sounded as if she would rather have vanished into the forward galley forever.

James pressed the door unlock. "Come in."

She stepped into the threshold, eyes trained on the carpet. Her tunic was now buttoned, her face as clean as makeup wipes could manage. Still, her hands fidgeted nervously with the hem of her skirt. "Captain Hart, I'm sorry for what happened. It was unprofessional. Won't happen again. I... I didn't think—"

James cut her off gently, but with no room for misinterpretation. "Miss Reznikova, you are very young in this job, and you made a mistake. That mistake is not to be repeated. What happens in this cockpit reflects on the safety and professionalism of everyone here—not just you, not just Mr Keegan, but the reputation of every crew who wears this badge. I will not be reporting this—today. But if I ever see or even hear of a repeat, I will not hesitate."

She looked up, relief and shame warring in her expression. "Yes, Captain. Thank you."

"Go and get yourself a drink of water. Compose yourself. Passengers deserve to see a professional when they board. Understood?"

She nodded, already halfway out the door, disappearing with a swiftness that spoke to a cabin crew member who knew how quickly a second chance could slip away.

James locked the door, then returned to the silence, finding Keegan watching him sidelong, the hint of a question in his posture. James ignored it. He continued his prep, entering performance data, cross-checking the route in the FMS, then running the initial flows aloud. The familiar script—"Batteries, ON... external power, disconnect..."—was the bedrock of their world, proof that order could be imposed on even the most absurd of days.

A few minutes later, as the terminal announcements echoed through the glass, the gate agent's voice crackled in through the interphone: "Captain Hart, we're ready to begin boarding in five. Any issues up front?"

James considered. "No. Proceed as normal. Let us know if you need anything."

Keegan, perhaps emboldened by the procedural comfort, finally spoke. "You want me to take the walkaround?"

James nodded. "Please. Take your time, do it by the book. Report anything out of the ordinary."

As Keegan grabbed his hi-vis and stepped out, James let his own facade fall, just for a moment. He rubbed his face, pressed his palms into his eyes until sparks danced in the darkness. This, he thought, was not how you kept an airline running. But then, this was AmericanoAir in 2025: half-Sprint, half-shadow, cobbled together by the ambitions of managers three time zones away, run by staff that changed faces faster than a London tube advert.

He straightened, found his composure, and reset himself for the task at hand.

* _ * _ * _ *

As they took off, James noticed that, as he was the pilot flying and Keegan the pilot monitoring, Keegan was busy pulling out a folder marked "Ohio Northern University Claude W. Pettit College of Law" from his flight bag, not even bothering monitoring the radios or inputting crossing restrictions. At first, James assumed it was a set of checklists or maybe a flight planning sheet—he'd seen

FOs use everything from bound Jeppesen manuals to battered iPads as crutches. But as the nose rotated up through VR, and Keegan's right hand hovered idly, James realised the folder was open not to anything aviation-related, but to pages of what looked suspiciously like civil law notes. Keegan's eyes flicked to the pages even as he called "positive rate" in a voice several beats behind the aircraft.

James kept his voice measured. "Gear up."

No response.

"Mr Keegan," James repeated, more pointedly this time. "Gear up."

The FO jerked his head upright, a flicker of annoyance—then embarrassment—crossing his face as he reached for the gear lever and raised it with a practised motion that should have been second nature. The thump of the gear retracting echoed through the frame, more intrusive for the lag in coordination. James could feel his teeth grind.

"Sorry. Gear up," Keegan mumbled, shoving the law notes back into his flight bag, almost dropping the folder in the process. He finally put both hands on the sidestick and thrust lever, but James was already revising his strategy for the rest of the flight. Distraction in the cockpit, *again*, and barely ten minutes since the last breach. The FO seemed intent on setting a record for procedural violations in a single rotation.

They climbed out into the peach-gold haze above Newark, the patchwork of New Jersey and the Atlantic blurring under the summer heat. James scanned the sky, the screens, and—discreetly—Keegan's posture. With every scan, the old lessons from RAF days came flooding back: trust, verify, and, when required, take over. Today was shaping up to be one of those days.

"Americano 5231, contact New York Departure, one-two-four decimal seven five," came the clipped handoff from Tower.

James acknowledged, flicking the radio and answering for both of them before Keegan could reach for the selector. "New York Departure, Americano 5231, passing three thousand, climbing five thousand."

As Departure responded, James completed the after-take-off flow alone, his hands darting from overhead switches to the MCP to the screens, almost daring Keegan to try and reclaim some measure of control. The FO, cowed but not quite apologetic, sat back, staring into the panel. It would have been comic, if it weren't so damned serious.

A minute passed, then James, voice carefully modulated, decided it was time to get ahead of the situation.

"Bryce," he said, keeping his tone neutral but direct, "let's agree: anything unrelated to flying, you stow it for the sector. Especially during critical phases. You know how this works."

A short pause, the radio hissed in the background. Keegan didn't quite meet his eye, but the words at least seemed to register.

"Yeah. Roger that. Sorry, Captain."

The silence between them stretched, broken only by the burble of ATC and the usual engine drone. James set climb power, let the aircraft find its step, and brought up the topic he had been dreading.

"I get it—you're probably juggling a lot right now. We all are. But when we're in this cockpit, you're either pilot flying or pilot monitoring. There's no room for outside distractions. You get that?"

Keegan nodded, slower this time. "I get it. It's just—I'm prepping for the bar exam. It's stupid. I know."

James raised an eyebrow. "You're sitting a law exam? In the middle of a block of duty?"

Keegan shrugged, a gesture that in another context might have passed for bravado. "Got roped into it before Americano called. Didn't want to drop it. But—yeah. I'll keep it out of the flight deck. Promise."

For a long moment, James considered his response. He knew the economics of AmericanoAir, of Sprint Group, of the entire battered airline world: everyone needed a backup plan. Law, property, crypto, TikTok. Still, the line between coping and dangerous distraction was a hard one, and his responsibility—to the company, the passengers, to the professional code—would not let him ignore it.

"Your personal life is your own. But you need to choose: law student or First Officer. Up here, it's the latter. Understood?"

Keegan finally looked him in the eye, chastened for the first time. "Understood, Captain."

James let out a breath he hadn't realised he'd been holding. He set the autopilot, glanced over the initial climb checks, and finally allowed himself to scan the weather radar—lines of thunderstorms ahead, a classic Miami descent on the cards. Behind them, the cabin settled to the drone of cruise, the PA chime occasionally cutting through with automated updates about delays and connecting flights.

For the next hour, the cockpit was a study in uneasy truce. James kept his eyes on the systems, guiding the aircraft by habit and calculation. Keegan, to his credit, abandoned all pretence of legal study and confined himself to the duties of PM, following the checklists with a crispness that suggested he was at least trying to recover ground.

It was during cruise, somewhere east of the Carolinas, that the third and most serious incident of the day occurred.

The cockpit door chimed, the standard two-tone, and Lena's voice came through the intercom: "Captain, I have your coffee. And Mr Keegan, I need you to assist me in the lavatory. My... erm... the plumbing is loose."

James stared at the intercom panel, certain he hadn't misheard, though for a fleeting moment he wished he had. "My… erm… the plumbing is loose."

Was this a coded call for help, or just another chapter in today's litany of cockpit absurdities?

He pressed the intercom. "Lena, repeat that please."

"I need Mr Keegan, Captain, not you, to assist me there."

James noticed that Keegan was grinning like a Cheshire cat—one eyebrow cocked, every inch the cheeky chancer now that the Captain was not the one being invited for "lavatory plumbing duty". It was as if the morning's embarrassment had faded to nothing, his attention now wholly focused on whatever game Lena was playing, or whatever script these two thought themselves to be starring in.

James pressed the intercom again, keeping his voice perfectly level. "Miss Reznikova, is this an urgent safety or medical issue?"

A heartbeat's pause. The static over the line pulsed with tension. Lena's voice, quieter now, almost sheepish, replied: "No, Captain. Just a minor problem. Not urgent."

"Then Mr Keegan is required on the flight deck," James said, his voice brooking no argument. "He'll be available to assist after we reach cruising altitude and there are no operational duties outstanding. I suggest you contact maintenance or another member of cabin crew if it's a technical matter."

He released the button and levelled a gaze at his First Officer that would have melted a less self-assured man. "You are not leaving the flight deck, Bryce. Not unless it's for an actual emergency, or I say so. Clear?"

Keegan's grin withered. "Yeah. Understood."

James let the silence linger, the drone of the engines a low, omnipresent judge. He watched Keegan as the FO shifted uncomfortably in his seat, every instinct of bravado suddenly checked by the iron bands of cockpit discipline.

For a moment, the atmosphere thickened into something almost physical—a wedge of tension, unspoken but undeniable, that hung between them like a storm cloud threatening rain.

Outside, the weather radar flickered with jagged bursts of yellow and red, the signature of summer thunderstorms building over the Atlantic coast. James busied himself with the upcoming approach into Miami, pulling up the latest ATIS on ACARS and confirming that, yes, the thunderstorms were expected right on top of the field, with gusty crosswinds and a ground stop in effect for at least the next half hour.

He let out a slow breath, sinking into the rhythm of the job. The cockpit became, for the next few minutes, what it always should have been: a sanctuary for precision, focus, and mutual trust. Keegan retreated into the PM role, managing comms with Miami Centre, calling out altitudes, backing up James's every move with a quiet diligence that almost made the Captain believe the lesson had landed.

For the rest of the cruise, the pair worked in a silence that was, if not companionable, at least professional. When Lena next knocked—this time for a routine coffee drop— she entered with eyes downcast, placed the cups carefully on the tray, and vanished as quickly as she'd arrived, as if trying to erase herself from the memory of the morning.

****

CHAPTER 7 – Flight 4352
Friday 18th July 2025

"Regan Tower, this is AmericanoAir Flight 4352, do you copy?" James Hart said over the radio, as they were at the outer marker for the transition between the gauntlet of summer storms rolling through the Potomac and the thick soup of Washington's late July haze. The call was clipped, measured—the voice of a man who had spent too many years threading the gaps between chaos and the performance of control.

No answer.

"Regan, this is AmericanoAir 4352, do you copy?" James asked again, hoping that the Airbus A321ceo that had been shipped in as part of the Sprint launch would be blessed with better luck than its usual stablemates. The radios hissed in reply, thunder muttering on the low frequency—no controller, just static, and the low, relentless percussion of summer.

Andreas Carlsen sat beside him in the right seat, his Scandinavian calm unruffled as he peered through the sweaty mist on the windscreen. On the centre pedestal, the transponder flickered with the latest squawk, and the ECAM spat out its usual complaints—ice crystals on the probe, predictive windshear advisory, a vague allusion to "NAV ACCUR DOWNGRAD"—the usual litany on a Washington evening.

James glanced left, then right. Ahead, the Potomac glistened in slats of late sunlight, shards of gold peeking between pillars of black cloud. Rain veiled the Virginia shore, sheets tumbling over glass towers and parkland; to the north, the city glowed sepia, fragile under a boiling sky.

And still, no answer from Tower.

He toggled the comms again, forcing his voice lower, firmer: "Regan Tower, AmericanoAir 4352, established ILS One-Niner, outer marker. Standing by for clearance."

"Nothing," Andreas said with a faint shrug, his voice a muted counterpoint to the fizz of static and the gentle whirr of the avionics. His finger flicked the volume knob, as if to summon some hidden controller from the ether.

James let the silence stretch for a moment, listening for the click of an answering call sign, a hint of humanity in the ether. Instead, the radio offered only the shudder of nearby lightning and the distant howl of wind across antennas. He exchanged a look with Andreas, a silent communion honed by countless approaches together—the unspoken language of those who have lived too long on the sharp end of uncertainty.

James toggled the second radio, switching to approach on VHF2. "Washington Approach, AmericanoAir 4352, ILS established, inbound outer marker, no response from Tower. Standing by for vectors or instructions." He leaned back, letting his mind drift for a fraction of a second through all the what-ifs—radio failure, controller overwhelmed, the remote chance of a security incident in the tower. The ECAM, mercifully, was quiet, but the storm outside was gathering pace.

Nothing.

118

James knew from his time in the USAF that silence on the radio in a city like Washington was rare, and rarely good. The Potomac River approach into Ronald Reagan Washington National Airport was not the sort of place where one could loiter and wait for the world to right itself. This was airspace threaded by rules and teeth, by Secret Service protocols and the constant, unseen hand of federal oversight. Still, the sky outside suggested there were bigger things on the move than any one air traffic controller could contain.

He glanced sidelong at Andreas. The FO had already prepped the go-around: next radial, minimum safe altitude, DCA 2 Departure in the box. Lightning stitched the horizon over Arlington, and the river, grey now beneath the cloud, curved towards the Capitol like a warning finger.

And then suddenly fighter jets. A pair of them.

James knew instantly what he was seeing: the distinct, predatory outline of two F-16s, call signs etched in sharp white against the cobalt flashes of storm light, each banking low over the Potomac as if conjured by the tension in the air. For a heartbeat, the cockpit of AmericanoAir 4352 held only the hum of avionics, the low vibration of the engines, and the primal recognition in James's bones—military eyes, quick decisions, no margin for error.

He keyed the mic once more, voice measured but now threaded with the subtlest steel. "Unidentified fast movers, AmericanoAir 4352, established ILS, unable to contact Tower, holding course for runway one-niner. Please advise if traffic in vicinity."

Nothing but the crackle of static. The lead F-16, trailing the pale afterburner flame that seemed oddly spectral in the gloom, swept across their nose from left to right. The second tucked in at their four o'clock, almost escorting, almost warning. There was something almost ceremonial about it—a ballet of power, of state-sanctioned muscle, a reminder that, in this airspace, commercial traffic flew at the pleasure of others.

Andreas flicked a glance at James, eyebrow quirking. "We are not in Copenhagen now," he said, deadpan.

"Nor Kansas," James replied. "Keep it stable, let's see what they want."

For a moment, both men fell into the choreography of silent teamwork, every movement deliberate. James dialled up 121.5—the international emergency frequency—and pressed transmit. "Any station, any station, this is AmericanoAir 4352, inbound Reagan National, ILS established, unable to contact Tower or Approach, being intercepted by military traffic. Request guidance."

Still nothing.

"F-15s on my side, this is Major James Hart, USAF retired, Captain of AmericanoAir 4352, do you copy?" James's voice was unwavering, the clipped consonants of military professionalism threading through the static.

Still no reply. The only answer was the thunder, that percussive bass note rolling down from the Maryland hills and across the Potomac, making the Airbus shudder and rattle as the first big drops of summer rain hammered the windscreen.

James pressed the transmit button again, his thumb digging into the ridged plastic, feeling the latent pulse of static through the bone. "Any station, any station, AmericanoAir 4352, established on the ILS, unable to contact Regan Tower or Approach, intercepted by F-16s, request guidance, over."

The only reply was the soft, jagged thrum of a world on the edge of a summer storm. To his left, the river arced beneath them, slate-grey, writhing, the bridges of the capital laid out like scars across the landscape. He caught the red glow of the Jefferson Memorial, a muted flicker in the haze, and for a fleeting instant, the surreal sense of being watched—every window below them, every antenna on every rooftop, trained upwards, waiting for something to go wrong.

Andreas leaned in, voice low, calm. "Checklist for lost comms?"

James nodded, flicking the standby card out of the holder on the glareshield. "Squawk 7600," he said, thumbing the transponder. He pressed the numbers deliberately, every motion slow and deliberate, the way only an old hand would in the midst of rising tension. "We do it by the book until we're told otherwise."

The F-16s swept closer, the lead jet's port wing rolling level with their own. For a moment, through the shimmer of rain on the windscreen, James could see the outline of the pilot: helmet, mask, the glint of a visor turned directly towards him. A waggling of wings. The international signal: *You are being intercepted. Follow me.*

James flicked the seatbelt sign to ON, then called back over the interphone. "Cabin crew to the flight deck." His voice was measured, devoid of panic but with a quality of clipped focus that any seasoned crew would recognise at once.

The intercom crackled as Natalie Tremblay, their purser for the sector, answered immediately. "Flight deck, Tremblay."

"Natalie, we've lost comms with Regan. We're squawking 7600, have a pair of F-16s off our port and starboard. Advise the cabin: this is not a drill, remain seated, follow all instructions from the flight deck. Secure galley. Secure doors. No one up, no one about. Prepare for possible diversion or go-around."

The interphone clicked off. Silence. Natalie's response was immediate and crisp—years at Air Canada Rouge and AmericanoAir had honed her professionalism, but James knew what he'd just asked her to do: take a cabin full of already delayed, irritable passengers and clamp it into iron discipline, without so much as an announcement to betray the full gravity of the situation. He could picture her now—standing in the forward galley, shoulders squared, tone even, hands folded just so.

Andreas, meanwhile, was already one step ahead. He'd pulled up the plates for Washington National—every alternate, every contingency runway, every missed approach procedure. The ECAM remained mercifully silent, but the weather radar now pulsed with lurid yellow, red, and a blooming sickle of magenta that promised hail to the north-east.

James's eyes flicked across the instrument panel, his mind a flurry of checklists and possibilities. He pictured the mental map of the Potomac approach—the snaking curve around Georgetown, the tight corridor that made Regan National the bane and pride of every pilot who ever touched down on its tarmac.

Still, the F-16s hovered in their periphery—one now edging ahead and descending fractionally, the classic "follow me" posture unmistakable.

"James," Andreas said quietly, "the lead wants us to descend. He's dropping to one thousand eight hundred feet, and he's doing it on the river track."

James met his FO's eyes—a quick flicker of trust, a centuries-old tradition in flight decks from Dakota to Dreamliner. "We keep our heading. If he signals, we follow. Squawk's set. You have the radios—such as they are. I have control."

Andreas nodded, his hands never leaving the thrust levers, as if his very fingertips could anchor the situation to reality. For a few breaths, all there was the thrum of the engines, the soft bleep of the altitude alert as they dropped into the thickening cloud.

Lightning seared the world outside, forked and sinuous, illuminating the endless tapestry of Washington's sprawl. Below, the Potomac's surface fractured the light into a thousand molten slivers.

James leaned forward, peering through the sheeting rain, willing the horizon to hold steady. The city's monuments—half-shrouded now, spectral—loomed in and out of view. He watched the lead F-16 waggle its wings again, then dip towards the river. Instinct, memory, and years of flying the circuit at Nellis AFB told him: this was not a drill, but neither was it an attack. This was choreography, a ballet with teeth, performed for the benefit of radar operators and nervous suits in windowless rooms beneath the city.

He keyed the PA, voice calm, shorn of all ornament. "Ladies and gentlemen, this is your Captain speaking. We're experiencing a communications issue and will be following standard procedure for arrival into Washington National. Please remain seated with your seatbelts fastened, and listen closely to instructions from our crew. Thank you for your cooperation and understanding."

He could almost hear, in the hush that followed, the ripple of unease through the cabin. But there was no time for second-guessing. The F-16s fell into position—one off the left wing, one astern. Their message was unmistakable: *do nothing rash, follow the choreography, trust the system.*

James knew the irony that a week earlier, due to a Federal Air Marshal leaving his firearm in the forward lavatory on his flight into Dulles, the entire DC law enforcement community had descended upon him with forms, incident logs, and thinly veiled accusations. Now, in the thickening murk above Washington, there was no radio, no ground guidance, and no cavalry except two F-16s dancing on his wingtip.

He let his mind run through the protocols as they descended, the measured logic that came from years of USAF training in F-16s. The Potomac approach, notoriously unforgiving, offered scant room for improvisation. It demanded precision, trust, and a faith that somewhere, unseen eyes were watching and judging your every action.

Andreas read off the altitudes, voice perfectly level. "Passing two thousand, cleared on the ILS. Lead F-16 maintaining parallel." The FO's Scandinavian accent, so often the butt of soft jokes in layovers, now seemed to carry the unyielding calm of northern granite.

James stole a glance at the ECAM. The NAV ACCUR warning still pulsed amber, but the aircraft was holding the localiser with admirable tenacity. In the cabin, Natalie would be moving down the aisle, ensuring tray tables were stowed and passengers braced—not for a crash, but for the unknown. He pictured her, lips set in that Canadian line between reassurance and authority, issuing instructions in English and passable Spanish to a fuselage of weary, anxious souls.

Outside, the world was a study in contrasts. Lightning flickered and strobed behind the marble pillars of the Lincoln Memorial, giving the city an ancient, haunted quality. Rain hammered the windscreen, sheeting sideways, turning the wipers into mere tokens against nature's onslaught. To the left, the lead F-16 kept station, its pilot visible as a pale skull behind the gold of a visor. For a moment, James felt the weight of the role he played—not just pilot, but steward of the old order, entrusted with the passage of lives and metal through contested skies.

A sudden movement on the ground caught his eye: the sweep of blue strobes and headlights along the perimeter taxiway, columns of emergency vehicles assembling in silent, purposeful choreography. They were preparing for every possibility—routine, disaster, act of God or man. James had seen this before: in Kandahar, in Cyprus, at Stansted on that long night of an engine-out return. The orchestration was always the same. Fire and Rescue, Security, the men with long-lens cameras who would file reports nobody read. And somewhere, above them all, the men in dark suits and earpieces, relaying updates to rooms full of generals and politicians.

"Speed's good," Andreas murmured, scanning the instruments. "One thousand to go. Localiser and glideslope captured."

James let his hands rest lightly on the sidestick, resisting the urge to squeeze. The muscle memory was there, old and comforting. "If they want us to break off, we break off," he said, quietly, to his FO. "Otherwise, we land as briefed."

The runway appeared through the haze—runway lights shimmering with a heat that was more memory than physical sensation. There was, James thought, a strange kind of poetry in this approach. Washington in storm season, a river curling like a sullen cat beneath the city, the green and gold wash of thunderstorm twilight, and here he was, an old pilot with Scandinavian steel beside him, watched by the full apparatus of American security as if he might, with a twitch of his fingers, change history.

"Five hundred," Andreas called out, still calm. "Land or go?"

James never took his eyes from the edge of the runway, the way the lights refracted through rain and the battered air. "Land. If we get the cross, or if either of those F-16s does anything rash, we'll go."

For all the choreography, it was still down to the man in the left seat, and James Hart, for all his years, felt his heartbeat notch up just one, two, three marks higher. He checked that the flaps were set, speed brake armed, gear three green, and cast his mind once more through the muscle memory of go-arounds: N1, TOGA, "Positive climb, gear up," and all the things that, in the end, separate a landing from a news story.

Outside, the rain sheared across the windscreen, thrumming with such force that even the wipers surrendered, leaving arcs of distortion over the runway lights. The F-16 to their left dropped lower, then pitched up sharply—a signal, deliberate and unmistakable. Continue. The runway threshold rushed towards them, the last seconds of uncertainty fading in the cold mathematics of approach.

James's hands guided the sidestick with that curious blend of relaxation and taut readiness that only comes with years. The wheels thudded onto wet tarmac, reversers biting as he gently steered through the yaw, a brief dance with hydroplaning and a final, decisive stab at the brakes. The spoilers clattered up, the aircraft shivered, and they slowed in the white roar of rain and reverse thrust.

"Sixty knots," Andreas said, voice the same as ever— calm, unobtrusive, necessary.

James exhaled, the sort of slow, deliberate breath that comes after a close shave on the A-road, or a child's near-miss at a zebra crossing. "Manual braking. Vacate left," he said, echoing the ritual.

He steered off onto the high-speed exit, slowing further as the tyres hissed on standing water. In the rearview of the cockpit window, he caught the flicker of the F-16 pulling a sharp wingover, a gesture as much of release as of order. On the taxiway ahead, fire engines and police SUVs formed a gauntlet—blue lights strobing, white headlights diffusing through the sheeting rain.

"AmericanoAir 4352, clear of one-niner at Echo," he called, with a sudden and irrational hope that the radio would come alive again, that the world would restore itself at the moment of their arrival.

Silence. Not even a flicker.

He taxied as rehearsed, holding the yellow line with the same respect he would offer a cathedral aisle. The F-16s peeled away in formation, roaring low over the river and vanishing into the storm as quickly as they'd appeared.

For a moment, the only connection James felt to the world outside was the drumming of rain on aluminium and the slow, flickering parade of emergency vehicles beside him.

"After landing checklist," Andreas intoned, almost in benediction.

James brought the aircraft to a halt just short of the line of emergency vehicles, brakes squealing as he held position, the Airbus idling in a puddle of its own noise. He glanced at Andreas—who had not so much as flinched—then down at the dark comm panel, the unbroken silence now heavy as a threat.

"Still nothing," Andreas confirmed, flicking the second and third radios out of habit. "Not even a squawk on guard. All aircraft on the field holding."

For a moment, James considered his options: attempt to taxi to the gate unbidden, or hold for further orders that might never come. His military training told him: hold position until instructed. His civilian brain, marinated in Sprint and AmericanoAir's just-get-it-done culture, was itching to get clear of the active taxiways.

He toggled the interphone, summoning Natalie. "Forward galley, flight deck. Natalie, we are holding short, surrounded by emergency services. I need everyone to remain seated, all bags stowed, and no cabin movement until I give the word."

She responded instantly, professionalism undimmed. "Understood, Captain. We are secure."

Rain battered the cockpit, making the world outside a theatre of movement and light. Firefighters, clad in yellow and silver, jogged forward, their faces rendered surreal by the lights and the storm. James saw the leading fire chief, a heavy-set woman with a radio clipped to each shoulder, gesture towards the aircraft—then raise a gloved hand, palm open in the universal command to wait.

James obeyed. Engines at idle, brakes held, he watched as a pair of police SUVs advanced, blue lights flickering, wipers struggling against the deluge. The forward-most officer stepped out, a waterproofed radio at his chin. He held up a small, laminated card: **STAY ON BOARD** in bold black print. The officer then, in a slow, deliberate motion, held up a finger: *one minute*.

"Guess we're waiting for the all-clear," Andreas murmured, eyes flicking between the officer and the ECAM. The rain continued to hammer at the fuselage, a relentless, numbing percussion.

James sat in the hum and dim of the cockpit, his pulse a low echo in the hush that follows crisis. Rain pours down in sheets, carving rivers across the flight deck windows, warping the blue of the strobes and the neon haze of the runway lights. For a moment, everything is still—suspended between the chaos that's just passed and the next instruction that might never come.

The world beyond the glass is abstract, as though the outside has become a kind of theatre: firemen in gleaming wet kit crouch beside their engines, radios pressed to their ears; the lead police officer stands by the nosewheel, a solitary figure outlined in sodium and lightning.

Overhead, the thunder rolled, the sounds reassuring in a way.

Andreas glanced at James, offering a wry half-smile. "Would be a bad moment for a cabin PA," he murmurs.

James allowed himself a fractional smile. "Let's not tempt fate."

Suddenly there was a flicker on the left MCDU—a print message from company dispatch, relayed by ACARS, somehow squeezing through the soup of electromagnetic chaos that the storm has laid over Washington.

FROM: *OCC JFK*

TO: *S7 4372*

MSG: *STAY ON ACFT. ATC INCIDENT UNDERWAY. WAIT FOR INSTRUCTIONS. CONTACT BY PHONE IF SAFE. ACK?*

James nods. "At least someone's watching us. That, or we've made the afternoon news."

He's only half joking. In 2025, nothing stays private—not in aviation, not in America. Half the passengers will have texted, tweeted, or TikTok'd something already: *"Our pilot says we're surrounded by SWAT, lol. Is this normal?"* Within minutes, the WhatsApp groups and Telegram channels, James knew, will be alive with theories—bomb threat, drone, lost comms, UFOs, a dog loose on the runway.

It is, in other words, a Friday.

Pulling out his phone, James loaded Teams up and phoned the East Coast Operations centre on the standard issue Pixel 9A, ringing out with its usual orchestral "corporate" jingle, and, just for a moment, James found himself missing the comforting monotone of an old airline VHF.

He put the call on speaker, keeping one eye on the movements outside. The emergency services had settled into what looked suspiciously like a holding pattern, firemen milling about the undercarriage, a pair of police officers now ducking under the nose to peer up at the cockpit windows. In the background, the curtain of rain wavered, sheets gusting sideways, lending everything a dreamlike, cinematic quality.

At last, the line connected. A tinny voice, New York-accented, barked through the static. "AmericanoAir OCC, this is Janine. Can I have your name, flight number and crew code please?"

James steadied himself, voice crisp, British-tinged professionalism cutting through the jumble of emotion. "Captain James Hart, AmericanoAir Flight 4352, crew code 61429H. Aircraft is an A321ceo, N940AA. We're clear of one-niner at Echo, holding short per instruction, surrounded by emergency vehicles. No radio contact with Tower or Approach for the last fifteen minutes, currently squawking 7600. Intercepted by a pair of F-16s on the ILS and followed to touchdown. Aircraft and passengers secure, awaiting further instruction."

There was a pause—static, the distant clatter of keyboards, the dull drone of other ops rooms behind Janine's voice. "Copy all, Captain. We're looped in with

FAA and DCA Emergency Command. Tower tried to get through to you but there was no answer. Cooperate with local law enforcement and airport fire as directed. DCA says all inbound traffic was put on hold after comms went down. The F-16s were scrambled as the Tower couldn't get you on radio and assumed that you were a hijack risk. You know the drill. They say sit tight. Someone from FAA incident command will make contact either at the aircraft or by airfield phone. Don't move unless told. Are you and your FO both fit, well, no security issues, no mechanical failures?"

James gave the short, clipped answers of a man who has weathered these storms before. "Both fit, all normal. Aircraft sound, no technicals as far as I know. Comms panel showing power but no output. Guard was dead as well. Only data link is functional." A pause, then, "Passengers are secure. No indications of smoke, fire, or unlawful interference."

The line to OCC crackled; Janine's voice returned, brisk now, more confident. "Understood, Captain. Maintain current status, keep ACARS open for text comms. You're top of the FAA's board at the moment—they've got the airport closed until they finish their security sweep. They may want you to deplane remotely or reposition. Expect company shortly, and try to keep the passengers calm. We'll keep this channel open for now."

"Copy, Janine. Thanks." James disconnected, pocketing the phone, and took a moment to roll his shoulders and let his hands settle on his knees. Beyond the cockpit windows, the tableau of rain-lashed emergency vehicles and silent officials became less threatening, more ritual.

At airports, everything was theatre; the audience merely shifted from hour to hour.

He breathed out—slow, meditative—and turned to Andreas. "Let's run the full comms reset," he said, voice low.

Andreas, ever methodical, had already begun, cycling power on the three VHF radios, resetting the audio panels, cross-checking circuit breakers. The ECAM, stubborn as a mule, continued to insist all was normal. Nothing, however, brought the radios back to life. They tested the headsets, the jump seats, even the cockpit speaker—every button, knob and switch.

Nothing. Silence.

Suddenly...

"AmericanoAir 4352, this is Regan Tower, do you copy, over?"

James felt his chest tighten. The voice—the blessed, tinny, real voice of a controller, half-swallowed by static but unmistakably human—cut through the cockpit. He glanced at Andreas, who sat upright, every fibre alert. It took James a moment to swallow the shock and click the transmit on VHF1, more out of habit than hope.

"Regan Tower, AmericanoAir 4352, reading you five-by-five now, over." He worked to keep his voice cool, betraying nothing of the fatigue and adrenaline humming beneath the surface.

There was a heavy pause, then a different voice—older, more controlled, with the unmistakable inflection of someone trying to keep their own nerves in check—came back. "Americano 4352, Regan. You've disappeared from our scope. Confirm location, airspeed, amount of souls and what damage you have, over?"

James glanced at Andreas, who raised his hands—palms open—giving a look that said, finally. James keyed the mic, voice steady, words rolling off as if this was a drill he'd rehearsed a hundred times, which, in a way, it was.

"Regan Tower, AmericanoAir 4352. We are holding short of Echo on the north side of one-niner, brakes set. Airspeed zero, aircraft intact, no damage, no injuries. Souls on board: 184 passengers, 7 crew. Negative smoke, negative fire, negative fuel leak. Awaiting your instructions. We've had complete VHF comms failure since the outer marker. Currently on backup power, ACARS functional. F-16s escorted us to touchdown. Request further instructions and permission to remain with engines running or to shut down."

There was a pause.

And then, over the static, "Americano 4352, repeat that? We have you last two zero miles east of the field, transponder intermittent, negative position update. Are you sure you're on the ground at Reagan National, Captain? Please confirm location, over."

James blinked—then, almost in unison with Andreas, gave a small, mirthless snort. "Regan Tower, affirmative, we are on the ground, holding short of Echo, runway one-niner, surrounded by emergency vehicles. I can see your fire chief, two police SUVs, and at least three perimeter security staff out my window. Request visual check from your ground units to confirm."

There was a long, shuffling pause—a sound, somehow, of pages turning, headsets exchanging hands, perhaps even a chair scraping back from a desk in the tower cab miles away, lost behind a veil of rain and static.

"You mean... you're the plane parked on my taxiway?" the controllers voice said in confusion, and James was surprised at the intelligence level displayed by the controller—a voice so obviously young, probably one of the new FAA contract hires out of Auburn or Embry-Riddle, trying desperately to sound as if this sort of thing happened every day. James felt a brief, wholly inappropriate flicker of sympathy: he'd been that kid, once, a thousand years and a dozen wars ago, watching the whole airfield move to the choreography of his voice and realising—suddenly, viscerally—how much could go wrong in a single radio call.

"That's correct, Regan," James replied, with the brittle patience of a man who'd just landed through thunderstorms, military intercept, and a full comms blackout. "We are stationary, engines running, all checklists complete. Request further instructions."

The radio hissed. Somewhere beyond the cockpit, the storm battered the fuselage, rain drumming the skin of the Airbus with such fury that it sounded like static, or applause, or a warning—James couldn't decide which. The rain, the heat of the day, the stench of ozone and kerosene and fear: all of it pressed in, flattening his world to the hundred square feet of glass and plastic and sweat.

And then, just as suddenly as the confusion had begun, the radio settled, another controller's voice came on, obviously older, more seasoned, the inflection that of someone who'd shepherded everything from a Gulfstream with a senator aboard to the occasional Cessna with a panicked student at the yoke. "Americano 4352, this is Regan Tower—Captain Hart, we have you visually, and the airport perimeter confirms. Maintain current position. Emergency services will approach on my command. Engines to idle, prepare for possible engine shutdown on request. Expect personnel at the left forward door. Do not deplane passengers unless instructed."

James felt, for the first time in nearly forty minutes, the icy thread of adrenaline that had been knotting his spine begin to slacken. Not gone—never gone, in a day like this—but now recognisable, familiar. The machinery of American aviation had finally, grudgingly, lurched back to life around him.

"Roger, Regan. Engines at idle, holding position. Standing by for ground personnel." He clicked off the transmit, allowing himself a dry, private smile. "They finally believe us."

Andreas' wry Scandinavian response came as he finished a scan of the upper ECAM and powerplant parameters. "It would be impolite to taxi to the White House and ask for directions."

James allowed himself a genuine chuckle, a release of the tension that had been accumulating since the outer marker. It was that particular breed of cockpit humour—dry, understated, a refuge from the absurdities that could arise whenever humanity, technology and weather decided to collude.

They worked the after-landing flows in silence: APU on, hydraulics checked, brakes cooling. In the back, Natalie would be repeating her earlier reassurance, perhaps now feeling the tiniest frisson of hope that the worst was behind them. Through the sodden glass, a small army of high-viz jackets was assembling: fire service, airport ops, police, even a couple of figures in business attire—a sure sign, James thought, that there was someone with a clipboard preparing to make this day even longer.

****

CHAPTER 8 – The Interrogations Begin

Friday 18th July 2025

The rain eased, but only just. The storm that had felled half the eastern seaboard still loomed on the horizon — a bruised mass of cloud curling over Washington like an animal reluctant to surrender the prey it had been stalking all evening. Inside the cockpit of AmericanoAir Flight 4352, there was that peculiar stillness that followed crisis: a sense that everyone was waiting for the next voice, the next decision, the next complication to announce itself.

James Hart flexed his fingers once, then again. The adrenaline of the approach had burned off, leaving in its wake a cold clarity — the same sensation that had followed his first emergency landing at Nellis AFB twenty years ago, and the one after that, and the one after that.

"So," Andreas said, after a long exhale, "shall we see what fresh nonsense awaits us?"

James let out a sound that hovered somewhere between a chuckle and a sigh. "No sense rushing it. If they need us, they'll bang on the door."

The pair of them watched the emergency crews standing by: firefighters in glistening silver aluminised suits, police in tactical jackets, airport ops staff nervously clutching clipboards as if paperwork alone could tame the chaos that had just unfolded. A row of blue lights shone through the downpour, refracting in beads across the windshield, casting the cockpit in an otherworldly glow.

The interphone buzzed.

"Captain," Natalie said. "Passenger situation is stable. A few are panicking, some are crying — but everyone's seated. Do you need anything?"

"Just keep them calm," James replied. "No announcements yet. We don't know the plan."

"Understood."

The line clicked dead.

"Coffee's going cold," Andreas murmured.

James huffed a quiet laugh. "I'd drink it if I thought I'd keep it down."

They sat for a moment, the hum of the engines at idle vibrating gently through their bones. The A321ceo felt oddly alive, as if the aircraft itself were holding its breath.

"AmericanoAir 4352, this is the ground," a voice from the radio, obviously someone who had plugged a headset into the airside comms panel below the cockpit window, finally broke the silence. The sound was muffled by rain and distance, the kind of squawk that came from a handheld, not the clarity of the VHF. James reached instinctively for the audio selector.

"Ground, 4352. Go ahead."

"Captain Hart, this is Sergeant Wilkins, MWAA Police. Stand by. We'll be approaching the aircraft on your left, near the L1 door. Engines must be off, brakes set, and cockpit secured. A GPU will be attached to the forward service panel. Please confirm Wi-Fi and cellular services are turned off and that you are ready for us to board."

James pressed transmit, glancing at Andreas as he replied. "Understood, Sergeant. Shutting down now. Wi-Fi and mobiles off, cockpit secured. Stand by."

He let go of the button and nodded to his First Officer, who was already moving with silent efficiency. The engine master switches thunked to OFF, hydraulics drooped, and the airframe gave a subtle shudder as the great fans spun down. Rain pattered against the glass with renewed force, then softened as if the storm itself, too, was winding down.

"APU's online, external power ready as soon as they plug in," Andreas said quietly, eyes on the overhead. The routine was comfort—a flow of buttons, levers, and lights that restored a sense of control in a world tilting on the fulcrum of uncertainty.

"Phones off, radios off," James replied, flicking the switch for the picocell and the Starlink Wi-Fi, the A321 having been fitted with it between its departure from the EU and its entry to US service under the 2023 FCC STC for the A320 family, as, even though Sprint had gone to Airbus who had issued a Supplementary Type Certificate, and the Lithuanian CAA had accepted the modification, the FAA's own rules required the Wi-Fi to be physically powered down for any law enforcement boarding or security event. James confirmed the green **'DISCONNECTED'** light illuminated above the overhead panel, then the same for the mobile cellular network—two worlds now cut off, the aircraft once more an island afloat in the soup of American summer rain. He gave Andreas a curt nod, one hand on the logbook, the other already moving to tidy away the flight paperwork with the same economy of motion that had gotten him through decades of both military and civilian command. Somewhere deep inside, James could feel the old patterns lock in: crisis response, check, checklist, check, de-escalation, check. Keep your crew calm, keep your voice measured, never let the passengers see the gears grinding.

"Ladies and gentlemen, this is your Captain speaking. May I remind you to keep all devices in flight mode until you are permitted to deplane, and certainly to remain seated for now. We have some procedures to complete with local authorities after our arrival—please continue to follow the instructions of our cabin crew. Thank you for your patience and cooperation."

He replaced the handset gently, let the PA chime fade, and rolled his shoulders back, feeling the slow release of tension. Behind them, he heard the soft murmur of Natalie passing down the aisle, voice low, soothing, a masterclass in poised reassurance. He caught Andreas' eye; the First Officer gave a small, approving nod.

A few moments later, a dull clang echoed from the forward fuselage—someone on the ground opening the nose equipment bay, hunting for the GPU socket. Through the rain, James glimpsed the pale gleam of an aluminium ladder and the bulky figure of a ground crew tech in waterproofs, wrestling the power umbilical into place. After a minute, the familiar blue "**EXT PWR AVAIL**" light illuminated overhead.

"Switching to external," Andreas murmured, and the subtle change in the aircraft's hum confirmed the transition.

The rain battered the skin of the Airbus in soft, relentless percussion, then faded to a moist whisper, a grey veil pressed against the vast windows of Ronald Reagan National. Inside the cockpit, James Hart listened to the engines whine down into the hush of shutdown, the propulsive heart of the aircraft stilling one fan blade at a time. He sat back for a moment, feeling every bone, every tendon, every weary synapse. The storm had not quite passed, merely stalled overhead; thunder rumbled far off, echoing down the Potomac, while the clouds moved like bruises over the city.

The moment was brittle and breathless, the world outside wrapped in a peculiar American hush—lights refracting through rain, the strobes of airport ops, the slow ballet of vehicles circling the jet in cautious, wary arcs. Emergency crews hung back, silver suits glinting, radios pressed to their faces, each waiting for the other to give the signal to advance. Police with hands on hips, fire officers squinting up at the cockpit windows. For James, it was déjà vu of every post-incident ramp scene he'd known from Afghanistan to Aberdeen: caution, choreography, and a kind of theatre that always came after the real danger had passed.

"External power's stable, APU shut down," Andreas reported softly. He was methodical, almost preternaturally calm—a presence that reminded James of why he hated to fly with anyone less than a full professional. Together they moved through the final flows, buttoning up the jet as if it might have one last surprise to offer.

The phone on the pedestal buzzed again. This time, Natalie's voice was edged with tension, but still the soul of competence. "Cabin's secure, all seated. Row 29 wants to know if the Wii's coming back."

James almost smiled. "Tell them the Starlink is temporarily out of service due to due to a very official government shutdown," he replied, voice just light enough for Natalie to carry a smile down the aisle. "We'll bring it back when the authorities have finished their show. And thank them for not live-tweeting the end of the world."

He could almost hear Natalie's dry smirk as she clicked off, the cabin doors now standing as the last boundary between the relative sanctuary of the crew and the orchestrated chaos waiting beyond.

Outside, the rain thinned to a sullen mist. Flashing blue and red lights cast fractured shadows up the sides of the fuselage. A ladder was wheeled to L1; a moment later, the low mechanical thunk of the airbridge locking into position vibrated through the floor. James straightened his tie—by now wilted with sweat and the day's exertions—checked his collar in the black reflection of the windscreen, and set his logbook square atop the centre pedestal.

"AmericanoAir 4352, this is the ground, prepare to open door Lima 1 and stand by for boarding," came Sergeant Wilkins' voice, a crackle of authority through the headset. "We will be sending a police officer and two representatives from FAA security onto the flight deck. Please remain seated and do not leave the cockpit until instructed."

James Hart thumbed the transmit. "Understood. L1 will be armed and opened on your command. We await your personnel."

He glanced to Andreas, who, as ever, betrayed nothing but the flicker of an eyebrow. "Ready for the parade?"

"Nothing like an audience at the end of a shift," James murmured, half to himself.

They waited. There was a strange hush now, a vacuum where the thrum of jet engines had once lived. The familiar scents of avionics and human occupation—acrylic, ozone, cheap aftershave—settled in the static air. James counted breaths, then seconds, then the click of the L1 door as the manual lever was thrown and the faint, wheezing sigh of the pressure seal releasing.

Natalie's voice came from the galley, subdued, professional. "Door's armed. Officers approaching."

There was the clatter of boots on aluminium, the bunched intensity of uniformed presence, then a polite but unmistakable rap at the cockpit. James opened the reinforced door himself—protocol, always—and in stepped Sergeant Wilkins, rain still trickling down the brim of his cap, his belt heavy with tools and radios.

He was followed by a lean, middle-aged woman in a navy FAA windbreaker, lanyard bristling with photo ID and the wary, apologetic look of someone who'd rather be anywhere else. Behind her, a second official: younger, hair cropped military-short, tablet already in hand.

"Captain Hart? I'm Sergeant Wilkins, Metropolitan Washington Airports Authority Police. This is Special Agent Parson from the FAA, and Mr. Taggart, also with the FAA's Air Carrier Compliance Division."

James shook hands with each in turn, then gestured to the jump seats. "Welcome to the circus."

Wilkins didn't crack a smile. He scanned the cockpit, gaze ticking over each switch and dial, as if expecting the radio to explode anew. "All electronics off, as requested?"

"Wi-Fi and cell disabled, per instruction," James confirmed. "No comms since the event. Cabin secure, doors armed, crew at stations."

Wilkins nodded, taking a position by the door—half guard, half witness, as if the cockpit was now a crime scene by default. Agent Parson, her lanyard gleaming with the faded hologram of federal clearance, perched carefully on the jump seat behind James, crossing her legs with the kind of mechanical neatness that suggested years of official visits to flight decks. Taggart remained standing, one hand on the overhead rail, scanning the panels and the pilots' faces as if he might decode the previous hour simply from posture and eye movement.

"Let's start with the basics, Captain," Parson said, her accent broad midwestern with a hint of forced calm. "Confirm the events leading up to the loss of communications. You were inbound ILS One-Niner at DCA, is that correct?"

James nodded, reciting the story he'd already begun to rehearse in his head—altitude, position, ATIS received, approach briefed, configuration set. He kept it stripped of any embellishment, tone matter-of-fact, hands folded over the logbook like a schoolboy giving an account of a fire drill.

"We were established on the ILS, outer marker inbound, unable to contact Tower or Approach. Both VHF1 and VHF2 gave static, no reply on Guard. ECAM warning on NAV ACCUR DOWNGRAD, predictive windshear advisory on descent, nothing out of the ordinary for this type of storm. Visual contact with two F-16s at ten o'clock and four o'clock positions, assumed to be Air National Guard scrambled for a comms loss event."

Parson nodded, fingers flickering over her tablet. "Did you deviate at any point from standard procedures, Captain?"

"No, ma'am. We squawked 7600, maintained heading and altitude per last clearance, followed all SOPs for loss of communications in controlled airspace."

Taggart chimed in, his voice sharper, the inflection that of a man who had once sat in a left seat but now found more security in regulatory detail. "And when did you first notice the comms panel was down?"

James exhaled, steady and deliberate. "After switching to Tower at the marker—no reply, repeated call. Checked both panels, headsets, boom and hand mics, swapped to Guard, no response. Standard reset, still dead."

Andreas, silent until now, added: "We confirmed with the cabin interphone—internal comms were functional, just no external transmit or receive."

The rain, having lost its earlier violence, lingered in a persistent, sullen drizzle—one that pressed against the glass and lent the airfield a perpetual dusk. The storm's legacy lingered everywhere: puddles pooled in the dips of the apron, blue strobes reflected on rain-slicked tarmac, and the spent energy of averted disaster clung to every rivet of the Airbus. Inside the cockpit of AmericanoAir 4352, James Hart found himself in that peculiar suspension unique to airline command—at once master of his domain and, suddenly, a subject under examination.

Agent Parson, her tablet balanced on one knee, listened with the attentive stillness of someone accustomed to being the least exciting presence in the room until, very suddenly, she was the most important. Wilkins remained by the door, rain still beading on the edge of his cap, his stance radiating both patience and low-level threat. Taggart, meanwhile, was the active observer, his gaze flicking between switches, logbooks, and faces—rarely resting, always assessing.

James felt the old compulsion for precision resurface; every phrase he chose was weighed, every technical detail carefully measured against memory and training. The cockpit became a courtroom and a confessional, his words parsed for deviation as much as for meaning.

"After the initial failed transmission," James continued, "we conducted a full audio panel reset, checked all headset jacks, swapped microphones. Andreas verified the circuit breakers. No tripped CBs, no sign of failure on the ECAM beyond the comms loss. We maintained the cleared approach profile, squawked 7600, and followed the book for lost communications in controlled airspace."

Agent Parson's stylus tapped a slow, staccato rhythm on her tablet. "And at no stage did you attempt to break off the approach or initiate a go-around?"

James kept his expression neutral, projecting the kind of calm that only came from years of being told off by both military instructors and civilian postholders. "Negative, ma'am. We had the ILS established, localiser and glideslope captured, aircraft fully configured for landing. Standard company policy in an extended comms loss event is to continue the approach if safely established, barring conflicting traffic or adverse indications. Weather was poor but within minima, no TCAS advisories, and the airfield was clear ahead—aside from the F-16s, who provided the only visible, er, 'guidance'."

Parson almost smiled at that—a brief, human flicker before her regulatory mask slid back into place. "And the F-16s: any attempt to communicate visually? Light signals, gestures?"

Andreas took that one, his English crisp but faintly melodic. "Lead F-16 executed a waggling of wings and a shallow descent on the river track, which we interpreted—correctly, I hope—as 'follow me, maintain approach'. No erratic manoeuvres, no indication we were to break off. It felt very much like choreography—if anything, they reassured us we were doing what was expected."

Wilkins made a note on his pad, his pen squeaking faintly against the waterproof pages. Taggart, meanwhile, pursed his lips in the way pilots do when confronted with someone else's emergency. "And after landing?"

James recounted the sequence: manual braking, vacating left, bringing the aircraft to a halt as instructed by emergency vehicles, running the after-landing flows, then holding for nearly twenty minutes while fire and police staged their cautious ballet around the aircraft. No attempts to move the aircraft without permission, no passenger movement, every door and hatch as per SOP.

Parson asked, "And the radio—was there any attempt to communicate with company, or via ACARS, prior to shut down?"

"We contacted AmericanoAir East Coast Ops via cellular before we shut down the flight deck completely," James answered. "ACARS was functional throughout the approach and after landing, so I reported our position, the comms failure, and the fact that we'd been intercepted. Once Sergeant Wilkins gave the order, all connectivity was powered off as per federal instruction."

Agent Parson's stylus skittered across her tablet. "Did you observe any system abnormalities that could indicate deliberate tampering, cyber interference, or evidence of unlawful interference with the comms system?"

James kept his voice even. "No evidence of sabotage. No unauthorised persons in the flight deck, no cockpit door breach, no reports from cabin crew of passenger disturbance or suspicious activity. The failure was total, but not malicious—just dead air, like someone had unplugged us from the world."

Taggart, standing, leaned forward to inspect the comms panel. "Would you permit me to take a photograph, Captain?"

"Of course." James slid sideways in his seat to give the man space. The old instinct to preserve chain-of-custody was so ingrained that even as he did so, he was checking his memory for every detail—what had been touched, toggled, cycled, checked. In the cabin, the same choreography was playing out: uniformed police checking galleys, verifying names against manifests, peering into overhead bins, asking for IDs from the handful of passengers who had raised concerns or simply sobbed too loudly to go unnoticed.

Agent Parson continued: "And you, First Officer Carlsen—any moment when you suspected something was amiss with the aircraft itself, beyond the comms?"

Andreas shook his head, his voice a balm of Scandinavian steadiness. "Aircraft was well-behaved. ECAM was noisy on descent, but nothing outside what we'd expect in convective weather. The comms loss was total but sudden, as if all radios had gone at once. We both ran resets, I checked the circuit breakers, Captain Hart checked again after touchdown."

"Hopefully CVR and FDR should have the information you need," Andreas said, his voice quiet but firm.

Taggart nodded, pulling a forensic tag from a pouch at his belt and affixing it, with a slow ceremony, to the comms panel. "We'll be downloading the cockpit voice and flight data recorders at the maintenance bay. For now, no one is to touch the centre pedestal, radios, or any comms equipment. Standard protocol. I assume you're familiar."

James smiled without mirth. "This isn't my first post-incident walk-through, Mr Taggart. We'll touch nothing."

A moment's hush lingered, filled only by the distant, watery rumble of thunder and the faint murmur of the forward galley, where Natalie and her team kept the curtain of professionalism stretched tight across the front row of anxious faces. James could almost picture them: crew hands folded, voices even, the older heads taking charge of the most rattled passengers, the younger ones huddled near the jump seats, all of them just waiting for the next instruction. Beyond the cockpit, the rain slackened a little, pattering now with a tired persistence against the hull.

Sergeant Wilkins cleared his throat, drawing James's gaze. "We'll need to take you both for statements once the initial handover's done. There's a secure interview suite in the terminal. Standard procedure—FAA, MWAA, and

TSA need your full accounts. Is there any reason you feel unfit to give a statement?"

James shook his head. "No. I'm fit and able."

Andreas simply replied, "Ready."

"Good." Parson looked at her screen, checking a prompt. "Once maintenance have checked the radios, and we've got preliminary data off the QAR, you'll both be escorted to the interview room. Sergeant Wilkins, could you organise a sweep of the flight deck and cabin? We need a record that nothing has been removed or tampered with."

Wilkins nodded, stepping out and murmuring instructions into his radio. The rain on his jacket left small, silver trails as he vanished aft.

Parson's tone softened, just for a moment. "Captain, First Officer—if there's anything you recall, no matter how minor, that seems out of place, this is the time to mention it. Small details matter in these events."

James, for the briefest instant, wanted to mention the look on Andreas's face at decision height—the flicker of concern, quickly masked, when the radios had failed entirely. The way the hush in the cockpit had felt thicker than simple silence, as if the jet itself had noticed the world had stopped talking to it. But he did not. He simply nodded. "Nothing, ma'am. Routine, right up until the world went quiet."

Parson studied him, something flickering behind her eyes. "Thank you."

Agent Parson and Mr Taggart exchanged a brief glance—one of those silent, bureaucratic conversations that could fill whole novels if anyone ever bothered to record them. Taggart finished with a last flourish of his stylus, then handed the tablet to Parson for her signature. For a moment, the only sound was the soft, staticky background of rain and the muted hum of external power, punctuated by the distant clatter of a catering truck repositioning across the ramp.

James glanced sidelong at Andreas, who was rolling his right shoulder, as if to shake off the coiled tension. There was nothing left to do, really. They were in the hands of procedure, and the gods of regulatory theatre.

A distant thud from the forward hold announced that someone was already busy tagging the luggage. On the ramp below, more yellow-jacketed staff had joined the tableau, wheeling out inspection steps, clipboards glinting in the arc-lights. To James it was all familiar: the slow-motion choreography of an airline in incident mode, every move watched, every word documented, every button-press potentially a line in a report destined for a regulator's inbox.

Sergeant Wilkins reappeared, his cap now off, hair plastered to his scalp. "Captain, we're ready to begin the sweep."
James nodded, stepped back from the seat, and stood to one side as Wilkins and Parson moved through the cockpit, torch beams dancing over panels and footwells. Taggart watched, hands clasped behind his back, the very picture of regulatory detachment.

After a few moments, Wilkins stepped into the forward galley, Parson in tow. James heard muffled conversation, the clatter of drawers opened and shut, the low, steady cadence of Natalie's voice as she responded to each question—calm, certain, a bulwark of experience.

Andreas stretched in his seat, rubbing his eyes. "Ever feel," he murmured, so softly only James could hear, "like you're the least important person in the room when something goes wrong? Yet everyone wants to hear your voice?"

James allowed himself a faint smile. "Welcome to airline command in 2025. The only job where you're always responsible, and almost never in charge."

The sweep did not take long. Sergeant Wilkins soon returned, damp but composed. "Cabin clear. No unauthorised items, no evidence of interference. Manifest matches headcount. Maintenance are on their way to the E/E bay."

Parson made a final note on her tablet, then stood. "Thank you for your cooperation. Please collect your essential belongings only—no bags, no paperwork. We'll escort you to the terminal. Your crew will be held separately for the time being. You'll have a chance to speak to them later, after your statements."

James nodded, flicking a glance at his battered flight bag, logbook tucked inside. "Just the essentials?"

"Just the essentials, Captain," Taggart confirmed, tone gentle but absolute.

James unclipped his ID from the lanyard around his neck, pocketed his wallet, and slung his rain-stained uniform jacket over one arm. The logbook, always the first essential, he kept cradled in his left hand. Andreas mirrored him: epaulettes straightened, tie loosely knotted, hair still perfectly in place despite the hours. The ritual of leaving the cockpit without the tools of command — no charts, no headset, not even the battered black bag he'd lugged across four continents — left James feeling oddly naked, as if the process itself was a test of humility.

Natalie appeared in the galley as the cockpit door swung open. She gave the two pilots a professional nod, her face set in lines of exhausted reassurance, but for just a second her eyes betrayed a question: *Is it over?* James replied with a quick, silent nod — not an answer, just a reassurance, a commander's promise that he was still in charge, for her sake if nothing else.

Wilkins led the way out onto the airbridge. The space was cold and humid, rain hammering in through the gap between jet and terminal. Two more police officers flanked the bridge, hands resting at their belts, watching the world with the practiced indifference of the over-exposed. Beyond the double glass doors was a cordoned-off holding area, fluorescent-lit and ringed with TSA in blue shirts, each armed with a tablet and the dull, slightly embarrassed authority of staff not used to handling real emergencies.

James and Andreas were ushered inside. The space had been hastily re-purposed: a sign reading "Welcome to Washington" stood incongruously behind a row of battered plastic chairs, and an ancient coffee vending machine whirred pointlessly in the corner. Someone had laid out a stack of paper towels to soak up the rain trailed in by the procession of uniforms. Two folding tables, draped with branded AmericanoAir throws, served as makeshift interview stations. A poster for "Know Your Rights at DCA" fluttered in the air conditioning.

A uniformed TSA agent — young, with a waxy, nervous complexion — handed them each a small bottle of water and a tightly wrapped snack bar. "You'll be called one at a time," he said, trying for calm and not quite making it. "Captain Hart, if you'd come this way first?"

James glanced at Andreas, who nodded. "I'll be here," the FO said quietly, settling into one of the plastic chairs with the stoic patience of someone who had sat through endless debriefs, and would likely sit through endless more.

The interview room was not so much a room as a repurposed office: two chairs, a table, a whiteboard with faded marker stains, and a ceiling vent that rattled every time the rain outside hit a certain pitch. Agent Parson sat on one side, her tablet ready, a legal pad beside it. Taggart stood by the door, arms crossed, leaning back as if he expected this to last hours.

"Captain Hart, this is a recorded interview under FAA and MWAA protocols. Are you fit to continue?"

James nodded, lowering himself into the chair with the careful precision of a man aware that every move, every breath, was now on the record. "Yes, ma'am. Fit and ready."

"Good. For the record, please confirm your name, rank, employer, and the flight operated today."

"James Simon Hart, Captain, AmericanoAir, operating flight 4352, service from Boston Logan to Washington Reagan National, Airbus A321, registration N940AA."

Parson tapped a few keys, then looked up, her eyes alert. "We'll begin with the sequence of events, then move on to operational details, then your impressions and any subjective observations. At any point, if you wish to clarify, please do."

James nodded. "Understood."

"Let's start at the top. Can you confirm, in your own words, the last communication received from ATC before comms failure?"

James drew a slow breath, casting his mind back over the last hour: "Washington Approach cleared us to intercept the ILS for runway one-niner. Cleared to descend and maintain two thousand feet. Last transmission was an acknowledgement — I replied, then switched to Tower on VHF1. Attempted to check in, but received only static. No response to repeated calls on Tower, or on Guard. Switched to VHF2, then to alternate frequencies, with the same result. Informed First Officer Carlsen, began comms failure checklist."

Taggart's voice cut in, precise and measured: "At this point, did you consider diverting?"

James shook his head. "No, sir. We were established on the ILS, fully configured for landing, no adverse indications beyond the comms failure. SOP is to continue the approach if established, weather and aircraft permitting."

Parson nodded. "And the F-16 intercept — can you elaborate on your interpretation of their actions?"

James allowed himself a tight smile. "Ma'am, I'm former USAF myself. The lead F-16 wagged wings, took up position off our port, then descended on the river track ahead of us. Standard intercept signalling: follow my lead, maintain course, do not deviate. No aggression. If anything, it was more reassurance than threat."

She made a note. "After touchdown — can you confirm you did not attempt to taxi without explicit instructions?"

"Affirmative. Brought aircraft to a halt on the taxiway, holding short of Echo, brakes set. Waited for visual signal from airport police and fire, acknowledged with landing lights. Awaited further instructions."

The questioning moved on: every switch, every call, every checklist was dissected. Parson's queries were detailed, never accusatory, but relentless in their thoroughness. She asked for exact times, for clarifications on radio resets, for confirmation of the chain of command in the cockpit and the sequence of crew briefings. She probed for any irregularities, any deviation from the manual, any subjective hunches or doubts.

At one point, she paused. "Did you ever feel, at any stage, that the aircraft or the operation was under threat? Sabotage, terrorism, unlawful interference?"

James shook his head, feeling the tiredness creep into his bones. "No, ma'am. This was a technical event, in my judgement. Total comms failure, but all other aircraft systems normal, no threat from cabin or passengers. My cabin crew reported no suspicious activity."

****

CHAPTER 9 – Seat 1A (Not In System)
Saturday 19th July 2025

Waking up in the Holiday Inn Express near Reagan National Airport, James knew that he'd have to have his schedule changed; as, due to the comms failure and the subsequent investigations, he had been unable to do the two sectors that had originally stood between him and a brief stretch of leave. He lay there for a moment, sheets tangled at his ankles, the muted whirr of the air-conditioning punctuated only by the occasional rattle of a departing Metro train, half a mile away. Rain, a persistent drizzle now rather than the biblical deluge of last night, traced thin lines down the windowpane.

He stared at the ceiling. Even now, nearly ten hours after touchdown, sleep had been brittle and unconvincing—a patchwork of short, restless segments, each punctured by the memory of the silent cockpit, the twitch of fighter wings on the periphery, the endless parade of officials with lanyards and iPads and apologetic smiles. In his mind, the sequence repeated itself: the quiet, the sweat prickling at the back of his neck, the hush that had followed every question in the interview room.

Loading up the Sprint Staff app, he noticed that he'd been allocated a 5 sector day, however, with the fatigue of the previous day, the notion of operating five sectors — even for Sprint's "get-it-done" breed of pilot — felt borderline masochistic. James stared blearily at his phone, thumb hovering over the 'fatigue report' button. He remembered too well the culture at some airlines where reporting tiredness was an act of professional treason. Here, with Sprint's pan-Atlantic chaos and AmericanoAir's still-embryonic corporate culture, he doubted anyone would care until he landed a jet in the wrong city.

Of course, Federal Regulations dictated that if a pilot felt fatigued, then he must report it—no excuses, no negotiation. Yet there was always a tension: if you did, you were "that pilot"—the one who got a reputation in the rostering office, the one who would be "forgotten" at bid time for a decent layover, the one whose emails about minimum rest would get buried beneath a tide of urgent requests for someone, anyone, to rescue a delayed sector. In the old days, with proper contracts and legacy union rules, it had been a straightforward matter.

Now, under Sprint's post-Brexit, post-pandemic, transatlantic Frankenstein of contracts and dodgy AOCs, it was all suggestion and corporate optimism, and very little of the sort of resilience that mattered when you'd been up for twenty-four hours and the weather was still closing in.

Tapping the button that would submit the fatigue report was, in the end, less a decision and more an act of self-preservation. James's thumb hovered, a mild battle of will and pride flickering in his chest, before the memory of last night—the storm, the silence, the blue strobe of police lights refracted through rain—nudged him over the line. He pressed "Submit". A dull click and the cheery notification—***FATIGUE REPORTED: CREW SCHEDULING TO CONTACT***—appeared with the clinical indifference of a computer that had never sweated through a comms blackout at minimums.

He set the phone aside. For a long while, he just lay there, mind spinning, body slow to respond. The room held that impersonal neutrality particular to all chain hotels: grey-blue carpet, a television bolted to the wall, one apologetic wardrobe, and a heavy curtain failing to keep the Washington dawn at bay. He'd known worse. He'd also known better.

Eventually, the phone buzzed with a new message.

Tamina Kent (Sprint Ops East Coast): *James, thank you for your report. As today would have been your second day in 6, you are required to deadhead to Boston Logan for tomorrow's 0412 to Panama City, Panama non-stop. Failure to acknowledge will be considered refusal of assignment, per contract. Please respond.*

James knew that the fact that as he had called fatigue, he couldn't be forced to fly that day, but the reality was, once you'd pressed the button and declared fatigue, the game shifted to a different set of rules: you were out of the loop until the scheduler needed you again, and any retaliation was strictly forbidden in theory, and practiced in subtler forms if anyone could get away with it.

He thumbed a reply, every word measured and civil, because that was the way these things had to be.

James Hart: *Tamina, acknowledged. As per my fatigue report, I am unavailable for operational duty today, including deadheading as crew. Please roster me as PAX only, and I will reposition to Boston as instructed for tomorrow's flight, provided minimum rest is achieved. Please confirm receipt and update my duty accordingly.*

Tamina Kent (Sprint Ops East Coast): *I had already booked you as pax on Delta 5682. It's a Delta Connection flight, so you'd need to check in by 1600hrs DC time for a 1700 departure. Seat 1A. Tickets will be for pickup.*

James looked at his phone, confused, as he knew that Delta would never issue a printed ticket, that they would request a PNR, as well as the feeling of being managed by an algorithm rather than a person. There was something bleakly comic in being handed "seat 1A" on a Delta Connection E175 for a deadhead, the software's sense of grandeur as hollow as the breakfast buffet below. James set the phone on the side table and swung his legs over the edge of the bed, feet finding cold carpet. He checked the time: 08:17. With nearly eight hours until check-in, he could almost convince himself he was on a real layover. Almost.

He let the shower run until the steam blurred the cheap bathroom mirror, letting the heat chase away what it could of last night's tension. When he finally dressed—Sprint-issue polo, battered Samsonite crew bag, AmericanoAir ID lanyard—he moved with the staccato efficiency of a man whose body ran on routine even when his mind was tired. The room's radio was stuck on NPR, voices droning through static about infrastructure and "aviation security events," the latter phrase making him pause for a moment with a wry, private smile.

Downstairs in the breakfast room, the scene was pure international crew: a handful of French and Brazilian pilots in Air France polos, a KLM captain with his hat perched atop a suitcase, a tired woman in a Delta uniform stirring packet oatmeal, and a group of Sprint Europe (for transatlantic runs) and Sprint US/AmericanoAir crews, all scattered across the bland landscape of beige tables, weak coffee, and the subtle etiquette of jet-lagged avoidance. There was, as ever, a kind of quiet hierarchy to these places: senior captains clinging to their window seats, junior first officers wolfing down calories in silence, a few cabin crew scrolling on phones, and the omnipresent sound of trolley wheels bumping over cheap carpet.

James helped himself to a cup of coffee, the kind that came out of a machine with more noise than substance, and eyed the buffet. The "hot" options—soggy scrambled eggs, limp bacon, pallid sausages—seemed as unappetising as the events of the last twelve hours. He settled for toast and some fruit, sliding into a corner seat with a view of the car park, where rain still lashed down in slow, relentless sheets.

He ate slowly, scrolling absently through the news feeds on his phone, every second headline reminding him that *"AVIATION INCIDENT AT REAGAN NATIONAL"* was now the clickbait du jour. The media's handling was as you'd expect: a heady mix of confusion, sensationalism, and earnest analysts who'd never seen a squawk code outside of an episode of *Mayday*. Some US outlets spoke gravely about "potential cyber threats to critical ATC infrastructure." A British tabloid ran with *Brit Pilot in D.C. Radio Silence Drama*, featuring an unflattering picture of a different, considerably younger pilot.

James put the phone down. At the next table, a Brazilian captain was arguing quietly with someone—possibly his union, judging by the fraying patience in his voice—about

EU 261 compensation. The Air France contingent dissected weather charts on a battered iPad, muttering about crosswinds at JFK. There was a universal weariness to the room: the solidarity of people who had all, at some point, been on the wrong side of a thunderstorm, a scheduler's whim, or the slow violence of a regulatory inquisition.

He watched rain sluice down the window, his mind turning over the sequence of events from the night before. The more he tried to dismiss it, the more his thoughts looped back: the F-16 off the port side, the flicker of a gold visor, the slow ballet of emergency vehicles on the tarmac. All performed in a climate of hair-trigger nerves, with nothing but a flickering transponder and muscle memory keeping order.

A message pinged on WhatsApp. It was from Andreas.

Andreas Carlsen: *Rested? The Swedes at the Hilton are buying the first round tonight if you fancy escaping. Heard the FAA are still camped in the crew room asking for my view on Norwegian airspace design. God help them.*

James smiled—wry, but grateful for the camaraderie. He tapped back:

James Hart: *Still in the land of the living. Got a deadhead up to Boston this evening. If I make it back to DC before the next flood, I'll take you up on that drink. Don't let them rope you into giving a PowerPoint.*

He finished his breakfast and nursed the last of the coffee, watching the crew room start to clear as various pilots and cabin crew began the day's slow, rain-soaked migration towards the shuttle bus, the Metro, or a rideshare.

The goodbyes were understated: a nod here, a raised cup there, the faintest mutter of "safe flight." It was the ritual of every layover, every city, every company.

He made his way back upstairs and forced himself to unpack and repack his kit, checking for the umpteenth time that his logbook, passport, and company ID were present and accounted for.

The habit was half paranoia, half necessity: when your world could shift with a single app notification, you learned to make sure the essentials were always to hand.

James spent the late morning in the numbed fugue familiar to every long-haul pilot out of synch with the local day. Shower, shave, the endless ritual of making the hotel room impersonal again.

He texted Natalie, the purser from the flight, to check she and her crew were safely on their way to wherever AmericanoAir had decided to put them up—she replied with a selfie of three stewards in raincoats outside the Smithsonian, all mock misery and forced smiles, captioned "Sightseeing in a cloud."

James felt a pang of gratitude for his crew: how, after hours of crisis, they'd kept calm, handed out water, soothed passengers, absorbed the brunt of confusion and irritation, all while knowing they'd be last off the aircraft, first into the arms of the authorities, and, if necessary, first to defend the captain's account.

James Hart: *Glad you got some time outside the aircraft! Try not to lose anyone to the National Gallery. Will see you in Boston, all being well.*

He checked his e-mails. The expected barrage had arrived: a formal notification from Sprint Legal reminding him not to speak to press (*"as you will appreciate, in the current environment, even the appearance of unauthorised communication may be misinterpreted by regulatory bodies and the travelling public"*); a dry note from the Fleet Office, requesting a written statement for the Company Safety Review Board; two company memos about "communications resilience protocols"; and one from HR inviting him to a "voluntary mental well-being session" via Teams. He made a mental note to ignore the last two until the next time a layover provided Wi-Fi decent enough to pretend to connect.

By lunchtime, the drizzle had eased to a fine mist, and the day had settled into a low, muggy heat. James ventured out for a walk, half-heartedly braving the heat and humidity of a Washington summer. The pavements along Crystal City were slick, reflecting a procession of shuttle buses, uniformed crews, hotel porters in disposable ponchos, and the odd jogger braving the weather. He skirted the perimeter of the airport, noting how the Potomac, swollen by the previous day's storms, ran brown and restless between the riverbanks. From across the water, the sound of jet engines and the periodic howl of police sirens drifted over the floodplain.

James paused by the long-term parking, watching a Southwest 737 lift off into the haze. In another life, he reflected, he'd have been the one rotating off runway one-niner, climbing out over Alexandria towards the Atlantic, never knowing how easily a line of thunderstorms or a crackle of static could turn routine into drama. The comfort of aviation was always its order—the infinite, comforting complexity of checklists, flows, callouts, and SOPs. What unnerved him, still, was not the chaos of the skies but the chaos of the system meant to keep everything tidy on the ground.

He returned to the hotel and, after a futile attempt at napping, packed his bags and headed for the airport shuttle. The bus was already half-full, a Babel of airline lanyards and accents. An Alitalia crew bickered quietly in Italian about whose turn it was to manage the crew paperwork; a United regional pilot snored quietly by the window; two young JetBlue cabin crew, eyes bright with the adrenaline of new jobs and new cities, scrolled TikTok and shared AirPods.

At Reagan National's terminal, the tension of the previous night had faded to the background hum of an airport returning to its usual churn. Security lines snaked in polite, efficient silence; the only nod to the previous day's drama was the increased presence of police, TSA, and what James recognised as a couple of plainclothes FAA types loitering with iPads by the checkpoint. No one gave him a second glance.

He made his way to the Delta ticket counter, passport and AmericanoAir ID at the ready, expecting the usual fuss over a ZED fare.

"Good afternoon, I was told by my Ops that there was a ticket for me. Name's Hart, James. Flight is Delta 5682."

"Do you have a PNR?" the Delta agent asked, and James knew that the Ops team never gave him a Passenger Name Record, because somewhere in the labyrinthine world of Sprint's crewing department, ticketing was still treated as an art rather than a science.

James summoned his driest smile. "I was told to collect it here. Perhaps there's something under company ID AmericanoAir, or Sprint Group?"

The agent, a trim woman with an unmistakable air of airline omnipotence, began clacking away on her keyboard. She asked for his passport, frowned at her screen, asked for his employee number, frowned again, and finally called someone in the back room. This, James reflected, was more inevitable than infuriating. He waited, suppressing the urge to check his phone, ignoring the faint ache at the base of his skull—a headache that had begun somewhere between the second interview with the FAA and the end of his second cup of bad hotel coffee.

"I'm sorry, there's nothing in the system for 'Hart, James' on Delta 5682, nor under Sprint Group or AmericanoAir," she announced, phone now pressed to her ear, as the queue behind him began to expand with the quiet grumbling of the travel-weary. "Let me check with ticketing. Can you step to the side, sir?"

James, seasoned in the lost art of not taking it personally, gave her a polite nod and moved off to the periphery of the check-in zone, where the linoleum had been dulled to a waxy sheen by decades of crew shoes and tired business travellers. He watched the ebb and flow of airport life— families clustered around bulging suitcases, the suited-

and-booted crowd eyeing their watches, pilots striding with the clipped certainty of those whose time is measured in block hours, not minutes.

"Right, I've just checked, and there's no such booking for you on Delta 5682. Did you receive an email confirmation, sir?"

James offered a rueful half-smile. "Not that I can see. My company—Sprint, or AmericanoAir depending on who you ask—promised there'd be a ticket at the counter. They're new to the US. Sometimes the paperwork... lags behind."

The agent, to her credit, didn't so much as roll her eyes. She had the poise of someone who'd dealt with Olympic-level incompetence before breakfast. She gave a professional nod and waved the next passenger forward. "Wait here, please. I'll see what we can do. Do you have a staff ID or anything from Delta?"

James patted down his lanyard. He'd flown for most of the alliances, but Delta wasn't one of them. He held up his AmericanoAir badge, the Sprint Group "globe" logo embossed with faux gravitas, and offered up his best, please-help-me face.

The agent took the badge and gave it a look that might have been amusement or disbelief. "I'll need a moment."

James retreated to a patch of terminal wall between a vending machine and a flight information screen. He set his bag down, stretched his shoulders, and braced himself for the next round of administrative theatre. Nearby, a TSA agent eyeballed him, clocking the pilot's stripes, then immediately lost interest when an actual argument broke out in the Precheck line.

He used the pause to check his email again—still nothing from Ops, and certainly no magic Delta confirmation. He fired off a curt Teams message to Tamina Kent, copying in the Sprint Crew Scheduling address as well, tapping it out with the sort of diplomatic brevity only a long-haul pilot could muster when dealing with ground staff incompetence:

James Hart: *At DCA. Delta counter says no ticket or PNR in system for Delta 5682. No email confirmation received. Please confirm booking, send PNR ASAP. Flight departs in under three hours. Standing by.*

He hit send and let his head tip back against the cold marble wall, eyes tracking the reflected chaos of the terminal in the shiny floor. Everything in aviation, he mused, was a kind of theatre: the passenger experience was an elaborate ritual of illusions, and for the crew, it was a tightrope of checklists, contracts, and increasingly desperate improvisation.

He'd landed in more countries than most people could point to on a map, but nothing made him feel quite as much like a stranded tourist as waiting for a crewing department to remember you exist.

He watched as a pair of United pilots breezed through priority check-in, laughing with the gate agent in a way that spoke of old friendships and well-trod routines.

Their ease made James feel all the more invisible, a guest at a party where he'd never quite learned the customs.

172

James looked at his watch, then at the now-quiet phone in his hand. Three hours until the scheduled departure and not so much as a line of reassurance from Sprint's "world-leading" crew logistics software. The terminal lights felt harsher by the minute, accentuating the edges of jetlag and adrenaline crash. Over by the window, a Southwest ramp crew scuttled like ants around a departing 737.

The Delta agent reappeared. Her patience was commendable, but the edge in her voice was that of someone on the third double shift of the week. "Sir, ticketing can't find you in the system, but if you can have your company send over an authority to bill or a ZED confirmation, we can reissue on the spot."

James offered his most neutral smile. "Thank you. I'll chase them up."

He typed another message, more urgent this time:

James Hart: *No record with Delta at DCA, agent needs ZED confirmation or billing authority. Please escalate— crew unable to travel without ticket.*

It was the sort of impasse that happened a hundred times a day in the tangled web of modern airline operations, where technology promised frictionless connections but often delivered little more than layers of obfuscation.

He checked his phone for any response, but there was nothing—no Teams ping, no email buzz. The air in the terminal grew close, thick with the scent of bad coffee and recirculated sweat. James tried to focus on his breath, on the slow movement of time. If he'd been a passenger, he'd have felt a kind of helpless indignation; as a crew member, it was just one more lesson in humility, the realisation that, in the great machinery of commercial aviation, everyone was disposable, no matter how many stripes adorned your epaulettes.

He shifted his weight, stretching the tension from his calves, aware of a familiar ache in his lower back—the kind that came from a career spent either folded into aircraft seats or standing in check-in queues waiting for other people's systems to remember he existed. In a corner of the terminal, a small TV was tuned to CNN, cycling through footage of yesterday's drama: looping animations of radar sweeps, the tail of an AmericanoAir A321 emerging through storm cloud, a scrolling chyron that read: *"PILOT RADIO BLACKOUT: DC FLIGHT LANDS WITH MILITARY ESCORT."* The newsreader was interviewing an "aviation security expert" who looked about twelve and had never flown further than Miami, opining gravely about the "new cyber-risks to critical aviation infrastructure." James couldn't help but grin, despite himself.

Give it two days, he thought, *and the world would have moved on to the next crisis*. For now, he was the latest non-story, fodder for the panel shows and the LinkedIn security consultants. By the time the report concluded, nobody in the terminal was even looking up.

He glanced across to the far end of the check-in zone where a Sprint Air First Officer—British by the look of her—was engaged in a parallel argument with an agent for JetBlue. He caught her eye as she waved her lanyard in explanation and saw the tired camaraderie that only airline staff can muster for one another. He nodded, received a tight-lipped smile in return, and wondered how many of Sprint's global army of pilots were right now wandering through terminals, bags in hand, waiting for the ghost of a ZED fare to materialise.

At last, his phone vibrated. A reply had landed, not from Tamina in Crew Scheduling, but from someone new:

Clara Vant (NYC Crew Liaison): *Captain Hart, apologies for the confusion. Delta 5682 booking was never finalised due to a block on the ZED agreement from the US end—system error flagged after auto-allocation. We are urgently working to secure a replacement sector, possibly via JetBlue B6 2354. Stand by for details. If you incur any expenses, please retain receipts for reimbursement.*

James let the phone sink to his side, a dull thud of disappointment blooming in his chest. The confirmation from Clara was at least human, though it did little to restore his sense of agency. A "system error" on the ZED agreement. Sprint Group's entire mythology was built on frictionless, borderless connectivity, yet every actual attempt to move a crew member from A to B seemed to collapse into the same friction, the same borders, and the same ever-mutable contracts. He couldn't even summon the energy for anger. He would wait, and he would adapt. It was the only way to survive.

He looked about the terminal, noticing how the ebb and flow of passengers never really changed—security theatre at the far end, the flickering promise of upgrades at the Delta Sky Club, the clatter of an overpriced Pret sandwich against the cash register. It was the same choreography at

Heathrow, Orly, O'Hare or Tegel. The only things that shifted were the accents and the colour of the carpets.

Ten minutes ticked by, then twenty. James fiddled with his phone, played a round of chess against the in-built app, lost in twelve moves, and watched a child in a soaked Nationals cap drag his mother, and an overburdened suitcase, past the check-in lines with a relentless determination that made him briefly nostalgic for his own childhood. At the window, the rain had eased further. Puddles reflected the harsh sodium glow of apron floodlights, now the only sign of drama on a day that promised little but waiting.

Another ping: this time, Clara again, brisk and to the point.

Clara Vant: *Captain Hart, JetBlue B6 2354 has been confirmed. JFK 1905. Booking ref E4J9V2. Boarding pass available at kiosk or B6 counter. Should be an A220. Seat 4E. Apologies again—please update us when checked in.*

It was, at last, something actionable. James thumbed his thanks, shouldered his bag, and threaded his way through the churning tides of the terminal to the JetBlue counters. He presented himself to the agent with the weary, hopeful look of a man whose day could still unravel at any moment.

The JetBlue agent was younger, more cheerful, and possessed of the brisk efficiency only found in New York-based staff who'd survived the pandemic without losing their sense of humour. She tapped in his reference, nodded once, and printed a boarding pass in a matter of seconds.

James offered a silent prayer of thanks for the JetBlue agent's professionalism. She slid the boarding pass across the counter with a conspiratorial wink and a low, "Godspeed, Captain." That single gesture, small as it was, undid some of the tightness in his chest. For the first time all day, he felt like a passenger rather than a stranded parcel lost in a logistical netherworld.

****

CHAPTER 10 – The Teams Meeting
Sunday 20th July 2025

Panama City, James had decided, was like hell on earth, especially after having to skirt Mexican airspace to avoid the war that the United States was raging on and off with the cartels. The new NOTAMs read like the Book of Revelations, each day adding new polygons of "military activity," "hazard to civil operations," and "increased risk due to possible kinetic action." In practical terms, it meant the flight plan that had once been a sleepy Atlantic arc from Boston down the coast now jogged erratically eastwards over Cuba, dicing with weather, fuel burn, and the very edge of American tolerance for Sprint's existence.

James's A321LR had landed at Tocumen at a shade past 09:00 local, in thick heat that made the jet bridge shudder and the ramp workers sweat through their Hi-Viz vests in minutes. His first officer—Rohit Sharma, a quick-witted, quietly sardonic New Yorker—handled the radios and ramp with a grace born of years navigating underfunded outstations and the patchwork of languages that was Sprint's global birthright. Their purser, Marisol Fernandez, wrangled the passengers—many of them connection-missers and overnighted businesspeople from Boston, clutching tickets marked "AmericanoAir by Sprint" with a rising sense of betrayal. Even the most tolerant traveller, James reflected, had their limits.

The cabin had been a pressure cooker on descent, with complaints about the fact the Wi-Fi was chargeable, being a regular Sprint service, and not a Sprint Max transatlantic run, erupting into a near-mutiny when the SprintReels function of the app, a function which was filled with the kind of vertical dramas that websites like DramaBox, GoodShorts and ReelShort had made a killing on, failed to load mid-flight. James had caught Marisol's eye through the galley curtain during the final hour, her expression a masterclass in weary professionalism as she deflected yet another demand for a free coffee because "the app said it was included." By the time they'd taxied to the gate, the cabin was a stew of muttered Spanish, English, and Portuguese grievances, with one passenger filming the overhead bins for what James could only assume was a future TikTok manifesto.

James had checked out the SprintReels function on a previous flight, and, if he was honest, he wasn't impressed with the selection of melodramatic mini-series that seemed to have been churned out by an algorithm with a vendetta against subtlety. The stories were all high-stakes, low-budget affairs—tales of betrayed lovers, corporate conspiracies, or implausible medical emergencies, each episode cut to fit a three-minute attention span. The fact each episode after the first 6 were chargeable, meaning that each passenger had to fork out $2.99 per episode or $19.99 for a season pass, only added fuel to the fire. The app's promise of "in-flight entertainment tailored to your journey" felt like a cruel jest when the Wi-Fi dropped over the Caribbean, leaving passengers staring at buffering icons and venting their fury at Marisol and her crew.

James had overheard one passenger when he went to the lavatory mid-flight, a suited man with a Miami accent, muttering about "false advertising" and "SEC violations" as he jabbed at his phone, presumably drafting a complaint to Sprint's non-existent customer service hotline. By the time the aircraft doors opened, James was grateful for the relative calm of the cockpit, where the only drama was the post-flight paperwork and the faint hum of the APU winding down.

The Tocumen crew room was a concrete box buried in the bowels of Terminal 2, its walls plastered with faded safety posters and a dog-eared noticeboard pinned with union flyers. The air conditioning rattled like a dying engine, barely denting the muggy heat that clung to everything. James, Rohit, and Marisol collapsed into plastic chairs, their uniforms creased and damp, while the rest of the cabin crew trickled in, lugging crew bags and trading tired banter in a mix of English and Spanish. The room smelled of instant coffee and the faint tang of jet fuel that seemed to permeate every airport outpost Sprint called home.

"2am wake up, and now this," James muttered with a tired shake of his head, loosening his tie as he sank deeper into the chair. The fluorescent lights buzzed overhead, casting a sterile glow that made everyone look half-dead. Rohit, scrolling through his phone, snorted without looking up.

"Mate, you're preaching to the choir. I got a text from Ops at 3 a.m. saying they'd 'optimised' my roster. Optimised, my arse—four sectors tomorrow, and one's a tech-prone A319 to bloody Managua. If that's optimisation, I'm the Pope."

Marisol, sipping from a chipped mug that read *Panama: Gateway to the Americas*, rolled her eyes. "You two think you've got it bad? I had a guy in 12C try to barter his vape for a gin and tonic. Said it was 'currency' now. Then he cried when I said no. Cried. I need a holiday, or at least a desk job."

The room chuckled, the kind of low, knowing laughter that only comes from shared misery. James felt a flicker of gratitude for this crew, this ragtag bunch of professionals who somehow kept Sprint's creaking machinery airborne despite the odds.

They were a microcosm of the airline's global sprawl—Rohit, the Queens-born son of Indian immigrants; Marisol, a Miami native with Cuban roots; the cabin crew, a mix of Panamanian locals and a lone Canadian who'd somehow ended up here after a stint with WestJet. Each of them carried the weight of Sprint's ambition, and each of them bore the scars of its dysfunction.

James glanced at his phone to see a notification for a Teams meeting half an hour before he was due to return to the A321.

HR Meeting – Fatigue Report – James Hart

James had been expecting this, as Sprint's HR processes, much like its ticketing system, were a labyrinth of bureaucracy layered over chaos. The notification for the Teams meeting, titled with clinical precision, carried the faint whiff of corporate retribution. James knew the drill: a fatigue report, while protected by regulation, was never just a report.

It was a signal flare, a declaration that you'd dared to prioritise safety over the relentless churn of the roster. In Sprint's world, where "operational resilience" was code for "do more with less," such declarations were met with a mix of suspicion and performative concern.

He swiped the notification away, not quite ready to face the inevitable. The crew room's hum of conversation provided a temporary shield, a bubble of camaraderie that felt like the last bastion of sanity in Sprint's sprawling empire. Rohit was now regaling the group with a story about a passenger who'd tried to board a flight to Bogotá with a live parrot in a shoebox, claiming it was "essential medical equipment." Marisol countered with her own tale of a woman who'd demanded a refund because the in-flight magazine didn't feature her horoscope. The stories, exaggerated or not, were the currency of the crew room—a way to alchemise frustration into something bearable.

James leaned back, letting the banter wash over him. His mind, though, kept circling back to the Teams meeting. He'd been through enough of these to know the script: a faceless HR rep, probably working from a call centre in Gdansk or Hyderabad, would recite a checklist of questions about his "well-being" while subtly probing for any hint of malingering. There'd be a nod to "regulatory compliance," a veiled reminder of his contractual obligations, and, if he was lucky, a promise to "review" his roster—code for "we'll bury you in short-haul sectors until you beg for mercy." The whole charade was designed to make you question whether pressing the fatigue button had been worth it.

He glanced at his watch: 09:45 local time. The meeting was scheduled for 10:15, which gave him just enough time to grab another coffee and brace himself. The crew room's machine spluttered out a tarry liquid that tasted like regret, but it was better than nothing. He stirred in a packet of sugar, the granules dissolving into the black abyss, and checked his emails again.

Sprint's email system was as reliable as its ticketing, which is to say it was a lottery. The inbox was a mess of automated alerts, crew scheduling updates, and the occasional missive from the C-suite, usually dripping with corporate jargon about "synergies" or "disruptive innovation." Today, there was a new email from HR, flagged urgent. James opened it, expecting the usual boilerplate, but the tone was sharper than he'd anticipated.

From: *hr.eastcoast@sprintair.com*

To: *james.hart.LAX@sprintair.com*

Subject: *Fatigue Report Acknowledgement – Immediate Action Required.*

Captain Hart,

Following your fatigue report submitted on 19th July 2025, you are required to attend a mandatory virtual consultation to assess your fitness for duty and discuss rostering adjustments. This meeting is scheduled for 11:15 AM EST on 20th July 2025 via Microsoft Teams. Failure to attend may result in temporary suspension from active duty pending further review. Please ensure a stable internet connection and a professional environment. A summary of your report and relevant CAA/FAA regulations is attached for your reference.

Regards,

Priya Malhotra

Senior HR Coordinator

East Coast Operations

Sprint Group

Attached was a PDF, a dense 12-page document titled *Crew Fatigue Management Protocol,* which James didn't bother opening. He'd seen it before—or versions of it— at every airline he'd flown for. It was the kind of thing written by lawyers to cover backsides, not to help pilots.

James set the phone down and rubbed his temples. The crew room was still buzzing, but the laughter had faded into a quieter rhythm as people checked rosters or napped in corners. Marisol was on her phone, scrolling through what looked like a family group chat, her face softening at a photo of a kid in a baseball cap. Rohit was now arguing with a cabin crew member about whether Panama's empanadas were better than Colombia's. It was the kind of debate that could only happen in a room full of people who'd eaten at every airport canteen from Reykjavik to Riyadh.

He envied their ability to switch off, even for a moment. His own mind was stuck in a loop, replaying the events of the past 48 hours: the storm, the silent cockpit, the F-16s, the endless questions from the FAA, and now this—a corporate inquisition dressed up as concern. He knew he'd done the right thing by reporting fatigue, but the system wasn't built to reward doing the right thing. It was built to keep planes in the air, costs down, and shareholders happy. Pilots, passengers, and common sense were all secondary considerations.

The Tocumen crew room was a microcosm of Sprint's global sprawl, a place where the airline's ambition and dysfunction collided in a haze of stale coffee and flickering fluorescent lights. James sipped his bitter brew, the plastic chair creaking beneath him as he stared at the cracked linoleum floor. The HR email lingered in his mind like a low-grade fever, its sharp tone a reminder that even in Panama, thousands of miles from Sprint's nominal headquarters in Luton, the corporate machine never slept. He checked his watch again: 09:52. Twenty-three minutes until the Teams meeting. Just enough time to mentally rehearse the tightrope walk of being honest without sounding like a troublemaker.

Rohit, now sprawled across two chairs, was still holding court. "I'm telling you, mate, the empanadas at Bogotá's crew canteen are the gold standard. Crispy, flaky, none of this soggy nonsense you get here." He gestured vaguely at the vending machine in the corner, its sad selection of packaged snacks a testament to Tocumen's culinary indifference.

The Canadian cabin crew member, a lanky guy named Ethan with a faded WestJet lanyard, shook his head. "You're all wrong. Winnipeg's got this hole-in-the-wall place near the airport—empanadas so good you'd cry. I'd trade a week of layovers for one right now."

Marisol, who'd been half-listening, snorted. "You lot are arguing about food when I'm still trying to forget the guy in 12C. Vape for a gin and tonic. Who even thinks like that?"

James managed a faint smile, but his thoughts were elsewhere. The crew room's banter was a lifeline, a way to tether himself to the present, but the weight of the past two days kept pulling him back. The F-16s, the FAA's relentless questions, the Delta ticket that never existed—it was all part of the same tapestry of chaos that defined Sprint's operation. And now, this Teams meeting loomed like a checkpoint in a game he hadn't signed up to play.

He stood, stretching his legs, and wandered to the noticeboard. The union flyers were a mix of Spanish and English, most of them outdated, their edges curling like autumn leaves.

"Safety, Efficiency, Innovation, Customer Focus," one poster said, and James wondered who'd written it—probably some consultant in a London high-rise who'd never set foot in a crew room like this one. Safety was non-negotiable, sure, but efficiency? That was code for cutting corners. Innovation meant half-baked apps like SprintReels. And customer focus? That was the biggest laugh of all, given the passenger complaints piling up faster than the bags at Tocumen's undersized baggage claim.

He returned to his seat, the coffee now cold in his hand. The crew room was emptying out as people headed for their next sectors or grabbed a quick nap in the bunks down the hall. Marisol was packing up, her crew bag slung over her shoulder. "You good, boss?" she asked, pausing by his chair. Her tone was light, but her eyes carried the sharp awareness of someone who'd seen too many captains burn out.

"Yeah, just bracing for the HR gauntlet," James said, holding up his phone. "Teams meeting in twenty. They're probably going to ask if I'm eating my vegetables and getting eight hours of sleep."

Marisol laughed, a short, dry sound. "Tell 'em you're thriving on instant coffee and existential dread. That's my secret." She gave him a mock salute and headed for the door, her heels clicking against the linoleum.

James watched Marisol disappear through the crew room door, her silhouette briefly framed against the harsh glare of the terminal corridor. The room felt quieter without her, the banter subsiding into a low hum of fatigue. Rohit was now engrossed in his phone, probably doom-scrolling through X or checking the latest NOTAMs, while Ethan and a Panamanian cabin crew member murmured about roster swaps in the corner. The air conditioning rattled on, its feeble efforts no match for the tropical heat seeping through the concrete walls. James glanced at his watch: 10:02. Thirteen minutes until the Teams meeting. He drained the last of his cold coffee, grimacing at the bitter aftertaste, and opened the Teams app on his phone to double-check the meeting details.

The invite was as sterile as expected: a generic calendar entry with a link, no agenda, and Priya Malhotra's name attached as the organiser. He didn't know Priya, but he could picture her—a young, overworked HR coordinator juggling a dozen time zones, probably reading from a script written by someone who thought "fatigue" was just a fancy word for laziness. James had been through enough of these meetings to know they were less about support and more about ticking boxes. Sprint's HR department, like its ticketing system, was a masterclass in performative competence—lots of noise, little substance.

He stood, stretching his shoulders, and wandered to the crew room's lone window, a narrow slit overlooking the ramp. The A321LR they'd flown in sat at the gate, its navy-blue Sprint livery glistening under the Panama sun. Ramp workers swarmed around it, unloading bags and refuelling, their movements precise despite the heat. Beyond the aircraft, the tarmac shimmered, and in the distance, the hazy outline of Panama City's skyline was just visible through the humidity. It was a world away from the storm-lashed chaos of Reagan National, but the same undercurrent of dysfunction ran through it all.

Sprint's global ambition was a house of cards, and James felt like he was perpetually one gust away from watching it collapse. He leaned against the window frame, the glass warm against his palm, and let his mind drift back to the flight from Boston. The NOTAMs had forced them to reroute over the Atlantic, adding an extra 200 miles to the journey and burning through fuel reserves that were already tight. Rohit had handled the flight planning with his usual precision, but even he'd raised an eyebrow when the latest update from Sprint's Ops centre came through mid-flight: a vague warning about "potential congestion" at Tocumen due to a baggage belt failure. It was the kind of half-arsed communication that had become Sprint's hallmark—enough information to make you worry, not enough to do anything useful with it.

The baggage belt issue had, predictably, turned into a full-blown fiasco by the time they landed. Passengers were already queuing at the lost-and-found desk, their voices a rising tide of frustration in Spanish, English, and a smattering of Portuguese. Marisol had stayed behind to help the ground staff, her fluency in Spanish making her the de facto liaison for a group of irate businessmen who'd missed their connection to São Paulo. James had caught her eye as he left the gate, her expression a mix of resignation and defiance. She'd be fine—she always was—but it was another reminder of how Sprint's frontline staff were left to clean up the messes created by corporate overreach.

Back in the crew room, James checked his phone again: 10:08. Seven minutes to go. He opened the Teams app and tested the connection, knowing that the provided Pixel 9A's data connection, as it was a data only SIM, meaning that Tigo, the local operator for Sprint's crew devices, was notoriously patchy in Tocumen's concrete maze. The signal bars flickered between two and three, a silent taunt. He sighed, resigned to the likelihood of a choppy video feed or a dropped call mid-sentence.

He paced back to his chair, the plastic creaking as he sat, and propped the phone against his crew bag to test the camera angle. The crew room's fluorescent glow wasn't exactly flattering, but it would have to do. James adjusted his tie, smoothed the creases in his Sprint-issue polo, and ran a hand through his hair, which was starting to grey at the temples—a reminder that two decades in aviation had aged him faster than the years alone. He wasn't vain, but he knew HR meetings were as much about appearances as answers. Look too tired, and they'd question your fitness;
190

look too polished, and they'd suspect you were gaming the system.

At 10:14, a minute early, he tapped the Teams link. Miraculously, the connection held, and the screen resolved into a virtual meeting room. Priya Malhotra's name appeared in a small tile, her camera off, with a placeholder avatar of a smiling cartoon pilot that felt jarringly out of place. Another tile showed "Sprint HR – Facilitator," also camera-off, and a third was labelled "Dr. Anil Gupta, Occupational Health Consultant," with a grainy feed of a middle-aged man in a suit, sitting in what looked like a home office with a potted plant and a stack of books in the background.

He paced back to his chair, the plastic creaking as he sat, and propped the phone against his crew bag to test the camera angle. The crew room's fluorescent glow wasn't exactly flattering, but it would have to do. James adjusted his tie, smoothed the creases in his Sprint-issue polo, and ran a hand through his hair, which was starting to grey at the temples—a reminder that two decades in aviation had aged him faster than the years alone. He wasn't vain, but he knew HR meetings were as much about appearances as answers. Look too tired, and they'd question your fitness; look too polished, and they'd suspect you were gaming the system.

At 10:14, a minute early, he tapped the Teams link. The app churned for a moment, the loading icon spinning like a slot machine, before the screen flickered to life. A generic Sprint logo filled the frame, followed by a prompt to "Join as Guest or Sign In." He signed in with his company credentials, the same ones that barely worked half the time on Sprint's rostering portal. Miraculously, the connection held, and the screen resolved into a virtual meeting room. Priya Malhotra's name appeared in a small tile, her camera off, with a placeholder avatar of a smiling cartoon pilot that felt jarringly out of place. Another tile showed "Sprint HR – Facilitator," also camera-off, and a third was labelled "Dr. Anil Gupta, Occupational Health Consultant," with a grainy feed of a middle-aged man in a suit, sitting in what looked like a home office with a potted plant and a stack of books in the background.

"Good morning, Captain Hart," Priya's voice came through, crisp but with the faint delay of a transcontinental connection. "Thank you for joining us. This is a mandatory consultation following your fatigue report submitted on 19th July. With me are Dr. Gupta, our occupational health consultant, and a facilitator from HR whose role is to ensure compliance with CAA and FAA regulations. This meeting is being recorded for training and quality assurance purposes. Do you have any objections?"

James cleared his throat, keeping his tone neutral. "No objections, Priya. I'm ready to proceed."

"Excellent. Let's begin with a brief overview. Your fatigue report was logged at 08:17 EST on 19th July, citing cumulative fatigue following an operational incident on Flight 4352 and subsequent regulatory interviews. Can you confirm this is accurate?"

"Yes, that's correct," James said, his voice steady. He'd learned long ago to keep answers short and factual in these settings. HR wasn't looking for a story—they wanted data points they could file away or, if necessary, weaponize.

Priya continued, her tone clipped and professional. "Thank you. Per Sprint's Crew Fatigue Management Protocol, we're required to assess your current fitness for duty and identify any factors contributing to your reported fatigue. Dr. Gupta will lead this portion. Dr. Gupta, over to you."

The consultant adjusted his glasses, his feed stuttering slightly as he leaned forward. "Captain Hart, good morning. I'd like to start by asking you to describe the events leading up to your fatigue report. Specifically, what physical or mental symptoms were you experiencing, and how did they impact your ability to perform your duties?"

James took a breath, choosing his words carefully. "The incident on Flight 4352 involved a complete loss of radio communications during approach into Reagan National, compounded by severe weather and a military escort. Post-landing, I underwent several hours of interviews with the FAA, MWAA Police, and other authorities, which extended into the early hours of 19th July. I had fragmented sleep—maybe three or four hours, broken up—and as yesterday was rostered to be a five-sector day. Physically, I was experiencing headaches, muscle tension, and a general sense of exhaustion. Mentally, I felt my focus was compromised—not enough to be unsafe, but enough to know I wasn't at my best. Given the regulatory requirement to report fatigue, I submitted the report to ensure I could meet safety standards."

Dr. Gupta nodded, scribbling something off-screen. "Thank you for the detail. Can you quantify the sleep disruption? For example, were there specific triggers, like noise or stress, that prevented rest?"

James resisted the urge to roll his eyes. Quantify sleep disruption? He wasn't a lab rat. "The hotel was standard—quiet enough, no major noise issues. The stress came from the incident itself: replaying the approach, the F-16s, the interviews. It's not something you switch off easily. I'd wake every hour or so, checking my phone for updates from Ops or the FAA. That's what broke the sleep."

Priya interjected, her voice cutting through the slight lag. "Captain Hart, you mentioned checking your phone. Were you engaging with work-related communications during your rest period?"

The question was a trap, and James knew it. Admitting to checking emails could be spun as "failure to disconnect," while denying it might raise suspicions of dishonesty. He kept his response measured. "I glanced at my phone when I woke naturally, as most pilots do. There were no urgent communications, but the habit's there—especially after an incident like 4352. You're waiting for the other shoe to drop."

"Understood," Priya said, her tone giving nothing away. The facilitator's tile remained silent, a mute observer in this carefully choreographed ritual. Dr. Gupta, however, leaned closer to his camera, his feed momentarily freezing before resuming with a slight pixelated stutter.

"Let's explore that further, Captain Hart," Gupta said, his voice carrying the measured cadence of someone who'd conducted a thousand such interviews. "You mentioned stress from the incident impacting your sleep. Can you describe how this manifested? For instance, were there specific thoughts or anxieties that kept you awake?"

James felt a flicker of irritation but kept it buried. The question was standard, designed to probe for psychological weaknesses or, worse, to fish for something that could be twisted into a case for grounding him. He'd seen it happen to colleagues before—pilots who'd been too candid about stress or fatigue, only to find themselves sidelined for "further evaluation" while the airline scrambled to fill their slots. Sprint, with its razor-thin margins and relentless schedules, had little patience for pilots who weren't ready to fly at a moment's notice.

"It wasn't anxiety in the clinical sense," James replied, keeping his voice even. "It was the natural aftermath of a high-stakes event. You're running through the sequence in your head—every decision, every callout, every moment where things could've gone differently. The F-16s weren't exactly a calming presence, and the FAA's questions were thorough, to put it mildly. That kind of mental replay doesn't stop just because you're in a hotel room. It's part of the job, but it takes a toll when you're already short on rest."

Gupta nodded, jotting another note. "And physically? You mentioned headaches and muscle tension. Were these new symptoms, or have you experienced them before under similar circumstances?"

James hesitated, sensing another potential trap. Admitting to recurring symptoms could flag him for a medical review, while dismissing them entirely might undermine his fatigue report. He opted for the middle ground. "The headache was new, likely from dehydration and lack of sleep. The muscle tension's par for the course—long sectors, cramped cockpits, and carrying a crew bag through terminals don't exactly leave you feeling like you've been to a spa. Nothing debilitating, but enough to know I wasn't operating at 100 percent."

Priya's voice cut in again, sharp and precise. "Captain Hart, you stated in your report that your focus was 'compromised' but not unsafe. Can you clarify what you mean by that? At what point did you determine that your condition warranted a fatigue report?"

James recognised the pivot—she was testing his judgement, looking for any crack in his reasoning that could be used to question his professionalism. He leaned slightly closer to the phone, his expression calm but firm. "As pilots, we're trained to self-assess constantly. My focus wasn't where I needed it to be for a five-sector day, especially after the incident and minimal rest. I could've flown one sector, maybe two, without issue, but five, with tight turnarounds and the complexity of Sprint's network? That's pushing the edge of what's safe. The FAA and CAA both require us to report when we're not at peak performance. I followed that requirement to ensure I wasn't putting the aircraft, crew, or passengers at risk."

****

CHAPTER 11 – The Drunk First Officer

Thursday 24th July 2025

The Las Vegas sun rose without ceremony, crawling across the tarmac, glinting off the battered jet bridges and glistening the air with heat haze by seven. James knew that, today, he was slated to work with one of AmericanoAir's rotating cast of First Officers, this time a recent arrival from a Dallas based regional which Sprint had, in the last week, acquired as it was close to collapse. The takeover was classic Sprint: rushed, brutal, and public. Crew bases uprooted, pilots reassigned via WhatsApp with zero notice, and a handful of contract FOs—barely finished with their line checks—scattered across the network like confetti at a shotgun wedding. That morning, James found himself cradling a cup of burnt crew room coffee, blinking grit from his eyes, as he scanned his iPad for the name of his next partner in crime.

"Evan Masters," the pairing app declared, helpfully listing a Dallas phone number, a stylised photo clearly cropped from a graduation party, and a licensing history which showed a suspiciously rapid progression from Cessna 172 to the right seat of an A321, his last employer, Dallas Express, a A321 cargo outfit that had gone belly-up so abruptly its pilots had barely had time to scrounge their last pay packet. James grimaced, swiping through the digital dossier: *ATPL (US, temp endorsement FAA/Sprint), total time: 1,730 hours, jet time: 440, A321 time*: "Less than you'd like," James muttered. Under 'training remarks': "Completed line check, observed for command presence, CRM awareness requires further reinforcement." A Sprint special, then. He took another sip of the bitter coffee. There would be no smooth handover, no detailed crew bulletin, just a "meet at gate 46A, D-Block," and the hope that Masters knew which way was up.

By the time James reached the crew briefing area—a windowless, over-air-conditioned cube beneath the departure concourse—Evan Masters was already there, slouched into the plasticky grey of a fixed-seat chair. He looked no older than twenty-six, Texan tan faded from weeks indoors, his uniform a slightly-too-tight Sprint knock-off with AmericanoAir's half-hearted US patch above the chest pocket.

The irony, being a Texan himself, James knew that he'd never been able to properly lose the twang from his own voice either, but at least he'd learned to switch it off when circumstances required. Masters, by contrast, seemed to wear his roots as both a badge of pride and a sort of armour, drawling through pleasantries with an ease that might have charmed, had it not been undercut by the dead-eyed exhaustion lurking behind his words.

"Morning, Cap'n," Masters greeted, squinting up at James as though surprised someone else had materialised. He didn't bother to rise. There was a Styrofoam cup clutched in his hand—crew room issue, probably even worse than what James had managed to choke down.

James set down his flight bag and extended a hand, waiting just long enough to make the lack of effort obvious. Masters seemed to register the cue, setting the cup aside with a shaky little movement and offering his grip, damp and a touch too limp.

"Evan, right?" James said, keeping his tone professional but not quite friendly. "James Hart. You all checked in, paperwork done?"

"Yessir. All set. Just got my last medical through, Sprint Docs sent it over on the app. All green." Masters blinked rapidly, his eyes bloodshot—was it just jetlag?—and produced a smile that did nothing to conceal the sour tang of last night's booze radiating faintly off him. The telltale notes of cheap whiskey, maybe something even rougher, clung to his breath, mingling with the stale aftertaste of the crew room.

James felt the first coil of tension tighten at the base of his neck. There was a ritual to these things, a way to feel out the mettle of a new FO before trusting them with lives and metal at 36,000 feet, but the timeline for that dance had evaporated somewhere between COVID, the collapse of half the regionals, and Sprint's relentless expansion. Now, you rolled the dice and hoped that your number didn't come up.

"You sleep at all?" James asked, more as a probe than a courtesy.

Masters shrugged, then forced a laugh. "Nah, got in late from Dallas last night, then hit the casinos. Spent most the night with a big titted hooker, and I think, but can't remember, something with an Elvis impersonator and one of y'all night wedding chapels. Vegas, right?"

The grin Masters gave was crooked, not quite devil-may-care so much as an attempted signal of belonging—a performance for the captain's benefit, or maybe his own. His eyes darted, briefly searching for camaraderie and not finding it.

James did not smile. He was acutely aware of the staleness in the air and the undercurrent of something more than just fatigue wafting off the man beside him. This was not the first time he'd smelled yesterday's bad decisions coming from his right-hand seat, but rarely had it felt so brazen.

He knew that Sprint had a zero-tolerance on drugs, alcohol and impaired crew rule, as they, being British and Jeff Young, the CEO of the Group, being formerly of easyJet, one of the 3 big European LCCs, had it written in block capitals on every digital noticeboard and on every aircraft door. Yet AmericanoAir, on the other hand, had one, albeit unwritten, rule, and that was every flight must take off, even if the engine has fallen off and Hades has already sent you a text message warning of delays at the River Styx. Operational necessity. Customer promise. Brand above all else. That was the culture James was forced to swim in, day in, day out, and here it was, distilled—no pun intended—into the twitchy, hungover form of Evan Masters.

He held the silence a little too long, letting the air con hum between them, the suggestion of rebuke unspoken. Masters stared down at his hands, rolling the cup between his palms, and for a moment looked younger still, shrunken by the too-bright LEDs, as if the reality of the day's job had only just begun to dawn on him.

"Right," James said at last, injecting briskness. "Let's get this done." He checked his watch—a battered Omega, gift from his first command—and gathered his tablet, flight plan, and paperwork. "I assume you're good for the walkaround?"

Masters nodded. "Sure, Cap. Did one with the examiner last week. All fresh." He sounded too eager, the words thickened by dehydration and residual intoxication. James let it go, for now. The choice, such as it was, was a simple one: scrub the flight, kick off a storm of paperwork, strand two hundred passengers at Las Vegas and probably land on the blacklist with both Sprint and AmericanoAir management; or keep Masters in sight, watch him like a hawk, and get airborne with as little drama as possible.

James hesitated only a heartbeat before motioning toward the door. "Come on, let's see what shape our bird's in."

Their aircraft for the morning rotation was N961AA, a brand new Airbus A319neo, one of 130 that Sprint had, since 2023, ordered, mainly for the UK and European markets, but which now found itself pressed into AmericanoAir's increasingly ragged domestic network. The jet had that new-plane smell that not even months of barely cleaned Las Vegas turns could erase, and the cabin still bore remnants of PanEuro-style mood lighting and a garish blue seat trim. Down on the ramp, as Masters stumbled through the walkaround—checking tyres with the distracted air of a student cramming for an exam— James followed behind, clipboard in hand, marking off each section and noting, with growing irritation, every fumbled latch and half-hearted glance.

A couple of rampers in faded AmericanoAir polos watched from the baggage belt, smirking at the "new guy" and his not-quite-straight cap. One whistled low, elbowing his mate, and Masters shot them a grin that was too wide to be genuine, the smile of a boy out of his depth and determined not to show it. James felt the edge of embarrassment on his behalf but said nothing, saving his energy for more critical moments.

In the flight deck, the temperature was already climbing. The APU had been powered up early—one tiny mercy from a ground staff otherwise renowned for losing paperwork and luggage in the same movement. James dropped into the left seat, his rituals so ingrained he barely registered each action: log-in, screens alive, checklists ready. Beside him, Masters sat down heavily, fishing in his kitbag for a battered set of David Clarks, their foam pads torn and held together with gaffer tape.

James waited as Masters struggled to buckle in, the FO's hands trembling just slightly as he fumbled through the FMGS initialisation, his fingers moving with mechanical correctness but none of the confidence of real experience.

"Right, today is a 8 segment run, mainly Nevada based, but with a Oakland and a Tijuana to finish today's run," James said, holding the EFB with the day's schedule and routing visible for Masters to peer at, the screen's white glare reflected in Masters' pupils as he squinted, reading the lines as if decoding a foreign script.

"Wait, we're overnighting in Tijuana?" Masters asked, voice cracking ever so slightly as the implication seemed to land—beyond just the haze of hangover, the dawning comprehension that today would be neither brief nor gentle.

"That's right," James replied, voice cool, eyes not leaving the EFB. "Our last leg, AAY418, lands us there around half-past midnight, assuming we're not held up at Oakland. Crew hotel's on the airport road. You got your passport on you?"

There was a small, almost pathetic, pause. Masters' mouth hung open just a fraction too long before started rummaging through his bag, and James noticed that the kid's hands, which had already betrayed him once with their tremor, were slow and uncoordinated, as if each compartment of the battered kitbag might yield something unpleasant. Out came a tangle of lanyards, a half-crushed bag of peanut M&Ms, the frayed edge of a Dallas Express security badge still clinging to the memory of his last airline. Then, with a muttered "Hang on," Masters tipped it out, revealing a half full bottle of whiskey and no passport.

James stared at the bottle for a beat too long, the silence between them swelling into something dangerous. The glint of the whiskey's cheap label in the morning cockpit sunlight was as damning as any breathalyser. For a split second, Masters didn't seem to register that anything was wrong, half-heartedly tugging aside a creased paper copy of his FAA certificate as if maybe, just maybe, the passport would materialise beneath the detritus of a pilot's half-lived life.

James let the silence do the heavy lifting. He kept his hands folded on his lap, the tip of his pen pressed to the checklist but not moving, eyes fixed with the unblinking intensity of a judge awaiting a confession. In the hush, a faint waft of alcohol, sweat, and last night's Las Vegas hung in the air, outdone only by the ozone tang of the aircraft's environmental system.

Eventually, Masters stopped rummaging, his hands stilled atop the jumble in his bag, as if realising all at once the absurdity of his own performance. For a moment, his eyes darted up, meeting James's with a flicker of defiance, then falling away into something softer—something that might have been shame, if not for the exhaustion that gnawed at his features.

"Cap... it's not what it looks like," Masters tried, too quickly, too rehearsed, but then didn't seem to have anywhere to go with the sentence.

James reached out, picked up the bottle by its neck, and held it up in front of the centre pedestal. He knew, from years in the US Air Force, that there were a hundred ways to destroy a man's career in a moment, and even more to ruin a day, a crew, or an operation. In the bright July sun filtering through the A319's side window, the bottle seemed to take on a grotesque significance—a monument to all the shortcuts, exhaustion, and unspoken desperation running through the veins of America's post-COVID regional airline industry. It was everything the manuals warned against, and everything the real world seemed to demand.

James held the bottle there, not as an accusation but as evidence, letting the seconds tick by until the discomfort became unbearable. Out on the ramp, baggage carts beeped and distant engines whined. Inside, the silence crackled with possibility.

"Evan, what does FAA Rule 91.17 say?" James asked, his voice flat as the Nevada basin, the bottle still held aloft like a totem of the day's moral crossroads.

Masters, for a moment, looked genuinely blank. Then he blinked, focus flickering behind his eyes, reciting from memory as if dragged from a half-forgotten exam. "No person may act or attempt to act as a crewmember of a civil aircraft... while under the influence of alcohol, or with... with a blood alcohol concentration of 0.04 or greater..." His voice trailed away, words withering in the oppressive hum of avionics.

"And how long since your last drink?" James pressed. It was a question neither rhetorical nor kind.

There was a long pause. Masters opened his mouth, closed it. "I... I dunno, Cap. Late. Real late. I lost track, honestly. Maybe, uh, three? Four? It was..." The admission hung in the air, naked and raw. The cockpit seemed to shrink around them, the A319 suddenly claustrophobic, a confessional box in a jet age cathedral.

James exhaled slowly. He was suddenly aware of his own heart thumping, of the layers of responsibility pressing in from every side—two hundred passengers, the AmericanoAir tail visible on the ramp, the phone calls he would have to make, the fallout, the paperwork, the shame. But mostly, the look in Masters' eyes—a cocktail of fear, pleading, and something deeper: the unmistakable look of a man who had finally reached the end of his rope.

He set the bottle down, keeping his tone as gentle as a captain could manage with lives on the line. "Evan, you know what this means, don't you?"

Masters nodded, but then pressed his palms hard into his eyes, hiding from the light. "Yeah, Cap. I do. I know." His voice cracked, Texan pride leaking out in ragged, hopeless strips. "If you tell them, I'm done. Career's over. Shit, I just… I just got here, man. I just—" He gulped in air, shoulders hunched. "I'm an alcoholic, ok. 3 years I was on the wagon, and then with Trump back in the White House, and Dallas Express gone bust, and my girl leaving—hell, Cap, I ain't even seen my kid since March. And they said it'd be a fresh start. They said Sprint was desperate enough to take anyone with a pulse and a ticket. I tried, I did. Shit, you're going to have to report me. You have to, right? I'd do the same. I just… I don't want to go back to nothing. I can't, Cap."

The words came out in a sort of hush, half-whispered, the bravado in Masters' Texas lilt suddenly hollowed, broken open. He kept his head bowed, staring at the patch of grey carpet between his boots, and James felt the whole sick machinery of the post-pandemic airline world grind to a halt in that narrow, sun-soaked cockpit. The procedure was clear. So was the law. There were protocols, checklists, and reporting lines for moments like this—a clear, well-trodden path that led inexorably to disciplinary hearings and medical reviews, possibly even the end of a short, embattled career.

James had flown with men like Masters before, in peacetime and in war, through turbulence both literal and metaphorical. There was something pitifully familiar in that battered, trembling silhouette—aviators who'd poured too much of themselves into the job, then found themselves wrung out and abandoned by the very industry that had promised adventure and belonging. The pandemic had only sharpened the edge of that particular sword. Once, pilots were knights of the sky. Now, they were day labourers in polyester, their fates as precarious as the cheap suitcases they hauled between cheap hotels.

He flicked a glance at the clock, then at his own reflection in the polished black of the standby instruments. How many times, over his years in the left seat, had he watched a good man come apart under pressure? And how many times had he looked the other way, weighed up the 'operational necessity' Sprint so loved to talk about against the ugly business of being responsible for another human being's self-destruction?

This was different. This was clear. There was no flying today—not with Evan in this state, not on his aircraft.

He took a slow breath, fighting back the sick knot of irritation and fatigue. He thought of two hundred-odd passengers, bags already in the hold, summer holidaymakers and road warriors and families with restless toddlers. The ground crew would be tapping their feet, the dispatcher already half-ready to ping him for a "quick release," the way AmericanoAir management so loved to demand in their relentless metrics war with the legacy carriers.

"Evan," James said, voice level, "I'm not going to dress this up. You're not fit to fly. Not today. And if I were you, I'd go see the base chief pilot before anyone else does. If you ask for help, you might just get a second chance. If you wait until you're called in for a 'chat' with the union guy and three people from HR, you won't."

He paused. Masters sat frozen, every muscle in his frame wound taut as wire. He nodded once, a tiny movement, then seemed to shrink even further into his chair.

"I get it," he croaked. "I just wanted to… I dunno. Prove I still could. That I wasn't finished."

James felt a surge of bitter sympathy—too many good pilots were losing the fight these days, chewed up by redundancy and roster roulette, cheered on by bottom-line executives who'd never set foot in a jump seat. He'd read enough accident reports to know where this path led: busted careers, ruined lives, the long, slow slide from airman to cautionary tale.

He kept his tone as gentle as possible. "Listen. I'll cover the paperwork. I'll tell the dispatcher there's a crew issue, and that you're reporting sick. You can walk yourself to Medical or I'll have them come get you, but you're not flying this jet with me, or anyone else, until you're cleared. And I'm writing this up for base management— by the book. Not because I want to screw you, but because you need help."

Masters's shoulders slumped. For a moment he looked like he might cry, but he just nodded again, a jerky, grateful, broken motion.

"Thank you, Cap," he said softly, voice hoarse. "For not making it a scene."

James nodded, refusing to let himself feel like the villain. He watched as Masters unplugged his battered headset, stuffed it back into his kitbag, and slung it over one shoulder. For a moment, Masters stood in the aisle, silhouetted against the sunlit terminal beyond, then gave James a last, awkward nod, and disappeared down the steps.

There was a brief, cathartic silence once he'd gone—James alone with the hum of the avionics, the weight of the day settling heavily on his shoulders. Already, his phone was vibrating: Ops wanted an update. The dispatcher's name—Amy, he recalled, a harried contract worker—flashed up, demanding to know the delay code. The union, meanwhile, would want to hear it was handled by the book. Management, for their part, would likely prefer he'd just kept quiet and pushed the day's revenue into the air.

James sat for a long moment, not moving, breathing in the dense, dry chill of the A319's conditioned air. Beneath the faint tang of Masters' whiskey, he could smell his own sweat and the rising metallic heat of the ramp. Out the window, the sun was now a white hammer, beating down on the apron, warping the horizon into a shimmer. A tug rolled past, trailing a chain of battered baggage carts. Somewhere below, a refueller was arguing with a ground handler over a missing nozzle. Vegas mornings, he thought—merciless, indifferent, and always too bright for bad news.

Pulling his work mobile phone from his pocket, the Google Pixel 9A's screen with the AmericanoAir logo on it and the Sprint Staff app, along with the Sprint Manifest and Sprint Perks app, all on the home screen, James had to chuckle at how the company had pre-installed the various apps, and had also added Microsoft Teams as the app to be the dialler.

Searching through the contacts, James chuckled as he typed in "US West Coast Ops" into the search and it came up with a +44 1843 telephone number for the base duty manager, even though she was based at Henderson Executive Airport on the other side of town. There was rumours, James knew, that Sprint had brought, back in 2022, a block of 40,000 UK telephone numbers, which was why the only plan on the Sprint supplied phones were data and Wi-Fi, with calls rerouted via Teams, not charged in-country. The economies of scale made sense to someone in the bowels of finance or procurement, James supposed, but it was still faintly surreal to phone Las Vegas and be answered by a fellow American, also based in the US, but using a British number.

He knew that, by law and FAA Regulation, Ops had to be ran in the US, and so the quirks of Sprint's telecoms strategy were a corporate eccentricity—one more layer in the absurd lasagne of AmericanoAir's existence. Still, it was a comfort of sorts: no matter how much the branding screamed red, white and blue, the machinery behind the curtain was inevitably British. Cost-cutting and clever regulatory footwork were as much the airline's true heritage as any flag stitched onto a uniform sleeve.

He thumbed the call icon, listening to the brittle digital ring. After three short bursts, a voice picked up—brisk, with the flattened vowels of the Pacific Northwest undercut by the easy cynicism of someone long since hardened to chaos.

"US West Coast Ops, Maddie Chen speaking."

"Maddie, it's James Hart, based at Vegas. Sorry to hit you with this at shift start, but I've got a crew problem on AAY410. First Officer's declared unfit. I'll be reporting it as a 'self-disclosed' to base and to Med. We're going to need a replacement."

There was the faint tap of a keyboard in the background, the sound of someone flicking through a digital rota. Maddie's sigh was audible.

"Roger, James. Name?"

"Evan Masters. Dallas transfer."

She gave a grunt of understanding. "He's not the first one this week. You mind putting that in writing on the Crew Safety Report so Med can pick it up? I'll have to mark the delay as 'Crew Unfit—SIC.' I'm not promising miracles on the replacement. Vegas pool is thinner than the bloody Thames. Standby could be a few hours."

"Copy all. I'll keep the cabin and gate in the loop. If you get a miracle, text me."

"Will do, Captain. Anything else?"

James shook his head, then remembered she couldn't see him. "Negative. Thanks, Maddie."

He ended the call, feeling the weight of the conversation—routine, professional, but threaded with the undertone of a crisis barely avoided. He pulled up the digital Crew Safety Report, filling out the necessary sections with practised precision: date, time, flight number, FO name, nature of the event. He wrote just enough: "FO declared unfit for duty, suspected alcohol impairment, self-disclosed, no incident or operational risk." He ticked the relevant boxes, attached his e-signature, and sent it sailing into the cloud, one more admission for the database, one more soul for the Sprint medical system to process.

James sat in the left seat, still, for a moment that was neither relief nor resignation, only the steady, methodical cooling of adrenaline as a bad situation slid—just—into the realm of procedure. For all the corporate chaos, AmericanoAir and Sprint, for all their legal gymnastics and sociopathic efficiency, still paid lip service to safety. There was a protocol, a flow of forms, a way to record the debris left behind by broken men and women. He'd done his part: the right thing, if not the easy thing.

He glanced at the clock. The aircraft's departure slot was already in jeopardy, and he knew exactly how the next hour would play out. Delays, angry customers, ground staff grumbling, the lurking threat of the local press if anyone caught the scent of scandal. It was never the airborne drama that undid you in the end, but the endless grind of waiting rooms, apologies, and the impossibility of explaining to the travelling public that a hungover pilot was, in its way, good news: proof that the system still sometimes worked.

****

CHAPTER 12 – Last Minute Changes
Thursday 24th July 2025

The final leg of the Nevada milk runs, as James called it, was nearly over, a light Reno to Las Vegas rotation on a late-spring afternoon where the air shimmered with that peculiar, dusty clarity which seemed unique to the high desert. Altitude 29,000, with a light southerly drift from the Sierras, and the sky ahead a patchwork quilt of baby blue and whispy, wind-sheared cirrus. In the right seat, instead of Evan Masters, a stand-in FO had been found by Ops after three hours of sweat, radio silence, and apologetic texts from Maddie Chen. Her name was Rebecca "Becky" Long, a former 960th Airborne Air Control Squadron navigator, more recently a first officer on AmericanoAir's newly-inherited A319s, and—crucially—one of the few available pilots with an FAA, EASA, and Sprint validation. She'd materialised at the gate with the studied calm of someone used to being dropped into chaos mid-rotation, a faded Ty Beanie Baby keychain swinging from her kitbag and a long-dormant RAF patch still stitched beneath the AmericanoAir insignia on her uniform.

James had only worked with her once before, and then it had been on a Vegas to San Diego quick turn, both running on fumes, neither with enough caffeine or patience to do much beyond the barest essentials of CRM. Today, though, there was a peculiar camaraderie in their silence—a sense of mutual recognition, of two pilots who had seen enough of post-pandemic aviation's grim absurdities to know when not to push a conversation.

For most of the flight, conversation was sparse. James let Becky handle the radios, noting her crisp, laconic replies to ATC, her professional focus as she double-checked approach plates and ran through the descent profile. The earlier stress, the grim bureaucratic ballet with Ops, felt like another world now—faded into the sunlit serenity of cruise. Below, the landscape shifted from the stark browns and ochres of the high desert to the faintest, ghostly greens where irrigation cut new lines across the earth.

"Y'know, I've just noticed, we're slated for a Tijuana run later, right?" Becky said suddenly, as they were in the hold sequence at Las Vegas, the notorious Camel Three Arrival, already halfway through a dull orbit over Jean, squinting at the monochrome wedge of McCarran's approach sector on the nav display. "Yet the Rude Rams are currently in theatre over Mexico."

James chuckled, as the Rude Rams, or 34th Fighter Squadron, a F-35 Lightning II squadron based at Hill AFB, were the sort of wildcards who turned up anywhere between Baja California and Baghdad. On the 12th July 2025, President Donald J Trump had issued a joint declaration on national television declaring the cartels in Mexico to be in "material alignment with non-state militant actors," a phrase so brazenly constructed to bypass any congressional vote that James had nearly choked on his instant coffee when he'd seen the live ticker scroll across the galley screen two weeks prior.

The Rude Rams, James knew from his time with the Gamblers, the 77th Fighter Squadron based out of Shaw Air Force Base, were rumoured not to be enjoying their deployment to Fort Bliss, their FOL, or Forward Operating Location, a US Army Base where the 'ground pounders', the name that USAF pilots universally used for anyone not certified to fly something with afterburners, were fond of reminding the flyboys that real fighting meant getting dust in places even a debrief couldn't reach.

"Yet Sprint haven't pulled us out of Mexico yet," James replied, keeping his tone light, though a thin vein of anxiety ran beneath his words. He scanned the latest ATIS for McCarran and flicked over to the secondary VHF, listening to the Ground frequency while also monitoring the Tower. "Probably waiting for some insurance clause to kick in, or for the FAA to decide if that new NOTAM blanket actually covers unilateral cartel zone incursions."

Becky gave a dry snort. "They'll wait until something explodes, as usual. Either a missile or the insurance market." She shifted slightly in her seat, keeping one hand on the yoke as the plane began a slow left turn, guided by the STAR arrival's predictable rhythm. "There again with all the federal firings because Trump thinks anyone whos a 'DEI hire' is secretly plotting Marxist puppet theatre in the Pentagon will probably interpret a weather delay as sedition. That and Musk's DOGE team cutting anything from the contingency budget not linked to some NFT-backed drone programme or genetically-engineered morale dog. How long did ATC say we'd be in the hold for again?"

James glanced at the hold timer on the FMS, noting they had another seven minutes before the next expected vector. The Camel Three Arrival was living up to its reputation—tedious, circuitous, and just unpredictable enough to keep them from fully relaxing.

"ATC's saying another 30 at least in the stack," he replied, adjusting the heading bug slightly. "We're close to the fuel limit for holding."

Becky's fingers danced over the fuel prediction page, then the alternate routing. "Yeah. If we don't get vectored in the next five, we could call Henderson, as we usually park overnight there, and we have a gate slot pre-approved in case of ATC overflow." Becky tapped at the ACARS interface. "I'll just ping Ops now in case we do have to make that call. Hey, Captain, at least we've only been doing Nevada milk runs, and we've just come from Reno, so it's not as if we're wrestling with a six-leg epic up from Tampa or some godforsaken field in West Texas," she added, her tone dry but with a ghost of a smile. "Beats flying a medical rescue out of Ciudad Obregón, anyway. Last time I did that, the ramp was full of Army, and the only fuel truck was a teenager who insisted on taking selfies with the plane."

"Yeah, I think Henderson is the best option," James agreed, allowing himself a brief smile at the thought of the farcical scene she'd described. "Still, it feels like this operation's just running on fumes and paperwork. But that's AmericanoAir in a nutshell, right? Always 'just about' managing to tick the boxes until someone says 'hold'."

"Americano 312, this is Las Vegas Tower, we have cleared you for descent. Expect a direct approach to runway 26R via the Camel Three Arrival. Arrival frequency will be 118.7, final descent will be in 3 minutes, over," The voice of the controller crackled over the radio, as routine and mechanical as ever.

"Copy that, Tower. descending on Camel Three, 118.7, final in 3 minutes, Americano 312, roger, thank you Tower," James responded, his voice carrying the practiced ease of someone who had long since mastered the art of flying with a calm façade. He adjusted the yoke slightly, guiding the aircraft through the final phase of the hold, watching the Nevada landscape tilt beneath them as the aircraft turned onto its final course towards McCarran.

James kept his focus sharp, though there was a small, tired part of him that just wanted to get this day over with. The routine of it all had become a blur, especially when it involved operations like AmericanoAir, where the rules bent to fit whatever operational need they had at the time. The disjointed nature of the airline, from its crew assignments to its ever-shifting schedules, left little room for relaxation. There was always something looming, like a deadline that had been given to you but not shared with anyone else. Still, he could see the end of this leg approaching.

Becky's hand moved swiftly across the cockpit controls as she monitored their systems, always alert despite the weariness in her eyes. The familiar hum of the aircraft and the soft rattle of the engines had become a kind of background noise for both of them, the familiar rhythm of aviation that was as comforting as it was unsettling.

"Approaching the IAF, Captain. You ready to take this one in?" Becky asked, her voice calm but carrying the weight of someone who had seen enough holds to know exactly when the descent would begin to feel like it was never going to end.

James glanced out of the cockpit window, spotting the desert horizon and the faint outline of Las Vegas sprawling beneath the wings. As he adjusted the descent rate, he reflected on just how surreal this flight had felt. The constant back-and-forth between Ops, the scrambled pilot assignments, and the impending questions about Mexico. He tried to keep it all in the background—after all, there was a job to be done—but the reality of the business he was now part of lingered.

It wasn't just the usual stress of operations, nor the endless churn of connecting flights and layovers. No, it was something deeper. It was the awareness that the industry he had once known so well, one based on pride in service and professionalism, had been infected by a creeping sense of chaos and desperation. This wasn't the proud, well-oiled machine that had once been PanEuro. This was something else entirely—a company constantly running behind, scrambling for whatever small victories it could find.

"Americano 312, Las Vegas Tower. You are cleared for final approach, runway 26R," the controller's voice crackled over the radio, snapping James out of his reverie. "Wind from 180 at 8 knots, clear to land. Expect a quick vacate after landing."

"Cleared for 26R, quick vacate, Americano 312, thank you Tower," James replied, his voice sounding almost like an echo in the sterile cockpit.

"Let's make this a smooth one, then," James muttered, more to himself than to Becky.

Becky shot him a quick glance, catching the weariness in his voice. "You okay there, Cap?" she asked, her voice genuine despite the dry tone.

James gave a short nod, adjusting the final descent profile as they crossed the last few miles. "Yeah. Just tired of this whole... everything," he admitted quietly, a rare moment of honesty slipping through the cracks. "It's like we're not flying anymore; we're just keeping the planes in the air for as long as we can before someone notices how messy it all is."

"Yeah," Becky said, her voice understanding. "Welcome to the world of AmericanoAir. If it wasn't for the constant deadlines and operational fire drills, we'd probably all have too much time to think. That's the real problem, isn't it?"

"Can't afford to think too much, especially with the way things are now. But at some point, you can't ignore it all. Just becomes... unbearable."

She didn't respond immediately, choosing instead to focus on the final stages of the approach. James understood—after all, they both knew the drill. The distractions were endless. But sometimes, it was the silence that spoke louder than the constant noise of operations.

With the runway approaching, James keyed in the final approach checklist. As they descended through 2,000 feet, the bright city lights of Las Vegas twinkled below them, a chaotic sea of neon and shadows that reflected the disjointed world they were flying through. The anticipation of landing, the final leg of a long and tense day, was always a bittersweet moment. They were nearly there, but the real challenges would come after the plane touched down.

"Americano 312, you are 5 miles out. Adjust to final heading, cleared to land 26R," Las Vegas Tower instructed.

"Cleared to land 26R, Americano 312," James replied, his hands steady on the yoke as he guided the aircraft in.

The aircraft sank lower, the runway growing larger in the cockpit window, a familiar sight for both pilots. The checklist ran through James's mind as he confirmed each step in the approach—flaps set, landing gear down, speed controlled. Everything was lining up just as it should.

"Don't let it get too tight on final," Becky cautioned quietly, her eyes glued to the instruments.

James nodded, adjusting the trim slightly to ensure a smooth landing. "Got it."

As they crossed the threshold of the runway, the wheels touched down with a firm but controlled bounce, the thud of the tires against the tarmac a welcome sound. The runway lights flickered in the periphery of their vision as they rolled down, the sound of reverse thrust roaring through the cockpit. They had made it.

The aircraft rolled smoothly to a stop as James flicked the landing lights off and disengaged the autopilot, guiding the plane onto the taxiway. He sighed in relief, feeling the last few ounces of tension melt away. It had been a chaotic rotation, but at least they were safely on the ground.

"Americano 312, vacate at Charlie 5, cross runway 19, contact Ground on 121.9," the controller instructed, and James acknowledged the clearance.

As they taxied toward the gate, Becky leaned back in her seat, unstrapping her harness with a quiet sigh of relief. "Another one done," she said, half-smiling despite the fatigue.

"Yeah," James replied, "another one done."

As they approached the gate, the usual haze of final paperwork and gate assignments loomed in the distance. The flight had been routine in its own strange way, but it was far from over. They still had the climb out to Tijuana ahead of them, and there were more things to consider than just the next leg. But for now, the world outside the cockpit faded as James steered the plane smoothly into the gate, the glow of Las Vegas's neon lights casting an otherworldly glow across the terminal.

"Americano 312, welcome to Las Vegas," came the final voice from the tower, cheerful despite the long day. "Hope your stay is short and sweet."

James gave a small chuckle, his fatigue momentarily lifted. "We'll see about that," he muttered, as they powered down the engines and started the usual post-flight routine.

It wasn't much, but it was the only way they could keep going. One flight at a time. One day at a time.

Becky unclipped her headset and gave him a nod. "Catch you after the turn," she said, already reaching for her bag.

"See you in a bit," James replied, as the cabin doors opened and the first wave of passengers started to shuffle toward the jet bridge. It was another routine landing. Another routine day in the endless cycle of flying and paperwork that seemed to define their world now.

But for now, the plane was on the ground, and for the moment, that was enough.

* _ * _ * _ *

As James and Becky entered the crew room at Las Vegas, as they had a hour break due to the fact the next two turns would be one to Oakland, followed by one from Oakland to the Mexican border town of Tijuana, they knew that the FAA would have their heads, as well as AmericanoAir's Air Operators Certificate, if they failed to have sufficient rest, as, being a ULCC and doing 8 sectors in one day, they were pushing the legal limits of duty time and rest requirements. James took a deep breath as he entered the crew room, the constant hum of overhead lights mingling with the chatter of other flight crews. They had an hour to kill, but it wasn't enough time to clear his mind from the intense, ever-present pressure that came with each sector.

The television, tuned into CNN, showed a Sprint plane on the ground at Tijuana, its tail destroyed, and a crater in the runway with a Breaking News banner flashing across the screen.

"...missiles from a US Air Force F-35 hit the runway while this Sprint Europe plane, scheduled to head to Madrid, was on the ground, empty due to air raid sirens in the area. Fortunately, no passengers were aboard at the time. The plane had arrived merely hours earlier from the Spanish capital, Madrid, when the incident occurred. Pentagon officials say that they were aiming at a cartel base in the Mexican border territory, and that the plane was mistakenly caught in the crossfire. There are no reports of injuries, but the runway has been severely damaged, and the airport remains closed indefinitely."

James stood still for a moment, his gaze fixed on the screen, the image of the destroyed tail section seared into his mind. He could feel Becky beside him, her expression unreadable, but he could tell she was just as shocked by the news. The steady background hum of the crew room felt suddenly distant, as if it had all faded into the background of something much larger than their own world of routine flights and flight times.

"Jesus Christ," Becky muttered, her voice barely audible over the buzz of the room.

James swallowed, the tension in his chest tightening as he exhaled slowly. "That's the last thing we need right now," he said, more to himself than to her. The idea of being anywhere near Tijuana, let alone flying into a zone that had now seen the reality of what it meant to be caught between cartel violence and military intervention, was terrifying. The fact that the F-35s—deployed as part of a controversial new policy—had accidentally hit a commercial aircraft, even an empty one, was a nightmare scenario in more ways than one.

They both knew how tenuous the whole situation was for AmericanoAir. Sprint and their other competitors had already been facing the fallout from shifting airspace rules, international incidents, and the growing global instability that had taken root ever since the pandemic. Now this—this was a mess that could easily spiral out of control.

A crew member from another flight wandered past, glancing up at the TV with mild interest. "You reckon Sprint's going to take a hit from this? That's one hell of a PR disaster."

"With Fernando Costas running Legal? He's ex Ryanair, so he's likely already drafting a 'we were collateral damage in a military operation' defence," James muttered. He rubbed his temples, trying to alleviate the tightness growing behind his eyes. The situation was precarious enough without adding an incident like this into the mix.

Becky leaned back against the wall, arms crossed as she glanced from the TV to James. "You don't think it'll get worse, do you?" she asked, the question heavy with concern. "This could be bigger than just a PR disaster. If it's found that civilians are getting caught up in these 'crossfire' situations, it could mean major fallout for any airline operating in these zones, especially with the US military involved."

"I don't know, Beck. What I do know is that Sprint's already walking a tightrope with this whole Mexican operation. Adding a missile strike to the mix isn't going to help. Not with the international scrutiny and the added regulatory attention we've been getting," James replied, his voice tired but firm. "And you know what this means for us. If Tijuana's officially marked as a no-go zone, we're stuck with those damned contingency flights to Henderson or wherever they want to send us next."

Suddenly James's phone rang, and he noticed it was Maddie Chen James hesitated for a moment before picking up the call. He could already feel the tension rising, a familiar weight in his chest. It was always a bad sign when Maddie was calling directly, especially during the short breaks between rotations.

"James," Maddie's voice crackled through, sharp and urgent. "We're changing your final sector. You're doing Oakland to San Diego instead of Oakland to Tijuana. FAA has closed the airspace south of the border. Your Vegas to Oakland has been brought forward 12 minutes too. We'll book you a deadhead on an Alaska flight back to LAX from San Diego."

James stood still for a moment, his fingers gripping the phone tighter, trying to grasp the weight of Maddie's words. Changing the final sector, shifting a flight from Tijuana to San Diego—it was all part of the endless scramble that was now second nature to him, yet it never felt any less disorienting.

"San Diego instead of Tijuana, got it," he muttered, more to himself than to Maddie. "And the Vegas to Oakland's pushed up? Fantastic. Just what I need today."

"Yeah, the FAA's pulled the plug on the Tijuana approach. Security risks in the region have escalated,"

Maddie explained, her voice clipped, the tone that of someone who had done this a hundred times before. "We're clearing the schedule for safety. You'll be back in San Diego before you know it, but you'll need to head over to Gate 6 at Oakland for your return leg. We've had a few slots shift, so the layover might be a bit tight."

"Understood," James replied, his voice losing a bit of its earlier composure. He rubbed the back of his neck, the fatigue settling back in like a blanket. "Just another day in paradise."

"Tell me about it," Maddie said, her voice light but with an edge of genuine sympathy. "Look, I'll keep you posted on any updates. Let me know if you need anything from us."

"Will do, Maddie. Thanks," James said, hanging up the phone with a sigh, running a hand through his hair. The whole day had started to feel like a blur, a carousel of confusion, bad news, and last-minute changes. He glanced at Becky, who was already rechecking her own schedules and making notes on the latest shift.

"Oakland to San Diego," James said, repeating the change as if to make it real. "No Tijuana today, I guess. You okay with the new routing?"

Becky's expression was unreadable for a moment, but then her lips twitched into a half-smile. "I've got to be. It's not like we've got many options right now. At least we'll avoid any missile shrapnel over the Mexican border," she added with a dry laugh, trying to inject a bit of levity into the situation.

James managed a tired smile. "Yeah, that would be nice. Could really do without the new PR mess Sprint's about to get from that."

"Probably a good thing we're not flying into Tijuana anymore," Becky replied, her voice lowering slightly. "You think they'll try and cancel the route for good?"

James took a deep breath. The implications were clear, and he didn't want to think about it. "Who knows? Sprint's always trying to cut costs and push boundaries, but I can't imagine flying over cartel zones and military operations is going to be in their top five 'most lucrative ideas'. If this gets worse, they'll have to pull the plug on the whole Mexico operation. That's a huge chunk of their US-Mexico routes."

Becky nodded, her lips pressed together in thought. "Yeah, and who knows where that leaves us. All these last-minute rotations... It's like we're just a cog in a machine that's rusting around us."

James's gaze drifted back to the TV, which was still showing the news footage of the damaged Sprint plane at Tijuana. He could see the crater where the runway had been impacted, the charred remains of the aircraft's tail. A small, sick feeling coiled in his stomach.

"Any word from Sprint HQ about this?" Becky asked quietly, breaking the silence that had stretched on too long.

James shook his head. "Nothing yet. But you can bet they're drafting some kind of statement or looking for a way to downplay the whole thing. The last thing they want is for this to hit the press and cause more regulatory nightmares."

"Yeah," Becky said, her voice tinged with a hint of bitterness, "and the first thing they'll do is remind us of the importance of operational efficiency. Never mind that some of us are running on fumes and dodging missiles just to keep the show going."

James couldn't help but let out a small chuckle, though it was more from frustration than humour. "AmericanoAir in a nutshell, right? Crisis after crisis, and yet we're still here, still flying."

Becky sighed, rubbing her eyes before taking a sip of her coffee. "One day, I swear, we'll look back on all of this and wonder how we survived."

"Maybe," James replied, his voice low. "But I'm not sure we'll ever get to the 'looking back' part. At this rate, we're just going to keep pushing forward, one day at a time."

Before Becky could respond, the crew room door swung open, and another flight crew entered, their voices rising as they joked and made their way to the break room. The noise seemed to snap James out of his momentary haze, and he stood up, checking his watch.

"Right," he muttered, more to himself now. "Oakland to San Diego. Let's get this over with."

Becky nodded and stood up as well, shouldering her bag. "Yeah, let's. Who knows what other curveballs they'll throw our way today?"

The two of them made their way back to the gate, the din of the crew room fading behind them. The terminal felt familiar, yet foreign in its own way, as if everything around them was part of a machine they were both a part of and yet increasingly disconnected from. The weight of the day hung heavy on their shoulders, but neither of them said anything more about it. There was no point in talking about the uncertainty of the future. There was only the next leg to focus on, and the next. Flight after flight, day after day.

As they boarded the aircraft for the next leg to Oakland, James settled into the captain's seat once more, Becky sitting beside him. The usual pre-flight checks went by in a blur of movements. They both knew the drill by now—prepare, fly, repeat.

"Americano 312, you're cleared to push back. Have a safe flight," the gate agent's voice came over the intercom, snapping James's attention back to the present.

"Cleared to push back, thank you," James replied, his voice steady despite the turmoil swirling in his mind. He flicked a glance at Becky, who was already focusing on the pre-flight checklist.

"Here we go again," he muttered under his breath, as the engines roared to life.

The aircraft moved slowly away from the gate, and for a moment, it felt as if the world was still. There was only the hum of the engines and the rush of air as they began to taxi. James kept his eyes forward, his hands steady on the controls.

In the back of his mind, he couldn't shake the thought that things were slipping further out of control. But for now, there was only the sky ahead of them, and the endless cycle of flying to get through. And that was enough for today.

****

CHAPTER 13 – The Führer Speaks
Friday 25th July 2025

The crew room at San Diego was less of a calm atmosphere and more of a full and standing riot of exhaustion, chatter, and resignation. The air smelled faintly of reheated burritos, cheap coffee, and the institutional tang of overworked air-conditioning. Screens mounted along the far wall flickered between the various networks, from Fox, who were describing the bombing of the Sprint Europe plane, which turned out to be a Sprint Max liveried one, meaning it was the Premium LCC and not the Euro ULCC style, as "deliberate agent provocateurs against President Trump's explicit instructions," to CNN, who were showing rolling footage of the ruined runway at Tijuana, the blackened tail cone of the Airbus still glinting amidst the wreckage, and the slow-motion close-ups of Pentagon spokespeople, each one managing to look both alarmed and entirely noncommittal at the same time.

MSNBC, on the other hand, was openly calling for Trump to be impeached again, citing the incident as evidence of "cascading executive dysfunction." Around the TV cluster, crews from five or six airlines were sprawled across every available sofa and table, all in various stages of paperwork, mobile phone scrolling, or just blank staring at the floor, as if hoping to fall through and escape duty time limitations by sheer force of will.

James Hart stood just inside the door, his kitbag slung over one shoulder, watching the chaos unfold. He'd long ago lost any illusions of peace or rest in airport crew rooms, but this—this was different. The air felt thick with the sense that something truly foundational had shifted overnight, that the industry's precarious hold on stability had finally, perhaps irretrievably, snapped.

Becky Long was already at a corner table, poring over a roster printout with all the haunted resignation of a condemned woman checking her own execution schedule. She waved him over, and he dropped his bag with a grunt, sinking into the battered faux-leather seat beside her.

"You hear that the Spirit lot in their crew room have got BBC News on, and the Big Boss is set to do a statement?" she asked, not looking up from the tangle of highlighter and biro that had become her next three days' existence.

James gave a dry, thin smile. "The Big Boss? Which one—ours, theirs, or the one currently playing tinpot dictator from the Oval Office?"

Becky didn't answer, and for a long moment, the two of them just listened to the ever-present din—the overlapping audio from TVs, the cackle of a Southwest crew celebrating their early finish, the anxious hum of a pair of Delta pilots debating whether to take the re-route via Houston or try to deadhead on JetBlue.

"It's supposed to be the real top," Becky said at last. "Jeff Young. Himself. The Führer."

James raised an eyebrow. In the world of Sprint, the CEO's rare public appearances were somewhere between a papal conclave and a hostage video. If Jeff Young was going to speak—live, on the BBC, to the transatlantic world—then something seismic was afoot.

"I'd have thought that Fernando Costas or that Frankie "I'd have thought that Fernando Costas or that Frankie Mendes woman would be up for the cameras before Jeff would let them haul him out," James said, his voice lowered as he leaned in, the background noise blurring to a dull, thumping hum. "If he's actually going live, then it's got to be either a full-blown PR disaster or he's trying to keep the shareholders from bolting for the exits. Maybe both."

Becky's lips twisted into a sardonic smile. "We're in the big leagues now, Hart. It's not just about irate passengers and lost bags any more. Now it's about who gets the blame when someone blows a crater in a runway and half the global news cycle spins off into orbit. He'll be wheeled out, do his Churchill act, and then quietly sack a handful of middle managers who couldn't have prevented it if they'd had a crystal ball and God on speed dial."

James grunted, glancing across the packed crew room. On one of the battered tables, a young Sprint captain was watching her phone intently, the BBC News feed loaded. The voice was tinny but audible:

"—and now, from Sprint Group headquarters in Kent, the Group Chief Executive, Jeff Young—"

A sudden hush spread in uneven waves as phones across the room switched to the same feed. The flickering screen showed the familiar backdrop: the fake-wood panelled wall, a plastic Sprint Max model perched on the sideboard, the company logo looming behind Jeff Young's broad shoulders.

Young's face looked greyer than usual, his expression forcibly composed. He wore a dark blue suit, an open-collared shirt—no tie, but not casual. Behind the practiced mask, his eyes flicked left and right, reading autocue or searching for cues from offstage handlers. When he spoke, his accent was halfway between easyJet calm, and generic business-English, modulated for maximum transatlantic comprehensibility.

"Ladies and gentlemen, colleagues across the Sprint Group family, and customers around the world. In the last twenty-four hours, we have all witnessed a most regrettable incident at Tijuana International Airport, in which one of our Sprint Max aircraft was damaged as a result of military action in the area. I want to begin by assuring all our passengers, crew, and partners that there were no injuries, and that our highest priority remains your safety and wellbeing at all times."

A faint, collective exhalation went around the room—somewhere between relief and cynicism. Becky snorted, eyes fixed on the screen. "That's the easy bit, then. Now comes the tap dance."

Young pressed on, the teleprompter rhythm smoothing his words. "We are working closely with local and international authorities to ascertain the facts of what occurred. Our team is already on the ground in Mexico, coordinating with the relevant agencies to ensure the runway is cleared and that the needs of our customers are being met. Unfortunately, we are only able to provide what the EU261 regulations, as the flight that is cancelled is to a Member states, requires, and will do so to the fullest extent of the law." Young paused, the hint of a smile—

234

almost apologetic—ghosting across his face as the autocue zipped him onwards. "To those passengers and crew affected, we offer our sincere apologies and our absolute commitment to returning you safely to your destinations as soon as practicable. To our staff across the Sprint Group—those who continue to show professionalism and resilience under the most difficult of circumstances—my deepest gratitude. Without you, we would not be able to keep the world connected as we do."

The screen flickered, compressing Young's image for a split second as the BBC's digital encoding stuttered. A low chorus of muttered sarcasm rippled through the crew room; nobody expected more than this. Becky's pen tapped against her roster. "I wonder if he even knows how many legs are being flown today," she murmured, so only James could hear.

Young continued, face never moving, voice perfectly pitched to be both authoritative and humble, a tightrope act for the age. "Let me be clear: at Sprint, we believe in accountability, in openness, and in learning from every incident. Our owners, the Oman Investment Authority and the UK Defence Corporation, have urged the North Atlantic Treaty Organisation, the European Union, the British Government and their allies to condemn the terrorist activities of Donald J Trump and his administration."

A stunned silence followed Jeff Young's last sentence. It lingered in the crew room like a pall of smoke, stunned even the most jaded of pilots into stillness. No one had expected that. Not even close.

"Jesus Christ," someone muttered near the vending machine, their voice thick with disbelief.

Becky Long's pen stopped moving mid-scribble. She looked at James, eyes wide. "Did he just—?"

"Yeah," James murmured, blinking. "He just called a sitting US president a terrorist. On the BBC. Wearing a Sprint badge."

He leaned forward as the broadcast continued, Young now delivering the rest of the statement with an oddly robotic calm, clearly aware of the enormity of what he'd just said.

"We regret deeply that the civil-military protocols intended to protect commercial aviation have failed in this instance. We will continue to advocate—loudly and unapologetically—for the protection of our crews, passengers and aircraft. Any further engagements of this nature, intentional or otherwise, represent a direct and unacceptable threat to civil society and global commerce. It must not happen again."

The silence that followed Jeff Young's words clung to the air like a thunderclap after lightning. For a moment, the San Diego crew room seemed almost to tilt around James Hart, the background noises suddenly muffled, as if someone had stuffed the entire airport with insulation. Conversations froze mid-sentence, paperwork slid from hands, and the fizzing, fluorescent anxiety that filled every corner of the airline industry's post-pandemic world spiked another level.

Becky was still staring at the screen, her biro hanging loosely in her hand. "That's it, then," she whispered, not quite believing her own words. "That's the end of the honeymoon. There's no walking that one back."

James was only dimly aware of the other crews in the room—an Alaska team, the distinctive yellow-vested Southwest pair, even the polished Delta pilots who always carried themselves with an almost military bearing—each of them craning towards the various screens, their own phones, every device now replaying Young's statement in a staccato echo of shocked disbelief. The clip, trimmed, clipped, and spliced, had already started to circulate online before the official broadcast even finished, spread by social media, WhatsApp groups, and the feverish grapevine that powered aviation at the speed of rumour.

Outside, the July sun glared hard against the tinted windows, bouncing off the apron where ground crews in faded Hi-Vis shirts toiled beneath the whine of APU units and the cough of baggage tugs. From somewhere distant—a different concourse, perhaps, or the other side of the glass—a burst of laughter broke through, jarring in its normality, a world away from the geopolitical aftershocks now vibrating through every airline in the Western hemisphere.

The television cut back to the news desk, the BBC anchor's face visibly strained as she attempted to inject a note of measured calm into the situation. "And that was Jeff Young, Group Chief Executive of Sprint, with what is undoubtedly the strongest language..."

The BBC Breaking News logo then came over the screen, and pictures of the inside of the press pit of Air Force One, hastily convened and bristling with the glacial tension of a political stand-off, replaced the Sprint backdrop.

"Hey, lads," one of the Brits who was on secondment to AmericanoAir and Sprint US, shouted, "Hitler's orange cousin is on the telly now!" His Midlands accent cut through the hush like a knife. "Let's see what the Orange One's got to say for himself, eh?"

A ripple of weary, gallows laughter fluttered across the crew room, even as most faces turned towards the nearest screen. James knew that Air Force One was on its way to Scotland, as it was an open secret that the Trump Turnberry, a golf course owned by the former president, was his preferred "bolt-hole" whenever Washington or New York got too hot. The press pack's camera focused on Trump's famous golden scalp, his face set in a mask of affronted calm as he strode to the makeshift podium at the back of the aircraft, flanked by his current Chief of Staff—whose name nobody could ever quite remember—and a Secret Service agent whose earpiece and body language screamed "do not approach." The blue-and-white presidential seal glinted beneath the harsh overheads, and for a moment, all other noise in the San Diego crew room seemed to dissolve.

Trump's voice, never less than theatrical, rang out in the staccato timbre that half the world had learned to dread or adore. "Let me be absolutely clear, ladies and gentlemen of the press," he began, his hands already waving in tight, controlled gestures. "This so-called airline boss, this… Young fellow—never heard of him before today, by the way, and believe me, I know all the important people—well, he's spreading fake news. More fake news than CNN, if you can believe that, and that's a lot. What happened in Tijuana was a tragedy, absolutely, but to call the President of the United States a terrorist? That's outrageous. It's a disgrace. And let me tell you, nobody, nobody, has done more for civil aviation than me. We brought jobs back. We fixed Boeing. We're keeping the skies safe. But what we're not going to do is be bullied by some lefty Eurocrat with a plastic aeroplane on his desk. Not on my watch."

He paused for effect, squinting down the press row as if daring anyone to interrupt. There was a cough, a rustle of laptops, but nobody spoke.

"Let's be clear. The F-35s were acting under the strictest rules of engagement, authorised by me personally, in coordination with our tremendous Mexican partners—very good people, very tough on the cartels, which, by the way, nobody else has managed to do. The damage to that aircraft—regrettable. Absolutely regrettable. But it was empty. No injuries, except maybe to Sprint's public relations team. Maybe they need to hire some Americans, huh? We're going to get to the bottom of this, but let's not be hysterical. This is an act of war? Give me a break. The only war I'm fighting is the war for American greatness, which is going very well, thank you. I will be personally filing a lawsuit against Sprint and its idiot board, and against Jeff Young, for slander, for inciting panic, and for whatever else my lawyers can find. We will not stand for this kind of language—especially not from some fly-by-night operator who couldn't fill an A319 in Albuquerque, let alone run a global airline. Frankly, I think their investors should be asking some very serious questions right now about who's really in charge. Maybe they want to hire some real leadership—maybe they want to call me! Nobody knows aviation like I do, folks. Nobody."

James snorted at the statement the President had made, as, despite being Texan, a red-blooded American and proud of it, he found something almost otherworldly in the collision of high office, reality TV bravado, and the surrealist politics that passed for daily news in the post-pandemic world. Becky gave him a sideways glance, one eyebrow cocked, her lips curling with the sort of gallows humour only those truly used to airline operations could muster.

"Maybe we should take him up on it," she whispered, voice dry as gin on a Sunday. "Hire him as our new fleet manager. See how he does with a bag of melted ice and a broken APU in Phoenix."

James almost laughed, but the mood in the room had turned again—this time, brittle and tense. Phones buzzed with group chats spinning into overdrive. Rumours were already hatching: Would the FAA suspend Sprint's US AOC? Would the Pentagon bar all Sprint aircraft from US airspace? Would the Mexican authorities throw the book at any operator with the wrong logo on the tail?

Watching, he saw that Trump's Press Secretary, Karoline Leavitt, was taking questions from the crowd of reporters, her smile brittle as spun sugar, her words rapid-fire, rehearsed, and yet barely keeping ahead of the spiralling narrative that had been unleashed. She called on someone from CNBC, who stood up.

"Is the Administration aware that technically, it was a Sprint Max flight, from their Lithuanian subsidiary, and not the US one, which is only 24.% owned by Sprint Group? Are there any plans to compensate Sprint for the hull loss, and, given Sprint is working with the Mobile plant of Airbus to build and maintain its 300 strong US fleet, certain US jobs could be at risk if Sprint is frozen out of the market?"

Leavitt's smile flickered. She adjusted her notes, buying a heartbeat. "The Administration is, of course, aware of the intricacies of modern global aviation partnerships. We're in close contact with Airbus, with Sprint's US subsidiary, and with our partners in the European Union. The president has made clear that American jobs remain the priority and that all actions will be taken in accordance with our national interests, regulatory frameworks, and the continuing investigation into the Tijuana incident. We are confident that our regulatory agencies will work closely with industry to ensure safety and continuity of service for the American people. Next question?"

That was all she gave them. The rest was a spiral of platitudes and noncommittal assurances. By the time the live feed ended, James Hart could feel his head buzzing with the fatigue of someone who'd lived through too many incident response calls and 3 a.m. operations telecons. Around the crew room, the mood was febrile— frantic messages on WhatsApp, urgent group chats between crews, a queue already forming for the payphones in the corner for those who still needed to check in with their unions or family.

"Yes, Peter from Fox News," Leavitt said on the television feeds, and James knew instantly that it would be an Administration love in from the US network which was owned by Rupert Murdoch, and the air in the crew room shifted yet again. Fox's Peter Doocy was already halfway out of his seat, his question rehearsed, the headline already drafted in the back of his mind.

"Ms Leavitt, how does the White House respond to Sprint's CEO not only calling the President a terrorist on live television but also suggesting NATO and the British government back that claim? Will the Administration be taking direct action against Sprint and its subsidiaries, and does the President see this as a challenge to American sovereignty?"

Karoline Leavitt's smile was razor-thin now, flickering at the edges. She took a shallow breath, the kind James recognised from hours spent watching cabin crew manage passengers who'd just realised their flight was overbooked and their connection impossible. "Peter, let me reiterate. The president is committed to a robust, competitive, and above all safe aviation market. We will not be intimidated by reckless statements from foreign executives, and we stand behind the actions of the US military and our partners. The Department of Transportation and the FAA are conducting a thorough review of Sprint's operations, both for safety and for compliance with US law. We will take whatever steps are necessary to protect our airspace, our jobs, and our reputation. As for foreign governments, we expect our allies to engage through proper diplomatic channels, not through televised provocations. That's all I'll say for now."

With that, the feed cut to a hastily assembled "expert panel" arguing about the meaning of "terrorist" in an aviation context, and whether NATO would really risk an Article 5 crisis for a low-cost carrier's CEO. The crew room hummed with low conversation, a sense of unreality thickening with each new angle to the story.

The room itself seemed to heave as the panel's bickering rose and fell—law professors and security experts and the inevitable old general in a suit at least a size too large, every one of them holding forth on the boundary between war and blunder, commerce and chaos. Becky closed her roster with a sigh and slumped back in her chair, her eyes half-shut as if she might doze right there and then, insulated by the drone of the televisions and the caffeine fug.

The crew room at San Diego did not so much settle as ferment. News travelled faster than the air-conditioning; the chill of collective anxiety competed with the muggy heat of too many bodies in too small a space. Some crews picked up their bags and drifted towards the door, abandoning pretence at rest, hoping for a more peaceful corner in which to process the shockwaves. Others huddled in tight knots, voices low, as if conspiracies and secrets would shield them from the fallout now drifting across the Atlantic, circling back on itself like the looping, broken news feeds overhead.

"Right lads, let's get these planes out or Herr Trump will demand we all sign loyalty oaths and swear allegiance to his next golf resort," came the gruff mutter from the far end of the battered table. A ripple of laughter, forced and nervous, passed through the nearest group of

AmericanoAir crew, but there was little real amusement in it. Even gallows humour felt played out, the punchlines exhausted by months—years—of lurching from one crisis to the next.

James closed his eyes for a moment, letting the soundscape blur: the omnipresent televisions, the shrill ring of a desk phone, the mechanical clatter from the ancient coffee vending machine, the fragmented snippets of anxious English, Spanish, and Lithuanian. This was the heart of modern airline life, he thought, not the glossy lounges or PR videos, but the battered, overbright crew rooms where everything happened and nothing changed.

When he opened them again, Becky was staring at him with an expression that combined curiosity, exasperation, and the bone-deep fatigue of a pilot who'd slept in hotel beds more nights than her own. "How long you reckon before we're grounded?" she asked, almost conversationally.

"Trump's full of bluster. He'll make life hell for a few hours then he'll get distracted by the Epstein files or someone else's tweet. FAA might go for a temporary grounding if they're told to, but that would kick off a row with the Europeans, and even the Gulf States, given how much of the Sprint Group's capital and aircraft are technically Omani or British on the books," James replied, keeping his voice low. "You shut down Sprint, you ground nearly 500 planes, not just ours but the ones that JetBlue, Spirit and even Delta wet lease off the mothership."

"Jesus H Christ, I didn't know Delta and Spirit leased from Sprint," Becky replied, her voice low but her eyes wide. "I thought they all did their own thing, but I suppose, with all the shifting AOCs and the way Sprint buys in bulk, it makes sense. Anyway, who've you got today for your flights?"

"An Anthony Devlin," James said, looking at the Sprint Staff app to scroll his pairings, "Supposedly ex-Allegiant, moved over when they started the SoCal bases. Haven't flown with him, but the briefing notes say he's solid on the paperwork. Good enough for me, unless today's the day we're all frogmarched off to some federal shed for enhanced 'debriefing'." He attempted a smile, but it faded quickly in the low blue glow of the television. "Assuming, of course, we're still flying after lunch."

Becky snorted. "If we're not, the only upside is I might finally sleep more than three hours." She pinched the bridge of her nose, as if the act alone might stave off another spike of exhaustion. "The world goes mad, and what do we do? Same as always. Get the bird out. File the paperwork. Try not to get shafted by Ops or the White House, whichever gets there first."

For a long, heavy moment, the two of them simply sat. Around them, the crew room's tension was now thick as oil—filled with those who'd stopped even pretending to be unaffected. A young cabin crew in AmericanoAir blues, probably not more than twenty-three, was crying quietly in the crook of her arm, her friend rubbing her back in awkward silence. Two veteran ground agents from Alaska Air whispered fiercely, heads close together. The TV now displayed a scrolling chyron.

SPRINT CEO CALLS PRESIDENT 'TERRORIST' – WHITE HOUSE THREATENS RETALIATION – TENSIONS RISE OVER TIJUANA STRIKE.

"Right," James said, a few minutes later, looking at the time, "I'm due for in half hour. I better go and check the plane to make sure its fit for anything other than becoming the next pawn in the White House's temper tantrum." He rose, the tired ache in his legs and shoulders echoing the heaviness in the room. He hauled his kitbag up, the battered Sprint Max tag swinging from the handle, and gave Becky a last, half-hearted grin. "If we're still airborne this time tomorrow, I'll buy the first round at McCarran."

She managed a weak smile, then turned back to her roster, the set of her shoulders speaking of someone ready to endure whatever came—if not unscathed, then at least unbroken.

****

CHAPTER 14 – Ryanair Style Diplomacy
Sunday 27th July 2025

The air around Dallas, Texas, was thick with heat and bravado, the kind that shimmered above concrete and aluminium alike, bending sound and patience in equal measure. It was already pushing forty degrees Celsius by mid-morning, the sort of day when even the jet fuel smelled more aggressive than usual, and the ramp at Dallas-Fort Worth radiated a dull, relentless glare that crept into cockpits, terminals, and tempers.

James Hart watched it through the slightly scratched window of the AmericanoAir crew room, a converted storage space tucked behind Gate D27 that still smelled faintly of bleach and old carpet glue. Outside, a line of aircraft sat baking on the apron: AmericanoAir A321s in their navy blue Sprint livery with the giant Stars and Stripes on the tail, Delta's widget tails glinting like polished coins, an American widebody trundling past with the weary dignity of a veteran, and, further out, a lonely JetBlue Airbus A220 parked nose-to-fence as if in time-out, a reminder that the world had grown teeth overnight.

Inside, the crew room hummed with a low, tired tension. It was not the electric panic of San Diego two days earlier, nor the stunned disbelief that had rippled through every WhatsApp group and secure channel in the industry. This was something more Texan, more grounded: a wary, pragmatic unease. People here expected trouble. They'd grown up with it. They just preferred it to arrive with paperwork.

James stood with a paper cup of coffee that had long since crossed the line from hot to hostile, watching a dispatcher argue quietly with a scheduler at the far end of the room. The wall-mounted television was mercifully muted, but the crawl of breaking news still ran along the bottom of the screen like a rash that refused to clear.

SPRINT GROUP UNDER FAA REVIEW – WHITE HOUSE CONSIDERS "ALL OPTIONS"

AIRCRAFT SEIZURES "NOT RULED OUT" SAYS SENIOR DHS OFFICIAL

SPRINT CEO SAYS "DHS WILL FACE LAWSUIT IF BRITISH OWNED AIRCRAFT ILLEGALLY SEIZED"

James drained the last of his acrid coffee, set the cup down, and took a breath through his nose, tasting ozone and machinery. All around him, the thrum of airline life was different now—tighter, more defensive. Dispatchers and pilots huddled over iPads and printouts, not so much collaborating as checking for loopholes, planning for the possibility that by the afternoon, the rules could have changed yet again.

At the nearest table, a trio of AmericanoAir first officers argued over who was to blame for the latest rumour—was it the White House, or the Sprint Group board, or simply the fact that every airline now seemed to live and die at the whim of some regulator or politician's tweet? The talk was animated but not hopeful. Everyone was waiting for the other shoe to drop.

Suddenly a Breaking News alert flashed across the TV screen, and James turned to see what fresh chaos had erupted. The volume was unmuted by a nearby scheduler, and the room fell into a jagged hush as the CNN anchor's voice cut through the ambient hum.

"—we're going live now to Dublin, where Ryanair CEO Michael O'Leary is holding a press conference in response to the escalating tensions between Sprint Group and the United States government. This follows Sprint CEO Jeff Young's controversial statement on Friday, where he labelled President Donald Trump a 'terrorist' after a US Air Force missile strike damaged a Sprint Max aircraft in Tijuana. Let's listen in."

The screen cut to a familiar sight: Michael O'Leary, in his trademark open-collared shirt and slightly rumpled blazer, standing behind a podium festooned with Ryanair's garish yellow-and-blue logo. The backdrop was a hangar at Dublin Airport, with a Boeing 737-8200 parked behind him, its nose pointed slightly upwards as if ready to bolt. O'Leary's face was a study in calculated mischief, his eyes glinting with the kind of glee that only comes from watching a competitor implode.

"Good morning, ladies and gentlemen of the press," O'Leary began, his Irish brogue sharp enough to cut through the transatlantic static. "I've called you here because, frankly, the world's gone mad, and someone's got to talk some sense. Jeff Young, the esteemed chief of Sprint Group—God help them—decided it was a grand idea to call the President of the United States a terrorist on live television. Now, I'm no fan of politicians myself, but if you're going to poke the bear, you'd best have a bloody big stick. Sprint, it seems, has a twig. A very small twig."

A ripple of laughter ran through the press pack, though the AmericanoAir crew room remained taut, faces fixed on the screen. O'Leary leaned forward, his grin widening. "Let's be clear: Sprint's in a right mess. Their aircraft's been blown to bits in Tijuana, their CEO's picking fights with superpowers, and now the FAA's circling like a shark that's smelled blood. I've got no dog in this fight, but as Europe's largest airline, Ryanair's got a duty to keep the skies moving. So, here's my offer: if Sprint's grounded—and let's face it, they're halfway there— Ryanair's ready to step in. We'll lease their slots, take their passengers, and maybe even buy their A321s at a discount. Call it charity. Or business. I'm not fussy."

James felt a wry smile tug at his lips. O'Leary's opportunism was as predictable as a sunrise, but there was something almost comforting in its brazenness. The man was a vulture, but at least he was upfront about it.

O'Leary wasn't done. "And to President Trump, if you're watching—and I know you are, sir, because you love a deal, Ryanair—"

Suddenly the TV pictures turned to Sprint's press conference room in Ramsgate, where Chief Press Officer of Sprint's UK and EU operations, Francesca 'Frankie' Mendes, was stood at a podium, and another group of press was gathered, their cameras and microphones bristling like a hedgehog's spines. The backdrop was the same fake-wood panelling and oversized Sprint logo that had framed Jeff Young's catastrophic statement two days earlier, but Frankie Mendes carried herself with a different energy—less corporate automaton, more seasoned street fighter. Her dark hair was pulled back tightly, her navy blazer crisp but unbuttoned, and her expression hovered somewhere between defiance and exasperation. She didn't wait for the room to settle before launching in, her voice carrying the clipped, no-nonsense cadence of someone who'd spent years wrangling crises.

"Ladies and gentlemen, thank you for coming on short notice," Frankie began, her eyes scanning the press pack with the precision of a radar. "Sprint Group has no intention of backing down from the truth. The destruction of our aircraft in Tijuana was a reckless act, and Jeff Young's statement on Friday was a necessary call for accountability. We stand by every word. The US administration's response—threatening our operations, our crews, and our passengers with sanctions and seizures—is nothing short of bullying. We're not here to play games. Sprint will defend its rights, its people, and its fleet through every legal avenue available, in the US, the UK, the EU, and beyond."

The Dallas crew room was a frozen tableau, every pair of eyes glued to the screen. James leaned against the wall, his arms crossed, feeling the weight of the moment settle like a lead blanket. Frankie's words were bold, but they were also a gamble—a high-stakes bet that Sprint could outlast the wrath of a superpower. He glanced at one of the female First Officers, who'd just entered the room, her kitbag slung over one shoulder. She caught his eye and mouthed a single word: "Madness."

Frankie pressed on, undeterred by the flashing cameras or the low murmur of the press. "To our passengers, we say this: your safety is our priority. We're working around the clock to maintain our schedules, despite the unprecedented pressure from US authorities. To our crews, I say: you are the backbone of this airline. Your professionalism in the face of this chaos is unmatched. And to President Trump, I would like to offer a one-to-one meeting to discuss our concerns and find a path forward that respects the sanctity of civil aviation." Frankie paused, letting the weight of her words hang in the air. Her tone softened, but her eyes remained steely. "Sprint Group is not the enemy. We're an airline, not a militia. We connect people, not conflicts. But we will not be intimidated into silence.

"Oh, and finally, I hear my old boss, Mick O'Leary was just doing his own press conference in Dublin, stirring the pot as usual. Let me be clear: Ryanair's not swooping in to save the day, no matter what Michael says. Sprint's slots, our aircraft, our passengers—they're not up for grabs. We're fighting for our place in the skies, and we'll do it our way, not his. Anyway, he claims Ryanair is the biggest European airline when Sprint in Europe has nearly 700 aircraft in its fleet, and we're not about to let a discount vulture pick our bones clean." Frankie's lips twitched into a half-smile, a fleeting nod to the absurdity of the moment before she straightened, her voice firm again. "I'll now take questions from the press."

The Dallas crew room seemed to contract under the weight of Frankie Mendes' words, the air growing denser with each syllable that crackled through the television. The hum of the overworked air-conditioning unit felt like a pulse, syncing with the collective heartbeat of a room full of pilots, cabin crew, and ground staff who knew they were witnessing a moment that could unravel their entire operation. James Hart stood rooted by the wall, his arms still crossed, the faint ache in his shoulders a reminder of too many hours in the cockpit and too few in a proper bed. The female First Officer who'd mouthed "madness" had now dropped her kitbag and joined the cluster of crew around the nearest table, her expression a mix of disbelief and grim amusement.

The television feed cut back to the CNN anchor, whose polished professionalism couldn't quite mask the strain in her eyes. "That was Francesca Mendes, Sprint Group's Chief Press Officer, doubling down on CEO Jeff Young's controversial remarks and issuing a direct challenge to both the US administration and Ryanair's Michael O'Leary. We'll have reaction from Washington shortly, but first, let's go to our aviation correspondent, Tom Bradley, at Reagan National Airport. Tom, what's the mood on the ground there?"

James didn't wait for Bradley's inevitable platitudes about "uncertainty" and "heightened tensions." He pushed off the wall and made his way to the coffee machine, which was less a dispenser of caffeine and more a monument to institutional neglect. As he jabbed at the buttons, coaxing a reluctant stream of something vaguely resembling espresso, he caught snippets of conversation from the crew around him.

"—she's got guts, I'll give her that," a grizzled captain was saying, his AmericanoAir lanyard swinging as he gestured at the screen. "But guts don't pay the bills when the FAA pulls your AOC."

"Or when Trump slaps a sanction on every Sprint tail," added a younger pilot, scrolling furiously on his phone. "X is already blowing up with memes. Someone's photoshopped Young's face onto Bin Laden's. It's brutal."

James snorted softly, the coffee machine finally surrendering a cup of lukewarm sludge. He took a sip, grimaced, and turned back to the room just as the television cut to a split-screen: one half showing the Trump National Golf Club, where Press Secretary Karoline Leavitt was stepping up to the podium, and the other replaying Frankie Mendes' defiant stare-down of the press. The contrast was stark—Leavitt's rehearsed poise against Frankie's raw, combative energy. James had seen enough of both types to know which one was more likely to survive a crisis, but survival wasn't the same as winning.

Leavitt adjusted the microphone with the practised ease of someone who'd spent the last few years dodging verbal grenades, her blonde hair catching the sunlight streaming through the golf club's ornate windows. The backdrop was a far cry from Sprint's utilitarian press room: manicured greens stretched out behind her, dotted with carts and flags, a subtle reminder that even in crisis, the administration projected leisure-class invincibility. "Good afternoon," she began, her voice steady but laced with that trademark edge of condescension. "The president has been briefed on the latest statements from Sprint Group's representatives, including this morning's remarks from their press officer, Ms Mendes. Let me be unequivocal: the United States will not tolerate baseless accusations or threats from foreign entities operating within our borders. Sprint Group's leadership seems intent on escalating a regrettable incident into an international spectacle, but make no mistake—we are committed to protecting American interests, American jobs, and American airspace."

A murmur ran through the Dallas crew room, a mix of groans and muttered expletives. James set his coffee down on the nearest table, the cup landing with a soft thud that seemed louder in the charged atmosphere. He knew the script by heart now: deflection, patriotism, veiled threats. It was the same playbook that had turned minor diplomatic spats into full-blown trade wars during Trump's first term, and now it was aimed squarely at their airline.

Leavitt continued, her eyes flicking to her notes before meeting the cameras head-on. "The Tijuana strike was a targeted operation against cartel elements that pose a direct threat to US national security. Any collateral damage—and I stress, there were no casualties—was unintentional and is being investigated thoroughly by our partners in Mexico. Sprint's attempt to portray this as an attack on civil aviation is not only inaccurate but inflammatory. As for Ms Mendes' invitation for a meeting, the president appreciates the gesture, but discussions of this nature will occur through appropriate channels, not publicity stunts. In the meantime, the FAA and DHS are reviewing Sprint's US operations for compliance with all federal regulations. We expect full cooperation. Failure to do so could result in enforcement actions up to and including suspension of operating privileges."

The room erupted into a cacophony of reactions. "Enforcement actions? That's code for grounding us," spat a cabin manager from the back, her Texas drawl thick with indignation. She was a stout woman in her fifties, with a Sprint lanyard that looked like it'd seen better days, and she slammed her iPad down on the table hard enough to make the nearby vending machine rattle. "We've got families to feed, and these suits are playing chicken with our livelihoods."

Beside her, a young flight attendant nodded vigorously, her ponytail bobbing. "I just got off a red-eye from Newark, and now this? If they ground us, what happens to our rosters? Do we just sit here twiddling our thumbs while the lawyers sort it?"

James didn't join the fray. Instead, he slipped his phone from his pocket and opened the Sprint Staff app, scrolling through the latest alerts. There were three new memos: one from Legal urging crews to "document all interactions with federal authorities meticulously," another from Ops warning of potential delays due to "enhanced security screenings," and a third from HR offering "voluntary unpaid leave" for those affected by roster changes. It was the airline equivalent of rearranging deckchairs on the Titanic—optimistic, but ultimately futile if the ship was going down.

His pairing for the day popped up: a Dallas to Chicago O'Hare sector, then on to Boston, with a turnaround back to DFW by evening. He was rostered with a First Officer named Elena Vasquez, a transfer from Volaris who'd joined AmericanoAir during the initial expansion frenzy. Solid on the stick, from what he'd heard, but green on Sprint's byzantine procedures. The aircraft was an A321neo, tail number N456SA, fresh from the Mobile assembly line but already showing the wear of Sprint's aggressive utilisation rates. James made a mental note to double-check the maintenance log; in times like these, even minor squawks could become major headaches if the FAA decided to play hardball.

As he pocketed his phone, the TV feed switched again, this time to a panel of pundits dissecting the morning's events like surgeons over a cadaver. A former FAA administrator in an ill-fitting suit was mid-rant: "—Sprint's walking a tightrope here. Their AOC is predicated on compliance with US regs, but with foreign ownership—Omani sovereign funds, British defence ties—they're vulnerable to CFIUS scrutiny. If DHS labels them a security risk, it's game over."

The door to the crew room swung open with a hydraulic hiss, admitting a blast of hot, fuel-scented air and a harried-looking station manager named Raul Jimenez. He was a lanky Mexican-American in his forties, with a clipboard clutched like a shield and sweat beading on his forehead despite the air-con. "Listen up, folks," he called, his voice cutting through the chatter. "We've got a briefing in five. FAA's ramping up inspections—every Sprint bird at DFW is getting a once-over before pushback. No exceptions. If you've got a flight today, expect delays. And for God's sake, keep your paperwork spotless. They're looking for reasons."

Groans rippled through the room, but James felt a familiar calm settle over him—the pilot's mindset kicking in, compartmentalising the chaos into manageable segments. He grabbed his kitbag and headed for the door, nodding to a couple of familiar faces as he went. Outside, the ramp was a symphony of organised frenzy: baggage carts zipping between aircraft, fuel trucks hooked up like IV lines, ground crew in ear defenders shouting over the whine of APUs. The heat hit him like a wall, but he welcomed it; better than the stale tension inside.

James made his way down the jet bridge access stairs, the metal clanging under his boots like a reluctant drumbeat. The ramp was alive with the usual choreography of ground operations, but today it felt off-kilter, as if everyone was moving a half-step slower, eyes darting towards the distant control tower or the unmarked SUVs that had started appearing at the edges of the apron. He spotted N456SA parked at Gate D29, her sleek lines marred by a thin film of Texas dust and the faint scorch marks from countless cycles of thrust and brake. The A321neo was a workhorse, efficient and unforgiving, much like the airline that flew her.

Elena Vasquez was already there, circling the aircraft with a flashlight despite the blinding sun, her uniform crisp but her expression guarded. She was in her early thirties, with sharp features and a ponytail that spoke of practicality over vanity. James had flown with her once before, on a milk run to Denver, and remembered her as competent but cautious—a product of Volaris's no-frills ethos, where fuel conservation was religion and delays were heresy.

"Morning, Captain," she said, straightening up as he approached. Her accent carried a faint Mexican lilt, softened by years in the US system. "Or what's left of it. You catch the circus on the telly?"

James nodded, dropping his kitbag by the nose gear. "Hard to miss. O'Leary sniffing around like a hyena, Mendes throwing punches, and Leavitt dodging them with that smile that could curdle milk. Feels like we're in a bad spy novel."

Elena chuckled, but it was mirthless. "Spy novel? More like a farce. Back at Volaris, we dealt with cartel threats and border politics, but this? Having the White House gunning for us because our CEO couldn't keep his gob shut? That's next level." She shone her torch into the engine inlet, checking for foreign object debris. "Raul says FAA's on the prowl. We might be here a while."

As if summoned, a pair of FAA inspectors emerged from a golf cart that had pulled up silently beside the aircraft. They were textbook bureaucrats: middle-aged men in polo shirts and khakis, clipboards in hand, badges gleaming like accusations. The lead one, a balding chap with a moustache that belonged in the 1980s, introduced himself as Inspector Harlan Brooks from the Dallas Flight Standards District Office. His partner, younger and more taciturn, simply nodded.

"Captain Hart?" Brooks asked, consulting his notes. "We're conducting a ramp check on this aircraft per enhanced oversight protocols. Shouldn't take long if everything's in order."

James kept his tone even, professional. "Understood, Inspector. We've got nothing to hide. Elena, let's walk them through the log."

What followed was a meticulous dissection of the aircraft's paperwork and systems. Brooks pored over the maintenance records, questioning a recent APU service that had been done in Toulouse under Sprint's EU arm by Sprint and Airbus's joint venture MRO. "This bird's got a mixed heritage," he muttered, flipping pages. "US registration, but half the parts are from across the pond. Any issues with supply chain compliance?"

"Do you see that bit there," James said, his USAF Major past coming into his muscle memory as he pointed at the bit where it was signed Toulouse. "That's Airbus, not some shoddy outfit in a back alley. It's all above board, certified under EASA and FAA cross-recognition agreements. We've got the certs right here if you need to see them."

Brooks grunted, his moustache twitching as he scribbled something on his clipboard. The younger inspector, whose name tag read 'Simmons,' peered into the engine with a torch, his face impassive. James exchanged a glance with Elena, who kept her expression neutral but her eyes alert. This wasn't just a routine spot-check; the air crackled with the subtext of higher directives, the kind that trickled down from Washington when politics infected procedure.

"Anyway, I thought you lot were short staffed due to the RIFs that President Trump and Elon had pushed through earlier this year," James added, his tone light but probing, referring to the Reduction in Force that had slashed federal budgets and staffing across agencies like the FAA. It was a calculated jab, testing whether Brooks would bite.

Brooks didn't look up from his clipboard. "We manage," he said curtly. "Got enough bodies to keep the skies safe, Captain. Especially when there's cause for concern." The implication hung heavy: Sprint's antics had put them squarely in the crosshairs, and no amount of charm or paperwork would fully shield them.

Elena stepped in smoothly, her voice calm but firm. "Inspector, the APU was serviced to spec, and we've got the digital trail in the maintenance app if you want to cross-check. Same for the engine work done in Mobile last month. All FAA-approved vendors, all logged in real-time." She tapped her tablet, pulling up the relevant records with a few deft swipes. Her efficiency was a quiet rebuke to Brooks' scepticism, and James noted the faint flicker of approval in Simmons' eyes, though the younger inspector stayed silent.

The ramp check dragged on for nearly an hour, Brooks and Simmons combing through everything from the weight-and-balance sheets to the crew's training records. James and Elena answered every question with precision, their responses a blend of military discipline and airline pragmatism. By the time Brooks finally signed off, the sun was higher, the heat more oppressive, and the aircraft's departure slot was teetering on the edge of delay. The inspectors climbed back into their golf cart without a word of thanks, leaving behind a faint air of bureaucratic menace.

"Charming blokes," Elena muttered, wiping sweat from her brow as she resumed her walkaround. "Think they found what they were looking for?"

"Not a chance," James replied, his voice low. "They're fishing. FAA's under pressure to make an example of us, but they won't ground us without something concrete. Too many jobs at stake, too much noise from Airbus and the EU. Still, doesn't mean they won't make our lives hell in the meantime."

Elena nodded, her flashlight sweeping the landing gear. "Back at Volaris, we had inspectors like that during the cartel crackdowns. They'd show up, nitpick, then vanish. Never grounded us, but it was death by a thousand cuts— fines, delays, extra audits. Sprint's got deeper pockets, but this?" She gestured vaguely at the sky, the airport, the invisible weight of geopolitics. "This feels bigger."

James didn't disagree. He hoisted his kitbag and followed her to the jet bridge, the clatter of their footsteps echoing in the empty tube. Inside the aircraft, the cabin crew were already at work, led by a wiry Purser named Marcus Tate, a former Spirit veteran who'd seen it all and forgotten none of it. Marcus greeted them with a nod, his expression a mix of resignation and defiance. "Heard the FAA's playing hardball," he said, stowing a stack of safety cards. "They gonna clip our wings, Captain?"

"Not today," James replied, forcing a confidence he didn't entirely feel. "Let's get this bird to Chicago. One sector at a time."

The pre-flight checks were a ritual of calm amid the storm, a reminder that the cockpit was still a sanctuary of procedure and control. James settled into the left seat, the familiar contours of the A321neo's flight deck grounding him. Elena ran through the co-pilot's checklist with quiet efficiency, her hands moving over switches and screens with the muscle memory of someone who'd flown more hours than she cared to count.

The screens glowed with data—fuel load, weather, NOTAMs—but the real challenge wasn't in the numbers. It was in the unspoken question: how long could they keep flying before the weight of Sprint's missteps crushed them?

As they waited for clearance, the radio crackled with the usual DFW chatter: American heavies negotiating pushback, Delta regionals squawking about gate changes, a FedEx freighter requesting priority.

But there was an edge to the exchanges, a clipped formality that hadn't been there a week ago. James caught Elena's eye, and she gave a small, knowing shake of her head. "Ground's twitchy," she murmured. "Bet they're getting heat from the tower, too."

Pushback came twenty minutes late, the ground crew's voices taut over the interphone. The tug driver, a grizzled Texan named Chet, muttered something about "Feds sniffing around the ramp like roaches." James didn't respond, but he filed it away. The FAA's presence was a virus, spreading unease from the cockpit to the tarmac.

****

CHAPTER 15 – ICE
Saturday 2nd August 2025

If there was one thing any pilot hated when he was at his base, which for James, was Las Vegas, it was ICE, Immigration and Customs Enforcement. Not the clear, cool stuff one might find in a drink at the Tropicana bar, nor the sleek frost he sometimes marvelled at on a dawn departure out of Denver, but rather the feds, their black jackets, and their near-ritual humiliation of airline crew and foreign passengers alike.

And right at that moment, as he sat in the crew room, he was watching his First Officer for the day, Theo Sullivan, being questioned quite heavily.

"Ever since Trump returned to the White House, it's been a bloody nightmare," muttered one of the older captains to James, who could only nod in silent agreement. The world might have expected that the chaos of 2020 was a one-off, but the United States of 2025 had doubled down. The second Trump administration—swaggering back into power on a wave of slogans and grievances—had brought with it a new ICE chief, a new mandate, and a sense of arbitrary authority that unsettled even the most battle-hardened crew.

James kept his head down, watching Theo try to keep his cool under the unblinking gaze of an officer who looked about twenty-five, crisp haircut, mirrored sunglasses even indoors. The young agent's fingers drummed impatiently on Theo's Green Card, named so because of the distinctive minty tint that belied the bureaucratic hell required to obtain one. Theo had been lucky to have married a LAPD Metro SWAT officer in a whirlwind marriage in London, only a few months after first meeting her on a PanEuro JFK to London rotation—a story that would have sounded far-fetched even in the wildest of airline crew bars. Their whirlwind romance had been chronicled in group chats and WhatsApp memes; the immigration paperwork, by contrast, was an unending slog, the punchline to every joke about "making it in America". Yet it was this very document—the literal green card—that now seemed the most fragile shield in the world, as ICE regarded Theo less as a professional aviator and more as a case file waiting to be dissected.

"It does look suspicious in a way," Kyler McMahon, one of the other Captains at Sprint US, or AmericanoAir as the official name was, even though the franchise agreement saw the fledgling airline take the Sprint name as they wanted a well-known brand to operate under, continued, "—but coming into the States 6 months ago, marring a LAPD Officer 2 months before that, getting the FAA approval to move from the Euro ATPL to the FAA ATP... Sullivan doesn't help his case with that, does he?"

James had to agree, as, being a Dallas born lad, moving to the USAF and then landing in LA, seeing a fellow pilot's luck—or audacity—always drew a mix of admiration and wariness. Theo, as a 25 year old, meant that he was among the youngest in the room, but also one of the most travelled. There was something about his Birmingham, British Midlands, not Alabama, accent, that that always seemed to amuse the American ground staff, and perhaps infuriate the bureaucrats who never quite knew what box to tick for him. He smiled a bit too much under pressure, the way some people did when nervous, and now that smile was getting him nowhere.

The ICE officer—badge reading HOFFMAN—snapped Theo's green card against the desk and flicked his eyes up. "So you're telling me, Mr Sullivan, that you just happened to meet a US citizen, marry her after two months, and now you're flying Airbus A320s within the United States 7 months after moving, a month after gaining this—" he said, dropping the green card on the desk, "and let's say for argument's sake, that's just how it worked out? No plans before you came here? Nothing irregular to declare?" The room was quiet except for the sound of an air conditioning vent ticking. Theo kept his hands visible, elbows on his knees, and tried to look as calm as a man can who knows his next meal depends on the whim of an ICE agent barely old enough to remember the first Trump term. "You know what, I've already decided. I'm going to have you deported under US Code Section 237(a)(1)(E)(i)," Hoffman continued, his voice low but firm, "for entering the United States under fraudulent circumstances." He leaned forward, eyes narrowing. "Care to explain to me, Mr Sullivan, why your passport shows multiple visits to the US before your supposed marriage?"

Theo swallowed. He knew this was a fishing expedition. They weren't interested in the truth; they were interested in control, in demonstrating power. "Sir," he said carefully, "I was working for PanEuro, a European airline. My flights took me frequently to the US for rotations. I've complied with every legal requirement to the letter."

Hoffman smirked. "Complied? That's a laugh. The government doesn't see it that way. Our job is to ensure these processes aren't abused. You think you're above it because you're a pilot? You're not. And frankly, your story doesn't hold water."

The tension in the room was thick enough to cut with a knife. Other crew members shifted uneasily in their seats, casting quick glances at James. James kept quiet. He'd seen this play before and knew there was little to be done except wait for the inevitable bureaucratic machine to grind through its motions.

"Get this dirtbag into cuffs, Agent Paulson," Hoffman then ordered, turning his attention briefly to a burly colleague standing by the door. The man—Agent Paulson, badge glinting with that casual arrogance only the truly secure possessed—stepped forward, flexing gloved hands, clearly relishing the little drama about to unfold. There was a quiet, collective intake of breath from the room: the other pilots, flight attendants and even the contracted ground staff all knew, as James did, that this was more than just a bad day for Theo. This was a warning, a chilling display meant for everyone in uniform.

James's pulse kicked up, but he forced his face to remain impassive, every muscle drilled by years of cockpit discipline. He locked eyes with Theo for half a heartbeat—a flicker of professional solidarity, the unspoken pilot's code: we look out for our own. Theo, for his part, only looked away for an instant, jaw clenched, every trace of that easy-going Brummie smile now gone. There was something else in his eyes: anger, yes, but also an odd resignation. As if he'd already guessed, long before stepping into this windowless room, that America was never going to let him just be a pilot.

Agent Paulson produced a pair of steel cuffs with the casual theatricality of a man who had never worked a day in commercial aviation, and stepped behind Theo. "Hands behind your back," he barked, and Theo obeyed, movements measured and deliberate—no sudden moves, nothing that would give them even the faintest excuse for violence. The click of the cuffs was absurdly loud.

"Come with me," Paulson said, and Theo was hauled to his feet and frogmarched from the room, leaving a vacuum of stunned silence behind him.

The moment the door closed, the chatter erupted—angry, nervous, muttered. One of the more senior flight attendants, Maria from San Juan, shook her head. "This is madness, man. Are we going to get someone from Crew Affairs? Union? Legal?"

James's reply was cut off as Agent Hoffman turned one of the cabin crew, who he knew was Guatemalan, and therefore likely to attract the same unwanted attention. "You," Hoffman said, pointing a finger at Ana, who had joined AmericanoAir after fleeing years of low-paid regional work back in Central America. "Documents, now."

Ana fumbled for her badge and her battered, navy-blue passport—Guatemala embossed in tired gold letters, its edges frayed by years of nervous handling. Her hands shook just enough for everyone to notice, but she managed to pass both across the table. Hoffman barely glanced at her ID, but took his time with the passport, flipping through the pages as if searching for a reason to prolong the ritual humiliation.

"Do you understand English?" Hoffman said with the sarcasm of a man not only convinced of his own superiority but determined to broadcast it to the room. His tone had shifted—less formal, more performative now, as though Ana were merely the next prop in his little power play.

Ana nodded, her eyes flicking nervously to James and then to the other crew, searching for support. The entire crew room had frozen, the air conditioning's click the only constant—an absurd white noise for this stage-managed cruelty. She managed, in accented but clear English, "Yes, sir. I am the lead cabin crew/purser for AmericanoAir 4553 to Reno–Tahoe International Airport, followed by flight 8472 from there to Dallas and back to Conroe-North Houston Regional."

Ana's voice quivered only slightly as she recited her itinerary—a statement she had repeated so many times it had become a liturgy. Hoffman regarded her as one might a suspect package, his gaze heavy, lingering far too long on the ragged edges of her travel documents. He held her passport up, squinting as if searching for invisible writing, then snapped it shut and placed it on the table with a force that made Ana jump.

"You're here on what visa, exactly?" he said, voice loaded with the kind of bureaucratic suspicion that seemed designed to trip up even the most careful answer.

Ana swallowed, keeping her hands folded. "I have a DV lottery green card, sir. Permanent resident." She placed the card on top of her passport, the laminate corners curling from years of wallet storage.

Hoffman picked it up and ran his thumb over the hologram, inspecting it with all the relish of a border official at a military coup. "You win the lottery, huh? Lucky girl." The sarcasm was deliberate; a minor humiliation to supplement the major one of being interrogated, like a criminal, in front of colleagues and subordinates.

James, in that moment, felt the oddest sense of dislocation. The room was lit with those harsh, sterile LEDs that made everyone look sickly and grey, and time seemed to slow. He watched Ana—her hands shaking, face pale—and remembered the first time he'd met her on a flight to Houston, a few months ago when they underwent AmericanoAir/Sprint customer service training, a three day course at a Holiday Inn Express somewhere on the edge of DFW airport. Even then, Ana had been the most diligent in the class, the sort who would double-check every emergency procedure, drill every service flow, and take the rules—such as they were in the world of low-cost American aviation—very seriously. Yet even back then, beneath the competence, there was an anxiety, an awareness that her right to be here was never quite secure, always a matter of someone else's paperwork and patience.

Now, with her life reduced to a handful of laminated cards and ink-stamped pages, Ana looked as if she was shrinking before them all, battered by the caprice of a man who had decided—long before he'd ever met her—that anyone foreign was, by definition, a problem to be solved.

She deserved better than this. They all did.

Hoffman, finished with his performance, tossed the green card and passport back onto the table so they skittered across the cheap wood towards Ana. "We'll see about this," he muttered, as if making a mental note. "Sit down, don't go anywhere. Someone will be in to talk to you. Next," he barked, scanning the room. The rest of the crew—AmericanoAir's patchwork of pilots, flight attendants, and ground agents, drawn from across the Americas and Europe—shifted uneasily, some rummaging for documents, others shooting furtive glances at the door through which Theo had disappeared.

"You!" James noticed that one of the Iraqi born flight attendants, Samir—always upbeat, quick with a joke, a dab hand with fussy business-class passengers—was the next to be singled out. He straightened his AmericanoAir uniform, eyes flicking to James for the briefest moment, seeking, if not comfort, at least the knowledge that someone was witnessing this.

Samir's story was infamous among the crew: fleeing Basra as a child, a long route via UN camps and Istanbul, eventually landing in Houston, then bouncing between low-cost carriers and survival jobs before finally finding his way to Sprint's American cousin. Samir had told his story once, in the back of a crew bus in Phoenix, to a flight attendant who'd cried at the sheer mad luck of it. Now he was just another name on a list.

Hoffman regarded Samir with a kind of predatory patience. "Papers," he snapped, holding out a hand. Samir produced his Texan residency card and his battered Iraqi passport, the two documents a contradiction in every way—one the product of a million regulations and interviews, the other a relic of chaos, stamped and stained.

"Your English is good," Hoffman commented, as if it were a compliment, as he flipped through the passport with a practised hand. "Where'd you learn?"

Samir forced a smile. "In Houston, sir. And before that, from YouTube. And school, when we had school."

Hoffman grunted, then held up the residency card. "This expires next year. Plan to renew?"

"Yes, sir. Already started the process," Samir replied, hands folded, voice even.

Hoffman eyed him. "We'll be in touch." He tossed the card back.

It was the same ritual—random, theatrical, ugly. The rest of the crew were called up one by one, each subjected to their own private humiliation. The Canadians—usually ignored at border checks—found themselves answering pointed questions about French-language ability, terrorist connections, and whether they'd ever travelled to Cuba. The British flight attendants were grilled about the finer points of Brexit and their feelings on the monarchy. An Irish co-pilot was quizzed about an Irish-language line on his passport; a Mexican crew chief was made to recite her entire travel history for the past five years, down to her last cross-border bus trip.

With that, Hoffman swept out of the room, leaving the door ajar and the assembled crew in a heavy, stifling silence. Agent Paulson had vanished with Theo, leaving only the faintest smell of aftershave and cheap authority. For a moment, nobody spoke.

Then Maria stood up and crossed the room, her hand landing gently on Ana's shoulder. "You okay, chica?" she whispered, her accent thick with Puerto Rican warmth. Ana nodded, but her eyes were wide and unfocused.

James looked at the clock. Every minute spent here was another minute lost to the Kafkaesque workings of the Trump-era TSA and ICE. If they didn't get released soon, their duty hours would tick past the legal limits. Another delay, another lost rotation, and more chaos for AmericanoAir's already fragile schedule.

He found himself glancing at his own passport in his kit bag—American by birth, Air Force veteran, son of a Texan lawyer and a mother who'd fought every school board and city council in their part of Dallas for a more just world. The stamp inside his passport that said he was "good to work" in the land of his own birth now felt like the most fragile assurance in the world.

James flexed his fingers, feeling the tension settle in his shoulders as the minutes dragged by. Around him, the crew room simmered with a suppressed, brittle anxiety. The air was thick with the scent of cheap cleaning products and nerves; someone's deodorant clung in the recirculated air. Out on the ramp, a distant jet engine howled as a Southwest 737 clawed itself off the runway, its roar as comforting as it was far away from the world of ICE and clipped authority.

He checked his watch. It was nearly 9am. The original report time for their Las Vegas–Reno leg had come and gone. No one from AmericanoAir's crew logistics had appeared, nor had anyone from the union—assuming the union had any real power in the first place. It occurred to James that, even in this "golden age" of pilot demand and relentless airline hiring, they were all still, fundamentally, replaceable. If ICE wanted to throw the book at Theo, there'd be another Brit or Aussie or out-of-luck American happy to take his place in the right seat.

He glanced at the remaining crew, trying to calculate who might break first. Maria was still murmuring to Ana in low Spanish. The rest milled about—checking phones (no signal, of course), shifting bags, quietly cursing. James had seen his share of crew crises—emergency landings, passenger medicals, engine failures—but there was a unique helplessness in being pinned down by paperwork and the state, with nothing to do but wait for someone else's whim.

He pulled out his phone anyway and flicked through his messages: a string of increasingly frantic pings from Ops, asking for updates, demanding estimated times, requesting an explanation for "unexplained crew delay at terminal 3." There were WhatsApp memes too—a shot of Theo's ICE officer with devil horns, someone's AI-generated Trump in a pilot's uniform, and a picture of their own A320's nose with the caption: "Waiting for clearance, much?"

But the real weight in the room was the absence of Theo, whose future now hung in the balance. James tried to picture where he might be—a bleak holding cell in the bowels of McCarran, perhaps, or a secondary inspection room filled with garish posters about "illegal entry" and "citizenship fraud." He hoped, at least, that someone from the British consulate would be contacted, but he doubted it. That would require a level of professionalism these ICE officers seemed to actively avoid.

At last, after what felt like hours, a new figure appeared in the doorway: a woman in a dark suit with a Department of Homeland Security badge clipped to her lapel. She surveyed the crew with clinical detachment and cleared her throat.

"Captain Hart?"

James stood, brushing non-existent dust from his AmericanoAir jacket, all careful calm. "Yes, ma'am."

"I'm Special Agent Rollins, DHS. You and your crew are being held for a secondary review. There are discrepancies in the paperwork of two crew members, as you've probably noticed." Her voice was flat, efficient. "We're working to clear up the matter. In the meantime, you are not free to leave the building, but you may use the crew lounge, the restrooms, and the café on this floor. Please do not attempt to go landside or approach the aircraft until further notice."

She paused. "Your First Officer, Mr Sullivan, is being processed. There may be further questions for another crew as needed. Thank you for your cooperation."

She turned to leave, but James forced himself to speak. "Agent Rollins, may I ask—what exactly is the allegation? Theo Sullivan is a permanent resident, fully vetted by both the FAA and ICE. He's married to a US citizen. What's the issue here?"

Rollins regarded him with the faintest flicker of empathy—or perhaps just fatigue. "You'd be surprised how often these things happen, Captain. There are questions about the timing of his marriage and visa, and about possible prior intent to immigrate. Until that's resolved, he's not flying anywhere."

James nodded tightly, resisting the urge to say something that would only make things worse. He sat down, muscles buzzing with frustration.

"You do know that if we have to wait around even longer during a secondary inspection," James began, striving for the casual composure of a man who hadn't just seen a friend marched away in handcuffs, "we'll be out of hours. You do realise you'll need another crew?"

Agent Rollins gave a minute nod, almost sympathetic—almost. "That's for your employer to worry about. But don't wander off. You'll be notified when you're free to leave."

And with that, she disappeared, the door swinging shut behind her with a finality that seemed to echo off every blank surface in the crew room. For a long moment, nobody spoke. The muffled hum of conversation and clatter from the airport's public concourse seeped through the double glazing—a reminder that the world outside went on as normal, heedless of the lives put on hold here.

James leaned against the table, the scuffed AmericanoAir pilot wings on his chest catching the overhead light. He watched the crew. Some paced, some sat, and others tried to busy themselves by re-checking baggage tags, manifests, or flicking endlessly through phones that showed only the same apologetic "no signal" icon.

It was Ana who broke the silence at last, whispering to Maria. "What if they send me back? My lease, my car, everything. Gone." Maria patted her hand in reassurance, murmuring words James couldn't catch. The rest watched with a mix of solidarity and helplessness, as if physical proximity could stave off the threat that any one of them, no matter how diligent or clean their record, might be next.

James was no stranger to this side of American authority. Born and bred Texan, son of a lawyer, former Air Force officer—he'd seen both the best and worst of officialdom. But this? This was something colder, the weight of bureaucracy wielded not as a shield, but as a weapon.

He made his way to the corner of the room where a battered coffee machine sat, its surface sticky with old sugar. The thing hissed and spat a meagre trickle of brown liquid into a paper cup. It tasted as bitter as the mood. He sipped anyway, eyes on the glass doors that separated them from the rest of the terminal, as if half-expecting Theo to be walked back in by a suitably abashed supervisor with apologies and paperwork in hand.

But that was a fantasy. He knew better.

He thought of the passengers. The ones who would already be queueing at the gate, grumbling about delays, muttering into iPhones and overpriced Starbucks cups, oblivious to the real drama unfolding just out of sight. To them, this would be another unexplained airline delay—another reason to hate AmericanoAir, or Sprint, or whoever happened to wear the right lanyard that day.

He thought, too, of the aircraft itself: an A320neo, barely six months old, still smelling faintly of factory plastics and new leather in the cockpit. Waiting for them on the ramp, now almost certainly being eyed up by airport ops and ground handlers, ticking away its scheduled maintenance window as the crew who should be prepping it for Reno were instead prisoners of administrative whim.

James returned to the group, finding his seat once more. Across the room, Samir had taken to sketching little figures in a battered notebook, each doodle more frantic than the last. The Canadians, Natalie and Juliette, had started a whispered French conversation, equal parts nervous and darkly comic.

James watched them—the microcosm of AmericanoAir, America itself in miniature: a Guatemalan, an Iraqi, two Québécoises, a Puerto Rican, a couple of Brits, an Irishman, a handful of Americans. All scrubbed, uniformed, compliant. All under the shadow of suspicion, as if the mere fact of holding a job that required international movement was itself a crime.

He wanted to say something that would help. That things would be fine, that this was a one-off, a bad morning, that the rules, for all their cruelty, had a limit. But to say so would be to lie, and he found he could not lie—not here, not now.

He saw Natalie shaking slightly as she peeled the sticker off her crew tag and re-affixed it, hands working the small adhesive label with the nervous energy of someone who has nothing else to control. She caught his eye, offered a tiny, tight smile, then turned away, muttering to Juliette in a French so clipped and Quebecois that it was practically code.

James's phone buzzed again—another message from Ops, this one more urgent, with a warning that DOT would be notified if the delay exceeded another thirty minutes.

He flicked it off, then caught sight of a younger ground agent—a new hire, probably barely twenty—hovering in the corridor. The young man kept glancing inside, checking on the crew with the expression of a caged animal, as if expecting the Feds to pounce on him, too, simply for being in the wrong place at the wrong time.

The air was growing thicker by the minute. The coffee, despite its bitterness, did nothing to steady his nerves.

He thought of Theo, running through scenarios in his head. Would they process him through the system? Call his wife? Deportation—was that a real threat, or just theatre? Would the British consulate be told? Would AmericanoAir's legal team intervene, or would they hang him out to dry? He knew from bitter experience—friends, acquaintances, even one ex-girlfriend—that when bureaucracy truly got its teeth into a foreign national, nothing was certain except that it would be expensive, slow, and humiliating.

****

CHAPTER 16 – ICE 2: Electric Boogaloo

Saturday 16th August 2025

"You know, love, I don't get why you hate AmericanoAir?" James heard from his wife, sitting back in seat 1F of the Sprinter service between Shannon and Providence, one of the European side of Sprint's ever-expanding transatlantic roster. They had been on holiday to Athens, and, instead of paying full fare or an ID90 fare on a full service airline, such as British Airways, they'd gambled on the one perk left to most airline families: staff travel, on the "parent company's" own low-cost long-haul brand. James, in his early fifties and sporting a tan that said *I've not seen an airport crew room in a week*," glanced over at Jane, who was busily stirring her plastic cup of white wine, her magazine open at an article about the latest budget hotel openings in Portugal.

"Because it's not an airline, it's a fever dream in a livery," James muttered, glancing sideways as a squat, freckled flight attendant bustled past, collecting the detritus from another round of paid snack boxes. "It's barely even a company, if you listen to what the Brits say about Sprint, they'd have a contrary if they saw our side of the pond. You remember that woman at Luton who was screaming at the check-in girl because the boarding pass said Sprint and the aircraft said we're on is carrying an Arabic registration and fleet names as it's an Omani AOC plane, love."

"Wait, this is a Muslim aircraft?" the man in 2D screamed from behind James, and he knew that just because they were half an hour out from landfall over Newfoundland, his day wasn't going to get any more peaceful. James turned to see the MAGA hat on the head of the person of 2D, and knew instantly that, as Trump had returned to the White House a mere eight months prior, and in that time had sent bombers into Iran, into Mexico, and was still threatening to take Greenland with a straight face on Truth Social, he would be getting no peace until the wheels were down and he was out of the terminal. The flight attendant, who James knew as Anka Horváthová, according to her badge, a Lead Flight Attendant, to her credit, ignored the outburst with the professional numbness of someone who had spent the summer traversing the Atlantic with a cabin full of people who saw every delay as a personal affront to their constitutional rights.

"Technically, sir, this aircraft is owned by SOMAN Leasing, sir, who lease it to Sprint Oman. We don't normally use this aircraft on the US routes, but the A319neo that we normally use was held up at Prestwick by a bird strike. It's still a Sprint plane, so your ticket and your safety are exactly the same," she replied in an Irish accent that rolled over the turbulence of his anger as smoothly as a Galway tide. "Would you like more peanuts?"

"No, I don't want halal peanuts!" the man barked, as though saying the word might summon a cleric from the galley to confiscate his bacon crisps. Jane shot James a glance—part amusement, part the exhausted disbelief of a woman who'd taught in a London comprehensive for thirty years. James just shrugged. He'd seen far worse in his cockpit, and, besides, the pandemic had made everyone a little odd. Travel brought it out in a certain class of American: that desperate, twitching defensiveness that made him grateful for his blue passport every time he cleared US Immigration, no matter the queue.

"No, they're German peanuts sir, from our German supplier," Anka said with a tiny flicker of a smile, betraying none of the disdain that lived behind her eyes. "And our captain is from Leicester, so you're in good hands."

"Leicester? Isn't that where Farage says Paki Muslims run the city?"

The man in 2D's voice cut through the hum of the A321's cabin, loud enough for a few heads to swivel. Anka didn't so much as blink.

"I couldn't possibly say, sir," she replied, the smile unwavering. "Would you like a drink? Beer, wine, or perhaps a whiskey?"

"I'll take the whiskey," he said, sulking.

"Of course, sir. That's $12.74."

"$12.74? I paid $20 at the Luton Duty Free for a 1L bottle of Bells and you're... wait, that pilot... he's Muslim."

James looked to see his fellow Sprint Captain, one of the British contingent based on the Union Flag on the name badge, had come out of the cockpit and one of the other flight attendants had gone in, as following London European Flight 341, the Channel crash where the Captain deliberately locked out the First Officer and the world had spent a fortnight convulsing over pilot background checks, Sprint's European operations had enforced an unbreakable two-person rule in the flight deck—one in, one out, always. It was security theatre for some, trauma balm for others. The British Captain, a tall, calm figure with a neat beard and a soft Midlands accent, was simply stretching his legs, doing the usual circuit for the sake of protocol and perhaps to reassure the cabin that, yes, someone was in charge.

James watched with the jaded eye of a veteran as the American in 2D squinted up, searching for signs of difference. "You one of them? You pray to Mecca, Captain?"

The Captain's mouth twitched in a smile that somehow managed to be neither amused nor offended, just infinitely patient. "I pray that we make it to Providence on time and with all the luggage, sir. That's about the only religious observance we manage up front. I'm sure my colleagues both here and Sprint America can confirm that my only vice is the Gunners."

James knew that the Gunners, or Arsenal FC, despite being a Texan and interested more in proper football, not soccer, were an English Premier League side, perennially disappointing and yet, in their own way, a global faith—one you might pray to in despair as often as to any god.

"Gunners?!" 2D shouted with the usual habits of a Trump and Farage fan boy. "Terrorist! I want off this plane now! I'm calling 911 and... shit, he's got a phone!"

James noticed the Captain was holding the same Pixel 9A that he himself had as part of being a Sprint Captain. The device was used for checking rosters, contacting Ops, looking at the Manifest and even WhatsApping colleagues on other flights. As they used data sims and the Starlink Wi-Fi that all Sprint planes were fitted with, James knew that his colleague would be using Teams to potentially call Ops, update the next crew on the inbound, or—more likely—just read the in-flight banter on the "Sprint Transatlantic Lunatics" WhatsApp group. Nothing remotely sinister, unless one's threshold for panic was set somewhere around 1995 and dialled up to eleven by years of social media rot.

And the Captain, Muhammed Rahman, as his badge stated in neat sans-serif, started talking on the phone, not in English but in Urdu, the Pakistani language of his grandparents—ordering extra special meals for the next crew change at Providence, if James had to guess, or maybe just checking with his wife about dinner plans if they got in on time. Whatever it was, the sight of a brown-skinned captain with a beard, speaking a foreign language, was enough to push 2D's panic into an entirely new key.

Jane, perhaps unconsciously, pressed her shoulder closer to James, as if to shield him from the second-hand embarrassment radiating from 2D. But James didn't flinch. He'd seen far worse, both in the cockpit and out of it, and the British Captain had the patient calm of someone who'd grown up with this sort of nonsense for decades.

"Is there a problem, sir?" Captain Rahman asked, returning to English with a soft, unthreatening smile.

"You seem upset. Is there something I can assist you with?"

2D was red-faced, tugging at his baseball cap. "You... you're flying this plane? With all this Muslim stuff? You know what happened with that plane in the Channel. That was terrorism. They covered it up—said it was mental health, but everyone knows. Everyone knows." His voice grew shrill.

Rahman didn't blink. "I'm flying this aircraft because I'm a licensed and experienced airline captain, sir. Sprint has, I assure you, the strictest checks of any carrier in Europe."

"The Captain's right," James said, knowing that he needed to come to the aid of his colleague—solidarity in the air meant standing up, even in civilian clothes. "Sprint's UK, European and Omani operations are as safe as Ryanair. They fly 550 aircraft a day in those areas, and they've not had a major incident since they launched in 2022."

James knew his Texan drawl still clung to his vowels despite decades in the cockpit. It had always been a small source of comfort to fellow expats in the air, but on days like this, it could be a red rag to the sort of American who wanted to believe he was surrounded by foreign plots and woke conspiracies. "I'd say you're in safer hands than most, friend. This is a modern Airbus, flown by some of the most audited pilots in the business. I should know, as I work for their American division, AmericanoAir. You might have seen the livery—same as the Euro planes but with a Stars and Stripes on the tail?"

"You're just a woke 'crat whos pissed that black bitch Harris lost to the one who has made America great again! I know how it is! You people and your 'diversity hires'. I'm not letting you fly me over the ocean. I want a white pilot, a Christian pilot! I'm calling the FAA, I'm calling my Congressman, I'm calling ICE."

"Listen, I've bled for America, I've had a Purple Heart, fighting in the USAF for fuckers like you," James said, his voice low and even, the hint of steel in it cutting through the hum of the galley. He didn't stand up, didn't need to. But the words, delivered in that measured, half-exhausted tone of someone who'd run out of patience with men like 2D, made the immediate three rows fall silent. "And you are embarrassing yourself. You're not in Kansas, and you're not the main character. You're on a Sprint Air flight, bound for Providence, with two qualified pilots up front, a crew who've dealt with more in an hour than you have in a year, and about three hundred witnesses to your tantrum. You want to make a scene, be my guest. But know this: we have the right to have you met by law enforcement at the gate, and I promise you, the authorities at Providence don't have much patience for folks who try to start international incidents at 38,000 feet."

The man in 3C stood up and walked towards James, a hand outstretched. "Thank you for your service, sir," the man said quietly, an unmistakable Midwestern twang lending a calm sincerity to his words. "Ignore him. He's not worth your time, or anybody else's." The nearby passengers—an exhausted mother with a toddler on her lap in 3A, a Portuguese businessman scrolling through LinkedIn in 3B, and a knot of gap-year students behind them—nodded in tacit agreement. There was a collective exhale, the subtle, grateful deflation of a cabin held taut by the possibility of mid-Atlantic drama.

Anka, ever the professional, leaned across James, dropping her voice. "Sir, would you like a top-up on your wine?" She grinned conspiratorially, a tiny flicker of solidarity passed between those who worked the skies and those who had, at some point, been called upon to keep order above the clouds.

"Make it a double, if you can, Anka," James replied, his mouth quirking upwards. "How much?"

"$1, sir, as you're staff," she said, and James knew that normally Sprint wouldn't give staff discounts on alcoholic drinks—some bean-counter at HQ would issue a sternly worded memo about "benefit in kind" by next week—but Anka understood the unwritten rules. Airline people looked after their own, when the pressure of the cabin squeezed just a bit too tight.

Jane squeezed his hand, and for a moment James let himself relax, letting the hum of the engines and the muted clink of glasses lull him back to something approaching contentment. The Atlantic beneath was streaked with cloud, the flight map on the seatback screen showing their path curling down past the Newfoundland coast, the green splotch of Ireland already a memory.

He glanced at the aisle. The man in 2D—whose passport, James wagered, would have "John" or "David" in the forename box and a string of Truth Social rants in his browsing history—sat with arms folded, a fortress of resentment. But for now, he was quiet. There was nothing left for him but to seethe and wait, plotting angry posts and Yelp reviews that would vanish into the same void as all the others.

*_*_*_*

As they arrived at Providence, James knew that, as they had passed CBP at Shannon, things would, normally, be as easy as waltzing through a domestic terminal in Kansas City. The preclearance at Shannon, an artefact of transatlantic bureaucracy and the post-9/11 obsession with layered security, had rendered their arrival almost comically mundane. No lines, no barking TSA agents, no stern CBP officers peering over their booths, demanding to know if you were carrying more than ten thousand dollars or a banana.

However, with 2D, James knew that there was something wrong as soon as Anka grabbed the internal phone from the jump seat, which he knew meant, as they had touched the ground and were taxiing, that something was afoot, and that they were, looking out of his window, not going to the usual remote stands, but to a secure apron marked with yellow chevrons and cordoned at two ends by bright orange cones and the rotating presence of two TSA vehicles. Not standard, not typical. Not just because this wasn't a major gateway like JFK or Dulles, but because Providence, sleepy and modest, didn't usually expect its Sprint flights to arrive bearing diplomatic crises in economy.

James raised an eyebrow. He'd flown into his share of trouble spots and special events, and this had the stink of "you've become the incident" written all over it. Anka's crisp announcement confirmed it.

"Ladies and gentlemen, welcome to Providence Theodore Francis Green International Airport. For safety reasons, we ask that you remain seated with your seatbelts fastened until the captain turns off the seatbelt sign. Please note that due to a special clearance procedure, there may be a slight delay before disembarkation. We appreciate your patience and cooperation."

Jane leaned in, whispering. "They've called the police for Mr Red Hat, haven't they?"

James nodded, watching out the window as a third vehicle pulled up. This one bore the deep blue shield of ICE— Immigration and Customs Enforcement. He felt his stomach sink, not because he feared any trouble for himself or the crew, but because he knew what it meant when ICE showed up early. It wasn't just to debrief a disruptive passenger. It was to make a point.

As the aircraft came to a halt, the forward door cracked open and a cool breeze swept through, mingling with the thrum of idling auxiliary power and the residual smell of galley coffee. Two men stepped aboard, one younger, square-jawed, with a buzzcut and mirrored sunglasses, and the other older, wearing a sport coat over khaki trousers like someone playing "senior lawman" on TV.

James had seen their kind before—Special Agents who preferred the optics of authority over the nuance of professionalism. He stayed seated but alert, watching from 1F as Anka intercepted them with a flight manifest and her best customer-service smile.

"Can I help you, officers?"

The older one flicked open a badge wallet. "Agent Harvey Ross, ICE. This is my partner, Agent Steve Paulson. We're here to check the immigration status of one Captain Muhammed Rahman. Now kindly open the cockpit door, or we shall arrest you on suspicion of aiding and abetting the unlawful entry of an inadmissible alien." He delivered the line in a tone that brooked no argument, but Anka's face remained a study in polite blankness—a thousand-yard stare honed from years of balancing safety, service, and the Kafkaesque theatre of border security.

"I'm afraid I'll need to call my supervisor and the Captain before I can open the cockpit door, sir. Company policy." Her Irish accent was as steady as ever, no hint of nerves. James, meanwhile, felt the old pilot's knot in his stomach tighten. He glanced sidelong at Jane, who had gone pale, her lips pressed in a hard line.

The junior agent, who identified himself as Donald Spencer, sneered. "Ma'am, you are now obstructing a federal investigation."

Anka didn't blink. "Not at all, sir. I am following company safety procedures and FAA regulations. Please give me one moment."

She leaned over to the nearest jump seat phone and punched in the intercom, her words low but firm. "Flight deck, this is Anka. We have ICE agents onboard requesting to speak to Captain Rahman regarding his immigration status. Please advise."

James, watching, pulled his Sprint issued Pixel, and was loading up Teams to contact Marnie Shaw, the East Coast Operations Duty Manager, who was as close to a guardian angel as anyone got in the sprawling world of Sprint's US operation. It was an instinct drilled in from a decade of American cockpit politics: whenever federal badges appeared, call Ops, call Legal, and—most of all—do not try to handle it solo. Especially not in 2025, with the ICE and CBP under pressure to prove themselves in a world of daily viral scandals and congressional hearings on aviation "security failures."

Jane gripped his hand, murmuring, "Do you think they'll actually haul him off? Just for being… well, you know—"

James gave a small shake of his head, forcing a wry smile. "Not if Marnie gets on the phone to the station manager before the agents get to the flight deck."

But the ICE men were already making their move. Anka's calm request for patience was bulldozed by the older man's glare.

"Open the cockpit, now, or you'll be detained with him."

That was enough. James stood, putting himself in the aisle—not quite blocking, but enough to be seen. "Officers, I can confirm you're about to cause an international incident for a man who is a British citizen, cleared by US preclearance in Shannon. Now, would you like to speak to the Operations Manager at JFK for Sprint
294

and AmericanoAir to clarify this or speak to the Consulate instead? Because your paperwork is going to hit a diplomatic brick wall if you touch a crew member without jurisdiction. Check your manifests—this is a scheduled service, operating under Open Skies, with preclearance already performed. You're not boarding a rickety migrant boat off Montauk. You're making yourselves the story."

James knew that he was interfering in a Federal process, but in a world where rules were weaponised as theatre, he also knew the choreography. He kept his voice steady, just this side of respectful, but carried that quiet authority born from thousands of hours behind locked cockpit doors.

The senior agent's mouth twisted. "And you are?"

"Major James Hart. USAF, retired, and AmericanoAir Captain. Off duty, but staff. Now, do you want to piss off Sprint Ops and have British and American lawyers, especially those who used to work for Carter Ruck and Ryanair, or speak to my Operations Manager on the phone?"

The next thing James knew, Ross pulled a pair of handcuffs from his belt and grabbed his arms, not even hesitating. "You are interfering in a federal investigation. Sit down and stay out of this or you'll spend the night in a cell."

Jane gasped, half-rising from her seat, but James twisted out of the man's grip with the fluidity of someone who had spent a lifetime in tight spaces, fixed the agent with a steady glare, and said, "You're about to put hands on a US veteran on a pre-cleared aircraft, in front of a planeload of witnesses. You'll want to reconsider that. Or I start a lawsuit in LA, New York, DC and my birth town of Texas just for good measure. And I guarantee you, the story will not be 'ICE bravely secures plane'—it'll be 'ICE assaults disabled veteran and airline crew on sovereign, pre-cleared flight.' Your call, Agent."

There was a taut, electric pause. The cabin, frozen in that terrible, collective inhale, watched the stand-off unfold with eyes wide, breaths held. Out on the apron, the engines whined down, the heat shimmered, and a faint whiff of jet fuel drifted through the open door, mingling with the cold bureaucratic violence about to be wrought in the name of "homeland security." Somewhere aft, a child started to cry, setting off a chorus of fretful murmurs.

Agent Ross, handcuffs hovering, seemed to wrestle with himself—torn between the brute theatre of power and the realisation that, for all his bluster, he had wandered onto a legal minefield. It was Agent Paulson who stepped in, laying a hand lightly on Ross's arm and speaking in a voice pitched just loud enough for the front few rows.

"Major Hart, Captain Rahman, Miss... Anka, let's all take a breath here. I see your points. If you're cleared through Shannon, and this is all above board, then I'm sure we can sort this out with the company and station manager. No need for this to become a... scene." He glared pointedly at his partner, who let the cuffs drop with visible reluctance.

James exhaled slowly, not backing down. "That's all we're asking, Agent. Run your checks, call the supervisor, do what you must. But this crew—this Captain—deserves respect and due process. And so does every passenger on board." He let the words hang in the air, not a threat, but the stone-cold reality of a world where law, aviation, and spectacle intersected in an unholy mess.

Rahman emerged from the flight deck, his face impassive but his eyes steely. "Agents, my passport, EASA and CAA ATPL licence, Sprint crew card. Take them, call your supervisors, call the embassy, call whoever you need. I'll wait here." His Midlands accent was calm, but every word snapped like a flag in a storm.

The ICE agents took the documents, their sudden caution a jarring contrast to the theatrical aggression of just minutes before. The senior man, Ross, glowered as if betrayed by the shifting winds of legal authority, but it was clear Paulson had read the cabin. A handful of passengers had phones out, discreetly filming; any rough stuff would be viral by the time they reached the baggage claim. There was a murmur from somewhere in the forward galley—another flight attendant, Maria, pressed herself flat against the bulkhead, eyes darting anxiously from Rahman to the ICE agents to the still-seated 2D, who looked torn between glee and indignation that his moment had somehow been hijacked.

James sat slowly, never quite turning his back to the officers. Jane squeezed his arm. "Let's hope your Marnie can sort this before they start dragging pilots off to Guantánamo," she whispered, half-joking, half not. He managed a wry smile. If he'd learned one thing in a lifetime of aviation, it was that the bureaucracy moved at two speeds—glacial, or all at once like an avalanche.

Agent Ross stalked to the front of the aircraft, phone already at his ear. Paulson, meanwhile, took Rahman's credentials, moving aft, stopping a few rows down to speak low into his own radio. James caught snippets of conversation in that coded, weary language of lawmen everywhere—"Shannon clearance… Sprint Group… yes, all in order… British passport, yes… manifest pre-screened…"—and slowly, almost imperceptibly, the pressure in the cabin began to ease. Anka caught James's eye, mouthed a silent "thank you," and made her way back to the galley, the model of composed efficiency.

The man in 2D, denied his YouTube moment of glory, slouched into his seat and glared at the window, fingers drumming furiously on the armrest.

For ten long minutes, nothing happened. James stared at the faded, chequered carpet. The air was thick with the smells of sweat, jet fuel, and over brewed coffee. Then, Paulson returned, his face now a picture of forced politeness.

"Captain Rahman," he said, voice formal, "thank you for your patience. We have confirmed with CBP and the Providence station manager that your status is in order. You are free to continue your duties. Our apologies for any inconvenience." He gave a shallow nod, the sort that meant "we were hoping for an easier collar." Rahman accepted his documents back with a calm, "Thank you, officer," and for a fleeting moment James saw the tension leave the man's jaw.

Ross, not to be outdone, turned to address the entire cabin. "We apologise for the delay, folks. Security procedures.

Welcome to Providence." His voice was a bark, not an apology. Then, in a lower tone, to Anka, "You might want to review your manifest procedures next time. We're only trying to keep Americans safe."

Anka, never missing a beat, smiled sweetly. "Thank you for your vigilance, sir. Our passengers always appreciate a thorough welcome to the United States."

There was a ripple of sardonic applause from the forward rows—just loud enough for the ICE men to hear, just quiet enough to avoid open defiance. The engines now fully silent, the crew quickly began the process of disembarkation. Bags clattered from overheads, passengers shuffled into the aisle, and Jane leaned in to James. "God, I need a drink," she muttered. "You always did pick the best flights for a holiday, love."

He kissed her forehead, feeling the tension in his own shoulders begin to unwind. "At least it's never dull," he murmured, eyes flicking back to Rahman, who was quietly speaking with Maria and Anka, the three of them moving through the rituals of post-drama clean-up— smiles, reassurances, a discreet offer of water in a paper cup, all the ordinary magic of airline professionalism in the face of chaos.

They filed off the aircraft into the sticky Rhode Island heat, the heavy scent of tarmac and ocean tang mixing as they stepped onto the mobile stairs. James squinted up at the terminal building, its faded signage and low-rise profile a far cry from the glass cathedrals of JFK or Heathrow. A handful of local police loitered near the door, their presence unnecessary now but keen, perhaps, for a glimpse of federal theatre. 2D stormed past, grumbling about lawsuits and "foreigners," his MAGA hat tilted at a sullen angle. James caught Anka's eye once more as she shepherded the last stragglers forward. He mouthed "Good luck," and she winked, a fleeting moment of mutual understanding shared by airline people everywhere—those who know the thin, invisible line between order and chaos at 35,000 feet.

****

CHAPTER 17 – Quid Pro Quo
Friday 22nd August 2025

"Ladies and Gentlemen, the President of the United States," the television intoned, the robotic solemnity of the White House press office broadcast echoing through the AmericanoAir crew room at JFK. A ripple of stifled groans spread through the ranks of crew, slumped at battered tables or hunched over takeaway coffee, the kind of collective exhale that had become as ritual as a morning checklist. Even here, half a world away from the West Wing, the shadow of politics fell long and dark across the gate piers and the cracked linoleum of the break room.

On the screen, Donald J. Trump appeared, hair more silver now than gold, but eyes as flinty as ever, squinting in the harsh summer glare on the South Lawn. Flanked by advisors, flags, and a new breed of press secretary, he radiated that particular, hardboiled triumphalism only a politician truly insulated from consequence could summon. The chyron below read *"US-UK AVIATION TALKS—LIVE"*.

James Hart was not a man given to watching politicians at breakfast, but today—today was different. Today, the fate of half the airline industry, and perhaps his own job, hung on the whims of men and women for whom flying was not a career, but a bargaining chip.

A muttered aside from the left: "What's the bet he mentions us before the first two minutes are up?"

James didn't look up from his phone. "Three to one. If he says 'America First', you buy me lunch."

The president wasted no time. "We are in negotiations, very tough negotiations, with the United Kingdom and the European Union—good friends, great allies—over the situation with Sprint, and, frankly, over the way American jobs and American skies have been treated by certain foreign companies. AmericanoAir, for example—supposedly American, but owned by British money, flying European crews, taking American routes. We're looking at that, and we're going to fix it. Believe me."

There it was. Less than thirty seconds.

Somewhere across the break room, a tired cheer went up, half-ironic, half-resigned. Someone threw a sachet of sugar at the TV; it bounced off the screen and landed by a stack of outdated flight manuals. The mood, as ever, oscillated between black humour and blacker dread.

Trump continued, undeterred by the muted jeers of a hundred pilots and cabin crew. "We have spoken to our partners in the industry, and, following discussions, big discussions, I have instructed the Department of Transport, the Federal Aviation Authority and the Department for Homeland Security to cease their investigations into AmericanoAir."

Trump paused, as if savouring the line, letting it hang in the humid August air. The reporters leaned forward in unison, a forest of microphones angling towards his mouth.

"—subject," he continued, holding up a finger, "to certain assurances. Fair assurances. Very reasonable assurances.

We believe in fair trade. We believe in reciprocity. Quid pro quo, you could say."

That phrase landed like a dropped tray in turbulence.

In the AmericanoAir crew room, the soundscape changed subtly. The muttering stopped. Phones were lifted a little higher. Someone near the coffee machine swore softly, not in anger, but in recognition. James felt the hair on the back of his neck prickle in a way that had nothing to do with air-conditioning.

Trump smiled, the thin, pleased smile of a man who knew he was holding cards other people needed badly. "We will allow AmericanoAir to continue operations without disruption. No more enhanced inspections. No more unnecessary delays. No more harassment of hard-working pilots and crew." He paused again, letting the benevolence of it all wash over the cameras. "In return, Sprint Group has agreed to make some important changes."

James looked up now.

The press secretary stepped forward, passing Trump a neatly clipped briefing card. He barely glanced at it.

"First," Trump said, "Sprint have agreed to purchase 50 Boeing 737 Max 8s for an as yet undisclosed operator who they have a beautiful partnership with," Trump continued, waving the card vaguely as though it were a restaurant bill he intended to dispute later. "Those aircraft will be built in America, by American workers, with American parts. That's jobs. A lot of jobs. Tremendous jobs."

The press pack erupted into a clamour of shouted questions, names being called, hands thrust forward. Trump ignored them with practised ease.

"Second," he said, holding up another finger, "Sprint has agreed that that their aircraft in the US will be maintained at the Mobile plant of Airbus, protecting thousands of American workers, thousands of jobs. And Sprint Group will increase its use of American-built engines from CFM International in Evendale, Ohio, a wonderful village, owned by GE Aerospace, a brilliant and all American company, by the way, you know that, everybody says so. And let me tell you, these are the best engines, the most reliable, absolutely fantastic," the President was saying, drawing out the syllables as though he had personally designed the turbines. "Sprint Group understands this. They know that to fly in America, you need to support American jobs. And now they're doing just that. So, we're going to let AmericanoAir, which we like, by the way, we want it to succeed—as long as it's fair, as long as American workers are protected. That's what this is about."

There was a lull as a correspondent from Reuters was acknowledged. The question was lost in a chorus of others, but the President pressed on, waving off a phalanx of microphones.

The president pressed on, barely pausing for breath, as if afraid that reality might catch up if he ever stopped moving forward. The reporters, meanwhile, jabbed questions in vain, their words snatched away by the breeze, by the press office, by the peculiar momentum of history as it unspooled in real time. The only thing louder than Trump's voice was the silence in the AmericanoAir crew room.

James felt it, viscerally: the stillness that came with realising you were, at last, at the mercy of events. All the drills, the briefings, the days spent negotiating delays and regulatory theatre with weary ground staff—none of it prepared you for the moment when the chessboard itself was picked up and shaken by hands far above your pay grade.

The President's smile never wavered. "We look forward to working with our partners in Europe and the UK," he finished, "to make sure that American skies remain the safest, and most competitive, in the world. That's what winning looks like. Thank you very much, everybody."

He raised a hand in a half-wave and turned from the podium, flanked by a clutch of aides in blue suits, the press secretary a step behind, all of them moving at that strange, ceremonial pace reserved for major announcements and state funerals.

The television flickered back to the CNN studio, where the anchor was already marshalling her panel of experts, analysts, and professional hand-wringers, all jostling to explain, in urgent soundbites, what it all meant for jobs, trade, and "the future of transatlantic aviation." No-one in the AmericanoAir crew room cared much for the analysis. They had lives to run and flights to operate, rosters to check, standby calls to dodge, and union reps to message. Yet for a few long moments after the broadcast faded, the air was thick with a silence that felt almost reverential—a collective recognition that something irreversible had happened, even if none of them yet knew quite what.

James broke the spell with the dry rustle of a paper coffee cup, crumpling it with the palm of his hand. "That's it, then. We're the new hostages."

"Fifty bloody Maxes," someone muttered from a table by the window, voice sour as week-old milk. "That'll go down well in Ramsgate."

Another pilot, a wiry New Englander with the wary eyes of someone who'd been through three Chapter 11s, snorted. "Quid pro quo. More like bend over backwards and smile for the cameras."

The conversation uncoiled, tense and fragmented. Someone scrolled feverishly through Twitter, reading out the early takes. *Sprint caves to Trump—jobs saved, for now.' 'Brits to pay the piper: White House leverages aircraft deal to save face.'* The memes were already flying—one was a doctored image of the Sprint boardroom, with Jeff Young and Francesca Mendes photoshopped as hostages, a grinning Boeing 737 Max hovering outside the window like a cartoon ransom note.

"Don't you get it," one of the Sprint Max First Officers said with a grin. "Sprint already runs CFM LEAPs and CFM56s, MRO is done at Mobile already, and Sprint is part owned by the Omanis, who own Oman Air, a 737 operator who's ordering Maxes, so…"

James looked at the First Officer of the premium LLC brand Sprint ran between Madrid and several Mexican and US cities and between Heathrow and JFK, and calculated what it meant, as Sprint was an all Airbus customer, meaning that fifty Boeing Maxes on the order book was not a business plan, but a flag of truce.

The fact that Sprint was only a month and half old in the US and three years old in the UK and Europe, meaning that the company was, in every sense that mattered, still in its infancy. It had only just found its feet in Britain— limping, perhaps, more than striding—by the time the first AmericanoAir jets landed in Las Vegas, painted up with the most enthusiastic Stars and Stripes ever committed to composite. James could recall, as if it were a bad dream, the scramble of their first JFK sector: the hired PRs, the bewildered American flight attendants in new lanyards, the Lithuanian mechanics in borrowed overalls, the piles of compliance paperwork signed in three languages and two alphabets. The fact that Sprint was now supposed to be buying a fleet of Boeings, for an operator "with a beautiful partnership"—God, Trump's words still hung in the air like old smoke—was a masterstroke of political sleight-of-hand. Boeing got a headline, Trump got a scalp, Sprint got a stay of execution, and nobody, least of all the crews, was asked what the hell they thought of any of it.

Now the WhatsApp groups were lighting up, as they always did when the company made a deal that would define everyone's fate before most had even finished their coffee. From Heathrow, from Ramsgate, from Vilnius, from the battered MacBooks of a hundred overnight crews in airport hotels with rattling windows and thin coffee, came a chorus of disbelief.

"Well, we're a Boeing airline now. Better brush up on the old 'tail strike on take-off' routine."

"Does anyone know if the 737 MAX can actually reach New York from Reykjavik with a full load and headwinds, or do we just carry extra prayer mats?"

"If we're flying 'American' jets, can we ask for American pay scales?"

James, though, simply stared at the television as the pundits, the self-appointed aviation analysts, and the parade of retired general managers took turns explaining the new world order. None of them, he thought, had ever had to face a ramp check at 0400 in a freezing wind, or argue with a Customs agent over the spelling of a Lithuanian engineer's name on a transit visa, or explain to a crew in a remote hotel in El Paso why their duty pay was still being "processed" by payroll in Riga.

"That's if what Roger said isn't true," one captain said to the one who'd joked about tail strikes, leaning back in his chair with the weary confidence of a man who had survived more airline restructurings than he cared to count. "He reckons those Maxes aren't even for us."

James looked at Roger, the Sprint Max First Officer who had been mid-sentence when the room had gone quiet again, and raised an eyebrow.

"Go on," James said. "Finish the thought."

Roger shrugged, the movement economical, professional—years of airline life distilled into a gesture that meant I've seen things. "I've got a mate at Boeing Commercial Sales. Drinks buddy from before he jumped ship. Says the order's real enough, but the delivery slots aren't. Not for years. And they're not badged Sprint. They're going to a 'strategic partner'."

"Define partner," someone said from the back.

Roger smiled thinly. "Oman Air. Our overlords."

There was a long, low exhale in the crew room, the collective sigh of people who'd spent careers living with the consequences of distant deals made by men in better suits. James, ever the observer, found himself watching Roger rather than the television.

Roger's face, lean and sharp beneath a Virgin Atlantic baseball cap he wore out of spite, was creased in a smile that didn't reach his eyes. "It's the Omanis, lads. That's what my mate says. These fifty Maxes will be routed via Muscat, rebadged for Oman Air. Sprint gets goodwill. Boeing gets the headlines. Trump gets to claim a British airline 'bought American.' And we—" he gestured around the crew room, "—we get another month without the feds up our arses."

Someone whistled. Another shook their head, but not in surprise—just in that slow, sad recognition that comes with knowing you've seen the trick before. Always a quid pro quo. Always a cost.

"Clever," said the wiry New Englander, now clearly warming to the role of unofficial cynic-in-chief. "But don't they know the FAA inspectors can count? They'll know if not one of those Maxes ever sees a JFK slot in anger."

Roger shrugged again. "Since when did reality have anything to do with politics? What matters is the contract signing. Press. Jobs. The rest's accounting. Sprint gets to keep AmericanoAir in the air. Oman gets new jets. Anyway, it's the first year of his Presidency, so he needs a win he can point to without having to explain it twice.

James let that settle. The truth of it felt depressingly plausible. Politics had always loved aviation because it looked solid and tangible on paper—aircraft orders, factory jobs, routes drawn on maps—yet the reality was fluid, leased, deferred, rebadged, shifted between jurisdictions with the flick of a pen and a change of registration. Fifty Boeing 737 Maxes might never see an AmericanoAir gate, but the headline would endure. Optics mattered. Metal less so.

The CNN anchor was now deep into speculation, flanked by a former DOT official and a defence analyst who seemed baffled to be talking about airlines rather than aircraft carriers. James tuned them out. Around him, the crew room had resumed motion, like a cabin after unexpected turbulence—low voices, sardonic laughter, the clatter of phones against tables as rosters were checked and rechecked, as if sheer vigilance might ward off whatever came next.

A buzz from his pocket. Sprint Ops. Not a call—yet—but a notification, flagged urgent. He didn't open it immediately. He'd learned, over the years, that bad news rarely improved with haste. Instead, he stood, stretched his back, and wandered to the window that overlooked the ramp.

Outside, JFK was doing what it always did: swallowing aircraft whole, spitting them back out again with mechanical indifference. A JetBlue A220 rolled past in powder-blue calm. An Emirates A380 loomed in the distance, arrogant and serene. Closer in, two AmericanoAir A321neos sat at adjacent gates, tails gleaming under the August sun, Stars and Stripes vivid against the concrete. They looked, James thought, absurdly patriotic—like props from a campaign rally rather than working machines flown by people who'd rather politics stayed firmly on the ground.

James watched the two AmericanoAir aircraft for a long moment, letting the hum of the ramp seep into him. He'd always found airports grounding in moments like this— not comforting, exactly, but clarifying. Politics could rage on screens and in boardrooms, but out here, aluminium still needed fuel, tyres still needed air, and pilots still needed to turn up sober, legal, and vaguely rested. The illusion of control lay in that repetition.

Behind him, the Sprint Ops notification chimed again. This time, he opened it.

SPRINT OPS – URGENT CREW NOTICE

Effective immediately, all AmericanoAir and Sprint US flight crew are requested to attend a mandatory briefing prior to next duty. Briefings will be conducted via Teams. Further guidance to follow.

James snorted quietly. Mandatory briefings were never good news. They were where corporate language went to launder bad decisions into something that sounded collaborative. He slipped the phone back into his pocket and turned as the crew room door swung open again.

The crew room door swung open with a hydraulic sigh, admitting a blast of recycled terminal air and a knot of fresh arrivals—two cabin crew still in coats despite the August heat, a dispatcher clutching a tablet like a flotation device, and a junior First Officer whose expression suggested he'd just read something on his phone that had permanently altered his blood pressure.

"Teams invite just dropped," the FO announced to nobody in particular, as if confirming a rumour rather than delivering news. "Mandatory. All flight crew. Thirty minutes."

A groan rippled through the room, the sort of low, communal sound airline people made when confronted with the inevitable. Thirty minutes was optimistic. Thirty minutes meant someone, somewhere, thought this could be wrapped up neatly. James doubted it.

He took his seat again, the vinyl chair squeaking in protest, and finally opened the Ops message thread properly. More detail had already begun to trickle in, each new line of text as carefully neutral as a NOTAM.

Briefing will cover regulatory developments, fleet strategy alignment, and operational continuity measures.

Fleet strategy alignment. James almost laughed. That phrase alone could keep an entire consulting firm in business for a year.

Around him, people were already rearranging themselves instinctively—finding sockets, angling screens, pulling on headsets that had long since lost any claim to hygiene. A few drifted out into the corridor, seeking better Wi-Fi or weaker supervision. Someone near the back had started a running commentary in a WhatsApp group titled, with admirable understatement, *Sprint: What the Actual*.

James watched them with the detached affection of a man who had spent most of his adult life in rooms just like this one. Different airlines, different logos on the lanyards, but always the same choreography when corporate gravity shifted: the jokes first, then the speculation, then the slow, dawning realisation that whatever had been decided was already done.

His phone buzzed again. This time it was a direct message.

Marnie Shaw: *You watching the circus?*

James Hart: *Front row seats.*

Marnie Shaw: *Brace yourself. Legal, Fleet, and Group Strategy all dialling in. Cameras optional, but "strongly encouraged".*

James snorted. Cameras optional was corporate for we'll remember who didn't turn theirs on.

The Teams chime sounded across the room in staggered waves as invites were accepted. Screens bloomed into life, filling with the familiar grid of faces: some sharp and well-lit from home offices with tasteful art; others grainy and backlit from hotel rooms, crew lounges, or the backs of crew buses. Names flickered beneath them—Ops East, Fleet Planning, Legal UK, Group Strategy, HR Business Partner—until the grid looked less like a meeting and more like a census.

James clicked in, camera off for now, audio muted. He leaned back and watched.

At the centre of the grid, inevitably, was Jeff Young.

The Sprint Group CEO looked… tired. Not haggard, exactly, but worn in that particular way men did when they'd spent the last fortnight oscillating between crisis calls, hostile interviews, and lawyers who charged by the syllable. His hair was immaculate, his tie perfectly knotted, but the spark—the evangelical confidence that had powered Sprint's improbable expansion—was muted, replaced by something harder and more guarded.

Beside him sat Francesca "Frankie" Mendes, expression composed, posture ramrod straight. She looked less tired than Jeff, but more coiled, like someone who'd spent days fighting fires and nights anticipating the next one.

To Jeff's other side, a man James didn't recognise— silver-haired, expensive glasses, the faintly abstracted air of someone who spoke fluent balance sheet—was labelled *Group Strategy – External Advisor*. That, James suspected, was code for the person who'd actually written the quid pro quo.

"Good afternoon, everyone," Jeff began, voice smooth but carrying an edge that betrayed how much effort it was costing him. "Thank you for joining at short notice. I know many of you are on duty, on rest, or somewhere in between, so we'll aim to keep this focused."

A few cameras flicked on. Others stayed dark.

"As you will have seen," Jeff continued, "the President has announced the outcome of ongoing discussions between Sprint Group, the US administration, and our European partners. I want to be absolutely clear from the outset: this agreement secures the continued operation of AmericanoAir and Sprint US. It removes the immediate regulatory pressures we've all been feeling, and it gives us breathing space."

Breathing space. James clocked the phrase. Not stability. Not certainty. Space.

"There's been a lot of noise," Jeff went on, "and some understandable concern. So today is about clarity— what's changing, what isn't, and what it means for you."

The Group Strategy advisor leaned forward slightly, as if preparing to translate.

Jeff nodded to him. "I'll hand over to Mark in a moment to cover fleet implications, but first, Frankie will address the regulatory position."

Frankie's camera flicked on. Her face filled one of the larger tiles, sharp and unflinching.

"Thank you, Jeff," she said. "I'll keep this factual."

James appreciated that. When Frankie said she'd keep something factual, it usually meant she'd strip it of any comforting illusions.

"The agreement reached with the US government halts enhanced FAA inspections, DHS secondary actions, and ad hoc enforcement measures against Sprint US and AmericanoAir effective immediately," she said. "It does not remove our obligation to comply with all applicable regulations. Nothing does. But it does restore a baseline of predictability."

Baseline predictability. Another phrase for the lexicon.

"In return," Frankie continued, "Sprint Group has committed to a set of commercial and operational undertakings designed to address US concerns around reciprocity, employment, and supply chains."

Her eyes flicked briefly to Jeff, then back to the camera.

"These undertakings do not affect pilot licensing, crew nationality, or day-to-day operating authority. There is no change to your legal right to work under existing contracts."

A ripple of relief moved through the grid. James felt it even through the screen—the collective unclenching of shoulders.

"What *does* change," Frankie said, "is our long-term fleet planning narrative in the US."

There it was.

She gestured subtly, and Mark—the Group Strategy advisor—took the floor.

"Afternoon," Mark said, with the practised ease of someone who'd briefed ministers and boards in equal measure. "I'll be brief, but I want to dispel a few misconceptions early."

He smiled faintly, the kind of smile that never reached the eyes.

"Yes, the President referenced an order for fifty Boeing 737 MAX aircraft. That order exists. It is binding. It is also not for AmericanoAir. As you know, Sprint is partly owned by the Oman Investment Authority, who also own Oman Air and SalamAir. Now, SalamAir is, like Sprint, an Airbus A320 operator. Oman Air is, however, a Boeing 737 operator. The fifty 737 Maxes will be delivered on Oman Air's books, through a lease vehicle controlled via Sprint Leasing DAC of Ireland. This arrangement—" Mark smiled a little, as if daring anyone to object, "—was proposed by Oman, accepted by Boeing, and blessed by the US administration as a sign of good faith. The President gets a domestic jobs headline. Oman gets new jets. Sprint gets regulatory relief in its biggest growth market. And none of you will have to retrain for a Max unless you fancy a transfer to Muscat."

There was a silence on the call, more profound than before. James took in the various faces, the slack jaws, the raised eyebrows, the careful, calculating stillness of those in management whose job it was to look like they'd known all this for weeks.

Frankie returned to the centre tile. "To summarise: nothing in your flying life changes tomorrow. No forced conversions. No layoffs, redundancies or demotions. Your contracts are protected, your routes secure. This is, as Jeff said, breathing space—purchased with a diplomatic fudge. The price is a lot of signatures, a bit of dignity, and a fleet order that will never touch down in JFK or Dallas."

Someone unmuted: "So the only real quid pro quo is we all get to keep flying?"

A ripple of nervous laughter followed, the sort only airline staff could manage. James almost smiled. He'd known, since his first days flying in Texas, that the secret of aviation survival was learning to laugh at the ground shifting under you.

"Correct," Mark replied, almost gracious. "And, in truth, that's not nothing."

****

CHAPTER 18 – Ooops... They Did It Again

Friday 29th August 2025

The airline industry, James knew, was a fickle thing, with sudden collapses as likely as likely as pop-up thunderstorms over the Rockies. He was reminded of this every time the news cycle shrieked about another failed carrier, but it was something altogether different to witness, up close, the particular choreography of disaster—where the music cut out mid-dance, and everyone realised, with the sort of cold clarity unique to aviation, that there was nowhere left to go but down.

He was standing in the corridor outside Crew Briefing, a battered blue folder of NOTAMs under one arm, as the news bled from the wall-mounted television in the break room.

"SPIRIT AIRLINES DECLARES CHAPTER 11 BANKRUPTCY PROTECTION. All flights to remain operational while restructuring efforts are underway."

The chyron rolled endlessly, a staccato warning, yellow and angry. James knew what that meant, even before the junior cabin crew began trading anxious looks, their mobile phones erupting in pings and alerts like the cockpit's ECAM in a rapid-fire emergency. In every airline break room in America, someone was standing just as James was—staring at a future unspooling with grim predictability. Spirit had only come out of Chapter 11 mere months earlier, and now, thanks to Sprint, it had collapsed with the gusto of a drunken Texan on a barstool.

This time, there would be no heroics, no private equity cavalry riding in to patch up the yellow planes with sticky tape and optimism. This time, James thought, the collapse had the inevitability of a controlled flight into terrain: slow at first, then terrifyingly fast, all alarms and chaos as the ground rushed up to meet you.

He watched as the CNN anchor moved on, the story shifting to scenes of stranded passengers at Fort Lauderdale and Dallas, all clutching discount suitcases and dayglo boarding passes, faces contorted in confusion and anger. Someone had left the volume high enough that he caught the words, "…could trigger a wave of industry consolidation…" before the scene switched to a harried-looking 'aviation expert' on a split-screen.

Behind him, the crew room hummed with a brittle, nervous energy. Flight attendants, some in AmericanoAir and Sprint navy blue, others in the ghostly green and yellow of Spirit, mingled in tense, whispered knots. James, ever the outsider, watched as alliances were recalibrated and little battlegrounds of rumour erupted between groups.

Suddenly his phone sounded the notification of the Sprint app, not the staffing one, but the public one where tickets and access to the SprintReels function, a clone of the ReelShort videos app, pinged up breaking alerts in the same digital font they used for boarding passes.

"Trapped with Spirit? Fly with Sprint for just a dollar in our Flash Sale. T&Cs apply."*

James scrolled through the notification, thumb flicking over the garish banner: a grinning, cartoonish cabin crew—neither recognisably Sprint nor Spirit, but an uncanny digital composite—waving a plastic boarding card at a plane which, in its pixelated enthusiasm, looked half Ryanair and half something Soviet. The asterisk after the dollar was as menacing as a flight manual footnote— promising nothing, warning of everything.

Before he could dwell, his own crew began to coalesce around him: Trent Pearson, a Boston native who was his First Officer for the day of transcontinental runs, was already in full uniform, tie slightly askew, scrolling furiously on his own phone. He looked up, caught James's eye, and pulled a face that managed to combine gallows humour and outright fear.

"Looks like I got out in time," the young man said, waving the device. "MSNBC say that Spirit will still be operating at its Chapter 11 bankruptcy protection, not Chapter 7, so they say that the banana bus will still be in the air for now. Funny how we turn us with the European model, and then a few weeks later, Spirit go back into Chapter 11 and decide to say "Oh, we might be cutting crew pay by 30 percent and parking half the fleet." He shook his head, the bitterness in his voice unmistakable. "My old roommate's still flying for them—says he hasn't slept in three days. Their WhatsApp group's all doom and memes. They've got some flying scheduled, but most of the bases are locked out."

James nodded, feeling the strange kinship of aviators everywhere—rivalry dissolved at the edge of disaster. He remembered the last time he'd watched an airline collapse, the death spiral of Monarch back in Europe, and how the staff had walked out into dawn carrying company-issue Samsonite, all looking like survivors from a shipwreck. "You know," he said quietly, "this isn't even the bad part yet. That'll come in about twelve hours, when the ops teams start playing musical chairs with all the slots and planes. And when the media calls it 'orderly', you'll know it's anything but."

Trent gave a half-laugh. "They'll all blame French ATC by this afternoon."

"Hey, that's our Brit cousins who blame the French for everything," a voice from over the other end of the corridor, Tanya Ramirez, one of the AmericanoAir pursers who had been around long enough to remember when Frontier, Spirit, and JetBlue all took turns pretending they were about to rule the world. She was leaning against the door of the briefing room, arms folded, lips painted a defiant red that clashed beautifully with the navy-blue cabin uniform.

Tanya kicked herself off the doorframe, heels clicking sharply against the linoleum as she joined them. Unlike most pursers, who carried themselves with the fatigued stoicism of people constantly one disruption away from a grievance filing, Tanya had a sort of unflappable glamour that came from surviving three airline mergers, two airline collapses, and a brief, ill-advised stint as a recruitment consultant. When Tanya spoke, people listened—not because she was senior, but because she sounded like she'd seen the future and wasn't impressed.

"Everyone's blaming everyone except themselves," she said breezily, her earrings swaying as she approached. "Spirit blames Sprint for undercutting them, Sprint blames the free market for Spirit's demise, Wall Street is blaming President Trump for the start of deregulation of the FAA in his second term, and the unions are blaming Wall Street for not supporting Spirit and Biden for blocking the merger between Spirit and JetBlue. It's musical chairs with lawsuits now, not seats. You just know, in the end, the passengers will get stuck with the bill. That, and us lot, picking up their 'displaced' gold members at the gate like lost puppies." She sighed, smoothing an imaginary crease on her skirt, her lacquered composure belying the tension in her jaw. "You know, I was walking through the terminal just now, and you know the Irish station manager here at here at Terminal C? He was charging Spirit pax who wanted to rebook on Sprint nearly $300 for a flight to Atlanta. Three hundred dollars! I mean, I knew the British HQ lot was ex Ryanair, easyJet and Wizz, but I didn't expect them to be so brazen about it. Three hundred for a seat on a 7am Sprint to Atlanta. And then he charged nearly $200 for a bag because apparently it was overweight by 5 kilos. I mean, kilos? Surely HQ in Delaware would insist on insist on pounds, surely? But no, 'company policy is metric now'. The poor sods barely knew which queue to join, let alone how much their suitcase weighed. And the station manager just shrugs, points at his phone and says, 'That's what it says on the app. Want to fly or not?' The whole thing's a farce. Corporate must be loving it—squeeze every last penny out before the regulators catch up."

James was not sure which was more grotesque: the sheer speed with which the vultures began to circle, or the grinning efficiency of those tasked with picking the bones clean. He was watching it in real time. As Tanya spoke, he half-imagined the boardrooms in London and Wilmington were all linked by a single red phone, flashing with opportunity. Nowhere was the theatre of capitalism more brazen than in the corridors of a failing airport terminal.

He set down his NOTAM folder on the ledge by the window, glancing out over the ramp. Even at this early hour, Fort Lauderdale's apron was already a kaleidoscope of liveries. The Sprint navy blue fuselages with the Stars and Stripes on it sat, smug as ever, alongside the fading Spirit jets—one, parked up and sealed with red tape on the airstairs, its APU whining in pointless defiance. Next to it, a Delta 737 loaded children, parents, and the business-casual stragglers of a broken Friday. Even the air seemed thick with apprehension and sweat.

He felt, absurdly, like he was standing at the edge of an archaeological dig. This was the way airlines died, not with the spectacular carnage of the old days—flights abandoned at far-flung outstations, staff breaking down in tears on live TV—but with a series of small indignities. Luggage abandoned on carousels. Staff not knowing who paid them anymore. The cheap boarding passes, spat out from dying printers, now worthless except as souvenirs of someone's failed dream.

"Did you hear," Tanya went on, "the rumour that Sprint's going to buy out the A320neo leases Spirit can't afford? Straight from the top. Jeff Young's people are already at the lessor's office in Miami, waving contracts. I'll bet you five dollars half the Spirit staff end up in Sprint uniforms by next month. That or Uber Eats lanyards."

One of the other Sprint First Officers chuckled, and, in a British accent, said, "Yeah, now you know how EASA feel. Fernando Costas is ex Ryanair legal, so when Fernando sees an aircraft with the paint still wet, he's already got a leasing term sheet drafted and a Maltese AOC on speed-dial." There was a ripple of weary laughter—a kind bred not of joy, but of exhausted, gallows amusement.

James glanced at the new arrival: Alistair Wright, a Londoner on secondment, whose dry commentary had found ready currency on both sides of the Atlantic. Alistair had the look of a man who had checked in at a Holiday Inn, been served by the Grim Reaper at reception, and decided to make the best of it with the breakfast buffet.

"Anyway lads," Alistair said, chuckling. "have any of you lot tried the 28 min turns that Sprint's just put on the roster for September?" Alistair's question, though delivered with a smirk, elicited groans from those who knew: the so-called "Euro-Turns," a legacy of Sprint's rapid expansion and relentless Ryanairification, were already infamous. "It's a piece of piss. I mean, I've done them loads while back home and its as mad here as it is in Stansted."

"Da, is good," an Estonian Captain sitting in the corner said with a grin. "I look forward to it."

"Wait, 28 minute turnarounds?" Trent spluttered, as if the concept had personally affronted him. "Is that even legal here? Didn't the FAA publish a thing after the Southwest ground handling scandal last year? Something about 'realistic safety buffers'?"

Alistair raised his eyebrows. "My dear boy, legality is for those who can afford to pay the fines. Jeff Young's counting on the fact that the regulators are about as awake as a Friday afternoon flight to Boise. Anyway, with your MAGA cult leader running the White House, Musky boy having gutted the NTSB's budget for 'efficiency,' and the FAA turning a blind eye to anything with an American flag painted on the tail, it's a free-for-all. Besides," he went on, "it's not about what's possible—it's about what Sprint's PR can plausibly blame on 'legacy systems' or 'unexpected operational demand.' They'll get away with it until someone gets hurt, and even then, they'll just blame a rogue ground handler from Lagos or a 'systems outage' in Hyderabad. Anyway, if ALPA complain... well, Sprint have already broke BALPA by installing a company union back home, so if you Yanks don't fall in line, they'll just swap you out for some Lithuanian or Portuguese wet-lease crew and call it diversity. It's all one big rotating raffle now, isn't it?"

A burst of cynical laughter swept the corridor. Tanya shook her head, but the edge in her smile softened. The crackle of public address announcements echoed faintly from the concourse—"Final boarding for Sprint 2284 to Dallas, all remaining passengers proceed immediately to Gate 32"—as James checked his watch and noted their own sign-in time was fast approaching.

Yet the break room was in no rush to resume business as usual. Every airline crew knew that, on a day like this, routines were for comfort only; the news could change in an instant, and the sudden shudder of a phone in one's pocket could mean a rescheduled flight, a cancelled sector, a sudden redundancy. That was the game: always flying with one eye on the exits, the other on the next opportunity.

Fortunately, as it was all Sprint crews in the room, as, by way of near enough trading for every slot that they could run, no one had to fear a last-second Spirit manager ordering them back to work, or the dread tap on the shoulder from some glassy-eyed HR rep. The room had the slightly febrile air of an airline crew in holding pattern, all bravado undercut by a sharp edge of dread. On another day, these same faces would be comparing outstation horror stories or teasing the latest round of uniform updates. Today, the banter had teeth.

Trent, after a moment, tucked his phone away and tried for nonchalance. "Suppose we should at least get the pre-flight out of the way. Otherwise Ops'll have us on the next Laredo shuttle." But his voice was thin, his eyes scanning the departure monitor as if expecting the news to spread, virus-like, to their own operation.

James nodded, though he knew every flight today would carry the taste of someone else's misfortune. "Come on, let's get it over with." He tried to sound reassuring, but it came out flat. The sense of witnessing something momentous, even historic, was growing. It was not a feeling of triumph or opportunity—rather the sombre realisation that aviation, in its modern form, was a zero-sum game. Someone's gain was always someone else's sudden loss.

They moved through the crew corridor, the world outside the terminal a swamp of Florida humidity. In the airside glass tunnels, groups of passengers drifted, still clutching boarding passes that no longer matched the tail numbers on their aircraft. Every so often, an announcement from the PA system—its accent oscillating between American and oddly British—reminded everyone that "due to operational changes, your flight may depart from a different gate." The code, James knew, for 'the schedule's gone to hell.'

Past the doors, airside security was a blur of yellow tabards and pink-faced supervisors. Luggage piled up like the aftermath of a coach party in Marbella. Spirit crew, the unlucky ones still rostered, stood in small groups near the coffee bar, trying to look invisible. Some wore the haunted look of people whose careers had just been made redundant by app notification. Others feigned indifference, talking too loudly, mugs of watery coffee clutched as talismans.

"We are sorry to announce that the 11:01 Sprint US service to Dallas will be delayed by approximately 56 minutes. This is due to Air Traffic Control Restrictions in Fr... sorry, ATC Restrictions in Florida, not France, Florida..."

The Tannoy's voice, an Irish lilt strained through the static of an overworked PA system, faltered as if even it was exhausted by the morning's mounting absurdities.

"…sorry, ATC restrictions in Florida, not France, Florida. Passengers are advised to remain in the gate area for further updates."

A ragged cheer rose from a cluster of Sprint flight attendants nearby, half-mocking, half-relieved. Nothing united a terminal quite like an announcement that blamed Florida rather than France. A few Spirit crew members — their yellow uniforms now almost sepia with accumulated despair — offered weak smiles before returning to their purgatorial waiting.

James scrubbed a hand over his jaw. Florida ATC restrictions. That old chestnut. As if the whole state had decided to take a lie-in. In truth, the congestion was probably caused by Spirit's meltdown, Sprint's opportunistic slot-snatching, Delta's determination to run forty-seven flights out of the same taxiway, and the fact that half the ground staff across Broward County were currently in a staffroom Googling "what does Chapter 11 mean for my job". The fact that French ATC was almost blamed was probably, James knew, due to how Sprint in the UK and EU blamed French ATC for everything from rain delays at Newcastle to missing sandwiches on the Amsterdam shuttle. Old habits died hard, and in the aviation world, scapegoats were international currency.

As James and Trent made their way through the glass tunnel, they caught the tail end of a conversation between two ground handlers, both of whom looked like they had slept in their high-vis vests. One was on the phone, muttering rapidly about "Spirit bag tags" and "last-minute Sprint rebookings," while the other, a middle-aged woman with a badge that read "Jackie—Ramp Lead," was alternately reassuring and scolding a trio of dazed passengers who had wandered airside looking for a Spirit gate that now existed only on the digital screens.

The terminal had become a living diorama of aviation failure. Screens blinked between cancelled and delayed, the letters SPRINT, DELTA, and SPIRIT flashing in dizzying alternation, like someone had left a child alone with the scheduler's keyboard. Over at Gate 17, a woman in a Spirit uniform, eyes rimmed with mascara and panic, was giving a performance worthy of any Broadway matinee—fists clenched, voice wobbling, telling a group of passengers that "your flight is… well, actually, I don't know what your flight is."

"I demand to speak to your manager!" James heard as he saw a woman approach a Sprint counter, and he nodded grimly. The phrase was as much a feature of modern aviation as turbulence or gate changes, a last-ditch attempt to summon authority from the chaos. Today, though, James doubted even the managers knew what to say. The rows of desks—some plastered with Sprint logos, others with haphazardly taped-over Spirit branding—were being manned by a shifting cast of ground staff, some familiar, some borrowed from who-knew-where, all moving with that desperate briskness of people pretending to be in charge.

The passengers were a cross-section of American chaos: retirees in matching tracksuits, families juggling Disney-themed luggage, businesspeople clutching phones and laptops with white-knuckled determination, and the odd budget traveller who looked as if they'd wandered into the terminal by accident. All of them, James knew, were united now by confusion. In moments like this, airlines lost their individuality; everyone was simply part of the same big, shambolic parade.

Trent, glancing sidelong at James, murmured, "You ever think, maybe, we should've done something normal? Banker, dentist, goat herder in Vermont? There's dignity in goat herding. You never have to explain to a goat why his bag's in Denver and his flight's been cancelled."

James snorted, the old joke making a welcome appearance. "Goats, unlike passengers, can't post on Twitter. Or threaten to sue. You know the Euro lot call passengers on Sprint 'Self Loading Freight', as they just pay the fees, board and then shut up and sit down. They've got the right idea."

They reached the gate for their own flight, AmericanoAir 417 to Atlanta, scheduled for an 11:45 pushback that everyone already knew was fantasy.

"No, I've already told you lot that the gate doesn't open for another 5 minutes," the gate agent said, and James knew, as it was one of the remote stands, the boarding process would be a logistical nightmare—buses, stairs, and a scramble across the tarmac in the oppressive Florida heat. The gate agent, a wiry man with a Sprint badge that looked suspiciously new, was already fending off a small knot of passengers waving boarding passes like battle flags. His voice, strained but resolute, carried the universal tone of someone who'd been explaining the unexplainable for hours.

"Five minutes, folks, five minutes," he repeated, holding up a hand as if to physically block their advance. "We're waiting on the bus from Ops, and the aircraft's still being turned. Please, just stay seated until we call zones."

James exchanged a glance with Trent, who muttered, "Zones? What is this, Delta? We're Sprint's ugly cousin. The only zones are those who need pre-boarding and those mugs who paid for priority boarding but still get stuck behind a pram the size of a Range Rover."

James gave a tight smile, the kind that didn't quite reach his eyes. He was used to the chaos—hell, he'd been forged in it, from his USAF days dodging SAMs over Basra to now, flying for AmericanoAir, the company that Sprint ran their operations through. But today felt different. The air was thicker, the stakes sharper. Spirit's collapse wasn't just a headline; it was a warning shot across the bow of every low-cost carrier, including AmericanoAir, which, despite its shiny new A321LRs and Jeff Young's relentless PR blitz, was still a patchwork operation skating on the edge of viability.

"Right, we need to get to the stand, so we'd better get moving," James said, his voice steady but carrying the weight of a man who knew the day was about to get worse. He adjusted the folder under his arm, the NOTAMs inside already feeling like relics of a simpler time when the biggest worry was a runway closure or a bird strike. Trent nodded, falling into step beside him, their polished shoes clicking in unison against the linoleum. Tanya followed, her heels adding a sharper, more deliberate rhythm, as if she were marching into battle rather than a pre-flight briefing.

The gate area for AmericanoAir 417 was a microcosm of the terminal's chaos. Passengers milled about, some clutching coffee cups from a nearby Dunkin' Donuts, others staring at their phones with the glazed intensity of people refreshing flight statuses. A young couple with a toddler in a Mickey Mouse backpack were arguing in hushed tones about whether they should rebook with Delta, while an older man in a crumpled blazer was loudly explaining to no one in particular that he'd "flown Pan Am in the '70s, and this would never have happened." James caught Tanya's eye, and she gave a subtle roll of hers, a silent agreement that every airport had its resident nostalgist, forever chasing the ghost of a golden age that never really existed.

The gate agent, still fending off the impatient crowd, spotted James and Trent approaching and waved them through with a relieved nod. "Captain Hart, right? Stand's ready, but the bus is stuck behind an inbound Spirit. I can get the Terminal Ops guys to get a van to take you out if you want to get set up?"

"Thanks," James replied, keeping his tone neutral. He didn't envy the gate agent, who was clearly new to the Sprint/AmericanoAir hybrid operation and already looked like he'd aged a decade in a single shift. The man's badge read "Carlos—Gate Ops," and his eyes had the haunted sheen of someone who'd been screamed at in three languages before breakfast.

As they moved through the jet bridge access door, Tanya leaned in, her voice low. "You know, I give Carlos here about two weeks before he's either running the show or running for the hills. Poor sod's got no idea what he's signed up for."

James grunted in agreement. "He'll learn. Or he won't. That's the Sprint way."

They stepped out of the air-conditioned terminal into the swampy heat of the Fort Lauderdale apron, where the air smelled of jet fuel, rubber, and the faint tang of desperation. The tarmac stretched out before them, a shimmering expanse dotted with aircraft in various stages of disarray. A Sprint A320neo, its navy-blue livery gleaming with corporate smugness, was being towed to a nearby stand, while a Spirit A321 sat forlornly at the edge of the apron, its yellow paint faded to a sickly mustard under the Florida sun. Ground crews in high-vis vests darted between vehicles, their radios crackling with urgent, half-intelligible instructions. Somewhere in the distance, a baggage cart had overturned, spilling suitcases like the aftermath of a piñata gone wrong.

James squinted against the glare, his eyes scanning the stand where their own aircraft—an AmericanoAir A321LR, tail number N457RA—waited. It was one of the newer additions to the fleet, a shiny beast that Jeff Young had touted as "the future of transcontinental low-cost travel" in a press release that read like it had been written by a man high on his own hype. The aircraft looked pristine, its red-white-and-blue livery catching the light, but James knew better than to trust appearances. Sprint's rapid expansion had stretched maintenance schedules thin, and he'd already caught whispers of deferred defects and logbooks that were more creative fiction than fact. Of course, those were rumours, as he had flew a A320 to

Mobile International, where Sprint's MRO joint venture with Airbus was based, and seen firsthand the meticulous care taken with their fleet. Still, in the world of low-cost carriers, where every penny was pinched until it screamed, vigilance was a pilot's best friend.

The van pulled up, a battered white Ford with "Sprint Ops" stencilled on the side in peeling letters. The driver, a wiry man with a sunburned neck and a name tag reading "Ricky," gave them a curt nod. "Hop in, folks. Gotta get you to the stand before this whole place turns into a car boot sale."

James slid into the front passenger seat, Trent and Tanya piling into the back with the practiced efficiency of crew who'd done this dance a thousand times. The van smelled of stale coffee and engine grease, and the dashboard was a museum of half-empty water bottles and crumpled Ops memos. Ricky gunned the engine, weaving through the chaos of the apron with the reckless precision of someone who'd long since stopped caring about near-misses.

"Spirit's really done it this time, huh?" Ricky said, glancing at James as he swerved around a slow-moving fuel truck. "Thank goodness it's Chapter 11 which means they can still operate while they reorganise, and not Chapter 7 where it's game over, planes grounded, and everyone's out of a job. Still, it's a mess. Heard they're already pulling aircraft off the ramp and sending them to Tucson for storage. Tucson! That's the aviation graveyard, man. Once your plane's parked there, it's not coming back unless it's for scrap."

James nodded, his eyes fixed on the chaos unfolding outside the van's grimy windows. "It's not just Spirit," he said, voice low but steady. "This is a domino effect. Sprint's grabbing slots and leases, but they're stretching themselves thin. You can't run a fleet of 600 Airbuses with a Ryanair playbook in the UK and nearly 300 here and expect it to hold forever. Something's got to give."

Ricky snorted, a sound that carried the weight of a man who'd seen too many airline promises turn to ash. "Yeah, well, it's the Omani's, ain't it?"

"Omanis?" Trent asked, and James turned to glance at Trent, catching the confusion on his First Officer's face. The van lurched slightly as Ricky dodged a stray baggage cart, his hands steady on the wheel despite the conversational detour.

"Yeah, the Omanis," Ricky repeated, as if it were the most obvious thing in the world. "Sprint's got that shadowy Omani trade union backing them, right? The one that's basically a front for their sovereign wealth fund. That's how they keep the cash flowing and the regulators off their backs. You think Jeff Young's got that kind of clout on his own? Nah, mate, it's Muscat pulling the strings. They've got their fingers in everything—aircraft leases, slots, even the new MRO in Mobile. Why do you think we're flying these shiny new A321LRs while Spirit's parking theirs in the desert? It's not just market savvy; it's deep pockets and deeper politics."

James raised an eyebrow but said nothing. Ricky's theory wasn't new—aviation was rife with whispers about Sprint's financial backers—but hearing it laid out so bluntly, in the middle of a sweltering Fort Lauderdale apron, gave it a certain weight. The Omani connection had been a topic of crew room speculation for months, ever since Sprint's inexplicable ability to snatch up Spirit's slots and leases became headline news. The trade union angle, though, was a particularly spicy bit of gossip, one that suggested Sprint's corporate structure was less a business model and more a geopolitical chess game.

Trent, still processing, leaned forward, his elbows resting on the back of James's seat. "Wait, so you're saying Sprint's basically a front for some Middle Eastern cash? That's… wild. I thought it was just Jeff Young being a Ryanair wannabe with better PR."

"Nah, he's ex easyJet, you know, that orange lot in Britain. His lawyer and finance guy in Britain, they're the former Ryanair lot, though—Fernando Costas and his crew, straight out of Dublin's legal shark tank. But yeah, the Omanis are the ones with the real muscle. They've got the cash to keep Sprint's wheels turning while everyone else is scrambling for scraps." Ricky's voice carried a mix of admiration and disdain, the kind of tone reserved for someone who'd seen the sausage factory and knew exactly how the meat got ground. "You heard one of the kids has got one of those new-fangled licences, that multiple thingy?"

Ricky's words hung in the van like the humidity outside, a mix of conspiracy and hard truth that James couldn't entirely dismiss. The Omani angle wasn't just crew-room gossip—it had been whispered in the margins of industry briefings, hinted at in the fine print of leasing agreements, and speculated over in WhatsApp groups that buzzed with the kind of insider knowledge only pilots and ground staff could muster. Sprint's meteoric rise, from a scrappy Manston-based ULCC to a transatlantic juggernaut with nearly 900 aircraft across two continents, had always felt too smooth, too perfectly timed. Jeff Young's brash charisma and ex-easyJet pedigree explained the PR blitz, but the money? That was another story, one written in the shadows of Muscat boardrooms and Delaware shell companies.

James shifted in his seat, the NOTAM folder digging into his side as the van jolted over a seam in the tarmac. "Multiple thingy?" he asked, glancing at Ricky, who was now grinning like a man who'd just let slip a juicy secret.

"Yeah, you know, one of them new licences," Ricky said, his eyes flicking to the rearview mirror to catch Trent's reaction. "The kid—some young FO out of the Sprint Europe operation, think his name's Adam or something, got one of those training things, MPL I think it was."

"MPL? Multi-crew Pilot Licence?" James asked, his tone measured but curious. He'd heard of the MPL, a relatively new training pathway that had stirred controversy in European aviation circles for its streamlined approach to getting pilots into the right seat. It was designed for rapid integration into multi-crew operations, often tailored to specific airlines, but it had its critics—those who argued it churned out "systems managers" rather than stick-and-rudder aviators. The idea that Sprint was dipping its toes into MPL waters wasn't surprising, but hearing it confirmed in the back of a rattling Ops van added a layer of gritty realism to the rumour.

"Yeah, they've got a whole factory in Lithuania. Sprint Europe has loads of 'em, and some of the kids shipped here have them," Ricky said with a shrug, as if the concept of an airline running its own pilot factory was as mundane as a baggage belt breakdown. "They're churning out FOs faster than you can say 'cabin secure.' Cheap, too. Word is, the Omanis bankroll the training, and in return, the kids sign contracts that lock them in for years. Like indentured servitude, but with better uniforms and a view from 35,000 feet."

James knew that the FAA required 1,500 hours of flight time for an Airline Transport Pilot (ATP) certificate, a far cry from the MPL's accelerated path, which could see pilots in the right seat with as little as 240 hours, heavily weighted toward simulator time. The FAA's reluctance to fully embrace the MPL had been a sticking point in US aviation, but Sprint's transatlantic ambitions—and their knack for exploiting regulatory grey zones—suggested they were finding workarounds. Perhaps through wet leases, or by funnelling MPL pilots through their European AOCs before transitioning them to FAA-validated credentials. It was the kind of legal acrobatics Fernando Costas, Sprint's ex-Ryanair legal eagle, was born to execute.

Trent, still leaning forward, shook his head in disbelief. "So, what, they're just shipping European kids with MPLs over here to fly A321s? That's… I mean, I've got 3,000 hours, and I'm still sweating line checks. These guys are barely out of flight school!"

Ricky chuckled, swerving the van around a slow-moving catering truck. "Welcome to Sprint, kid. It's not about hours; it's about cost. You think Jeff Young cares if his FOs can hand-fly a raw-data ILS in a crosswind? Nah, he wants butts in seats—pilots and passengers. The Omanis pay for the training, Sprint gets cheap labour, and the regulators look the other way because, well, who's got time to audit a 900-aircraft fleet when the FAA's budget's been slashed to ribbons? There again remember when Jeff called the President a terrorist on live television?" Ricky's grin widened, relishing the memory of Jeff Young's BBC outburst that had set the aviation world alight. "That's the kind of balls you need to pull this off. Call the President a nutter, then turn around and lease fifty A320neos before the ink's dry on the last deal. Respect, in a twisted sort of way."

James stayed silent, his mind turning over the implications. The MPL pipeline, if true, was a classic Sprint move—ruthlessly efficient, questionably ethical, and cloaked in just enough legal plausibility to keep the regulators at bay. It explained the influx of young, wide-eyed First Officers he'd noticed in recent months, their accents a mishmash of Eastern Europe and the Home Counties, their logbooks suspiciously light but their simulator proficiency eerily polished. He'd flown with a few—competent, if a bit robotic, their training clearly tailored to Sprint's SOPs rather than the broader art of flying. The thought didn't sit well, but then, little about Sprint's operation did. It was a machine built for profit, not permanence, and James had long since accepted that his role was to keep it airborne, not to question the wiring.

****

CHAPTER 19 – The Paramount+ Penalty Box

Friday 29th August 2025

Atlanta, Georgia, and James knew his next journey was going to be interesting as it was a cross over Kentucky into Indiana, a route that promised not just the usual operational hurdles but the added spice of Sprint's relentless ambition. The flight, AmericanoAir 672 to Indianapolis, was a bread-and-butter domestic hop, but with Sprint's fingerprints all over the operation, nothing was ever as simple as it seemed. The crew briefing had been a whirlwind of last-minute changes—revised slot times, a swapped aircraft, and whispers of yet another Spirit slot grab pushing their departure back by 40 minutes. The gate agent, a harried woman named LaToya with a badge that looked like it had been printed that morning, had warned them of a three quarters full load: 189 passengers, including a group of college football fans already three beers deep and a gaggle of corporate types clutching laptops like life rafts. Add to that the lingering fallout from Spirit's Chapter 11 announcement, and the terminal felt like a pressure cooker with a dodgy valve.

James stood by the gate, his NOTAM folder now tucked into his flight bag, watching the apron through the floor-to-ceiling windows of Hartsfield-Jackson's Terminal C. The tarmac was a hive of activity, with Sprint's navy-blue A321LR—tail number N457RA—being fuelled and loaded under the watchful eye of a ground crew that moved with the frenetic energy of people who knew Ops was breathing down their necks. Nearby, a Delta 757 gleamed in the late summer sun, its silver livery a stark contrast to the faded yellow of a Spirit A320 being towed to a remote stand, its fate uncertain. The scene was a microcosm of the industry's churn: winners and losers, all jockeying for position in a game where the rules kept changing.

The flight from Fort Lauderdale had been an uneventful one, except when in Orlando airspace when a Virgin Atlantic A350 had to declare a minor hydraulic issue, forcing a brief hold over Lake Apopka while ATC sorted the mess. James had handled it with his usual calm, coordinating with Trent and Tanya to keep the cabin settled while he worked the radios. The passengers, blissfully unaware of the temporary chaos, had disembarked in Atlanta with the usual mix of grumbles and gratitude, leaving James and his crew to regroup for the Indianapolis leg. Now, as he scanned the gate area, he felt the familiar weight of responsibility settle over him— not just for the flight, but for navigating the increasingly surreal world of Sprint's transatlantic empire.

Trent Pearson, his First Officer, was already at the gate podium, double-checking the flight plan on his tablet with a furrowed brow. The young Bostonian had a knack for spotting discrepancies in the paperwork, a skill honed during his days at Spirit before he'd jumped ship to AmericanoAir just in time to avoid the latest collapse. "They've got us on a reroute over Chattanooga to avoid some weather building over Nashville," Trent said, glancing up as James approached. "Adds about 15 minutes, but the fuel burn's within limits. Barely. Ops is cutting it fine again."

James nodded, his eyes flicking to the weather radar app on his own phone. A line of thunderstorms was indeed brewing across Tennessee, their angry red and yellow blobs pulsing on the screen like a warning. "As long as we've got enough to hold over Indy if it gets messy," he said, his voice steady but laced with the caution of a pilot who'd seen too many "optimistic" fuel loads turn into nail-biting diversions. "Anything else I should know?"

Trent hesitated, then lowered his voice. "Yeah, uh, we're swapping planes to a 194Y A320 neo with ACTs."

James raised an eyebrow, his hand pausing on the strap of his flight bag. "A 194Y A320neo with ACTs? When did that happen?" The switch from the A321LR to a smaller, denser A320neo wasn't unheard of, but the addition of Auxiliary Centre Tanks (ACTs) suggested Sprint was squeezing every last mile out of the aircraft's range— likely to avoid a tech stop on a later leg. It also meant a tighter cabin, less wiggle room for passengers, and a potential headache for the crew if the load was as rowdy as LaToya had warned.

Trent shrugged, his expression a mix of resignation and mild annoyance. "Ops sent the update while we were grabbing coffee. Apparently, the A321's needed for a last-minute charter to Dallas—something about poaching Spirit's stranded pax. So, we get the neo, tail number N592EL. It's fresh out of Mobile apparently. And yes, 194 seats with 28" pitch in a nation where 41% of the adult population are obese. Good luck to Tanya keeping that lot settled." He flashed a wry grin, but the tension in his eyes betrayed his unease. Sprint's habit of last-minute aircraft swaps was par for the course, but it always carried the risk of cascading problems—mismatched catering, incorrect weight and balance calculations, or, worse, a plane with a logbook full of deferred defects.

"How fresh out of Mobile is it?" James asked, hoping it was a new one and not a few months or years old clunker patched up to look shiny. He'd seen enough of Sprint's "fresh" aircraft to know that Mobile's MRO, while meticulous on paper, sometimes churned out planes with quirks that only revealed themselves at 35,000 feet.

Trent tapped his tablet, pulling up the maintenance log. "Accepted into service this morning by Sprint. Came off the FAL last month, did its test runs, and then straight into B Check for Sprint before it was put on a Mobile International to here this morning. Mobile yesterday. No major snags reported, but you know how that goes—new planes, new gremlins. They've got it loaded with ACTs so when its used on transcons, it can actually make it without a fuel stop, but it's still a tight squeeze for 194 souls. Tanya's already grumbling about the galley space—says it's barely enough for a coffee run, let alone a full service." He paused, then added with a smirk, "And the seats are the Recaro R1s Sprint UK and Europe have been running on their latest A320s—those ultra-slim ones with about as much padding as a yoga mat. Passengers are going to love that."

James let out a low whistle, picturing the cabin layout: 194 seats crammed into an A320neo, with the Recaro R1s offering all the comfort of a park bench. The 28-inch pitch was a bold move, even for Sprint, especially in a country where, as Trent had pointed out, obesity rates meant half the passengers would be spilling into their neighbour's personal space. Tanya Ramirez, their purser, would have her work cut out keeping the peace, especially with a load that included boisterous football fans and stressed-out business travellers. The ACTs, meanwhile, were a classic Sprint gambit—extending the A320's range to compete with longer-haul routes, but at the cost of added weight and complexity. It was the kind of decision that looked brilliant on a spreadsheet in Wilmington but could turn into a nightmare at FL350 if the fuel burn didn't match the projections.

"Alright," James said, adjusting his cap and squaring his shoulders. "Let's get to the aircraft and give it a proper once-over. I want to see those ACTs for myself, and we'll double-check the weight and balance before we sign off. Last thing we need is a surprise when we're dodging thunderstorms over Tennessee." His tone was calm but carried the weight of experience—a pilot who'd learned the hard way that Sprint's optimism often outpaced reality.

Trent nodded, slinging his flight bag over his shoulder. "On it, boss. I'll grab the load sheet from LaToya and meet you at the stand. Tanya's already out there, probably giving the ground crew an earful about the catering." He flashed another grin, but it was tinged with the same wary anticipation James felt. They both knew the day was shaping up to be one of those where every decision would feel like a tightrope walk.

As they stepped out of the terminal into the muggy Atlanta heat, the apron was a cacophony of jet engines, beeping ground vehicles, and shouted instructions. The A320neo, N592EL, sat at Stand 34, its navy-blue livery gleaming under the Georgia sun, but unlike the other A320s that Sprint US, or AmericanoAir, had, this one didn't have the Stars and Stripes. Instead it had a tail which was advertising Paramount+, obviously a deal had been done to advertise the streaming service in bold, eye-catching graphics—a swirling purple and white logo that screamed corporate synergy. James squinted at the tail, the Paramount+ branding a stark reminder of Sprint's knack for monetising every inch of their operation. The aircraft looked sleek, almost too pristine, as if it had rolled straight out of Mobile's final assembly line with the plastic wrap barely removed. But James knew better than to trust a shiny exterior. New planes, especially ones rushed into service to capitalise on a rival's collapse, had a habit of hiding surprises—loose fittings, glitchy avionics, or, worse, maintenance oversights buried in the logbook under a mountain of deferrals.

The walk to the stand was a gauntlet of organised chaos. Ground handlers in high-vis vests darted between baggage carts and fuel trucks, their radios crackling with urgent bursts of jargon. A Delta A330 was pushing back from an adjacent gate, its engines whining as it taxied toward the runway, while a Southwest 737 rolled in, its blue-and-red livery a cheerful counterpoint to the forlorn Spirit A320 still languishing at the edge of the apron.

James paused at the edge of the stand, his eyes scanning the A320neo with the practiced scrutiny of a pilot who'd seen too many "new" aircraft turn out to be anything but. The Paramount+ branding on the tail was a garish distraction, but his focus was on the airframe itself— every seam, every rivet, every hint of wear or haste.

"Right, I've got 10 trollies, $1500 in preordered F&B off the app, and more Michelob Ultra than a Super Bowl weekend party," Tanya Ramirez called out as she emerged from the aircraft's forward galley, her clipboard in one hand and a look of exasperation on her face. Her navy-blue uniform was immaculate despite the heat, her red lipstick a defiant statement against the chaos swirling around them. She spotted James and Trent approaching and gave a mock salute. "Welcome to the Paramount+ Express, gentlemen. Hope you're ready for a cabin full of frat boys and suits who think 'low-cost' means 'all-you-can-drink.'"

James chuckled, the tension in his shoulders easing slightly at Tanya's familiar blend of sarcasm and competence. "Sounds like a blast. What's the catering situation? Trent says you're already short on galley space."

Tanya rolled her eyes, gesturing toward the aircraft's open forward door, where a ground handler was wrestling with a stack of meal trays that looked one jolt away from toppling. "Short? Try non-existent. They've crammed ten trolleys into a space designed for four, and half the pre-orders are for Michelob Ultras and Bud Lite. You do know it's Georgia Tech at Colorado Buffaloes this weekend, so they're probably heading to Indy for another plane to we're due to push back." She sighed, tucking a stray lock of hair behind her ear. "And don't get me started on the Recaro R1s. These seats are so tight, I'm half-expecting a riot when the linebackers try to squeeze in. You boys better fly smooth, or I'll have a mutiny on my hands before we hit cruising altitude."

James gave a sympathetic nod, his gaze drifting back to the aircraft. "We'll do our best, Tanya. Let's get the preflight sorted, and I'll check the ACTs myself. Trent, you've got the load sheet?"

"On it," Trent replied, already striding toward the gate podium where LaToya was buried in a flurry of paperwork and passenger queries. The terminal's chaos seemed to spill onto the apron, with ground staff weaving through the crowd like dancers in a high-stakes ballet. James took a deep breath, the humid air thick with jet fuel and anticipation, and headed for the aircraft's forward door.

The interior of N592EL was as pristine as its exterior suggested, but the cabin felt claustrophobic, the 194-seat configuration pushing the limits of what an A320neo could reasonably hold. The Recaro R1 seats, with their sleek, minimalist design and 28-inch pitch, looked more like a design statement than a place to spend three hours. The overhead bins were already half-full of crew bags and catering supplies, and the galley at the front was a tangle of trolleys and plastic-wrapped trays. Tanya wasn't exaggerating—the space was barely functional, a testament to Sprint's obsession with maximising revenue at the expense of practicality.

James made his way to the cockpit, his flight bag slung over one shoulder, and settled into the left seat. The flight deck was a stark contrast to the cabin: clean, modern, and reassuringly familiar, with the Airbus's glass cockpit glowing softly under the midday sun filtering through the windows. The smell of new leather and electronics lingered, a reminder that this aircraft had barely clocked a hundred hours since leaving Mobile. He ran his hands over the controls, a ritual as old as his career, and began the pre-flight checks, his fingers moving with the muscle memory of thousands of flights.

Trent joined him a moment later, sliding into the right seat with the load sheet in hand. "LaToya says we're at 189 pax, 8 crew including us, and a hold mainly of what the European station manager is calling a "normal Ryanair mess'—oversized bags, sports gear, and a few dodgy suitcases that probably weigh more than the paperwork claims. Total ZFW's within limits, but the count of football fans is 112, so the CoG is slightly aft-heavy, just shy of the envelope. We're good, but I've asked for a recheck on the baggage weights. Those frat boys aren't travelling light, and I don't trust the scales when Ops is in a rush." Trent's voice was steady, but the faint edge of caution mirrored James's own instincts. In Sprint's world, "within limits" often meant "barely legal," and neither pilot was keen on testing the margins over a stormy Tennessee sky.

"If it's one of the Euro boys running the station here, then they've probably done what happened at Lauderdale, charged them for every pound and ounce of luggage to bleed the passengers dry before they even board," James said, his tone dry but tinged with resignation. He'd seen Sprint's European station managers in action—ex-Ryanair and Wizz Air types who treated every check-in as a personal mission to extract maximum revenue. Sprint's US operation, under the AmericanoAir banner, was still finding its feet, but the European influence was unmistakable: ruthless efficiency, creative fee structures, and a knack for turning chaos into profit. It was a model that worked—until it didn't.

"Ah, yes, the $100 for a "20 kilos" bag, and then $20 for every additional kilo over," Trent said, shaking his head as he input the load sheet data into the FMS. "You know the new Terms of Sale on the app says that guns are explicitly banned, even though Federal law already bans the transport of firearms in carry-on luggage? They're just covering their backsides after that incident with the air marshal's Glock. Still, I bet half these football fans are trying to sneak hunting rifles into their checked bags, thinking Indy's some sort of Wild West. Tanya's going to have a field day with the security sweeps."

James grunted, his eyes scanning the ECAM as he powered up the avionics. The screens flickered to life, displaying a clean slate—no deferred defects, no maintenance alerts, just the sterile glow of a brand-new aircraft. It was almost too good to be true, and James's instincts, honed over decades in cockpits from Basra to Boston, told him to dig deeper. "Let's run the full checklist, no shortcuts," he said, his voice firm. "And I want a look at the ACTs' installation records before we push. If Mobile rushed this bird out to catch Spirit's collapse, I'm not betting my licence on their paperwork being spotless."

Trent nodded, already flipping through the digital logbook on his tablet. "Way ahead of you. The ACTs were fitted during the B Check last week. Certified by Airbus's Mobile team, signed off by Sprint's MRO lead. No reported issues, but there's a note about a minor fuel transfer glitch during the test flight—fixed with a software update, allegedly. I'll double-check the fuel distribution once we're powered up. If it's off by even a litre, we're not going anywhere until Ops sorts it."

James gave a tight smile, appreciating Trent's diligence. The younger pilot's time at Spirit had left him with a healthy scepticism of airline operations, a trait that served him well in Sprint's cut-throat world. The Multi-crew Pilot Licence (MPL) rumours Ricky had mentioned in the van were still nagging at James, though. He'd flown with a few of Sprint's European FOs—bright kids, barely out of their teens, with simulator-polished skills but logbooks thinner than a boarding pass. They were competent, no question, but there was something unsettling about their robotic adherence to SOPs, as if flying was just a sequence of button presses rather than an art. The thought of Sprint flooding the US operation with MPL pilots, trained in Lithuanian academies and bankrolled by Omani cash, felt like a gamble too far, even for Jeff Young's audacious standards.

"You know, I might have a look at that MPL stuff when we get to top of climb. Anyway, for this flight, you're monitoring, I'm flying, right?" Trent said, mainly for the purpose of the cockpit voice recorder, which been running since they powered up the aircraft. His voice was casual, but the formality of the statement was a nod to the meticulous professionalism that kept them grounded in Sprint's chaotic orbit. James nodded, confirming the roles with a quick, "Affirm, I'm flying, you're monitoring," as he continued his pre-flight checks, his hands moving with the precision of a surgeon across the overhead panel.

The cockpit of the A320neo was a marvel of modern aviation—sleek, digital, and deceptively simple, with its twin ECAM screens and sidestick controls. But James knew that simplicity was a lie; beneath the glossy interface lay a labyrinth of systems, any one of which could turn a routine hop into a high-stakes drama if mishandled. The ACTs, in particular, were on his mind. Auxiliary Centre Tanks were a clever way to stretch the A320's range, but they added complexity to the fuel system, requiring careful monitoring to ensure proper transfer and balance. If Mobile's maintenance team had rushed the installation to meet Sprint's aggressive schedule, a "minor fuel transfer glitch" could easily become a major headache at 35,000 feet.

"Fuel pumps on, cross feed checked," Trent called out, his eyes flicking between the ECAM and the checklist on his tablet. "Left and right tanks balanced, ACTs showing full and stable. Software update seems to be holding—for now." He tapped the screen, pulling up the fuel distribution schematic, a web of green lines and numbers that confirmed the aircraft's readiness. "We've got 14,200 kilos total, enough for Indy with a 45-minute hold and a divert to Louisville if it gets dicey. Ops is playing it tight, but we're legal."

James grunted, his gaze lingering on the ECAM's fuel page. "Legal's one thing. Comfortable's another. If those storms over Tennessee tighten up, I want enough juice to loiter without sweating the gauges. Let's have a word with the fueller before we close up, make sure they've topped off exactly as planned." His tone was calm but carried the weight of a pilot who'd learned to trust his instincts over company promises. Sprint's fuel-saving ethos—pinching every litre to boost margins—was notorious, and James wasn't about to let a bean-counter's spreadsheet dictate his safety margins.

"Roger that," Trent replied, jotting a note on his tablet. "I'll get the fueller's paperwork when I do the walkaround. Want me to check the ACT fittings while I'm out there? Make sure Mobile didn't leave any bolts loose?" His grin was half-joking, but the question was serious. New aircraft, especially ones rushed into service, had a habit of revealing quirks under scrutiny, and Trent's time at Spirit had taught him to look for the cracks beneath the polish.

"Do it," James said, his voice firm. "And take a good look at the landing gear while you're at it. If this bird's fresh from Mobile, I want to know it's not going to shed a tyre on take-off. We've got 189 pax and a cabin full of beer-soaked football fans—last thing we need is a mechanical on climb-out." He leaned back in his seat, the leather creaking softly, and began configuring the FMS, inputting the reroute over Chattanooga with methodical precision. The flight plan was straightforward enough—depart Atlanta's Runway 27R, climb to FL350, and skirt the thunderstorms before descending into Indianapolis—but the added variables of a new aircraft, a dense passenger load, and Sprint's relentless cost-cutting made James's instincts hum with caution. He wasn't paranoid, but he'd been around long enough to know that aviation punished complacency with ruthless efficiency.

Outside, the Atlanta apron was a swirl of activity as the ground crew hustled to turn the A320neo. A fuel truck was parked under the wing, its hose connected to the aircraft's belly, while baggage handlers tossed suitcases into the hold with the practiced nonchalance of people who'd long since stopped caring about "fragile" stickers. Tanya was visible through the cockpit window, directing a catering team with the authority of a drill sergeant, her clipboard a weapon against the chaos. James caught her eye and gave a nod, which she returned with a raised eyebrow that said, *This is going to be a long day.*

Trent slipped out of the cockpit to conduct the walkaround, his high-vis vest a bright splash against the tarmac's grey. James watched him go, then turned his attention back to the FMS, double-checking the waypoints and fuel calculations. The reroute over Chattanooga added a slight dogleg to the flight path, but it kept them clear of the thunderstorms brewing over Nashville. The METAR for Indianapolis showed scattered clouds and a light crosswind—manageable, but he'd need to keep an eye on the weather as they approached. Sprint's Ops team had a habit of underestimating headwinds, and James wasn't about to let their optimism turn into a low-fuel bingo call over Indiana.

The cockpit door swung open, and Tanya poked her head in, her expression a mix of exasperation and grim amusement. "You boys ready for the circus? We've got 112 football fans, half of whom are already demanding their booze. Honestly, at $15 a can of Michelob Ultra, I don't blame them for wanting to pre-game, but I'm not running a frat house at 35,000 feet. Also, the corporate lot in rows 1 to 3 are already whining about the seat pitch—surprise, surprise. We're going to need a smooth push if we want to keep this lot from turning into a riot." Her voice was sharp but carried the warmth of someone who thrived under pressure, her years of surviving airline chaos lending her an unshakable calm.

James gave a wry smile, his hands still moving across the FMS. "We'll do our bit up here, Tanya. Just keep the galley locked until we're at cruise, or we'll have a conga line to the cockpit demanding refills. Any VIPs or special requests I should know about?"

Tanya snorted, leaning against the doorframe. "Just a request from half the pax to delay our flight in the air so they can drink their booze. Also, as the pre-orders are 90% booze, they want to know if they can take it off the plane with them or if they have to drink it all before we land. I told them Indy's not a dry state, but they're treating this flight like it's their last chance at a pint. No VIPs, unless you count the bloke in 4C who claims he's a 'regional sales influencer' and wants a free upgrade. I shut that down quick—told him the only upgrade available is a window seat in the emergency exit row, and he'd have to pay $50 for the privilege." She smirked, her red lipstick catching the cockpit's dim light. "Anything else you need from me before I go wrangle the masses?"

James shook his head, his focus still on the FMS. "Just keep them strapped in and sober until we're airborne. We've got a reroute over Chattanooga to dodge some weather, so it might get bumpy. If anyone starts a riot, you've got my permission to duct-tape them to their seat."

"Deal," Tanya said, her grin widening as she slipped back into the cabin, her heels clicking sharply against the floor. The cockpit door swung shut behind her, leaving James and the hum of the avionics in a momentary bubble of calm.

He leaned back, his eyes scanning the ECAM one last time before switching to the fuel page. The numbers were reassuring—14,200 kilos, enough for the flight to Indianapolis, a 45-minute hold, and a divert to Louisville if needed—but the memory of Ricky's MPL gossip lingered like a bad aftertaste. The idea of Sprint flooding their US operation with barely-seasoned First Officers, trained in Eastern European academies and bankrolled by shadowy Omani funds, was unsettling. Not because they were incompetent—James had flown with enough MPL pilots to know they could handle the Airbus's systems with eerie precision—but because their training felt like a shortcut, a factory line churning out pilots optimised for Sprint's SOPs rather than the unpredictable chaos of real-world aviation. Flying wasn't just about pressing buttons; it was about instinct, experience, and the ability to stay calm when the ECAM lit up like a Christmas tree and ATC started barking conflicting instructions. Could a 22-year-old with 240 hours, most of it in a simulator, handle a sudden depressurisation over the Appalachians? James wasn't sure, and the thought made his jaw tighten.

Trent reappeared, ducking into the cockpit with a faint sheen of sweat on his forehead from the Atlanta heat. He tossed his high-vis vest onto the jump seat and slid into the right seat, his tablet balanced on his knee. "Walkaround's done," he said, his voice clipped but professional. "No loose bolts, no tyre issues, and the ACT fittings look solid—Mobile did a decent job, at least on the outside. Fueller confirms we're topped off as planned, and I double-checked the paperwork. Baggage weights are, surprisingly, exact. Loadmaster took some off as a sample, and his scales showed what the labels said, so we're good there. Only oddity was a couple of football bags with what looked like extra padding—probably jerseys or something, but I flagged it for Tanya to keep an eye on. No rifles, thank God." He paused, wiping his brow with the back of his hand. "Oh, and the ground crew's moaning about the catering load. Apparently, Ops underestimated the booze demand, and they're short a trolley. Tanya's going to love that."

James nodded, his eyes still on the ECAM as he cross-checked the fuel distribution. "Good work. Let's hope those bags are just jerseys and not a DIY bar setup. Tanya's got enough to deal with without pax smuggling their own kegs." He tapped the screen, confirming the ACTs were balanced and the fuel transfer system was nominal. "Anything else?"

Trent hesitated, then leaned in slightly, his voice dropping to a conspiratorial whisper. "Not about the aircraft, but… I overheard some of the ground crew talking while I was out there. They're saying that some of the other rampies, the ones who United and AA deal with, are looking at moving to Europe. Mainly because, well, we're in a Trump presidency and the pay's better over there, and they're sick of the States' rollercoaster politics. Y'know, Heathrow's wanting more ramp and baggage handlers, and word is they're offering visas to anyone with apron experience."

The rumour about ground staff eyeing Europe was a major red flag. Sprint's US operation relied on a lean, often underpaid ground crew; if the experienced ones started defecting to Heathrow or Schiphol, the resulting brain drain could turn their already brittle logistics into a house of cards.

James absorbed Trent's words, the implications settling like a low-pressure system on the horizon. The rumour about ground staff eyeing Europe wasn't just idle gossip—it was a symptom of an industry stretched to breaking point, where even the unsung heroes of the apron were starting to look for the exits. Sprint's US operation, branded as AmericanoAir, was already a patchwork of ambition and improvisation, held together by overworked crews and a relentless drive to undercut the competition. If the ground handlers—those vital cogs who kept baggage moving, planes fuelled, and turnarounds on schedule—started jumping ship for better pay and stability in Europe, the fallout could be catastrophic. A single missed connection in Atlanta could cascade into delays across Sprint's sprawling network, and with Spirit's collapse still clogging the system, the timing couldn't be worse.

He leaned back in the captain's seat, the leather creaking under his weight, and let his eyes drift to the ECAM display. The fuel numbers were still green, the ACTs stable, but the cockpit's sterile calm felt like a thin veneer over the chaos outside. "Heathrow's poaching rampies?" he said, his tone measured but laced with a grim curiosity. "That's a new one. Last I heard, they were struggling to staff their own terminals post-Brexit. What's the draw— better wages or just fed up with the States?"

Trent shrugged, his fingers tapping idly on his tablet as he pulled up the latest NOTAMs. "Bit of both, from what I heard. The guy I was chatting to—some baggage lead with Delta—said Heathrow's offering £35,000 a year for experienced handlers, plus relocation bonuses and fast-tracked visas. That's nearly double what most rampies make here, especially with Sprint's 'competitive' pay scale." He snorted, the sarcasm dripping. "Add in the fact that Trump's second term has everyone on edge—new tariffs, FAA deregulation, all that noise—and it's no wonder they're looking across the pond. One of them even mentioned Schiphol. Apparently, the Dutch are desperate for apron crews too, and they don't care if you're American, Mexican, or Martian as long as you can sling bags and drive a tug."

James grunted, his mind turning over the logistics. The UK and Europe had been grappling with labour shortages in aviation since Brexit slammed the door on free movement, but the idea of US ground staff being lured across the Atlantic was a twist he hadn't seen coming. It made a certain grim sense, though. The US aviation industry, battered by post-COVID recovery, political volatility, and now Spirit's high-profile collapse, was a pressure cooker. Ground handlers, often the lowest-paid and most overworked, were the first to feel the squeeze. If Heathrow or Schiphol were dangling better prospects, it was only a matter of time before the exodus began. And Sprint, with its razor-thin margins and relentless cost-cutting, would be hit hardest.

"Let's hope Ops doesn't get wind of that rumour," James said, his voice dry. "Last thing we need is a skeleton crew on the apron when we're trying to make a 28-minute turn in Indy. Tanya's already got her hands full with the booze brigade." He glanced out the cockpit window, where

Tanya was now orchestrating the boarding process with the precision of a conductor, her clipboard a baton against the rising tide of passengers. The football fans, identifiable by their garish team jerseys and boisterous energy, were already clogging the jet bridge, their voices carrying through the open door like a distant roar.

Trent chuckled, but the sound was tinged with unease. "Yeah, well, if the rampies bail, we'll be loading our own bags soon. Or Ops'll just outsource it to some dodgy contractor in a tax haven. Wouldn't put it past Jeff Young to have a shell company in Muscat ready to go." He paused, then added, "Speaking of Young, you think there's any truth to that Omani trade union stuff Ricky was banging on about? I mean, I get the sovereign fund rumours—Sprint's got way too much cash for a ULCC—but a trade union as a front? That's next-level shady."

****

CHAPTER 20 – War Is Over, MPLs Aren't

Monday 29th September 2025

James Hart sat in the cockpit of the A320neo, tail number N592EL, now parked at a remote stand at Indianapolis International Airport. The engines were silent, the ECAM screens dimmed, and the hum of the auxiliary power unit was the only sound breaking the stillness.

The post-flight lull always felt oddly intimate to him, like the hush after a performance before the audience rose from their seats. But this evening there was no sense of applause, no satisfaction in another sector flown. Instead, James sat with his arms folded over his chest, watching fat drops of rain trace their way down the windscreen as the Midwestern dusk bled across the horizon. In the overhead locker, his battered flight bag waited for him to decide when, or whether, to go.

He let his eyes wander across the darkened displays, seeking comfort in routine. Fuel totaliser—zero difference. Hydraulics—steady. Cabin pressure—normal, now venting to atmosphere. Every check complete. In truth, he was only stalling, giving himself a moment to decompress before facing the administrative tangle he knew was about to descend on him.

Today's schedule, a LAX to Indianapolis to Dallas/Fort Worth to College Station-Easterwood, and then a trip to Houston Intercontinental, finishing at Ellington Airport and an Uber to the hotel was always going to be a grind— five legs, four states, and a relentless march across the fractured skeleton of the American midcontinent. But what set today apart wasn't the fatigue, nor the drama of a Paramount+-branded A320 packed with college football fans, but the rumour that had run like wildfire through crew rooms, WhatsApp chats, and even the cockpit PA: Sprint's importing of pilots from Europe, some with European Air Transport licenses barely a year old, others—most alarmingly—with Multi-Crew Pilot Licences (MPL) from Lithuanian and Spanish academies, and a handful allegedly with even less actual command time than the cabin crew they worked alongside, had reached the FAA and was now being investigated at the very highest levels. The phrase "MPL scandal" was now being muttered by American crew with the same bitterness as "regional pay" or "maxed FTLs." For James Hart the day felt like the eve of something tectonic.

All this, so the Sprint Group could staff its new AmericanoAir venture at breakneck speed, cashing in on Spirit's collapse and exploiting every regulatory loophole the FAA and EASA would allow.

James let the reality settle, quietly rolling the side-stick in his palm, thumb resting idly on the trim switch. On the glare shield, his First Officer, a MPL himself, named Mihai Ciobanu, was looking over the shutdown checklist for the third time, his movements just a little too precise, a little too eager. The young Romanian's jaw was tight, eyes flicking up to James with the nervous anticipation of a cadet desperate for approval. It was always there, James thought—a kind of haunted readiness he saw in the youngest Sprint pilots, especially those with less than a year's experience and more hours in a simulator than in actual weather.

Mihai finally broke the silence. "All secure, Captain. Logbook's up to date."

He spoke in a crisp, slightly mechanical accent that betrayed hours of ICAO-standard English drills but little of the casual American cockpit banter James preferred. It wasn't the accent that bothered him; it was the way Mihai seemed to perform every action as if the room was full of examiners, always just slightly too careful, as if missing some essential human looseness.

James nodded, gave a thin smile, and reached for the flight log.

"Thanks, Mihai. You can head out now. Ask Celine in so we can keep the two man rule going while I close out the tech log," James said, keeping his voice neutral. He tried to offer Mihai the faintest warmth—just enough to let the lad know he was trusted, but not so much that he invited a confession. The last thing he needed tonight was a conversation about training hours or licences. They'd all heard the stories: fast-tracked FOs with two-hundred real hours, cross-qualified on PowerPoint, flown in to fill gaps and keep jets moving. Some, like Mihai, were technically excellent. But excellent wasn't the same as experienced.

Mihai nodded, almost bowing as he backed out of the cockpit. A second later, Celine — the purser, a Canadian who was as old-school as they came — appeared at the cockpit door. Celine Marchand was a familiar presence on these transcontinental hybrids: a Montréal native with a sardonic wit, always one eyebrow raised, always two steps ahead of cabin drama. She gave a little knock on the frame, glanced at James, then Mihai as he ducked past, and eased herself into the jump seat, clicking the harness with the muscle memory of three decades of long-haul.

"Was that another one?" she asked, voice pitched low. Her French-Canadian lilt gave her words a certain musicality. "MPL? Or just another kid who looks twelve?"

James didn't answer at first, just kept writing. Eventually, he capped the pen, set down the logbook, and met her gaze. "MPL. Sim hours for days. Actual line time… well, he's done about 9 months at Sprint Europe, and since July here at AmericanoAir. I checked his training file before pushback. He's technically sharp, I'll give him that. But if he's ever flown a visual approach at night in a thunderstorm, I'll eat my epaulettes."

Celine pursed her lips, folding her arms. She didn't need to say "typical." It was in the arch of her brow, the slight shake of her head. "The passengers don't care about hours in a box. Not until something goes wrong."

James let the words hang between them, heavy with the memory of every scare story: the Ryanair Faro overrun, the Flydubai crash in Rostov, the TikTok clips of twenty-something FOs botching crosswinds in full public view. For all the jokes about "children flying Airbuses," it wasn't age or accent that worried James. It was the sense of something foundational, some steadying ballast, being hollowed out and replaced with metrics and risk models designed in offices.

Celine watched him closely. "You think it's going to stick? The investigation?"

"I think," James replied, "that Washington can only ignore it for so long. Word is, two of the new FOs botched go-arounds in Philly last week. ATC caught it on the tapes. They were both MPL, both new in from Vilnius. It's only a matter of time before the unions get blood in the water. ALPA's already filed a grievance. You know it's only a couple of days until a shutdown, right? And yet the DoD... sorry, Department of War... is still at war with Mexico over the cartels."

James let his head fall back against the headrest, throat tight. He felt older than he ought, and not just in the knees. Some days, the energy it took to remain the calming centre of an operation like this—especially now, especially with the world in such feverish flux—left him as drained as if he'd run the entire concourse at O'Hare with a week's sleep debt. He gazed at the rain, following the fat beads as they meandered across the outside of the windscreen, blending and dividing, blurring the halogen apron into an impressionist's afterthought.

"Want the honest answer, Celine?" he said, voice rough as gravel. "I think the unions will make it stick. It's not just ALPA anymore. The IAM, the Teamsters, they're all circling now. They can smell blood—and a chance to bloody Sprint's nose. Especially after what happened last week in Philly. FAA's rattled. DOT too, for what it's worth. This could get ugly."

Celine considered him, head tilted, lips pursed in a way that made her look, for an instant, every inch the teacher she'd once been before aviation. "Is it true what they say about the cadets? I mean, I know Sprint Europe's always been, well, inventive—but this?" She nodded at the empty right seat, at the tablet resting where Mihai had left it. "He looks about seventeen. My grandson's not far off."

James grunted. "He's 24. And he's… fine. Most of the time." He let the sentence trail, searching for a phrase that wouldn't be unfair and yet not dishonest either. "But you can see it, can't you? He flies the airplane beautifully. He can brief a non-precision into Dayton or Chicago with all the right words, but you sense it's just that—words. Give him an ECAM warning at top of descent and he'll checklist it in three different accents. But if you switched off the screens, gave him a horizon and a wet runway, I'm not sure he'd trust himself."

He scrubbed his face with one hand. "Christ, Celine. Do you remember when being a First Officer meant you'd sweated through fifteen winters in Aberdeen, or dodged Cessnas around Wichita for half a decade before they let you loose on an Airbus?"

She gave a dry, short laugh. "My first captain was a guy named Dan Ouellette. Used to fly DC-8s up to Frobisher Bay. Smoked so much you could light a galley oven off his uniform. He told me once, 'There's no substitute for getting your arse kicked by the weather, kid.'"

James tried to grin. "And now? Now it's just a PowerPoint, a credit agreement, and a one-way ticket to wherever Jeff Young's running a ground school this month." He gestured vaguely towards the terminal, the horizon, the world. "But I suppose it's progress, eh?"

James let the last echo of laughter die between them, a sound softened by the hush of the shut-down cockpit.

Outside, the rain had intensified, the rivulets thickening and racing down the Perspex, distorting the sodium-lit apron until the Delta and United tails became mere smears of colour in the night. Indianapolis was not a beautiful airport, but it had the kind of midwestern dusk that made everything momentarily seem a little softer, a little less harsh—if you didn't look too closely.

Inside the cockpit, the sense of liminality was almost sacred: post-shutdown, pre-crew bus, that twilight intermission where pilots and senior cabin crew could be honest in ways the relentless churn of the operation never permitted elsewhere. James unclipped his harness, stretching his back and shoulders, feeling every knot of the day's tension resist and then yield.

He glanced at Celine, who still sat poised, hands folded, gaze not on him but fixed somewhere beyond the wipers, as if searching the tarmac for the ghosts of old friends. There was a certain stillness to her—an old-school poise rarely seen in the younger generation, especially those who wore the uniform like a temporary costume, knowing they'd be gone to another airline, another continent, before the next winter.

"You know what frightens me most?" Celine said at length, her voice soft, almost confidential. "It's not the young ones themselves. It's the way the system seems built to push them through so fast. Everything's about throughput. More cadets, more hours, more sectors. I used to look at a captain and see someone who'd survived. Now I see a spreadsheet."

James nodded, reaching for his water bottle, swallowing against the arid dryness in his throat. "It's all just risk tolerance now. How many line training captains can you burn out before the system seizes? How many eighteen-hour days can a twenty-two-year-old fly before they make a mistake no checklist can catch?"

Celine's lips curled in a wry smile. "Remember when a pilot's logbook was a storybook? Not just line checks and zero-flights, but scrawled notes about snow at LaGuardia, a dodgy approach in Faro, a near-miss over the Bay of Biscay…"

"Now it's all digital," James said. "They finish a leg, sign the iPad, it's already in the cloud before the engines spool down. Half of them couldn't tell you what runway they landed on two sectors ago. It's all just numbers."

A movement outside caught his eye—a pair of ramp agents, heads bowed under the hoods of their high-vis jackets, splashing through puddles as they disconnected the ground power and wrangled baggage containers onto a battered tug. Their movements were methodical but tired, and James wondered—again—how many were ex-Delta, ex-United, even ex-Brits lured over by the rumoured pay rises in Europe.

"You know their website says 'You'll take to the sky for the first time in Phoenix, Arizona in the US. The brilliant weather conditions there make it the perfect place to learn how to fly. During the roughly 28 weeks you're there, you'll get to explore and make friends too. It's the memories of a lifetime kind of deal', and that it's basically a 'study abroad' scheme with sidestick authority, isn't it?"

James murmured, his voice equal parts mockery and melancholy.

Celine made a sound between a sigh and a laugh. "It's all the same brochure, whatever continent you're on. 'See the world, make friends, become a captain at twenty-three.' They never mention the bit about holding over Peoria on minimum fuel because Ops wanted to save a hundred quid on Jet A, do they?"

James shook his head, rolling his shoulders to relieve a growing ache. "I've flown with cadets who couldn't find Peoria on a map. But give them an ECAM memo and they'll recite Airbus FCOM verbatim. It's not their fault. It's the pipeline. Fast track to the right seat and pray the weather stays VMC."

"You know, I almost did flight school, back in 2000, but then, with United 93 happening and everything that came after, my mum begged me to think again," Celine said, her eyes distant with a kind of survivor's nostalgia. "Did a year at the University of Montreal, then—well, you know the story. Found the airline, fell in love, lost more than I kept. Never did get my wings, but ended up on a jump seat more times than not. Funny how the world turns."

James smiled, but it was the smile of an old comrade, not of comfort. "Back then you'd have been in a queue with a hundred others, all paying their dues, hoping for a slot when the music stopped. I went USAF, F-16s, the whole song and dance, chasing tail codes round Texas and Arizona. Did you know I didn't set foot in a glass cockpit till I was thirty-two? Now half the captains I fly with would be lost without their MCDU to tell them which way up to hold the checklist."

Celine laughed softly, a sound mingling irony with fatigue. "Funny how the further we go, the more we end up circling back. Everyone wants progress until progress means trusting your life to a spreadsheet."

They shared a look—one of those wordless exchanges that only comes with years at the sharp end, where laughter and resignation were often closer than anyone on the ground ever suspected.

Outside, the drizzle thickened, drumming faintly on the roof of the crew centre. Through the rain-streaked glass, James could just make out the silhouette of N592EL in the gloom, the Paramount+ tail illuminated by sodium floodlights. He wondered idly who'd be flying her out next—some ex-Ryanair chancer with a bag full of duty-free, or another of the Lithuanian cadets, eyes wide, checklist clutched like a talisman.

Suddenly his phone sounded, a notification from the NBC News app.

James let his head sink briefly, heart sinking with it—he'd set alerts for "AmericanoAir", "Sprint Group", and "FAA" long ago, a relic of habit, but lately it felt as if the world's news was always half a page ahead of him. He flicked the phone from aeroplane mode, screen glowing with the blue-white of after-dark news. Celine craned over with the slightly hungry curiosity of any crew member in a storm, each of them trained by years of operations to expect only one thing from a breaking alert: trouble.

NBC BREAKING: PRESIDENT TRUMP TO SPEAK ABOUT US-MEXICO WAR. WATCH LIVE.

James let the headline register, the words bright and insistent beneath his thumb. For a heartbeat he sat in the hush of the cockpit, hearing only the distant rattle of rain on aluminium, and the faint echo of the jet bridge bumping against the forward door as ground crew prepared the plane. The silence was broken only by the soft exhale of Celine beside him.

James's first thought was—God, not another one. In the past year, every time Trump's face appeared on a breaking alert, it had meant something for the aviation industry: airspace closures, snap tariffs, sabre-rattling about open skies, or most recently, the fever dream of a war with the Mexican cartels that had half of Texas in a state of perpetual hair-trigger anxiety. In practical terms, it had meant more delays, more operational chaos, more pilots and crew stranded in the wrong city at the wrong time. In less practical terms, it meant the sensation of flying on shifting sand, the world's axis groaning as it sought some new, less rational alignment.

But this alert—the promise of a speech—felt heavier. He showed Celine the phone. She read the headline, then handed it back with the grim fatalism of a woman who had seen enough "big news" for a dozen lifetimes.

"He'll declare victory, mark my words," she murmured, eyes on the rain. "War is over, we won. Next crisis, please."

James allowed himself a small, sardonic smile. "Maybe he'll nationalise Delta this time. Or start selling off border airports to pay for the next Paramount+ livery."

She snorted—equal parts amusement and scorn—and stood, flexing her knees. "Come on, Captain. You want to watch history or wait until CNN tells us what to think about it?"

He didn't answer immediately, just reached for his flight bag, unbuckling and gathering up the stack of logbooks and spare checklists he carried everywhere—still a tactile man in an increasingly digital world. They walked out together, stepping down the crew steps, jackets zipped tight against the drizzle.

The ramp was a world of muted colours and urgent motion: ground crew ferrying baggage and canisters under floodlights, the snaking outline of a Delta 737 pushing back into the rain, Sprint's own battered A320neo gleaming a little too new, a little too bold in its sponsored livery. The world of commercial aviation—gaudy, improvised, both proud and ridiculous—compressed into one sodden tableau.

Inside the terminal, things felt almost normal. The bright white lighting, the low hum of vending machines, the weary crowd at Gate 22—a cluster of stranded passengers wrapped in branded sweatshirts, the odd child asleep across three seats, the perpetual queue at Starbucks. James and Celine blended with other crews in hi-vis, the subtle choreography of badges and bags marking them as kin in this strange tribe. Beyond the news screens, nothing seemed to be happening. Just another Monday, if you didn't look at the ticker tape.

But as they crossed toward the crew centre, a ripple passed through the crowd: heads turning, murmurs rising, the CNN anchor's voice suddenly louder, strident with that American mix of solemnity and showbiz.

"We cut now to Washington, D.C., where President Trump is about to address the nation regarding ongoing operations on the southern border and the conclusion of military engagement in Mexico—"

Celine elbowed James, and together they joined a knot of Delta pilots and AmericanoAir crew clustered near a muted television. The image was grainy, rain-fogged, the Rose Garden shot through with floodlights, the American flag limp in the humidity. Trump stood behind the podium, that familiar lean-in posture, flanked by the usual array of generals and aides, each looking as though they'd rather be anywhere else.

"Ladies and Gentlemen," President Donald J. Trump began, eyes squinting into the early morning light of the South Lawn, "I am proud to announce that, due to strong, beautiful negotiations with our friends—and yes, they are friends—in Mexico, we have secured a total and complete ceasefire. Starting tonight at 11:59pm. For 120 days. That's four months, folks. Big number. Huge." He paused, letting the cameras flash, his signature smirk returning.

"There will be a binational commission," he drawled, "headed by some of the best people. Smart people.

Patriots. Who are going to look into what happened. Because—let's be clear—there was bad stuff. Very bad. Horrible things. And I said—no more! I told the military, we're not going to go in and risk American lives when we can lead with peace, from strength."

He made the familiar hand gestures—flattened palms, circling fingers, the occasional jab to emphasise strength—and then, with a grin: "And to our friends in international racing—I know both Formula 1 and WARS are meeting today in Singapore and Montreal, I'm looking forward to seeing WARS in Indiana and Formula 1 in Texas, big, beautiful sports, especially WARS with its V10 beasts, I asked them to have proper V10s, not this lawnmowers. I love that. Big, angry engines. They got this guy, Jordie Whiting—used to be in Formula 1, now runs the American team, great guy, doing tremendous things."

"However, the United States will not be accepting any citizens of Mexico until we've completed a very strong vetting process. Very strong. The strongest. And I've directed Homeland Security to increase the border presence. We're talking military-grade fences, drones, patrols—everything. We're going to keep Americans safe. And if international sporting events—like WARS— want to race near the border, well, let me tell you: they're going to see America leading the way, safely. Beautifully."

James stood back, letting the flood of words and bluster roll over him. It was the same performance as every other Trump address he'd watched in the past year: the bravado, the exaggerations, the odd detours into sport, the carefully-placed jabs at enemies real and imagined. Only now, it was happening in real time as a small circle of aviation professionals—AmericanoAir, Delta, even a Southwestern FO stranded by a codeshare misconnection—gathered near the TV, their faces lit blue-white by the screen, their moods oscillating between disbelief and gallows amusement.

"Four months?" Celine murmured, half to herself. "Plenty of time for another war."

James smirked, then glanced around at the other pilots. The American captains looked relieved but wary—nobody quite trusted a Trump ceasefire to last, and already the whispers had begun about what the new "vetting" measures would mean for airlines, for crew, for passengers with dual nationality. He could see the gears turning: more delays, more queues at passport control, more operational notes on the iPad, all for the sake of one more layer of political theatre.

The speech went on, veering wildly between "America First" rhetoric and a surreal riff about sports—NASCAR, the Indy 500, even a rambling anecdote about his time in Atlantic City with "the finest pilots I ever met, all military, all beautiful, strong, American." It was the kind of broadcast James had learned to half-ignore, picking out only the keywords that would matter for flight ops.

The anchor cut in, summarising: "—the US-Mexico war, now on a temporary halt. But the aviation industry still faces significant disruption. FAA guidance remains in place for border airspace. Airlines are advised to check NOTAMs, expect delays at all major southern hubs, and plan for ongoing uncertainty regarding Mexican crew and dual citizens."

James felt a subtle tightening in his gut. The "guidance" was already legendary among line pilots: hastily written, patched with amendments, full of contradictory advice about who could and couldn't operate, which routes might be suspended at a moment's notice, and how to handle everything from cargo pre-clearance to crew layover restrictions.

"Furthermore, the crooked Democrats with their with their endless obstruction—nasty people, by the way, just nasty—tried to stop this deal, but we got it done. And let me tell you, nobody does deals like we do deals. So, effective tonight, American airspace remains secure. Mexico? Very secure. We're bringing back stability to our border. Thank you, God bless you, and God bless the United States of America."

The cameras flashed, the network cut to talking heads, and the terminal crowd collectively exhaled—a few cheers from an Army vet in fatigues, but mostly that low, animal sigh of a nation used to living on tenterhooks. For a moment, the news anchor's baritone was lost beneath the scurry of the concourse, the scratch of wheels on tiles, and the distant squall of a child dropped by a weary mother.

James let it all wash over him, chest tight, as if he'd been holding his breath for an entire news cycle. He found himself glancing around, taking stock of the faces—Delta crews murmuring into their phones, AmericanoAir's own Mihai hovering by the vending machines, a young Southwest FO frowning at the departure board as if willing her next sector to materialise. The war was, for now, "over." But the work of flying in its wake—the confusion, the doubt, the whiplash from today's operational norms to tomorrow's political decrees—was only beginning.

"Mr President, what do you plan to do about Sprint importing European pilots with so-called 'MPL' licences—training schemes that some American pilots claim are unsafe, that have led to incidents at Philly and Houston, and which are now under FAA review?" came the reporter's question, thrown from somewhere beyond the Rose Garden hedges. The President paused, pursed his lips, and adopted a look of studied concern—part showman, part school principal feigning patience.

"Well, it's a very big issue, a very serious issue," he said, wagging a finger. "We want American jobs for American pilots, that's what I've always said, and you know that. These European licences, some of them, frankly, not the best, not what we would do here—some are very good, beautiful pilots, but others... not so much. So we're going to look at it. The FAA, wonderful people, are going to make sure that if you're flying an American flag, you have American training—real training, the best. We're not going to risk safety. You see what's happened—other countries, not always up to our standards. We're going to make sure American passengers have American pilots. That's what I've always said, and that's what we'll do. Next!"

The answer was classic Trump—rambling, self-congratulatory, and almost totally lacking in specifics. For the cluster of pilots in the terminal, it was more noise:

enough ambiguity for every side to find a threat, a promise, or a loophole. Already James saw Mihai stiffen near the vending machines, the young Romanian clutching his can of Sprite as if it were a lifeline, eyes darting from the screen to James as if seeking assurance.

"Mr President, with a Government Shutdown looming thanks to the Democrats refusing to sign the Continuing Resolution, will the FAA even have the staff to enforce any new rules? And what about the airspace NOTAMs still active on the Texas–New Mexico–Arizona corridor?"

James watched as Trump flapped a dismissive hand, his voice blaring through the tinny airport speaker and the CNN feed alike. "We have people—good people—essential people. The FAA will do their job. The government will do its job, shutdown or no shutdown. The Democrats want chaos, we bring order. American skies will stay safe, believe me. And if Sprint or anyone else thinks they can pull a fast one, we'll know. Our pilots are the best. We look after them. We will not be importing problems, that I can tell you."

"Justin Harper, Newsmax. You said that Sprint is facing questions about importing European pilots. Does the White House support a review and ban of all foreign airlines unless their pilots are FAA accredited and ALPA members?"

Trump grinned for the cameras, rolling his shoulders as if limbering up for a prize fight. "Listen, we're looking very closely at all these issues. If you're flying in America, you follow American rules. You follow our standards, our great standards. If you want to operate here, you use

American pilots, or pilots who meet our highest, toughest criteria. No shortcuts. We're not going to have pilots who barely finished flight school landing jets in Indianapolis or Houston. Our people—real pilots—will keep America flying. You know, ALPA, great folks, very strong. They'll be happy with what we're doing. And if you're a foreign airline and you don't like it? Well, maybe you should fly somewhere else."

James watched as an advisor whispered in Trump's ear, and then the President suddenly u-turned.

"Of course, AmericanoAir, Sprint, are an exception as they do great things for America, great things, the best really. They've reduced fares for hard working Americans that low that they've basically turned air travel into the new Greyhound. That's what competition looks like, folks—real American innovation, even if the owners are from, you know, across the pond, Oman, Britain, wherever. But we'll look at it, we'll make sure only the best are flying the flag. I've spoken to Jeff Young—great guy, tremendous, real winner, brought jobs. They buy Airbuses from Mobile, you know, meaning loads of American jobs in the South—Alabama, great state, loves me. And I always said, if it's made in America, flown in America, that's good for America. And if the Europeans have beaten the ALPA enforced shortage, then maybe the FAA should look at this MPL thing, maybe bring it to the States, do it properly, make it even better—because we always make things better. American pilots, American planes, American skies. No question."

For a moment, James simply stood there—shoulder-to-shoulder with Celine, his bag hanging at his side, his mind flicking between the half-remembered rhythms of old, easier days and the sharp, fluorescent realities of modern airline life. He let the president's words echo off the tiles, filtering through the crowd in the terminal like an approaching thunderstorm. The conversations around him ebbed and flowed: some pilots shaking their heads in disbelief, others grinning at the latest presidential U-turn, a handful already speculating about what new "guidance" would be in their inbox before block time tomorrow.

He watched Mihai drift closer, awkward in his hi-vis, clearly unsure if he should stay or disappear. The Romanian FO hovered, then, seeing Celine's quick, reassuring nod, came over.

"Captain," Mihai said quietly, as if not wanting to interrupt whatever secret ritual these senior crew might be observing, "are we—am I—still on the Houston leg? Or will they… you know, change things?"

James offered the briefest of smiles. "We're all still on until Crew Scheduling finds someone more American than apple pie, Mihai. It'll be fine. If anything changes, Ops will call, and then we'll all go for a very long lunch. Until then, it's business as usual—just with a bit more paperwork."

The younger man nodded, a faint blush of relief crossing his cheeks, and Celine caught James's eye with a look that said: *See? It's not their fault. They're kids, in a world that keeps rewriting the rules.*

The TV was now playing pundit panels: experts, ex-ALPA spokesmen, retired generals, economists, and even a gurning YouTuber who once vlogged a night stuck at O'Hare. It was all white noise—wheels turning, content generated, no answers found. In the background, a chime called a final boarding at Gate 25, and for a brief second, James considered walking down there, buying a standby to anywhere, and just riding the night out above the weather.

Instead, he shouldered his bag. "Come on," he said, "let's see what our next mess looks like."

****

CHAPTER 21 – The Shutdown of a Government

Tuesday 30th September 2025

It had been less than twenty-four hours since the press conference by President Trump, and the news wasn't about Sprint, James noticed, sitting in the crew room at the southern end of Dallas/Fort Worth's Terminal D. For once, the screens weren't looping delayed footage of rowdy boarding at LAX, or pundits speculating on the latest AmericanoAir near-miss. Instead, CNN, NBC, and Fox alternated between ***"GOVERNMENT SHUTDOWN: LIVE"*** graphics and countdown timers until the Government would, in fact, shut down with the force of a gale. Even the local ABC affiliate, which normally confined itself to stories of burnt barbecue and high school football, had rolled in the breaking-news banners and sombre-voiced anchors.

James Hart sat hunched on a battered blue sofa, a Styrofoam cup of coffee in one hand and his company-issued iPad balanced precariously on his knee. The air in the room was thick with a kind of false calm, the collective energy of dozens of crews on duty or reserve—waiting for something to happen. Flight bags and roller boards formed a hedge by the door. Uniformed men and women—AmericanoAir in their Sprint uniforms, Southwest, Frontier, Spirit, even a handful of Delta and United crews clustered in corners, their lanyards and epaulettes making strange tribal patterns across the tatty, fraying upholstery. It was a scene James had known in three continents and a dozen cities, but never before with this particular edge of anticipatory dread. He sipped the dreadful, over-extracted coffee, feeling his pulse quicken not from the caffeine but the churn of uncertainty. Outside the wide plate-glass windows, the Texas morning was bruised with cloud, yellow sunlight struggling through the haze, illuminating the unending choreography of ramp traffic and the distant shimmer of jet fuel on hot concrete.

Someone had left the crew room door ajar, letting in bursts of airport noise: the rumble of baggage carts, the metallic groan of a jetway, the blare of a PA system announcing yet another delayed shuttle to Charlotte. A fresh-faced pair of AmericanoAir FOs, both wearing "*I FLY FOR AMERICA*" pins on their ties, played a slow, silent game of chess at the far end of the room. On the telly above, the government shutdown coverage flickered relentlessly. ***FEDERAL EMPLOYEES TO BE FURLOUGHED AT MIDNIGHT. AIR TRAFFIC CONTROLLERS TO REMAIN 'ESSENTIAL'—BUT FOR HOW LONG?***

James checked his phone again. The WhatsApp groups—**AmericanoAir US East Schedulers**, **Sprint Europe Deadhead Refugees**, **DFW Line Pilots**, and a private thread with Celine—were all popping off with frantic speculation: Would the FAA still staff the towers? Would the TSA walk out? Would the Tijuana–San Diego–Houston corridor get shut down for good? It was a strange thing, James reflected, to fly every day through the world's most complex airspace and realise, for the first time, that the entire system was now held together by a single Congressional vote and a handful of emergency orders.

He forced himself to scroll through the latest NOTAMs. There was something comic, if you had the stomach for it, about reading "*UNTIL FURTHER NOTICE DUE TO FUNDING LAPSE, SERVICES AT [LOCATION] MAY BE INTERRUPTED*" and realising that this was now the official language of American aviation. The digital deluge from HQ didn't help—one after another, Sprint memos arrived, each one more anodyne than the last: **"Crews are reminded to observe all company SOPs during the shutdown period and report any irregularities to local base managers or by submitting an AIMS incident."** Someone had even added a cheery "Stay positive, team!" at the end, which was about as much use as a chocolate teapot.

James glanced up as the door banged, letting in a short, humid breath of Texan air. Another crew—Delta by the look of them, neat navy epaulettes and the faintly put-upon expression of pilots who'd done too many shuttle legs that week—filed in, shaking drizzle off their jackets. No one spoke; the room had taken on the hush of a waiting room before a difficult diagnosis.

Across from him, Danielle Howe, his First Officer for the day, set down her Starbucks and cracked her knuckles. She gave James a look of dry amusement.

"I don't understand you Yanks. Back home, we don't have these continuing resolutions. Instead we have Rachael Reeves pretending to know the price of bread for a week, the Tories falling over their own expense claims, and somehow the lights stay on. Here, the whole circus comes to a halt every time Congress can't agree how many billions to chuck at the Pentagon."

James allowed himself a thin, grateful smile. Danielle was London-born, one of the growing handful of British expats populating Sprint Group's US operations, and her humour was always sharpest at the darkest moments. She still wore her old BA pilot's wings beneath the AmericanoAir badge, a small act of quiet rebellion. He'd come to appreciate her wry take on American absurdities. There was something steadying about a colleague who could talk you through a CAT3B Autoland and the entire plot arc of Line of Duty without missing a beat.

He stretched out his legs, the bones in his knees audibly clicking. "Well, Danielle, here, everything is drama. In Britain, you can't get a sandwich after 10pm. Here, you might not get paid tomorrow but you can order a loaded shotgun on Amazon Prime."

"Well, actually, Tesco's have 24 hour stores, and Deliveroo has petrol station sandwiches until three in the morning," Danielle fired back, arching an eyebrow as she stretched. "But point taken. Only here does a government running out of cash feel like the prelude to an alien invasion. No one knows what'll still work in the morning – except the vending machines, obviously. Those things would survive nuclear winter."

James snorted, savouring the rare chance for gallows humour. The room, full of strangers forced into proximity by circumstance and nerves, seemed to shift a little closer to normality.

"Maybe that's the solution," he mused. "Replace Congress with vending machines. You pay a dollar, get a randomly assigned policy. At least you know what you're getting, and you can always try again if it's inedible."

The sound of stifled laughter from a nearby jump seater – a wiry, bespectacled man in a battered SkyWest jacket – punctuated the moment. "Would still be better odds than getting a rest break through Houston this week."

The coffee machine spat out another faintly metallic stream. A tired Spirit captain, his cap askew, flicked through his phone and muttered to nobody in particular, "At least if they shut down the FAA, the bloody managers won't be able to send us so many emails."

A ripple of knowing smirks passed around the room. Crew rooms had always been equal parts confessional, war room, and sanctuary. Today they were something closer to a life raft, bobbing on the rising tide of governmental idiocy.

James glanced at Danielle, lowering his voice. "Have you flown during a shutdown before?"

She shook her head. "No, but I did fly through Brexit. That was chaos enough. Five sets of rules for every passenger, half the crew rostered across the wrong continent, and the only thing anyone agreed on was how much they missed the Swissport biscuits." Her eyes flicked to the TV, which was looping images of deserted government offices and queues outside Social Security. "This is different, though. Feels like the whole system's about to seize up."

James nodded, feeling the tension like an ache beneath his collarbone. He watched the news ticker crawl along the bottom of the screen: *"FAA SAYS TOWERS TO REMAIN OPEN FOR NOW,"* followed by, *"AIRPORTS WARN OF POSSIBLE TSA ABSENCES."* None of it was comforting. In the cockpit, you always knew your backup plans: alternate, fuel, a holding pattern, another airport somewhere within range. Here, on the ground, there was no such thing—just a fog of speculation, and the sense that the people making decisions had never worked a midnight at O'Hare with a 200-foot ceiling.

He sipped his coffee, already cooling to the ambient chill of over-conditioned air. The room around him felt more like a weather system than a workplace: clusters of crew blowing together, shifting with rumour and necessity, some moving on a schedule, others simply waiting to see which way the winds of fate would gust next. It was a kind of human holding pattern—expectant, uneasy, the steady drone of cable news their only horizon.

A young woman in AmericanoAir uniform—Caitlyn, a Chicago-based flight attendant he half-recognised from previous rotations—approached with a nervous energy. She hovered at the edge of the sofa, iPad in hand, her voice pitched just above a whisper. "Captain Hart? Ops just called me. There's a rumour going round about a system reboot tonight—something about flight plans needing to be filed by hand if the FAA systems go offline. Any idea if it's true?"

James managed a half-smile, not unkind. "Only thing I know is, if they want us to file by hand, we'll need more than a biro and a clipboard. We'll need a small army of ex-NASA engineers and a bottle of bourbon."

She giggled—a brittle, grateful sound. "So… business as usual, then?"

"Business as usual," he agreed, glancing at Danielle, who grinned in sympathy. "Only with a bit more panic."

The sofa cushions under James gave a resentful squeak as he shifted, the fake leather clinging to the back of his shirt. For a moment he was acutely aware of his own sweat: not the old, healthy kind that came from a sprint down a jet bridge in July, but the anxious perspiration of a day spent in institutional air, of too many hours waiting for someone else to decide if you would work, eat, or even fly tomorrow.

He let his head fall back and listened to the room: voices in various accents—Texan twang, New York clipped, Atlanta's smooth vowels, the London and Liverpool edges of Sprint's British imports—murmured and sometimes rose in frustration. It was a symphony of simmering tension, punctuated by the dull, periodic thuds of roller bags on tile and the relentless, tinny newsfeed that seemed intent on charting the apocalypse in half-hour increments.

Caitlyn had wandered away, reassured or at least reassigned, and James watched her retreat to a knot of fellow flight attendants all scrolling through doom-laden group chats. Danielle caught his gaze and rolled her eyes.

"I used to think British rail strikes were bad," she said. "But at least when the trains stop, you can see it coming. There's a sense of inevitability. Here, everything's fine until it isn't, and by the time you notice, you're already at cruise altitude with a NOTAM that says 'Good luck, mate'."

James smiled, though his heart wasn't in it. "You're assuming we'll have ATC in the morning. Last shutdown, I ended up circling over St Louis for forty minutes waiting for a guy from maintenance to come off his break and answer the radio."

A nearby United captain, white-haired and wry-faced, interjected. "Be grateful they didn't close the runways. Back in '13, I watched a TSA supervisor try to direct ground traffic at Denver. Nearly sent a Southwest 737 into a snowplough."

That drew a scatter of chuckles—gallows humour, aviation's lifeblood. Someone at the back of the room suggested, not entirely facetiously, that now might be the time for the return of the London–Sydney Kangaroo Route, via Auckland and Manila. "At least then if the FAA goes down, you're someone else's problem for a day or two."

Danielle fished her phone from her bag, the screen glowing with a barrage of WhatsApps.

"Anything?" James asked.

She snorted. "My girlfriend at BA says they've just briefed LHR crews to expect inbound US flights to be delayed, but outbound are still a go—unless something goes properly sideways. Apparently American's briefing is 'turn up, see what happens.' Good to know the joint venture is keeping up the tradition of making it up as they go along." Danielle offered a dry smile, but James could sense the shadow behind it—a deep fatigue, one that wasn't about hours or time zones, but the sense that grown adults were being asked to play make-believe with systems too vast and brittle for such games.

He took another sip of coffee, the bitterness now familiar, almost welcome. "I've had more coherent briefings from Ryanair," he said. "At least Michael O'Leary would call you an idiot to your face."

"Or just make you pay to use the loo," Danielle replied, raising her cup in mock salute. "God, I'd kill for a strong Irish tea and a packet of Hobnobs."

For a moment, the conversation drifted. The crew room's noise ebbed and flowed. Some pilots, better adapted to waiting than others, had dozed off in odd corners, heads tipped back and feet stretched out. A knot of younger flight attendants gathered by the window, their laughter brittle, phones held high for selfies against the runway backdrop—proof, perhaps, that they'd survived the day, or simply the hope that if they documented enough of it, the world might stay real.

"...IN THE TOILETS? YOU YOUNG LOT SHOULD BE OUT ON THE LINE, NOT MAKING... WHOOPIE... IN THE TOILETS!"

The bellow from a Southwest captain, who James saw was waiting for the lavatory and berating a pair of Sprint uniformed AmericanoAir crew members, and, the first face he saw was none other than Bryce Keegan, who, back in July, had been on one of James's flights as a thoroughly useless First Officer. James watched, equal parts amused and appalled, as Keegan—still far too smug for a man who'd been nearly fired for his in-flight antics—emerged from the loo, sheepish and dishevelled, trailed by a young woman with a Sprint badge askew on her lapel, her stockings laddered, and her shirt only half done, while Bryce's trousers were still unzipped and his belt was undone.

"At least he didn't do it in my flight deck again," James said with a sigh. "Who's got this idiot on their crew today?"

"Me," Toyah O'Hara, one of the other Sprint Captains who was in the middle of packing away her iPad, called out, her Brooklyn vowels slicing through the general hum. She didn't look up from the screen, simply shook her head and muttered, "I've already told him that if he left my flight deck without completing his checklist, I'd run him over with a catering truck." She caught James's eye and gave a look of such long-suffering exasperation that he felt an unexpected flicker of camaraderie. "Honestly, Hart, I don't know where Sprint finds them. Is there a special finishing school for overconfident halfwits, or is it just the ones who failed Ryanair's psychometric?"

A ripple of laughter rolled across the room. Keegan, face flushed, tried to recover his dignity and sloped off towards the vending machines, avoiding eye contact with everyone—especially the Southwest captain, who continued muttering about "kids these days" and "no wonder we're in the mess we are."

James exchanged a look with Danielle, both of them shaking their heads in that universal pilot's semaphore for "seen it all now." Toyah, now joined by Bryce, who, James noticed, was guiding the flight attendant by his hand on her rump to Toyah, started to get up with a frown.

James noticed how the Brooklyn born Captain fixed Bryce Keegan with a glare so withering that even the coffee machine seemed to hesitate. "Touch her arse again, Keegan, and I'll swap your jump seat for the galley jump and tell Purser Kevin to leave you there at 39,000 feet with the cold plates."

The flight attendant gave Toyah a grateful, slightly mortified smile, straightening her uniform. Bryce, suddenly all boyish repentance, attempted a joke about "team bonding" that went over about as well as a thunderstorm in finals. Toyah ignored him, turning instead to James and Danielle with the air of someone who'd survived worse.

"I've flown with some divas, but I swear, if we get through today without him starting a TikTok, it'll be a miracle."

James grinned, grateful for Toyah's granite backbone and the way she radiated that special kind of authority only New York pilots seemed to possess. He reached for the remote and muted the TV, the low drone of shutdown speculation replaced by the immediate soundtrack of the crew room—murmured banter, the click of trolley wheels, and the ever-present hum of tension. Even the flight bags by the door seemed to be listening.

He nodded to Toyah, who now found a place on the sagging armrest beside Danielle, their mutual exhaustion transcending airlines and continents. "I'll buy you a round if he doesn't end up on the evening news," James said. "And two if he manages a flight without chatting up the gate agent mid-boarding."

Toyah snorted. "You're on, Hart. Not holding my breath."

A brief lull fell, punctuated by the rhythmic tapping of a rainstorm finally breaking over the terminal roof. Outside, the horizon vanished into shimmering grey. It was the kind of Texan downpour that grounded anything not already airborne. From the far corner, a JetBlue pilot in a bright blue jumper murmured to his FO about alternate fuel requirements. At the table by the window, two older United pilots thumbed quietly through the new FAR amendments, one shaking his head every few lines.

Danielle caught James's eye and, with a conspiratorial glance at Toyah, whispered, "How long do you reckon before Keegan tries to get furloughed as a political statement?"

James stifled a laugh. "He'd probably demand they fly him home in the left seat, then claim 'constructive dismissal' when they don't."

The gallows humour—sharp, dry, fundamentally human—rolled on. The room swelled with low voices and the scent of spilt coffee, fried onions from the concourse, and just a hint of jet fuel. Beyond the windows, the apron had become a mirror, streaked with rain and the distorted forms of ground crew in hi-vis splashing from one aircraft to the next. Airport life, undeterred by the storm, pushed on in its own language of routine and barely contained chaos.

The screens in the crew room blinked, and all at once a ripple of attention snapped back to the TV as CNN cut live to a press conference from the FAA. The Administrator—a florid, jowly man in a suit far too sharp for the hour who had been appointed by Trump—spoke into the hush.

"Ladies and gentlemen of the press, airline representatives, and the American public watching at home," he intoned, "as you know, at midnight tonight, due to a lapse in federal appropriations, the United States Government will begin an orderly shutdown of all non-essential services."

A long pause—clearly deliberate, intended for dramatic effect, but only heightening the sense of encroaching disaster among the assembled airline professionals.

"We at the Federal Aviation Administration want to assure the travelling public and all stakeholders that the National Airspace System will remain operational. Air Traffic Control services will continue. However,"—here he paused again, and the camera did a slow zoom—"all certification, oversight, and administrative processes will be suspended. Pilots requiring renewals, medicals, or licensing updates are advised to contact their airline's designated representatives. TSA staff are considered essential, but local arrangements may lead to variable coverage. Please refer to individual airport bulletins."

The Administrator took a breath, his composure beginning to crack around the edges. "In practical terms, this means: expect delays, reduced staffing, and a potential for operational disruption at short notice. Any NOTAMs issued in the last forty-eight hours will remain in effect unless specifically cancelled by an essential operations officer. The FAA website may experience outages due to IT support limitations. Please check with your airline for guidance. We urge all aviation professionals to exercise patience, flexibility, and above all, professionalism during this unprecedented time caused by the Democrats not signing the continuing resolution. President Trump has advised that he will not negotiate with the woke liberals who'd rather, quote, 'see the planes grounded than agree to real American values'. The FAA will, of course, remain apolitical and focused on maintaining safe operations." The Administrator's eye twitched slightly, as if he'd read that last line for the first time in the moment.

The feed cut, replaced by a studio anchor wearing the same grave expression now universal across American news. Danielle groaned quietly, Toyah rolled her eyes, and James felt the mood in the crew room constrict, like cabin pressure falling by invisible degrees.

"That's us told, then," Toyah muttered. "Delay, confusion, and blame it on the Democrats. No mention of actually paying the controllers. Y'know, I voted Harris back in November last year, as I didn't trust Trump then, and I don't trust him now. But if the system holds, it'll be the controllers and ramp staff saving our skins, not the politicians."

Her voice was dry, low, edged with the kind of brittle fatigue that settles in after too many months living at the sharp end of airline chaos. Danielle gave a little nod of agreement, eyes on her phone, scrolling the latest from WhatsApp.

James watched the crew room settle into a strange, weightless hush: a shared sense of anticipation, dread, and faint disbelief. There was the odd burst of laughter, always dark, but mostly there was the slow, methodical business of getting ready for the unknown. Uniform jackets were shrugged on, hats pinned in place, logbooks flicked through for the tenth time. The pilots and flight attendants moved as one, an odd, silent ballet of professionals who'd learned long ago how to keep their cool while the world outside spun in circles.

A Delta FO by the coffee machine murmured to his captain, "Atlanta just bumped our slot again. Operations say it's a staffing issue, but I think half their team are already on the beer."

His captain only shrugged. "Good luck, son. Keep the wheels down and the complaints up."

James found himself staring at the rain-streaked tarmac, watching a ground crew run a baggage tug past a lineup of widebodies. The day's flight—a Dallas to San Diego to Portland run, followed by a redeye to Chicago—was still technically on. The aircraft was sitting at gate D33, refuelled, packed, and ready for boarding. But the whispers were everywhere: some flights were already cancelled for "resource reasons," others running on skeleton crews, and a handful of desperate regional jets stuck at remote stands with nobody to marshal them.

He glanced at Danielle, who met his gaze with an unspoken question: "Do we fly or do we wait?"

He shrugged. "We prep. Until someone tells us not to."

It was then that James's Sprint issued Pixel 9A's Teams app pinged—just as the room's collective mood shifted from grim patience to simmering frustration. The sound was echoed across the room by a chorus of phones and iPads vibrating with urgent company messages. For a moment, James simply watched the lights of notification banners bloom and fade, as if the digital world was more real than the airport outside.

Sprint US East Coast Operations: *All crews are to operate flights as scheduled. Any changes will be relayed via the Sprint Staff app to all planes, and to all planes via ACARS, in the event of a comms failure. Please monitor all company channels, ensure you check-in per usual procedure, and report any staffing or TSA issues via your base manager or duty controller. If in doubt, do not push. Safety is paramount. We appreciate your flexibility in these exceptional circumstances.*

James read the company message twice, the clipped phrases already familiar from a dozen previous operational "incidents"—weather, strikes, border closures, once a volcanic eruption. "*Operate as scheduled*" was airline code for "Pretend everything's fine until it isn't, then improvise." He pocketed his phone and looked around the room, noting the way the collective mood had subtly shifted—phones now out, heads bowed, everyone plugged into their own particular digital lifeline.

Danielle was flicking through her own phone, her jaw tight. "Same from crew control. They're saying TSA are short at gates B and F, but our departure's holding for now. I'd put a fiver on it changing by the time we get to security."

Toyah groaned from the armrest, stretching her arms above her head. "San Diego's already delayed ninety minutes. Portland's worse. Oh, and there's a rumour of a walkout by the refuellers." She eyed James over the rim of her mug, her Brooklyn vowels flattening in exasperation.

The room was moving now—people packing up, zipping jackets, checking watches. There was an almost military efficiency to it, the swift, practised ballet of professionals who'd spent years working in environments designed by bureaucrats who had never flown a sector in their lives. James drained his coffee and stood, rolling his shoulders as if bracing for turbulence.

"Right," he said to Danielle. "Let's see what kind of mess the terminal's in."

They gathered their things—flight bags, iPads, logbooks, ID lanyards—performed the little ritual of pocket-pats and mutual checks for hat, pass, pens. The rituals mattered. They were the only constants when the world outside insisted on rewriting the rules each day.

The terminal concourse was a river of fluorescent light, nervous energy, and rolling luggage. Even before they reached the security checkpoint, it was clear something was wrong: the usual zigzag queue snaked far beyond the stanchions, curling past the newsagent and halfway to the escalators, dense with frustrated passengers and the occasional frantic gate agent darting from queue to queue with a sheaf of printed lists.

Danielle blew out her cheeks. "Bloody hell. Is this just us, or is every airport in America having a meltdown today?"

James scanned the crowd—business travellers scowling into their phones, families marooned on suitcases, an elderly woman in a floral blouse frantically repacking a mountain of cosmetics at the front of the queue. There were more uniforms than usual: off-duty pilots, jump seaters, cabin crew all queued up like regular mortals, their usual security shortcuts evidently suspended by staff shortages.

He and Danielle joined the end of the crew queue. It moved glacially, held up by the broken scanner at the staff lane and the single weary officer manning the ID check.

A plump, red-faced man in AmericanoAir epaulettes a few places ahead turned and said in a low voice, "Rumour is, half the Dallas TSA walked out when they found out they'd be working without pay. Management's got a skeleton crew—mostly contractors, retirees, anyone with a pulse and a badge."

****

CHAPTER 22 – WARS Checks In, PanEuro Checks Out
Tuesday 6th October 2025

If there was one thing that was obvious in Indianapolis to James Hart, it was that the city was electric with anticipation. The World Apex Racing Series (WARS) had rolled into town for the Indianapolis Grand Prix, transforming the normally sedate Midwest capital into a pulsating hub of motorsport mania. Full billboard advertisements, advertising Dodge's team, its two stars—Louis Andretti and Alex Walker—plastered across the city, their faces looming over Interstate 70 and the downtown skyline, their retro-spec V10 Kestrels gleaming in high-definition glory. The streets buzzed with fans in team colours, food trucks slinging tacos and craft beer, and the distant roar of engines warming up at the Indianapolis Motor Speedway. For a city accustomed to the Indy 500's annual pilgrimage, WARS was a new beast—raw, aggressive, and unapologetically nostalgic, with its V10-powered machines evoking a bygone era of motorsport untainted by hybrid tech or corporate sanitisation.

Vauxhall Racing was the name on everyone's lips, their star driver Montoya "Monty" Potter's brash charisma and on-track audacity making him a lightning rod for adoration and controversy. His rivalry with now former teammate Luca Pascali, an Italian with Ferrari's weight behind him, had already spilled into the headlines after their clash at Imola, and the Indianapolis Grand Prix promised to be another chapter in their volatile saga.

The third-placed driver, Lorenzo Bellandi, a steady but less flamboyant Italian from Scuderia Tempesta, was quietly gaining ground in the championship, his consistent points-scoring a counterpoint to the Potter-Pascali fireworks, however the Italian suffered from what was called "Ferrari Syndrome", the same that Charles Leclerc and his teammate Lewis Hamilton was also suffering from, also known as strategy errors and poor pit-stop decisions that had plagued Ferrari for decades. Bellandi's methodical approach, while effective, lacked the headline-grabbing bravado of Potter or the raw passion of Pascali, leaving him as the dark horse in a championship increasingly defined by chaos. The Indianapolis Motor Speedway road course was a track that rewarded precision as much as aggression—a perfect stage for Bellandi to close the gap, or for Potter and Pascali to self-destruct in spectacular fashion.

James, however, wasn't here for the motorsport spectacle. He was in Indianapolis for work, captaining an AmericanoAir A321neo on a transcontinental rotation that had started in Las Vegas the previous day and would end, after a gruelling series of sectors, in Newark. The city's WARS fever was an incidental backdrop, a vibrant distraction from the operational grind that defined his days. The crew hotel, a Holiday Inn Express just off Interstate 495 meant that the crew bus had had to do a near enough circuit of I 495 east instead of I 495 west due to a major pile up that had cost 4 people their lives and closed the westbound lanes for hours. The detour had added an extra 40 minutes to the journey from the airport, leaving James and his crew—a Brit with a MPL named Oliver Finch, a twenty-three-year-old Londoner with the wide-eyed earnestness of someone who still believed that airline operations followed logic—utterly exhausted by the time they arrived at the hotel. Oliver, known in the crew room as "Finchy", had spent most of the diversion grumbling about the FTLs and how the detour would "destroy the duty day calculations." The rest of the crew—two cabin crew from the Miami base and a pursuer from Los Angeles—were equally relieved when the shuttle finally pulled into the hotel car park at half one in the morning.

The irony, James knew from his discussions with Oliver, about the British love for Monty Potter and his feud with Luca Pascali, was that it had turned WARS into a cultural phenomenon back in the UK, where motorsport fans were lapping up the drama like it was a soap opera with horsepower. Oliver, despite his fatigue, had been scrolling through X posts on the crew bus, chuckling at memes of Monty's dive bomb at the Canadian round, which had, surprisingly been unsuccessful, Mosport Park having been the venue the final weekend of September, leading to a P4 finish for the Brit.

That, however, according to Oliver, meant that Potter needed to finish only in the top 3 at the Brickyard to win the WARS World Driver Championship, the inaugural season, which was on NBC in the prime time slot for the first time in years. Potter's rise had captured the British imagination: half "James Hunt for the TikTok era," half professional troublemaker, a hero to the tabloid sports columns and a curse for the Vauxhall Racing PR department. Even as the city throbbed to a new rhythm—American fans drawn by the noise, the spectacle, the promise of something a little more dangerous than the usual Indy fare—James could see the soft power of motorsport stretching across oceans and time zones, its threads linking a night-shift captain on a bread-and-butter US rotation with a grandstand full of blue-collar Indiana fans.

Of course, that had been the previous night, and now, after a long detour due to the Interstate being blocked by a mangled tangle of semi-trailers and SUVs, it was morning at Indianapolis Airport, and James was in the monotone grip of another pre-flight, coffee in hand, standing at the crew room window with a view across a grey, rain-washed apron. The Holiday Inn Express had delivered precisely what it always did—lukewarm coffee, polyester sheets, and a free breakfast that, on this occasion, had been devoured by an entire tour group of Dutch WARS fans in matching Max Verstappen bucket hats before James or his crew could even sniff a bagel. As he watched an elderly ramp agent marshal a caravan of Sprint-branded baggage carts past a line of idling low-cost jets, he reflected on the strange collisions of spectacle and slog that defined modern aviation.

Behind him, the crew room hummed with the low-key chaos of an AmericanoAir morning: gate changes, last-minute roster swaps, and that particularly American habit of blaring cable news on a 75-inch TV, the sound off but the headlines screaming anyway. Today, the news ticker was an endless loop of Trump's latest trade war bluster, Spirit's ongoing bankruptcy fire-sale, and rumours that Monty Potter was still in Monaco and hadn't even departed for the States yet, much to the horror of the WARS paddock and the delight of social media, which was busy speculating whether the championship leader would even make it to the Brickyard in time for free practice. Even the gate agents seemed caught up in the circus; James could overhear a pair of Delta staffers at the next table debating whether Monty's rumoured last-minute flight out of Nice was on a Vauxhall-branded Dassault Falcon, or some chartered Sprint Max. The entire terminal buzzed with the sense that something big was about to happen—either the coronation of a new global motorsport superstar or an infamous American cock-up for the ages.

James checked his watch—just after 08:10. The roster had them operating AmericanoAir 1510, a routine Indianapolis to Newark sector, before returning back to Indianapolis, then off to Boston for the final leg of a 4 leg day, a short hop by transcontinental standards but an eternity by the measure of post-pandemic, post-ULCC operational chaos. He glanced at the FTL calculations on his phone, knowing that the earlier detour and late check-in would mean the whole crew would be running dangerously close to their legal maximums by the end of the day. In theory, everything would work; in practice, the odds of a rolling delay, an inbound aircraft swap, or a catering SNAFU were as high as the nose of a Dodge Kestrel at full throttle down the Brickyard straight.

He drained the last of his mediocre coffee and surveyed his team: Finchy already nervously double-checking his bag tags and pouring over the iPad, the two Miami-based cabin crew—Lupita and Clara—animatedly debating whether to brave the "Hoosier hashbrowns" from the staff canteen, and their LA-based purser, Marnie, fixing her hair in the reflection of the vending machine. Despite the hour, they all looked far more ready for battle than he felt.

There was an easy camaraderie to this group, the kind forged on hotel shuttles, early showtimes, and endless reboots of the same app-crashed crew rostering software.

"Alright, troops," James announced, nodding to the departures screen, where AA, Delta, and Sprint flights to Chicago and Atlanta blinked with the expected delays. "Our chariot's on Stand B23. A321neo, N484AT. Two trolleys of breakfast bagels, cola and also, for some random reason, $400 worth of pre-orders of cold brew and jalapeño poppers. Don't ask me why. NOTAMs have come in, with reduced service due to the Government Shutdown being in the 6th day. Reduced controllers in DC's FIR, so expect a reroute via Cleveland Centre and possible delays at push. New York's still stacking up from last night's thunderstorms, and Ops says we're third in line for fuel, so if anyone wants to put the kettle on, now's your chance."

That earned a groan from Lupita and a resigned eye roll from Marnie, who was already mentally calculating how many times she'd have to explain to hungry Hoosiers that, no, AmericanoAir didn't serve breakfast burritos at 30,000 feet, and no, you couldn't take your jalapeño poppers off the aircraft because of "FAA food hygiene protocol."

Finchy looked up from his iPad, pale from lack of sleep and nerves. "I take it that means we're not leaving on time, then?"

James smiled, the kind of smile that was half commiseration, half gallows humour. "It means we leave when the fuel truck turns up, and when ATC lets us."

James watched as Finchy packed away his iPad, tucking it under his arm with the care of someone who half-expected it to be snatched by a passing supervisor desperate to justify a roster reshuffle. The morning lull was already giving way to the low-level hum of an airport gearing up for a day of high drama: bleary-eyed businessmen, families in Pacers jerseys, and packs of WARS fans in blue-and-gold Andretti merchandise jostling at the gates. Somewhere, a group of British students—likely on a gap year and already three beers deep by breakfast—argued about the difference between "real Indy racing" and "F1 with muscle cars." Lupita, watching them, shook her head and muttered, "If they start a singalong, I'm hiding in the rear galley."

James offered a sympathetic grimace. "That's your right. Just don't let them near the jalapeño poppers. FAA's still got rules about that."

As the crew filed out towards security, James caught the fleeting scent of rain and jet fuel—an odd comfort, the perfume of his profession. The terminal, while modern, already bore the scars of Sprint's relentless expansion: brand new self-bag-drop kiosk, staff trained in the Ryanair Way of Revenue Extraction from Americans who aren't used to charging for everything that didn't physically fit in a rucksack, and endless "Sprint Extra" banners promising faster boarding for a fee. James threaded through the security queue, exchanging tired but friendly nods with Delta and JetBlue crews, all caught in the same operational undertow.

On the walk to the stand, the windows of the concourse framed a panorama of activity: various 737s and A320s squeezed into every available gate, an Sprint A320neo being towed with a new Disney+ tail ad, and of course a United Express liveried CRJ200 that looked like it had been held together with little more than gaffer tape and nostalgia, its ground crew studiously ignoring the puddle of something viscous pooling beneath the nosewheel. James watched, half-smiling, as a pair of rampers bickered over whether the "liquid" was hydraulic fluid or the remains of last night's nachos, a dispute resolved when one flicked a cigarette butt perilously close and both scuttled away in mock horror.

It was just another Tuesday in twenty-first-century aviation—corporate slogans painted on tails, global sports events warping the traffic flow, and everyone at ground level improvising through the gaps in the system.

Suddenly his phone sounded, an NBC News alert.

"PANEURO COLLAPSES WITH NO WARNING – STAFF LEFT STRANDED

Hundreds of crew and thousands of passengers across Europe and the United States wake to chaos as retro airline ceases operations overnight. PanEuro, a British airline who had promised in 2020 to 'revitalise travel' has this morning collapsed.

The full service operator, owned by private equity specialists Thomas Industries, has confirmed that the company, acquired during the Trump tariffs of April 2025 when the company had undergone an initial public offering on Britain's AIM market, has entered administration. UK Civil Aviation Authority officials have grounded the fleet. Stranded crews in Berlin, Birmingham and Miami are reportedly being told to 'make their own arrangements'. Early indications suggest a liquidity crisis following a failed refinancing round with Omani sovereign investors and a collapse in forward bookings after last month's incident at Prague, when a PanEuro flight was intercepted by a USAF F-35 after a 'security misunderstanding'.

The airline, introduced in December 2020 by a consortium of Rothschilds and several members of the British House of Lords, had a chequered past, including sexual assault by a captain on a transatlantic flight, a near-miss incident involving a Russian MiG-31, and a high-profile security debacle in Prague. These events, coupled with a string of operational missteps and a retro glamour model that alienated as many passengers as it charmed, had eroded confidence in PanEuro's viability.

Melissa Thompson, CEO of Thomas Industries said to Sky News "We are deeply saddened by the collapse of PanEuro. We exhausted every possible avenue to secure additional funding and keep the airline flying. However, the combination of rising fuel costs, post-pandemic travel volatility, and the impact of recent security incidents rendered the business unsustainable. Our priority now is to support our colleagues and passengers as best we can during this difficult time."

It was a boilerplate statement—impersonal, corporate, the kind of empty reassurance James had heard too many times over the years. He scrolled further, skimming through testimonies from angry passengers stuck in Prague, bewildered stewardesses at Manchester, and a clip of a tired pilot in what was PanEuro's new uniform, it having been amended since June from its former Pan Am style to a more British Airways meets 2020s practicality, with less of the pillbox hats and more focus on functionality, standing outside Rome Airport, his cap in hand, looking like he'd just aged a decade overnight. The pilot's voice cracked as he told a Sky News reporter, "We were told to report for duty as normal. Got to the crew room, and the system was locked. No flights, no roster, no nothing. Just an email saying the company's gone bust and we're on our own. I've got a mortgage, a family—how am I supposed to get home from here?"

What made James laugh was the next paragraphs.

"The move from Manston Terminal 1 for the Summer 2025 schedule to Heathrow was, in retrospect, the most spectacular miscalculation of the lot.

For a few short years, PanEuro had made nostalgia a business model. Their 707-blue seat covers, the daily social media campaigns about "bringing back the romance of flight", the fluted champagne glasses on transatlantic services—they'd seemed, briefly, to bottle lightning. In the end, nobody really wanted to pay full-service prices for a brand-new facsimile of the past when you could get to Malaga or Mykonos for £29 with Sprint or EasyJet.

PanEuro's demise is a story of hubris, nostalgia, and the brutal arithmetic of low-cost competition. In a world where consumers crave Wi-Fi and legroom but won't pay for either, old-school glamour has little chance."

The push notification was still glowing on James's phone as he led the crew through the final crew ID check at Gate B23. He glanced sideways at Finchy, who looked up from his own phone with wide eyes and a look of genuine sorrow.

James found himself thinking, not for the first time, how thin the veneer of security in aviation really was. One day you were an airline with new uniforms, a marketing campaign, and a roster of flights; the next, a ghost. Pilots grounded, cabin crew marooned, planes impounded and creditors picking over the bones.

But operational reality didn't pause for corporate disaster, and Gate B23 was already alive with the usual morning chaos. There was a line of boarding passengers, a chorus of moans about bag fees, and a Sprint supervisor remonstrating with a Delta rampie over the use of a shared tug. James forced himself into the rhythm of the morning. He led the crew out onto the damp apron, where the A321neo sat waiting—tail still slick with last night's rain, the "AmericanoAir" titling so fresh it looked like it might rub off on your sleeve.

Finchy fell into step beside him, lowering his voice. "You ever fly with any of the PanEuro lot?" he asked.

"Not as far as I'm aware," James replied, stepping around a stubborn puddle on the tarmac as he angled towards the forward airstairs. "They're the lot who were involved in that scandal where a Captain where a Captain got decked by his own FO on a New York sector, weren't they?" He shook his head, suppressing a wry smile. "They always seemed a bit like aviation cosplay, to be honest. I mean—

proper coffee, hot towels, a menu in French and English, and every week some poor sod in a pillbox hat was in the papers moaning about the make-up policy. It was never going to last against six quid fares and paying a tenner for carry-on."

Finchy nodded, but he wasn't laughing. He looked troubled—part empathy, part the rising worry every young pilot feels when the fragility of the business becomes real. "It's grim though, isn't it? I mean—half of my course from CTC went to PanEuro. There's a WhatsApp going now—people stranded in Berlin, Paris, even DC. One bloke said he was halfway to Calgary when the ops desk sent a message saying 'don't land—return to London, CAA's grounded you'. The FO's stuck out there now, says they're making them all buy their own tickets home."

James reached the bottom of the steps, giving the cold, slick fuselage an affectionate pat—his own ritual. "Yeah. Doesn't matter how big your fleet or how pretty your Instagram—when the cash runs out, nobody's immune. Thank goodness I was USAF before going into commercial aviation, so I knew never to trust an airline with more branding consultants than spare wheels," James said, his tone softening as he stepped onto the first metal stair. He turned and glanced at Finchy, who stood a moment, rain spitting against his navy Sprint/AmericanoAir parka, caught between admiration for the "glamour" PanEuro had promised and the cold realisation that in the end, glamour was just another line item for the liquidators. "They all look solid until payday vanishes."

Inside the forward galley, Marnie was wrestling with the trolleys and a stack of cold brew cans that looked like a miniature Mount Fuji. "Who's bright idea was it to load a football flight's worth of caffeine on a Tuesday morning?" she called, looking over her glasses at James. "And did you see the news? PanEuro's gone. Kaput. Poof. Done." She snapped her fingers, the sound sharp against the hum of the aircraft's auxiliary power unit. "Half my mates from LAX training are texting me."

James stepped into the galley, the familiar scent of fresh plastic and cleaning fluid mingling with the faint tang of coffee. The A321neo's interior was still showroom-new, its navy-blue seats and sleek overhead bins a testament to Sprint's knack for making budget look premium—at least until you sat down. "Yeah, just saw it," he said, setting his flight bag on the jump seat. "Sounds like a proper mess. You know anyone at PanEuro personally?"

Marnie shrugged, shoving a tray of jalapeño poppers into a storage compartment with more force than strictly necessary. "Nope, not really. Anyway, one of their girl's been posting on X about how she's got no savings, no ticket home, and her landlord's already threatening to chuck her stuff out. It's brutal."

James nodded, his jaw tightening. The human cost always hit hardest: crews stranded in foreign crew rooms, pilots with type ratings suddenly worth less than the paper they were printed on, and passengers left to fend for themselves in terminals from Berlin to Birmingham. PanEuro's fall was just the latest chapter in an industry that chewed up dreams as fast as it burned jet fuel.

"Let's focus on getting this lot to Newark," he said, his voice steady but not unkind. "We've got enough on our plate without borrowing PanEuro's troubles. Finchy's got the load sheet, and I'll do the walkaround. You and the girls keep the pax calm—especially the jalapeño popper brigade. Last thing we need is a riot over cold brew."

The Indianapolis apron was a damp, bustling chaos, the rain having eased to a fine mist that clung to his uniform like a second skin. The A321neo, tail number N484AT, gleamed under the overcast sky, its Sprint livery with the AmericanoAir logo by the door and the advert where the Stars and Stripes on the tail a subtle nod to its American ambitions, though the paint job still screamed budget efficiency over patriotic flair.

James began his walkaround, his boots splashing through shallow puddles as he scanned the airframe with the meticulous eye of a pilot who'd seen too many "new" aircraft hide costly surprises. The A321neo was pristine, fresh from Airbus's Mobile plant, but he wasn't about to trust a shiny exterior. He checked the tyres, the flaps, the pitot tubes, and the engine inlets, pausing to run his fingers along the seams of the auxiliary fuel tanks. The ACTs, a Sprint staple for stretching range, looked solid— no loose fittings, no telltale oil streaks—but he made a mental note to double-check the fuel transfer system once they were powered up. A "minor glitch" in Mobile's logbook could easily become a major headache at 35,000 feet.

The ground crew, a mix of Sprint's navy-vested locals and a few Delta contractors pressed into service, moved with the frenetic energy of people racing against a departure slot. A fuel truck was parked under the wing, its hose snaking into the belly, while baggage handlers tossed suitcases into the hold with the kind of nonchalance that suggested "fragile" was just a suggestion. One of them, a wiry kid with a Hoosiers cap pulled low, caught James's eye and gave a thumbs-up, shouting over the whine of a nearby APU, "Fuel's on, Cap! You're good for Newark and back, no sweat!"

James returned the thumbs-up, though his expression remained guarded. "Cheers, mate. Double-check the paperwork, yeah? I don't want any surprises when we're over Ohio." The kid nodded, already turning back to his clipboard, and James continued his circuit, satisfied but not complacent. The Indianapolis apron was a microcosm of the industry's churn, all coexisting in a fragile ecosystem held together by overworked ground staff and sheer bloody-mindedness.

Back at the forward airstairs, Finchy was waiting, his iPad glowing with the latest load sheet. "We're at 176 pax, seven crew including us," he reported, his voice clipped with the precision of someone still proving himself. "Hold's got 82 bags, mostly standard. Total ZFW's within limits, CoG's nicely balanced. Fuel's at 15,300 kilos, enough for Newark, a 45-minute hold, and a divert to LaGuardia, JFK, Philly and even Boston if we need it. Catering's loaded, but Marnie's already kicking off about the cold brew cans—they're stacked so high she reckons they'll avalanche when we hit turbulence." He paused, a faint grin breaking through his fatigue.

James chuckled, the mental image of Marnie fending off a mob of Vauxhall fans with a tray of spicy snacks briefly lightening the morning's weight. "She'll manage. Always does. Let's get the cockpit sorted, and I'll run the fuel transfer check myself. If those ACTs are as fresh as Mobile claims, I want to know they're behaving before we're dodging thunderstorms over Pennsylvania." He clapped Finchy on the shoulder, a gesture of camaraderie that doubled as a nudge to keep moving. The younger pilot nodded, falling into step as they climbed the airstairs, the damp metal creaking under their boots.

The cockpit of N484AT was a familiar sanctuary, its glass displays and sidestick controls a stark contrast to the chaos outside. The smell of new electronics and leather lingered, a reminder that this A321neo had barely clocked 200 hours since leaving the factory. James settled into the left seat, his flight bag stowed beside him, and began powering up the systems, his fingers moving with the muscle memory of decades in the air. The ECAM flickered to life, its green readouts confirming a clean bill of health—no deferred defects, no maintenance alerts, just the sterile glow of a brand-new aircraft. It was almost too perfect.

****

CHAPTER 23 – News From London
Thursday 31ˢᵗ October 2025

"They're calling it the Miracle on the Thames, Sprint UK Flight 1549," the voice on NBC News crackled through the crew room's ancient television, its flickering screen casting a pale glow over the cluttered space at Las Vegas McCarran International Airport. Captain James Hart leaned against the chipped Formica counter, a Styrofoam cup of lukewarm coffee in hand, his eyes narrowing as the anchor's voice droned on. The room was a mess of mismatched chairs, half-eaten donuts, and dog-eared flight manuals, the kind of place that screamed temporary but had been limping along for decades. Outside, the Nevada sun beat down on the tarmac, glinting off the MGM Grand liveried tail of an AmericanoAir A320neo, a brand new aircraft fresh from Mobile's assembly line, its bold navy blue livery a stark contrast to the faded Spirit Airlines A320s languishing at the edge of the apron.

The news segment replayed footage from London, captured by a bystander's phone: a Sprint UK A318, G-SATC, gliding low over the Thames, its engines eerily silent, before executing a textbook ditching just past RSPB Rainham Marshes, the video footage showing it was a departure from London City service, heading east out of the airport, according to the anchor, from a local aviation enthusiast who'd been plane-spotting at the time.

The segment replayed, grainy and shaky, the A318's low silhouette somehow stately above the murky ribbon of the Thames. As it passed the towers of Canary Wharf, traffic on the Woolwich Ferry froze, cameras rose. There was an audible gasp from those watching in the background as the jet, gliding lower than seemed survivable, flared—just barely above the water—before settling with a great white splash that fanned spray up over the mudflats and startled a flock of wintering lapwings into flight. Someone's voice, thick with disbelief, exclaimed, "Bloody hell, he's put it in the river!"

The anchor's commentary faded back in, American vowels unable to do justice to the moment: "All one hundred and twenty-four souls on board were safely rescued by London's emergency services, with minor injuries only—miraculously, no fatalities." The banner at the bottom of the screen read, in all-caps, "**_SPRINT MIRACLE: UK JET DITCHES IN THAMES, EVERYONE SURVIVES_**." As the camera cut to images of shivering passengers wrapped in foil blankets, James caught a glimpse of the Sprint logo on a steward's sodden uniform, the navy unmistakable even on an NBC feed.

James set his coffee down and let out a long, low whistle. All around him, the hum of the crew room had stilled; the usual back-and-forth between shifts had faded as the television seized everyone's attention. Kyle Richards, a Canadian, who was the purser for the upcoming Oakland run, looked up from his phone and caught his eye, Kyle's expression one of naked shock.

"London City to Amsterdam," Kyle murmured, voice hushed as if the events were happening right there in front of them. "That's a river, not a runway. It's Sully all over again."

James nodded, the edges of the news broadcast seeping through his brain in fragments: *G-SATC… Sprint UK… 1549… Rainham Marshes… all survived.* He sipped his coffee absently, barely tasting the bitter dregs. The room was tense, as if a cold draught had found its way through the sun-bleached cinderblock. Even in Nevada, a world away from London's autumnal greys, the impact of what had just happened felt personal. There was a quiet awe in the crew room, something almost reverential—the sort of hush reserved for miracles, or disasters narrowly averted.

He caught the tail end of the segment: an interview with the A318's captain, still dripping, being led away from the riverbank by two fluorescent-jacketed paramedics and a dozen camera flashes. The captain's accent was pure Essex, all stoic understatement and clipped vowels: "We lost both engines, and my First Officer said to me "Boss, we're going to have to do a Hudson. It ain't worth continuing to try for Southend or Manston." So we set up for the Thames—couldn't make London City back, not a prayer. Kept her clean, kept her flying, and—well, we're all here, aren't we? Credit to my crew, and the river was smoother than the Docklands Approach on a Monday."

James watched, transfixed, as the captain's battered dignity played out on the screen—a thousand miles from this stale American crew room, yet so immediate he could almost smell the cold river water. The paramedics ushered the flight crew toward an ambulance, news microphones thrust like blunt weapons in their faces, but the captain only paused long enough to say, "Couldn't have asked for better discipline from my lot. Cabin crew made the difference." The newscast rolled in footage of lifeboats, Metropolitan Police RIBs, and bobbing orange rafts; a surreal, almost orderly scene on a river more accustomed to traffic jams and tourist boats than rescue operations.

The room began to stir. Someone—James didn't catch who—exhaled sharply, breaking the spell.

"Bloody hell," muttered a woman from Southwest, her lanyard still half-tucked in her shirt, "if that was one of ours, it'd be all over TikTok before the ATIS updated."

Kyle nodded, pushing back his chair with a scraping sound. "We've had plenty of maydays out here, but nobody puts it down in the Bellagio fountain and walks away." His quip drew a thin smile, a crack in the tension.

But James's thoughts were elsewhere, already drifting eastward, imagining the chaos unfolding at Sprint's Kent HQ, the press vultures, the regulators, the armchair pilots, the families waiting by phones for news. He pictured the aircraft, still afloat in the chill Thames, the water lapping at the underbelly, the rear, like Cactus 1549, deeper than the nose, the aft galley already a sodden archive of high-vis jackets. James remembered the procedural diagrams in every Airbus manual—*'Ditching: gear up, spoilers retracted, flare as required'*—but the reality, that battered jet now bobbing in the brown water, was never in the books.

A silence lingered, the crew room suspended between admiration and something rawer: fear, maybe, or the dreadful empathy of those who know how fine the margins are.

Kyle sat forward, fingers drumming restlessly. "Think they'll salvage it?"

James shrugged, the movement slow, uncertain. "The insurers will have kittens, but the Thames is shallow out that way. They might just patch her and tow her out, if the media circus lets them."

James's mind wandered, lost in thoughts of the A318's fate. Outside, the endless sun on the Nevada tarmac now seemed incongruous—a world away from the slick, chill surface of the Thames and the wreckage of G-SATC, its Sprint blue already smudged brown with river mud.

For a few minutes, the Las Vegas crew room dissolved into quiet speculation. Someone tapped at a phone, searching for new video. Flight crews clustered in small, instinctive knots—Southwest, JetBlue, even a United pair who'd turned up on a deadhead to Phoenix, all half-watching, half-remembering. It wasn't just morbid curiosity. Everyone in that room had run "the scenario" in their heads, in simulators, or in quiet, sleepless moments. Everyone had wondered how, or if, they'd have made the same decisions.

The TV shifted to commercials, and the spell broke. James shook himself and stretched, feeling the ache of another overnight layover in his bones. He still had three sectors left that day: Las Vegas to Oakland, Oakland to San Diego, then a deadhead home to Los Angeles for a week off. It all felt remote now, routine set against something that, by luck or fate, hadn't happened to him. Yet.

James left his coffee to go cold and made his way to the window overlooking the shimmering apron, needing movement to shake the chill left by the broadcast. The

Nevada heat pressed in through the glass, a reminder that life, flights, and pay-to-play chaos rolled on regardless of miracles or catastrophes elsewhere.

But the world outside felt slightly less real now—a tableau of service trucks, pushback tugs, and bustling rampies in Hi-Viz vests, all too busy or too jaded to pause for the news from London. Sprint's navy A320neo sat at Gate 14, a dog-eared manifest tucked under a windscreen wiper, ground staff arguing with a third-party caterer about the absence of the right vegan meal boxes. For a moment, James wondered how many of these people had seen the news, or cared, or would wake up in the dead of night with the sound of silence in both engines, the brown water of the Thames looming up.

He leaned his forehead against the glass, the cool touch a little grounding, and allowed himself a few moments of imagined connection with the sodden Sprint UK crew somewhere in a hospital or a sterile police interview suite by now. The River Thames had never felt so close, or so inevitable.

By the time James returned to the crew room, the news cycle had moved on—election adverts, a feel-good segment about a local dog rescue, a garish promo for a Nevada wedding chapel. But the Sprint miracle lingered in the undertone of every conversation: the volume was lower, the jokes softer, and the sense of shared vulnerability more acute.

"First the MPL scandal you lot have," a United captain was saying to Kyle, his drawl half-mocking but edged with unease, "then the Government shutting down meaning the FAA and ATC is flying on good faith and borrowed time, and now your British cousins manage to turn the Thames into a runway. They ought to shut you lot and your cowboy outfit down, before you try it with the Hudson or the Charles River. I mean, your deathtrap Airbuses-"

James didn't even need to say a word, as Kyle got up and, shockingly for a Canadian, punched the United captain square in the face. It wasn't a hard blow, more the kind that made a statement—enough for the room to pause, half the assembled crews turning, not quite sure if this was a fight or just the normal heat of layover banter.

"That's it!" The United pilot snarled, getting up and attempting a return punch, catching Kyle in the eye, causing the Canadian to stagger backwards, colliding with a stack of ancient, battered coffee trays. The thud silenced the room for a heartbeat, everyone frozen between the urge to intervene and the half-amused, half-appalled instinct to let it play out.

"You can hardly talk," Kyle said, taking another swing at the United pilot with a look half hurt, half contemptuous. "You want to talk about deathtraps?" he shot back, nursing his bruised cheek. "Last I checked, you lot run fucking Maxes and Airbuses, and how many people have died because MCAS decided to go sightseeing? Sorry, but no one here needs a lecture about aircraft from a country that let the 737 Max fly for nearly two years before grounding it. Sprint's had one crash, and that A321XLR that got bombed by Trump's terrorist Air Farce-"

James knew, being a retired USAF Major, that calling the USAF a bunch of 'terrorists' was a line he wouldn't usually let slide, but the room was too stunned, too exhausted, and too full of adrenaline to react.

"Everyone knows that the Max deaths were the idiots at the pointy end not knowing their CRM and how MCAS operates. The Europeans overreacted as per usual," the United pilot snarled, before headbutting Kyle in the face, the crack of bone on bone echoing round the linoleum and battered tables.

"Oh, so those who died in the Lion Air and Ethiopian Airlines crashes were all their own fault, then?" Kyle's voice cracked a little, blood trickling from his eyebrow, his Canadian composure entirely lost to adrenaline and fatigue. "What would you have done—reset the circuit breakers with your arse? And what about Alaska Airlines Flight 1282?" Kyle shot back, voice cracking. "Or do you lot not read your own NTSB reports?"

The crew room had fallen into an uneasy hush, punctuated only by the low buzz of a vending machine and the muted thunder of departing jets. All eyes flicked between the two men, now separated only by the battered laminate table. For a moment, it looked as if fists might continue to fly, but James, stepping forward with the authority of years in the left seat and the weariness of one who'd seen layovers sour too many times, held up a calming hand.

"Enough," he said, voice level, but edged with steel. "We're all on the same side, right? It's a miracle, what happened in London. Let's not let the media circus in here make us forget it."

Kyle, blood still trickling from his eyebrow, glared at the United captain. The American, to his credit, dropped his gaze, running a hand through thinning hair, a flush creeping up his neck. There was, James knew, an unspoken bond in the room: all of them understood the peril of the sky, the caprice of engines, and the sheer bloody luck sometimes needed to bring everyone home.

"Sorry," Kyle muttered at last, voice grudging. "It's just—" He shook his head, wiping the blood from his cheek with the back of his hand. "We all know it could've been any one of us."

"Fucking got my contacts, you Yankee twat," Kyle muttered, "I'm going to have to go to the ER as you've got it smashed straight up behind the eyelid." He blinked furiously, tears streaming down his cheek as he fumbled for his phone, voice strained between anger and embarrassment. "This is the last bloody thing I need before a triple-sector day."

"You Sprint lot think you're all heroes now, just because you've put one in the drink and everyone walked away," the United captain shot back, voice full of American bluster, but the force behind it had faded. He was already aware he'd crossed a line, and more aware still of the half-circle of crew now watching for escalation—or entertainment.

James stepped in, calm but loaded with years of command authority. "That's enough," he said, drawing on his experience as a USAF Major to steady the room. "Kyle, get yourself checked at medical—Union's got a hotline if you need it. And you," he turned his cool gaze on the

United captain, "are welcome to file a report if you feel hard done by, but you'll do it outside this crew room. We're all professionals, and if you can't behave like one, there's a shuttle back to the terminal with your name on it."

A tense hush hung, broken only by the whine of the vending machine kicking in as if to mock the drama. For a long, awkward moment, neither pilot moved. Then Kyle, blinking hard, muttered, "Thanks, James," and shouldered his bag, heading for the door. The United captain snorted but sat, deflated, staring at the scuffed tiles as if they'd yield some better outcome.

James looked around the crew room, catching the eyes of each group—JetBlue, Southwest, AmericanoAir, even a pair of Spirit crew stranded by the latest slot grab. "You know, every one of us will have a day when the rules break down and only airmanship keeps the score even. No matter what's on your badge." He turned to the television, now showing another breathless recap of "the Miracle on the Thames," as if the anchors themselves were trying to grasp how a jetliner could end up in a river and nobody die. "That crew in London… they deserve your respect. Only them and Sully and Skiles ever pulled off something like that and got everyone out alive. You can call it luck, you can call it skill, but in this job, anyone who's honest knows it's a bit of both. And if ever I meet them two, I'm going to buy them a pint and a plate of chips and ask how the hell they kept their hands steady with a city watching and the water coming up."

He let the words hang for a moment, his accent gone a touch more Midlands as fatigue and the surreal aftershock of the broadcast caught up with him. Then he straightened, rolled his shoulders, and reached for his flight bag. "Right. Let's get back to doing the job. We've all got flights, and nobody needs to add a punch-up to the paperwork pile."

As the room's tension dissolved, the old rituals reasserted themselves: crews comparing sector lengths, swapping aircraft tales, someone checking their watch and grumbling about minimum rest. James found his focus drifting back to his own schedule, the prospect of three more flights before he could collapse in a hotel bed. But his mind, still fogged by the news from London, replayed every simulator session where he'd briefed for a ditching, every time he'd run through the checklists—gear up, ditching button, brace, wait, hope. He wondered how he'd do, if the unthinkable ever came.

He stepped outside into the desert heat, blinking against the sun, and let his gaze travel over the sprawling apron. The MGM Grand-tailed AmericanoAir A320neo glinted, engines whirring as a ground crew finished a hurried turnaround. Overhead, a JetBlue A321 banked north towards Salt Lake, and a Southwest 737 rumbled down the runway on another milk run to San Diego.

James lingered for a moment on the service road, the taste of adrenaline and coffee mixing uneasily as he watched the ballet of ground ops unfold. He could sense, even here under the crystalline Las Vegas sky, that something had shifted. There was a gravity to what had happened in London, a collective shiver of mortality that ran through every uniformed soul on the ramp, whether they admitted it or not.

He made his way to the operations desk. His badge pinged the scanner and the dispatch supervisor, Lila, glanced up, her phone pinned between ear and shoulder. She was fielding a call from someone in AmericanoAir's Wilmington HQ, all the usual background chaos: boarding bridges stuck, last-minute slot swaps, the fallout of Spirit's latest route collapse.

"Hey, James, just got your revised release," she called, covering the phone. "Oakland slot's back fifteen—ATC holding all departures for a ground stop due to… fog?" She gave him a look that said she knew that was code for slot juggling. "And Ops says catering is only half loaded. Apparently, the vendor sent a truck to the wrong terminal—again."

James accepted the latest stack of paperwork, a thick sheaf of forms—release, NOTAMs, last-minute flight plan amendments. Everything looked routine, but his mind kept looping back to the image of G-SATC on the Thames, bobbing gently, encircled by lifeboats and the metallic flutter of foil blankets.

"Any word from London?" he asked, mostly to make conversation, partly because he wanted some tangible link back to that other world.

Lila shook her head, her voice dropping. "Just the news, same as you. Sprint UK's phones are off the hook. FAA sent a circular. There'll be briefings. You know the drill." She paused, lowering her voice. "Lot of people in here are shaken up, James. Even the rampies. It's a small world."

He nodded, the reassurance hollow. He found his FO, a young woman named Mia Choudhury, already at the gate, crosschecking the digital log on her iPad. Mia had that brittle, over-caffeinated focus he recognised from the new generation—sharp, competent, sometimes bristling, but underneath it all, just as vulnerable as anyone when the curtain ripped and the chaos showed through.

She looked up. "Got the new plan? They want us out of here five minutes after wheels up from the last inbound. But catering's a joke—half the coffee, twice the beer. And Dispatch says the weather's still holding over the Bay." She offered a lopsided grin. "You ever think we'd see the day when the Thames is the safest place to land in London?"

James managed a ghost of a smile. "Honestly, Mia? After today, I'm ready to believe anything. All bets are off. Thames, Hudson, the Paddington Canal—if you can put it down and get everyone out, it's a runway as far as I'm concerned. You know, I wonder if it's one of the MPL lot who was in the right seat or if the Brits had put an ATP as FO. I mean, it's been a month since the MPL scandal here was released, and the FAA still haven't decided whether AmericanoAir is to be shut down or not because the DC lot have cut the funding due to the Shutdown, and if they do shut us down, we're all out of a job overnight."

Mia looked at a looked at him, eyes wide and tired, the lines of a long run of double turns etched beneath her eyeliner. "If they close AmericanoAir, I'll just sign up for Sprint UK—though after today, maybe I'll ask for seaplane conversion. I hear the City Airport Yacht Club are recruiting." Her smile was brittle, forced through the uncertainty that haunted all new pilots—especially the ones on these contract gigs, forever waiting for the next audit, scandal or economic axe.

James gave a dry chuckle, though nothing about it felt funny. "Sprint will take you, if you're willing to sign a thirty-year NDA and promise never to mention Brexit, Omani investment or the meaning of 'fuel planning' in a public place." He checked the manifest: nearly full, mostly westbound business refugees, a handful of retirees in airport wheelchairs, and a group of middle-aged British men in matching T-shirts reading "Viva Las Vegas— Mick's Stag Do 2025" who, even at 11:30 am, had a dangerous gleam in their eye.

He turned back to Mia. "You good to fly? I know it's just Oakland, but if you want to stand down, I'll cover you. Day like today, no shame in it."

She shook her head, gathering herself. "I'm fine, Captain. If anything, I'd rather be up there than down here watching another 'Miracle on the Thames' special report. Up front, there's something to do. Down here, there's just—" She trailed off, waving at the TV, where the news had cycled back to endless speculation, split-screened with nervous politicians and aviation 'experts' from YouTube. "Anyway, let's get these punters to Oakland and see if Dispatch has left us enough fuel to divert to Reno when the slot collapses."

James nodded, falling easily into the rhythm of preflight. "Alright. You take the walkaround—if anyone from NBC or the Review-Journal tries to interview you, tell them we're just actors from Cirque du Soleil. I'll get on the radios and find out if we're actually going to get the coffee before push."

Mia grinned, slinging her bright orange vest over her blazer as she headed out onto the jet bridge, ducking the throng of inbound passengers, most too engrossed in their phones to notice her. She had the springy walk of someone clinging to discipline through exhaustion, dodging the stares of the "Mick's Stag Do" lot, who were busy debating the merits of gambling versus "pacing themselves" before take-off.

He scanned the ramp through the plate-glass window. The sun was brutal, shimmering off the white concrete and corrugated metal, broken only by the scurrying figures of baggage handlers with their battered carts and sunburnt faces. Somewhere, a ground crewman in an old Sprint UK vest, faded and torn, was balancing two mismatched crates marked "Fragile" on one arm while swigging from a Red Bull can. Above, the tail of the MGM Grand jet loomed like a billboard for a different reality, a reminder of the relentless churn that kept AmericanoAir, Sprint, Spirit — whoever — barely in the air.

"I'm surprised they had a jet bridge allocated, as normally we use remote stands," James muttered to himself, lips quirking in the ghost of a smile as he surveyed the gate. Out here, even the little graces felt like rare luck—though maybe, after London, luck was being rationed worldwide.

He moved along the gate, clipboard in hand, ticking boxes with half his attention, ears pricked to the background chatter of operations—flight delays blamed on "weather," whispers of yet another AmericanoAir IT outage, the slightly panicked bark of a new supervisor fielding a call from Wilmington HQ about "brand reputation management." No one said it aloud, but he could feel it in the air: today, the brand's reputation was floating in the Thames.

He scrawled his initials on the fuel slip, checked the load sheet Mia had sent via the SharePoint that Sprint US used, and nodded to the ramp supervisor—a genial man with an old Sun Country badge on his lanyard, who looked like he'd done twenty winters in Minnesota and two careers before this one.

"Full load, all bags, one electric wheelchair with a dodgy battery clearance," the man reported. "Stag party are behaving so far, but I give it until the safety demo. Good luck up there, Cap."

James grinned, trading that familiar look of gallows humour all frontline staff shared—the unspoken, *this will all make sense in the memoirs*.

Back on board, the flight deck was cool and quiet, the Airbus's hum a steady anchor. Mia returned, cheeks flushed from the heat, sunglasses pushed up into her dark hair.

"Walkaround's clean," she said. "Only oddity is the galley trolley marked 'Fragile'—feels empty, might be another catering screw-up. And some joker chalked 'Miracle 2: Coming Soon?' on the main gear."

James snorted, shaking his head. "Well, at least it's not 'This Side Up.' Cabin good?"

Mia nodded. "Cabin's mostly fine. Kyle's not returned, so we're missing a Purser."

James pulled his Pixel 9A from his pocket and, loading Teams, dialled West Coast Operations. He spoke into the phone, his voice pitched low to avoid being overheard by the boarding stag party already chanting the opening bars of "Wonderwall."

"Thank you for calling Sprint Ops Europe, please hold and we will connect you to an Operations Officer," an automated voice said, and James was surprised, as the line wasn't supposed to connect to Budapest, but to the US West Coast.

James swore under his breath, holding for a real voice, as the minutes ticked by. Every second the stag party in Row 21 grew louder. The plane reverberated with a jumbled mix of British accents, Elvis impressions, and the hollow slam of galley trolleys as cabin crew tried to get ahead of the chaos. It would have been funny, if the edge in the room wasn't so acute—everyone riding their own nerves from the "Miracle on the Thames" news, everyone thinking about their own briefings, checklists, and the moments that don't go to plan.

The Teams call finally clicked over to a harried-sounding woman, the faint echo of Hungarian vowels betraying the "Sprint Europe" call centre in Budapest. "Sprint Europe, you're through to Katalin, can I have your name, flight number and crew code please?"

James exhaled and forced a professional calm. "James Hart, Captain, AmericanoAir 2187 to Oakland, crew code

Delta Romeo Two-One-Niner. We're at Las Vegas, Gate 14. We're short a Purser—Kyle Richards took a hit in the crew room and is being checked at medical. Need a qualified replacement or guidance to dispatch with a Senior in his place."

A pause, the staccato clatter of keyboards, and the low murmur of voices conferring in Hungarian and English. Behind Katalin's voice, James could hear the layered chaos of a global airline: calls from Boston, Frankfurt, Dubai, someone complaining about Luton's lost bags, a Romanian accent demanding "legal rest" after a 14-hour duty. For a second, he was viscerally aware of the threadbare seams that held this industry together: people, rules, a little luck, and sometimes, duct tape.

"Understood, Captain. You say AmericanoAir? You are through to the wrong number. Sprint does not run American Airline routes. You should call your own dispatcher."

American Airlines? James thought as the line went dead, as if the Europeans thought he was calling from AA and not Sprint's own American operation—a symptom of the chaos that had followed the group's panicked expansion stateside. He gritted his teeth, took a breath, and redialled.

"Thank you for calling Sprint Ops Europe, please hold and we will connect you to an Operations Officer," an automated voice said, and James waited, listening to the tinny hold music—some generic Europop loop, designed more to discourage than to entertain. Behind him, the ambient cabin noise was building: the stag party now halfway through "Sweet Caroline," cabin crew trying to enforce basic decorum with the weary resignation of people who knew defeat when they saw it, and the sporadic squawk of the PA system as a junior flight attendant attempted her first proper boarding announcements. The sense of unreality that had hovered all morning only deepened. Even now, with the Thames miracle still rippling through aviation's collective psyche, it seemed Sprint's own transatlantic chaos would not be delayed for mere drama.

The hold music cut off. At last, a real voice—male this time, but German and rough, as if he'd been awake for two shifts too many. "Sprint Network Control, Wolfgang speaking. Sorry for the wait. Can I have your name, flight number and crew code please?"

James steadied himself, voice crisp, British-tinged professionalism cutting through the jumble of emotion. "Captain James Hart, AmericanoAir two-one-eight-seven, crew code Delta Romeo two-one-niner. I need a replacement for Purser Kyle Richards—medical, following a crew room incident. We're short a qualified number one at Vegas, Gate Fourteen, and departure's supposed to be in—" he checked the old digital clock above the door, "—twenty-seven minutes. Guidance, please."

On the other end, Wolfgang sighed, the sound of a long shift and too many operational fires to fight. "You are AmericanoAir, yes? But routing through Sprint Europe ops? Ach, that's a problem. You should be through West Coast Ops. Please hold and I will connect you—though if you're already through here, I'll see what I can do." There was the clatter of more typing, an audible sigh, and muffled consultation with someone else in the background. James heard the drone of Budapest Ops— German, English, Hungarian and the odd streak of Polish.

Wolfgang came back, his voice rougher. "I am unable to get through to West Coast Operations. Please hold and I will try US East Operations."

James pinched the bridge of his nose, feeling the start of a headache building behind his right eye. On another day he might have found the Kafkaesque absurdity of Sprint's global patchwork operation amusing, but with the spectre of the Thames ditching still fresh and the clock ticking ever closer to their slot time, his patience was on a knife edge.

The background noise on the line swelled: phones ringing, someone shouting in Hungarian, a clipped British voice from Luton barking about de-icing fluid, then Wolfgang returned to the line.

"I'm unable to get through to Sprint US East Coast. Let me have a look on my end to see what is available."

James waited, knuckles white around the handset, heart thumping not with drama but with the sickly, bureaucratic dread that every airline pilot knows too well: the sense that the whole edifice could be brought down not by failure of engines or a river landing, but by a missing phone number or a half-trained dispatcher two continents away.

The cabin's drone was intensifying: the stag party now hammering on the overhead bins in rhythm with "Don't Look Back in Anger," punctuated by the electronic chime of PA and a chorus of shushing from the more sedate retirees up front. A short, red-haired flight attendant—Emily, he remembered—hovered at the flight deck door, iPad clutched to her chest.

"Sorry, Captain, but we're going to have a situation with 21A and B," she whispered, glancing anxiously at the stag group. "They're already arguing over seat assignments. I think they want to swap with the lads in 31 so they can sit together."

"Tell them we'll swap them at cruise if everyone's behaving," James said, not looking up. "We're short a Purser, so everyone needs to do double. Do your best. If you get any aggro, tell them that they'll be removed from the flight and can sing "Wonderwall" to airport security instead." He tried to inject a note of dry humour, but Emily's taut smile told him she wasn't convinced. Still, she nodded and vanished back into the fray, leaving James alone with the endless holding music, the humming worry of a missing senior crew, and the low-grade headache of operations gone global.

On the line, Wolfgang returned, sounding like a man out of solutions. "Captain Hart, I have found a standby Senior Cabin Crew—Susan Eldridge, badge 3298—who just landed from Portland. She is in the terminal and can make it in fifteen minutes, maybe ten if ramp security cooperate. I will send her details to your gate and update Dispatch. If she does not arrive in time, you may need to delay for crew legalities. Sorry for the inconvenience."

****

CHAPTER 24 – The Thanksgiving Blessing

Thursday 27th November 2025

"Jane, honey, have you seen my shirt?" James said, his voice bouncing off the yellowed walls of the kitchen, a faint note of panic threading through his early morning calm. The condo that the couple shared in the LA Valley was chaos, as usual—half-packed suitcases scattered across the dining room floor, Jane's gardening gloves discarded by the back door, and a battered AmericanoAir flight bag perched precariously atop a tottering stack of aviation magazines. In the distance, the first whine of leaf blowers mingled with the slow percolation of the old filter coffee machine, promising caffeine and comfort, but only if he could get out the door in the next twelve minutes.

His mission? Meeting his in-laws off the Denver to LAX United flight that they had booked on, the elder McDonalds being Premier Gold and thus entitled to every conceivable privilege, short of a personal carriage from gate to curb. James, meanwhile, would have settled for finding two matching socks and a moment to gather his thoughts before the next round of familial turbulence.

Jane's voice drifted in from the bathroom, already filtered through the steam of a running shower. "Did you check the laundry basket? You left it there after you finished work yesterday and I haven't washed the others-"

"No, I mean the non-work one, the holiday one with the collar. The blue one. The only shirt I own that your mum actually complimented."

James's hand dug fruitlessly through a mountain of still-warm laundry in the hall, mostly leggings and gardening shorts, before pulling free a crumpled pale-blue Oxford, smelling faintly of jet fuel and last week's garlic. He gave it a once-over and shrugged—this would do, because nothing else could.

Out in the hallway, Jane's laugh rolled through the steam and the clatter of her make-up case. "She complimented it because it hid the sweat patches, darling. Try to be nice—Dad's knee is playing up, and their flight has only just left Denver, so you've got an hour at least before they start demanding to be picked up curbside in violation of three separate airport regulations."

James grinned to himself, the smile equal parts fondness and dread. He dragged the battered flight bag off the stack, dislodging a copy of Flying magazine from 2018 and a yellowing Lufthansa safety card that he was fairly certain belonged in a museum. He grabbed the coffee carafe, poured himself a mug, and tried not to think about the magnitude of the day ahead.

This was Thanksgiving in America, and the former USAF Major knew it came with rules—some written, most not, all enforced more rigorously than FAA ops manuals. LA was still quiet, the city's grid of boulevards yawning itself awake, but James could already feel the thrum of a thousand delayed flights, a million anxious families, and the knowledge that, in a few hours, his condo would be ground zero for one of America's greatest exercises in mass-delusion: the Thanksgiving dinner.

James took his first sip of coffee, the liquid scorching but necessary, and braced himself against the counter as he ran through a silent checklist. Shirts, socks, keys, wallet, ID, the battered old Pixel with its cracked screen—the only thing that reliably worked on it was the WhatsApp notification for crew swaps and, lately, the running commentary from AmericanoAir's ever-more-frazzled dispatch. Somewhere out in the garage his car sat sulking, half-cleaned from last week's San Diego turn, still carrying the faint odour of cold French fries and spilled cold brew.

Thanksgiving. For years, the word had meant nothing but a line of tiny print on a duty roster, a reason for check-in queues to snake out into car parks and for US airport security to get even more jittery than usual. But now, in the strange comfort of domesticity, it was about the in-laws, Jane's mashed sweet potato, and the annual family skirmish over whether stuffing belonged in the bird or on the side. He let out a breath he didn't know he'd been holding and forced himself into action.

He hunted down his battered trainers by the back door, brushing off the worst of the garden soil, and called out, "Jane, do you want coffee?" No answer—just the thunk of a hairdryer and some muffled cursing about her eyeliner. James poured her a mug anyway, knowing she'd forget it until it was tepid and then complain, as she always did, that he'd made it too strong.

He padded into the bedroom, dodging piles of clothing and the half-zipped suitcases, and looked in on Jane. She was, as always, a blur of efficiency, her hair twisted into a towel, face already half-done, her phone wedged between shoulder and cheek as she fielded a call from her mother.

"Yes, Mum, James will be there on time… No, I told you, LAX has changed the drop-off again, you can't just stand outside Terminal 7 and expect someone to find you in the chaos—yes, Dad can have a wheelchair if he asks at the gate, but if he pretends he doesn't need one he's just going to get left behind by the United Golds." She rolled her eyes at James, gave him a conspiratorial smile, and mimed strangling herself with the towel. He grinned and mouthed, "I'll survive."

Downstairs, the kitchen filled with the smells of impending war—sage, onion, the faint, medicinal whiff of cranberry from a jar Jane's mother insisted on bringing every year "in case the fresh stuff isn't right." James watched the digital clock on the oven tick over. His phone buzzed: a dispatch update from AmericanoAir, something about reserve standby for Dallas on Friday. He thumbed back a polite "UNAVAILABLE" and dropped the phone face-down.

He stood for a moment in the warm chaos, trying to assemble his thoughts. It struck him that, for all the years in uniform—first USAF, then endless hours in Airbus cockpits, then the surreal hell of AmericanoAir—nothing in training had prepared him for the logistical nightmare of a domestic Thanksgiving. He'd managed LA ground holds, Category III approaches into O'Hare in freezing fog, even once a bomb threat at Houston Hobby, but the thought of shepherding two seventy-something in-laws through the gauntlet of LAX Arrivals was enough to raise his pulse. He checked his watch—forty minutes until touchdown.

The drive to LAX was mercifully uneventful for Thanksgiving morning, the 405 sluggish but not the parking lot of legend. On the radio, NPR muttered on about supply chains and the price of turkey per pound; James idly calculated what that would be in kilos, then in the number of crew meals you could buy wholesale for the same money, and gave up. The skies over Inglewood shimmered blue and empty—a trick of the air or a brief window in the usual conga line for Runway 25L.

At Terminal 7, the traffic was already in full swing: families dragging wheeled suitcases, uniformed cabin crew clutching Starbucks, rideshare drivers double-parked and yelling into earpieces, police waving off anyone lingering a second too long. Suddenly, his phone, not his personal one, but the Sprint issued Pixel 9A buzzed, the bland, insistent vibration that never meant anything good. James risked a glance and saw that it was Maddie Chen from West Coast Ops, her name highlighted with the scarlet urgency of a dispatcher's last nerve. James considered ignoring it—he was off duty, in-laws inbound, and as far as he was concerned, AmericanoAir could weather a Thanksgiving without him. But old habits died hard, and he thumbed the call open, holding the phone low as he nosed the Prius into the only available bay between a Hertz shuttle and an UberXL with hazard lights flashing.

"Maddie, I'm not in uniform. If you need someone for Dallas, you'll have to find another mug."

Her voice came through with the kind of forced cheer that suggested she was already on her third shift, or perhaps her third Red Bull. "James, happy Thanksgiving—no Dallas, I promise. But I do have a very short day if you want it. We've got a 321LR needing moved from LAX to Long Beach and a 320LR returned if you fancy a full day's pay for a hours work?"

James let out a snort. "On Thanksgiving? What's the catch—does it have an engine missing, or am I supposed to ferry it dressed as a turkey?"

Maddie actually chuckled, and he could hear the low rumble of chaos in the background—phones ringing, radios squawking, the ambient stress of Ops on a holiday. "No feathers required. Just a repositioning job. Half the network is a mess because EASA have released a Bulletin about the A320 types, something about needing to roll back software following an incident last month with a JetBlue flight, and all A320 types, so the 318s, 319s and the 321s all need a software patch—yes, even the old ones, and yes, the LRs too. FAA haven't said anything but the HQ in the UK have told us to ground anything that hasn't had the update by midnight. You're not flying punters, just ferrying from LAX to Long Beach, drop-off, back in time for turkey. It's all on the company, full pay, only an hours work, two at the most. I told Dispatch you'd say no, but figured I'd ask."

James took a long, measured breath. Through the windscreen, LAX Arrivals was a fever dream of America in motion—families waving signs, children in matching turkey hats, a priest arguing with a rideshare driver. He weighed the offer: a guilt-free bolt for a few hours, with all the legitimate excuses in the world, a quick shuttle down the 405 and back, and, for once, a guaranteed on-time return for dinner. Not to mention, full pay at the Thanksgiving rate—a nice little bonus, and one less slot for some unlucky junior to cover. He pressed the phone to his ear, glancing in the mirror as he saw Jane's parents' flight blinked "LANDED" on the United tracker.

"Alright, Maddie. As long as I'm back by four. And if this thing so much as chirps an ECAM at me, I'm turning it straight round. You want a call after, or just the usual sign-off on the EFB?"

A sigh of relief from Maddie. "Just the sign-off, James. You're saving my bacon here—if it were anyone else, I'd have to send a contractor, and you know what that does to the insurance. LAX South Ramp, Bay 52. She's already powered and ground crew will brief you. I've got you as PIC, and I've got… erm… you'll hate this, but it's Bryce Keegan who's your SIC."

James closed his eyes.

Of all the names Maddie could have uttered, that one—the human equivalent of an unexpected hydraulic leak—rose like smoke from a burning galley oven. For a moment he genuinely wondered if this was punishment: for ignoring the last three reserve calls, for telling Dispatch that if they sent him to Tijuana again he'd defect to Hawaiian Airlines, for denying Maddie's insistence that he "smile more in the crew photos."

Bryce bloody Keegan.

The only First Officer James had ever flown with who behaved like the cockpit was a Tinder date and the Airbus a booth in a nightclub. The same Keegan who had been caught (1) fraternising in the left-hand seat, (2) studying for his law degree mid-sector, (3) falling asleep in the jump seat during a go-around at Oakland, and (4) once trying to charm a TruJet cabin crew member into giving him her WhatsApp number during an emergency descent.

James inhaled slowly. "Tell me you're joking."

Maddie didn't miss a beat. "James, if I had the staffing for jokes, I'd be in the Maldives. I've got pilots diverted all over the country—San Diego, Albuquerque, even a few stuck in Santa Barbara because someone in Maintenance decided to rotate tyres on Thanksgiving. Keegan's in LAX and legal to fly. He's… well, available."

"I'd rather fly solo," James muttered.

"You can't, FAA says no, as well you know. If I could swap him for another FO, I would do. Oh, and you know you asked me to keep an ear out about Flight 1549 and the cause of its downing… geese."

James froze in the car, his hand hovering between the gearstick and his phone, mind suddenly split between the looming threat of Bryce Keegan and the lingering trauma of geese—real or metaphorical—haunting every Airbus pilot since the Miracle on the Hudson. Maddie's voice rattled on, oblivious to the existential weariness settling into his bones.

"Geese. Actual Canada Geese, James. The British AAIB preliminary says the Sprint UK A318 hit a flock departing

City, right over the river. Same as Sully, twenty-odd years on. Apparently, the ATC tapes are all over the BBC and the Daily Mail's already trying to get the crew to sign a book deal before the CAA even finishes their breath tests. It's chaos in London—Sprint UK are briefing every network, all the pilots are checking their bird strike drills, and, well… you can imagine. Anyway, I'm on until 5, and then I'm handing over to Adam for the night shift."

James let Maddie's voice fade into the crackling air between them. For a moment he didn't speak, watching a family of five in matching USC hoodies squabble at the crosswalk, the father gesticulating with a sign reading "GO BRUINS!" as if the universe might realign for him, just this once, on Thanksgiving.

"Geese," James repeated, half to himself. "Of course it's geese. Has anyone called Sully for a comment yet, or are we still pretending he's in retirement?"

"Trust me, the BBC have probably got him on standby," Maddie replied. "Look, I've got to go—Ops line's lighting up and I think someone's set off the fire alarm at SFO. I'll send the full ferry brief to your EFB. Oh, and, James—happy Thanksgiving."

"Take care, and happy Thanksgiving, Maddie. Enjoy your turkey, and if you haven't seen it yet, enjoy the Macy's parade."

James ended the call with a thumb swipe, his mind still on geese, the Sprint UK miracle, and Bryce Keegan's myriad offences against common sense. He barely noticed the parade of Uber drivers honking at each other over the curbside queue until a battered United wheelchair handler began to shepherd Jane's parents through the sliding doors, their progress as slow and stately as a state procession.

Jane's father, Douglas, wore the haggard look of a man who'd battled turbulence and recalcitrant snack service at 38,000 feet; her mother, Ruth, carried herself with the ferocious dignity of the well-travelled matron, every inch the Premier Gold, her matching Samsonite gliding behind her as though it, too, held status. Ruth's face lit up in a smile the moment she spotted James. He stepped forward, trading a tired but genuine hug with Douglas, who gripped his hand like an old adversary who'd called a truce.

"Well, there he is," Ruth said, as if producing a son-in-law on demand was a small miracle in itself. "Did you get stuck in that dreadful 405 traffic?"

"Bit slow, but not terminal," James said, resisting the urge to make an aviation joke about holding patterns. He took Douglas's bag, bracing himself for the smell of Ruth's preferred lavender fabric softener, and nodded toward the Prius. "You both alright?"

Douglas snorted, shifting his weight onto the wheelchair arm. "Depends on if you call United's First this week luxury. The plane we had was as old as a Braniff credit card," Douglas was muttering as James lifted the Samsonite into the Prius' boot with a grunt. "And the food was—what do they call it—'artisanal'? Means there's not enough of it to feed a child. Tell me, James, do you ever eat those crew meals on your airline?"

James shot him a grin, slamming the boot and guiding Douglas to the front passenger seat. "Sprint is like Spirit and Frontier," he said, sighing. "When it comes to crew meals, we have to have to pay for anything that isn't a teabag and a stale muffin, and half the time, the hot food is still frozen in the middle. But at least the coffee's strong enough to wake the dead. Or kill them, depending on who brewed it." He winked at Douglas, who managed a grunt that might have been a laugh or a memory of a better meal. "Look, I've got to work in half hour, so, how would you two like a meal at a restaurant near here while I do a quick work flight while you relax? The place next to the airfield does a decent turkey club and the fries aren't as soggy as they look."

Ruth's brow furrowed. "James, you promised, no working on Thanksgiving! That's what you said, wasn't it, Douglas? He promised Jane and me that we'd have a proper American holiday, not one of those… what do you call them? 'Tech stops' you pilots always mutter about at Christmas."

James winced, glancing at his watch and then at Jane's mother's determined face, which suggested that her love was only ever half a step from exasperation. "It's literally an hour. Less, if Bryce doesn't cock it up. You'll barely have time to finish your coffee before I'm back, and I'll be home well before Jane's started on the stuffing, I promise. Besides—" He gave Ruth a look of pure sincerity. "—I owe Maddie in Ops, and I'll never hear the end of it if I say no. You'd be amazed how fast a dispatcher's grudge travels."

Douglas gave a dry snort. "He says it'll be an hour. Like that time he said he'd only be gone for a 'short hop' and came back four days later with a tan and a story about snow in El Paso."

Ruth relented, a reluctant smile tugging at her lips. "Fine. But if you miss dinner, I'm feeding you nothing but that cranberry sauce Jane's trying to pawn off on us. And you'll be peeling potatoes next year."

"I wouldn't dream of letting you down," James said, and, meaning it for once, led the way to the Prius.

James knew, even as he drove the short mile from the arrivals kerb to the chain restaurant overlooking the perimeter fence at Long Beach, that he would pay for this small act of professional loyalty later. Ruth and Douglas were settled at a faux-wood table with plastic menus and a view of the runways, eyeing the glassy-eyed waitress who'd survived three dawn shifts of pumpkin spice lattes and would probably mistake an Americano for a dessert. James gave Jane's mum his best "forgive me" smile and promised again he'd be back before the gravy congealed. In truth, it was a relief—a chance to step back into a world where things (mostly) made sense, where a checklist was a checklist and a cockpit argument could be resolved with a sharp word, not a round of mashed potatoes and family politics.

The drive north up the 405 was classic California: slow, bright, and edged with the tension of everyone else trying to get somewhere else. Billboards hawked Black Friday sales and rainless snow tyres, while local radio flickered between sports, traffic, and breathless updates about the

"Thames Miracle"—the London City ditching now fully mythologised by every transatlantic anchor with a passing interest in aviation. By the time James swung the Prius into the staff car park at LAX, the air was already warm with the tang of jet exhaust, and the airport looked like an anthill kicked by God.

It didn't take long to clear Security; the Thanksgiving morning crew were too busy gossiping about overtime to properly check badges, and James was waved through with a muttered, "Happy holiday, Cap." On the South Ramp, Bay 52, the A321LR sat squat and gleaming, shimmering in the late-morning sun—a thin haze of heat rising off her dark blue paint. The jet was a recent transfer from Sprint Europe, the registration half-heartedly re-stickered for FAA compliance, the old Sprint call sign still stencilled beneath the captain's window in ghostly outline.

At the foot of the air stairs, a ramp supervisor gave James a nod. "You're Captain Hart for the ferry? Good. She's been ground powered since six. Avionics techs cleared the software. She's light—no bags, no galley, just the flight deck and the basic ops kit. Maintenance want her in Long Beach before two for the patch, so if you see any ECAMs, just bring her back. Don't risk a reject. Oh, and Keegan's up there—said he was doing preflight." He rolled his eyes in the way of all ground staff who've met more pilots than they care to remember.

James made his way up the steps, every sense tuned for the worst. As he entered the cockpit, the familiar plasticky scent of Airbus hit him: recycled air, sweat, and the acrid tang of cheap cleaning fluid. Bryce Keegan was already in the right seat, feet up on the glare shield, headset hanging around his neck, scrolling through TikTok on his phone and humming a tune James didn't recognise.

"Morning, Captain!" Bryce grinned, the picture of youthful enthusiasm and utter lack of self-awareness. "Happy Turkey Day. Can you believe Maddie roped me into working this morning? I had to ditch a brunch date for this. At least it's a ferry, yeah? Low stress. I got the walkaround done, all good, except the pitot cover on two was stuck, so I got one of the rampies to bash it off with a torch. Classic Sprint maintenance, am I right?" He winked.

James set his bag behind the seat, ignoring the prickle of irritation up his neck. "You didn't break the probe, did you?" he asked, flipping through the journey log with quick, professional detachment.

"Nah, mate. Little tap, job's a good 'un. Everything else is green. APU started first go, fuel's as per the slip, and Dispatch sent me the new OFP. I even loaded the patch for the EFB. Not that we'll need it for a twenty-minute hop." Bryce swung his feet down, finally, and stretched like a man untroubled by career or consequence. "Oh, and happy Thanksgiving, Cap. No hard feelings about, you know, the other thing."

James let that pass. "You set up the FMS yet?"

Bryce nodded, spinning the right CDU around to show his work—direct LAX-LGB, cost index zero, block fuel to the kilo, a landing weight that'd make a Cessna jealous. "I got it all from Dispatch. The only NOTAM is the usual about the construction at Long Beach—short taxi, left at Charlie. You want to fly it or shall I?"

James hesitated, then decided it was safer to keep his hands on the controls, both literally and figuratively. "I'll take the sector. You can monitor. Let's get her fired up."

****

Books by Thomas Brant

Broadcasting Boundaries
BROADCASTING BOUNDARIES
BROADCASTING CHAOS
BROADCASTING DISRUPTION

Fallen
IRELAND IS DOWN

PanEuro
STICK AND LIPSTICK
SPRINTER OF THE SKIES
LANE @ CHECK IN
BORROWED AIRSPACE

The Manic Collective Candidate
THE MANIC COLLECTIVE CANDIDATE

The Wirral Gal
IN SPEKE
NOW A MAM

Other Shared Universe Novels
THE BROOKES BABES
THE DAY THE QUEEN DIED
VIXEN
RED ROSE ACADEMY